THE HEART OF DANGER

D Cleland
Heathrow
Easter 1995

GERALD SEYMOUR

THE HEART OF DANGER

HarperCollins*Publishers*

HarperCollins*Publishers*
77–85 Fulham Palace Road,
Hammersmith, London W6 8JB

Published by HarperCollins*Publishers* 1995
1   3   5   7   9   8   6   4   2

A catalogue record for this book is
available from the British Library

ISBN 0 00 649682 2

Photoset in Linotron Plantin by
Rowland Phototypesetting Ltd
Bury St Edmunds, Suffolk

Printed and bound in Great Britain by
HarperCollinsManufacturing Glasgow

To Gillian, Nicholas and James

PROLOGUE

'*Back again?*'

Yes, he was back again. Back again in Library. A smile for the supervisor that was not returned, as it had not been returned on either of the two days that he had been in Library the previous month, nor the two days of the month before that. Henry Carter's smile was brief, just enough to be polite. He looked for a table that was free.

'*Train was late, I'm afraid,*' *he said mildly. He wiped the rain from his scalp.* '*It's a dreadful service.*'

He was the interloper, really, an unwanted male in a feminine world, and he supposed that he inhibited conversation on men, cystitis, brassieres, mortgage rates, curtain hanging, school meals, Gilts versus Equities, tampons, whatever women talked about these days. The table that was free was placed furthest from the small supply of natural light permitted to filter through to the half basement floor of Library. Pretty poor light anyway because the windows were of blast-proof glass that distorted and were copper-tinted to block the electromagnetic signals from the computers being monitored by any electronic surveillance from across Vauxhall Bridge. Different from his day. Seemed to have managed without lead-lined rooms and copper-tinted windows and computers in silicon casings and finger-print recognition locks on interior doors, managed pretty well, and kept a few secrets . . . He should not complain. He found space on the coat stand for his overcoat. His pension, even index-linked, was inadequate. He stood his umbrella, dripping, against the wall. The two days a month back in the Library were welcome, well, damned necessary. At the free table, watched by the girls and the women and their day shift supervisor, he unlocked his briefcase. The old one, of course, the one that he had carried day in and day out for twenty-three years from Waterloo Station and along the pavement beside the river

7

and into the concrete tower of Century House, with the EIIR gold print faded from the flap. The morning newspaper, crossword started on the train, was first out. Then his sandwiches, cheddar and pickle and made by himself. Then his thermos (milk and sugar and sufficient for four measures). Then the magazine of the Royal Society for the Protection of Birds, a pleasure to be saved for the hour's statutory lunch break. If the RSPB had been prepared to have him for more than a single day a week, working on their membership register, then he would not have needed to grovel in gratitude for two days a month in Library . . .

The supervisor stood over his table. She had the file in its cardboard folder clasped to her shallow bosom. She apologized, without sincerity, 'It's a bit of a mess.'

Well, there were so many files these days that were a bit of a mess. Old files needed tidying and editing before being fed to the computer disks. Henry Carter was good at tidying and editing which was why he was called back those two days a month and sat at a table away from the natural light. He supposed that the women regarded the part-time labour as a threat to their own work security, because there was never a greeting, never any friendship.

'I expect we can sort it out . . . Interesting one, is it?'

'I wouldn't know.'

The file was dropped on the table. She turned and walked away from him, clattering her heels on the composite flooring. There had been carpeting in Library at Century House. Carpet had been good enough for the old building, not for the Babylon on Thames that was the new monstrosity at Vauxhall Cross. Too vulgar, too flash, for a headquarters building for the Secret Intelligence Service, inappropriate . . .

He peeled the elastic band from the file's folder. Words, typed and handwritten and printed, were leaping at him. He looked up at the ceiling, at the battery of recessed lights. A little indulgence, but Henry Carter lived with nostalgia. Somewhere close by, perhaps in the annexe, perhaps already transferred to disk, would be the files of operations that had involved him from the start, when he had not just been the road sweeper, hired at £5.47 an hour for sixteen hours a month, to clear the litter of others. A little tremor, as there always was when he indulged himself. No need for a retired has-been, some

8

*never-was, to be called in to sift the files of Henry Carter's operations
. . . He recalled the days when he had controlled a man sent across
the inner German border to Magdeburg. He remembered the night
long interrogation when he had reduced a desk head, one of their
own, to a weeping and shamed creature. Decent files he had left
behind him. He . . . They were watching from behind their silly
screens. It would have been a good day to have been up on the former
railway line at Tregaron, mid-Wales, because it was just the right
time of year for the rare red kites, Milvus milvus, to be feeding.
Glorious birds . . .He dropped his head. He began to read.*

The file was, indeed, a mess, no order and no shape.

*He turned the pages fast. Fifteen typed sheets, four faxes, nine
Foreign and Commonwealth Office signals, thirteen foolscap sheets
covered by three different sets of handwriting, and a buff envelope
of photographs. The old desk warrior gutted the pages, his training
taking over. Henry Carter would have said if he was asked, and he
never was, that there was a narcotic addiction from a file that was
fresh to him. He was hooked, caught. Almost without looking up he
called to the supervisor.*

'I'd like a map, please.'

'Of what?'

*Because of what he had read, because of the images already in
his mind, a scratch of irritation clawed him. It was not a joke, nor
was it mischief.*

*'Hardly the sea front at Bognor Regis, no thank you . . . Large
scale, 1:1000, if that's possible. Former Yugoslavia, what they call
Croatia. The area that the United Nations Protection Force desig-
nates as Sector North . . .'*

*He turned back the sheets of paper spread now haphazardly across
the table. He was reaching for his thermos flask and Henry Carter's
elbow, the leather patch on his sports jacket, caught the envelope
that held the photographs. The envelope fell from the table. The
photographs spilled. He looked down at them. He looked down onto
the grotesque image of the young face. Worse than those of the old
man shot to death on the ploughed strip beside that revolting German
fence. Worse than those of the hanged Iranian woman suspended
from a hideous construction crane in Tabrīz. He shuddered.*

He barely heard the shrill voice. 'A map like that, you'll have to wait until tomorrow for it. Can't get it before tomorrow. You know, Mr Carter, it's not our job to . . .'

He bent to pick up the photographs. He gazed into the face. He wondered if she had been pretty before the decay of burial had swollen the features. His fingers were scrabbling for the photographs and were unresponsive, and he felt the cold sweat streaming to the small of his back. His body weight swayed in the chair. He gulped deep air. He lifted the photographs onto the table and then he gripped the edge of the table that he might restore his balance. Too damned old for it . . .

The voice beat at him. 'Are you all right, Mr Carter?'

The woman at the computer desk nearest him giggled out loud. It was the giggle that probably saved him from fainting. It made his anger surge. It was rare for him to let his temper show. The woman was feeding her face with squares of milk chocolate. He took the photograph that was second from the top of the pile and walked the five strides, briskly, to the woman's desk and he laid the photograph on her keyboard. A photograph of a young face with a head wound and a throat wound and a close-quarters bullet wound. The woman belched chocolate over her blouse.

Henry Carter went back to his table.

He called across the silence, 'I'm fine, thank you. Tomorrow would be grand for the map.'

He settled. For a moment he drummed his fingers on the table surface, then he reached again for his thermos and poured himself a half-measure into the plastic cup. He drank. He took from his brief-case a bag of sharpened pencils and biro pens in three colours. The moment had passed, it was as if the photographs had ambushed him. He began to search the sheets of paper for date stamps and he laid them out over the width of the table and then began to number them in red from the first date. Wouldn't take him long to knock the file into shape. If the map came he would most certainly be finished by tomorrow lunch time. That would be excellent. It would give him time to be out of London before the afternoon rush for home, and on the road comfortably for the Powys mountains, and the railway line from which the red kites, Milvus milvus, could be seen.

The date stamp on the first sheet of paper was 3 April 1993. For a moment, idly, he tried to remember what he would have been doing that day twenty-three months before, and failed. The paper was letter-headed 'Physicians for Human Rights' . . . It was easy for him to picture it.

There was a village and a lane and foul mud, and a grave.

1

The area for the digging was outlined by a rude rectangle of white tape.

The rectangle was approximately ten metres by four metres, as measured out by the Professor's full strides. It had been easy to recognize the rectangle where they had dug because only weeds had grown in that disturbed corner of the field.

Around the edge of the rectangle, heaped on the grass beyond the white tape, was the new boundary marker of piled muddy earth. Four policemen had done the digging at the Professor's direction.

The long-handled spades with the wide blades were now tossed onto the low mud wall.

The four policemen and the Professor knelt in the pit they had made. When they had started, their overalls had been pure white, they were now smeared in the grey-black mud of the field. There was no talking amongst the policemen and they responded only to the curt instructions of the Professor. Each could recognize that the light was starting to fall and would go quickly because the rain cloud was already below the level of the summit of the wooded hill that rose above the farmhouse. They had the one chance to excavate and exhume, and the chance would not come again, and they had brought no portable generator and no lights. It must be finished that afternoon. The rain spat on them, beat at their shoulders and their buttocks and at the backs of their knees. The rain made muddied pools in the pit around the bodies that were already retrieved. If the Professor had been working at home, if he had been called out by the Police Department's homicide team, then he would have been protected by a tent of stout tarpaulin. If the Professor had been working at home, crouched over the cadaver of a murder victim, then he would have had his own team with him, all expert, and there would have been no pressure of time. There was a way of doing things, there was a pattern of procedure, and he abided by the procedure because that was the bible to which he worked. He thought they were fine men, the four policemen with whom he uncovered the corpses, the tall young Canadian and the cheerful Frenchman and the droll balding Portuguese and the slim-waisted Kenyan, and they worked in silence to his abrupt instructions that were muffled through his face mask. Each time he looked up he saw that the rain cloud crept further down the wooded slope of the hill, and he saw that the lights burned brighter in the houses on the far side of the valley beyond the stream.

If it had been possible to have erected a tent cover over the grave, if they could have worked at a slower speed, then they could have used the scalpels and the narrow brushes. The rain fell in the pit, destroyed his hopes of minute care. The policemen had learned from him, watched him and copied, and they scraped the clinging clay mud from the bodies with small trowels, the sort of trowels that his wife used in the garden back home in north Los Angeles. When they had taken as much mud from each body as was possible with the trowels, then they wiped the faces of the dead with the sodden cloths that he had brought. When he was satisfied that each face had been cleaned to the best of their ability, then the policemen would stand back and he would photograph the body in wide shot and then operate the automatic zoom on his pocket Nikon and photograph the face in close-up.

There were nine bodies photographed in wide shot, nine faces captured in close-up, nine bodybags zipped and lying close together beyond the earth wall around his white marker tape.

The Professor used a clipboard of note paper that was covered by a clear plastic bag. He had made a small sketch map of the grave site, and had detailed each corpse before it was lifted to the bodybag. SSK9 wore around his throat a gold chain to which was attached a thin gold cross and an inscribed medallion. The left foot of SSK9 was gone, taken off at the ankle. The forehead of SSK9 showed the bullet hole, central.

A single boot protruded from the mud layer alongside the indentation, now filling fast from the rain, from which they had taken SSK9.

'OK, guys, should be the last one . . .' The Professor's voice was a growl.

He kept his words brief and his voice low because that way he reckoned he was better able to prevent the bile spilling up from his throat. It was the smell that made him want to vomit. The face mask was a token against the smell of putrefaction. He had been told that the bodies were reckoned to have been buried in the month of December in the year of 1991, but the clay of the earth had been dense enough to keep out foxes and dogs from the grave and had slowed the process of decomposition.

The Professor stood for a moment and tried to stretch his back to arch out the stiffness.

Back from the pit and the tape and the low earth wall, back from the white painted jeeps of the United Nations Civilian Police, a small crowd watched. He had seen them gather during the course of the day. They watched and they made no sign. He had seen them come from the tight cluster of houses around the church on the far side of the stream. There were women in the crowd, the old in black and the young in bright coats; there were children with ravaged mature faces, holding an unnatural quiet; there were men in the crowd, some wearing the drab clothes of farm work, some in poor-fitting damp uniforms, some armed with shotguns and automatic rifles. He wondered what they thought, the crowd that had come across the stream to watch the excavation of the grave. His eyes wandered. He looked from the field and on down the lane where the grass had grown across the old tractor ruts and on towards the ruin of the village and on to the church tower where the upper stonework that would have housed the bell had been taken away by tank or artillery fire. He wondered what they thought. He turned to stare back at the crowd . . .

The Canadian murmured, 'Don't make eye contact with them,

Professor. Always smile at them, keep the smile glued.'

The Kenyan muttered, 'We want to get it wrapped and we want to get the shit out. Don't expect to be loved . . .'

He thought them fine young men. He was in his seventieth year. He had taken two months of unpaid leave from the hospital in north Los Angeles where he headed the Department of Pathology. Back home, those who had been his contemporaries through medical school had long retired to the beach houses of Santa Monica and Santa Barbara. He thought them fools. Dear to his heart was the charity Physicians for Human Rights. And dearer to him than the charity was the knowledge that his Abigail, in the forty-fifth year of their marriage, held a pride in her husband for taking himself off to Croatia for two months. He'd tell her about the Canadian and the Frenchman and the Portuguese and the Kenyan, great young guys who could chide, gently, a vague old man who let his eyes wander. He had the one day at the grave, and the day was nearly done.

'Sorry, guys.'

The Kenyan was out of the pit and had gone to where the mine detector lay in shelter alongside the wheel of a jeep. He jumped back into the pit and ran the machine over the last part of the earth, beyond the protruding leg. It was the fourth time that the mine detector had been used to sweep the site. They were all in the pit again. The crowd who watched from the edge of the field would only have seen their shoulders and their buttocks, and the trowels of dripping mud that were tossed from the pit to the earth wall.

It would be the last body. The growing gloom brought a new pace to their work. An army boot, a leg in disintegrating camouflage fatigues, a hand that wore a cheap and dulled ring, a wristwatch, an arm that was bent crazily because the central bone had been broken. The Professor was scraping for the skull. The Portuguese policeman tapped at his shoulder, asked for his attention. He turned. He saw the small trainer shoe revealed alongside the second boot. His wife, Abigail, liked to tell him that he was a tough old goat of a man, that his humour when dealing with the dead was black as night, gas chamber mirth. He gagged. He felt the emotion swell in him because he had not expected to

16

find a woman's body in the grave. Sure, he could handle female cadavers when he was out with the Police Department homicide unit, but he had not expected a woman's body, not here . . . They were entwined, the camouflage trousers and the blue jeans. They were locked together, the camouflage tunic arms and the grey windcheater arms. They were against each other, the skull of a young man and the skull of a young woman.

The Canadian crouched above them and held a flashlight with the beam directed down . . . He would have liked to have stood his full height and shouted to the crowd to come close, the women and the children and the men with their guns, he would have liked to have invited them to see the bodies of the young man and woman who were entwined, and he wondered how many of them who waited in the rain would have known what would be found. The chest of the young man was wrapped in stained bandages. The Professor understood. All of the bodies of the men showed the marks of combat wounds, bullet holes, shrapnel gouges, field amputations. They had been the wounded. It had been a shit little war in a shit little corner of Europe and the wounded had gotten themselves left behind when the fit guys had run out on them. He looked down into the swollen and decayed face of the young woman. His own daughter was forty-one years old, his own granddaughter was nineteen years old. His own daughter had said he was an idiot to involve himself in a shit little war, and his own granddaughter had asked him, the night before he had flown, to tell her why this shit little war was worth caring about. He could go cold. It was useful to go cold when he was looking into a young woman's face where the putre-faction had started, but not gone so far as to hide the killing wounds. There was a bullet entry wound in what remained of the fair hair above the right ear. There was a knife wound at the throat that had cut deep through muscles. There was a bludgeon wound across the bridge of the nose and the lower part of the forehead. They were all killing wounds.

'Sorry to hurry you, Professor . . .' the Canadian pleaded. 'We ought to get the hell out . . .'

He realized then that all the light he had been working to had been from the torch held by the Canadian.

17

The Kenyan brought two bodybags forward. He took his photographs, and made the necessary notes, and nodded his head to tell them that he was satisfied. They prised the stinking corpse of the young man apart from the stinking corpse of the young woman. It was when they lifted the body of the young woman out of the pit that the Professor felt the bulk of the money bag. The bag was under her windcheater, sweater and T-shirt. He delayed them while his rubber-gloved fingers struggled with the bag's clip fastening that was against the small of her back. He put the bag into the pocket pouch on the leg of his overalls.

Bent under the weight of them, they loaded the eleven body-bags through the tail doors of the two Cherokee jeeps.

They drove away. When they turned to reach the lane, as the rain pattered on the windscreen, beaten away by the wipers, the Professor saw that the crowd had broken and now meandered away towards the houses and the lights across the stream. Off the lane, in the ruined village, the Cherokee swerved to avoid a rusted and burned-out car, and then again to go past a collapsed farm cart; it was only when they were on the metalled road, going towards Glina and the Sisak crossing point through the front line, that the Professor asked the Canadian for the loan of the light.

He opened the money bag.

He took out an empty purse and a single sodden traveller's cheque to the value of twenty US dollars, and the passport.

He squinted tired eyes at the passport, at the nationality and the name. He took his handkerchief and wiped the discoloured photograph. He wondered what she had been doing there, caught in a shit little war in a shit little corner of Europe.

The engines were cut.

There was a moment of quiet, before the scuffled stampede as the passengers surged for the cabin door.

She sat three rows from the far end of the cabin. She stayed in her seat as it had been suggested to her that she should. She was tall, did not fit easily into the tourist accommodation but the senior purser on the flight had, in kindness, arranged that neither of the seats beside her should be taken. She had the look and the elegance of a woman who was used to being noticed, as she had been by the other passengers, dark hair well cut and short, careful cosmetics, a string of pearls at her throat that were real, and confident dress. She wore a titian-coloured blouse and a deep-green skirt that had the length to cover her bent knees and its hem was over the upper part of her well-shined boots. Several of the salesmen on the flight, those who had been away from home the longest, had looked at her, wondered what her business had been in that dismal city they were so relieved to be gone from. The cabin was clearing, the canned music was now supreme, but she seemed not to hear the forced cheerfulness of the Viennese waltz that drove her fellow passengers towards the immigration desks and the baggage carousel and the Customs quiz. She ignored the movement around her, she leafed the pages of *Vogue* magazine. A small man, one of the last to go, bulged his stomach near to the diamond stud in her ear as he reached to lift down a shopping bag from the compartment above her head, and when he breathed an apology she seemed not to hear him. She gave the appearance of being quite engrossed in the colour advertisements that her eyes flitted over.

She was a sham.

The purser thought she was just brave.

She was still turning the pages of the magazine when the hostess came up the empty aisle of the cabin. The cleaners were following, whistling and laughing and grabbing paper debris from the floor and from the backs of the vacated seats. She smiled up at the hostess and began to collect her possessions that were discarded over the empty seats beside her. A handbag, an over-night grip, a raincoat, a packet of cigarettes and a slim gold lighter, a spectacle case, and a patterned headscarf, and a single red rose of which the bloom was not quite opened and the stem was wrapped in tinfoil. She craned forward and looked through the porthole window and saw the low grey cloud and the puddles on the tarmac and made a small joke about the weather. The hostess offered a hand in help and her eyes showed her sympathy. Again the smile, as if the concern of the hostess were quite unnecessary, out of place and not required, and she stood and shrugged into her raincoat. She looked behind her, once and briefly, to make sure she had left nothing. She laid the scarf over her head, then loosely knotted it under her chin. She had the rose. It was a small gesture, but she laid her hand quickly on the hostess's sun-coloured arm, to show her gratitude. She could cope, no problem, but the concern was appreciated.

She was led by the hostess down the length of the aisle to the cabin door.

The pilot, coming from the cockpit, ducked his head to her in embarrassment.

The purser shook her hand, said something into his chest that she could not understand, but she smiled back at him warmly, the sham smile.

There was an official from the Airport Authority at the hatch of the aircraft. She thought that he had probably done it before. He had no smile for her and no handshake, and no anodyne small talk. He took her grip bag. He unlocked an outside door at the start of the extended tunnel from the aircraft and gestured that she should follow him. The rain and the wind caught her, trapped her skirt against her thighs and billowed her raincoat. She followed him down the steep staircase, skipping the last step onto the apron. The handlers had already started to unload the baggage from the cargo hatch, and they took the suitcases and string-tied cardboard boxes from the hatch and threw them carelessly onto the open trailer. There was a young woman from Customs edging towards her, unsure, and pushing the documentation under her nose. She signed with the pen she was offered and the ink ran as the rain dripped on the paper. Two men in black suits, the one working his jaw round spent chewing gum and the other cradling in the palm of his hand a dead briar pipe, waited statue-still beside the hearse. There were no more suitcases, no more cardboard boxes coming from the hatch. The men from the hearse moved forward as if to a signal. She heard the noise of the scraping from inside the cargo hold.

The coffin was of grey sheet metal and it was heavy and awkward to manoeuvre in the confined space.

The pipe was pocketed, the chewing gum was spat out.

The coffin was lifted clear. She stepped forward. She laid the single rose on the coffin's lid beside the documentation that was fastened to it with adhesive tape. The wind seemed to come fiercer off the tarmac and she walked beside the coffin with her fingers steadying the rose until they were sheltered by the length of the hearse. The back door closed on the coffin and she could see her rose through the rain-blurred windows. It was driven away.

Was she being met? No, she had her own car . . .

Did she need a lift? Yes, that would be very kind, to the long-stay car park . . .

Mary Braddock had brought her daughter, her Dorrie, home.

'I said we could go out and get something in a pub. I said I'd have a go at knocking something up. She wouldn't hear of it. Said something about being too tired to go out, and something about me needing a proper meal. She was into her kitchen and putting it all together.'

'She's so strong, she's a grand woman.'

'Sorry, Arnold, but it's a facade. It was all over her face, she'd been weeping, the poor darling, all the way home. I couldn't go with her, you see. Well, you know that . . . The contract is eleven million sterling, it's got to be in day after tomorrow. She said, anyway, quite definite, that she was going and going alone. Damn the little bitch . . . I married Mary, not her bloody daughter . . . You'll have another?'

Charles Braddock's hideaway, what he called his 'snug', was at the bottom right corner of the acre of garden behind the Manor House. The Manor House, Elizabethan brick and good timber, was hidden from them except for the tall chimneys by a succession of screens provided by the old azaleas and rhododendrons, and a yew hedge, and the wooden frame that supported honeysuckle and climbing roses, and the flintstone wall of the vegetable garden. Under the big bare branches of the oak and beech trees that separated the garden from a farmer's fields, he had designed, then built, the wooden hut that was his hideaway.

There was power in the hut for a small fridge, and space for a small cabinet. He came to his 'snug' to read, meditate on problems at work, sleep through weekend summer afternoons, and curse. Alongside the hut was the boundary fence to his neighbour's smaller garden, and set in the fence alongside the cage for compost and grass cuttings was a stout stile that provided his neighbour access to the ice and Scotch and gin. It was the way of things that when Arnold climbed heavily over the stile and took the offered plastic cup Charles Braddock would do much, most, of the talking.

'She wasn't easy . . .'

'God, and that classifies as understatement. She was hopeless, impossible . . .'

'And dead, Charles.'

'Are you going to read me the lecture? Mustn't speak ill, that sort of stuff? If she hadn't been Mary's girl I tell you what, I would have said "bloody good riddance". I would have said . . .'

'Best you don't, Charles. Not many medals to be won there. I think we all know what sort of young person was Dorrie. Thank you . . .'

Charles Braddock passed the refilled plastic cup. It was always plastic cups that were used in the 'snug', no washing up afterwards, and a bin bag in the corner for the throwaways. He valued Arnold. He thought of him as sensible and logical and calm. Probably, he used Arnold. Senior partner in the practice, major architectural projects, country-hopping for business, taking home before tax a minimum of £300,000 a year, he found from Arnold a patience and an understanding. God, the man knew just about every secret in the life of Charles Braddock and his second wife, Mary . . . But then Arnold was good with secrets.

And it was secrets that paid him a salary considerably less than fifteen per cent of Charles's gross. They talked about Charles's work, interminably, and about Charles's domestic scene, often. Charles knew the exact nature of Arnold's job, and it was off limits and his family was not mentioned. They stood in the front of the hut, huddled in their overcoats straight from the day's work in London and the 6.17 train from the capital. Charles knew that Arnold was always on the 6.17 down to the Surrey and Sussex border village, and he had made the big effort to be on the same train and home early.

'Is there anything I can do, or say?'

'She doesn't know how Dorrie died, in the middle of a war zone. She doesn't know what the wretched girl was doing there, in a village that was fought through. She doesn't know what happened. She says that she's the right to know . . . You know Mary, it'll nag and fret and worry with her. The bitch, living, damn near ruined our marriage, now the bitch, dead . . .'

'I'd like to speak to Mary.'

The cups were finished, thrown into the plastic bag. The Scotch was placed back in the cabinet. The light was switched off and the door of the hut slammed and locked. They hurried in the dark along the path of slab paving that wound around the azaleas and rhododendrons and under the wooden frame and past the vegetable garden wall. Charles was a big man, sixteen stones, and his neighbour was slighter and barely filled out his high-street coat. They ran as best they could through the rain and towards the kitchen door. They came to the long thrown light from the kitchen window.

His wife was sitting at the wide refectory table in front of the Aga cooker.

Charles Braddock cursed. 'The bloody girl, dead, and hurting worse . . .'

His wife had her head in her hands.

'She's the right to know,' Arnold said quietly. 'I promise that I'll do what I can.'

His wife shook in her sobbing.

The journey had taken all of the day and all of the night.

It had taken all of the day because the tyres of the car had been bald and the front left had punctured on the road between Belgrade and Bijeljina, and it had been at pistol point that they had persuaded the owner of the garage in Bijeljina to replace it. And the rear left had gone between Derventa and Miškovci which was a bad place and close to the front line, and not even a pistol had won a replacement tyre from the garage in Miškovci because there were none, and they had had to wait while the puncture slash was repaired.

It had taken all of the night because, after the punctures, in darkness, the car had run out of gasoline on the road between Banja Luka and Prijedor, under the Losina mountain of the Kozara range, and the youngest of them had walked to Prijedor to the barracks, and taken four hours for it. No tyres and a shortage of gasoline, the bastard sanctions, and dawn before the car had reached the bridge over the Una river which was the crossing point from Bosnia, and they had reached Dvor.

Always the rain. The whole of the journey in rain, and uncomfortable in the Mercedes of the man from Knin because there were three of them on the bench seat in the front and four of them crammed onto the back seat.

No break in the rain, but the bitter angry mood of Milan Stanković had lessened as they approached Glina. Coming closer to home, coming closer to the fields, farms, villages, woods, hills that were his place. The policeman was to be dropped at Glina, he would be next after the policeman, and then the car would head on south for Knin. And when he had been let off then, see if he cared, they could have four punctures, and they could have a dry tank, and they could walk ten kilometres for new tyres and new gasoline . . . The policeman insisted they stopped, all of them, in Glina. They banged up the café on the main street, by the bridge, and they hit the brandy. He was close to home, and the brandy was good. Banter and laughter in the car and talk of the meeting in Belgrade, and the hotel into which they had been put, and the fine sheets in the hotel, and the bar in which nothing was paid. And good speeches for them in Belgrade, and the hall full for each of the five days. Speeches of the Serb nation, and the Serb victory, and the Serb future, and nothing about the bastard sanctions and no tyres to be had and no gasoline . . . They took the Bović road beyond Glina and they came into the village that was his home and his place. He wanted the big Mercedes to be seen in Salika, and he wanted to

24

be seen with the big men from Knin. He took his time at the door of the Mercedes, punching shoulders through the opened window and slapping cheeks and clasping hands. There would be enough in Salika who would see that Milan Stanković was the friend of the big men from the government in Knin, and those that did not see it would be told.

He walked home.

He wore his suit, his best suit that was usual for weddings in the village, the suit that had been right for the speeches in Belgrade, and he carried a small suitcase and slung on his shoulder was his AK47 assault rifle with the metal stock folded back. The brandy was in him and he smiled and waved and called out his greeting to those who were already out in the street of Salika, his home, and it puzzled him, through the alcohol, that none came forward to him.

When he was near to the river, when he turned into the narrow lane beside the wire farm fencing that led to his home, he called the name of his son and smiled.

The boy was running to him. Heh, the little ape, and not out of his pyjamas, barefoot and running in the mud of the lane. The boy, his boy, Marko, six years old, was running to him and jumping at him. He dropped his small case and he held the boy and hugged him, and the boy was chirping excitement, and the head of his boy was against the barrel of the AK47. He carried his Marko the last metres to his house and the mud from his Marko's feet was wiped against the jacket of his best suit. And the German shepherd was leaping at him, paws beating at him and the back of Marko and catching in the webbing belt from which the rifle hung. She came to him, his Evica, crisp in the blue linen dress in which she went to work, schoolteaching, and they were all together on the step of his house. His home, his place, his safety. His boy hugged him and his wife kissed him and his dog whimpered pleasure.

He climbed the stairs. The bed in their room, the room that looked away from the village and over the valley and the stream, was not made, and he could see from the bed that his Marko had slept the night waiting for him with his Evica. He threw down the case, and unhooked the AK47 assault rifle from his

25

shoulder. He started to strip out of his suit with the mud marks and his white shirt with the mud smears. They were behind him. He was telling her fast, the brandy warm in him, fast and with pride, of how he had been in a group that Milošević had spoken to, more than ten minutes. And he had talked with Seselj, the Red Duke, one to one for at least a quarter of an hour. And he had been congratulated, personally, by Kertesz who was Chief of Intelligence. And he had shaken the hand of Bokan who commanded the White Eagles.

'. . . All of the big men were there, and I was there.'

He bent to the floor. He wore only his socks, vest and underpants. He unfastened his case. He rummaged amongst his used clothes for the parcels, for the blouse and the plastic toy pistol, that he had bought in Belgrade with American dollars.

His Evica said, flat, 'I tried to telephone you, it was impossible . . .'

Milan grimaced. Of course the telephone did not work between the village of Salika and Belgrade. The telephone did not work, often, between the village and Glina, nor between the village and Petrinja, not to Vojnić, nor to Vrginmost; of course it was not possible to reach Belgrade. He gave the wrapped parcel to his Marko. He watched the boy rip at the thin paper.

'I tried to telephone you to tell you that they had come.'

Marko had the plastic pistol free and made the noise of firing and whooped his excitement. He gave his Evica her parcel. She took it and was gazing into his face, and he could see her fear. Confused, tired, and the wash of the early brandy still in him, Milan did it for her, and took the paper from the blouse, and held it in front of her and against her shoulders and her chest. She pushed him away. She ignored the blouse and went to the window. Her back and her head and her neck were in shadow.

'It was the day after you had gone that they came and dug for them.'

He held the blouse limp against his leg. He went to her and

26

stood behind her. He looked out through the window and over her shoulder. He looked across the fence at the end of his garden, where she grew their vegetables, and across the field where the grass was greening in the spring rain, and across the stream that was swollen from the winter's snow. He looked into the village of Rosenovici. He saw the scattered homes that had been burned and the tower of the church that had been hit with shell fire and the roof of the school that was a skeleton of wood beams. He knew where he should look. On down the distant lane and he could make out, faintly, the new tyre marks in the grass that covered the old tractor ruts. At the end of the lane, where it went into the field, was the rough rectangle of disturbed black-grey earth.

'We did not know, without you, what to do. They dug for them and they took them away.'

Arnold Browne closed the file.

He thought he might have met the man, once or possibly twice, when he had been briefing F Branch recruits long ago, or in that short period of a few months when he had headed 1(D) section of A Branch. He thought he recognized the likeness but the file photograph was poor and thirteen years old. From what he remembered, he was quite an alert and resourceful young fellow. In his opinion, and professional suicide to voice it, there should have been room in Five for men like that. He looked up and noted that the door to the outer office was closed. He had what his wife described, without sympathy, as a siege mentality to his work now. He pushed the file away across his empty desk, empty because little of substance in the affairs of the Security Service these days came his way. He reached for his direct-line telephone, dialled, and spoke quietly so that his voice would not carry through the prefabricated walls of his office and the closed door. He valued his neighbour's friendship, something that excited him about the power of decision that no longer came his way.

'Charles, it's Arnold . . . Can't speak much. Mary, she most definitely has the right to know. There's a man who was once on our books . . . If Mary wanted someone to peck around a bit then I've a telephone number . . . I'll have all the details tomorrow for her, and I'll mark his card meantime . . . Yes, I would recommend him.'

2

He had been sat in the Sierra since before first light. He had the engine idling and the heater going and every few minutes it was necessary for him to wipe the inside of the windscreen hard, bully it, to clear the mist that hazed his view of the target house. He had parked up in a side street a full fifty yards from the main road on which the target house was one of a line of low-set terraced homes. Four hours back, when he had first parked his Sierra in the side street, he had felt a small glow of satisfaction; it was a good place to be parked because it gave him the option of going right or left up the road without the clumsiness of a three-point turn, it was the way he would have done it before the slip, slide, out of the Service. But it was different now from his Service days, and this was solo surveillance and he was working cheapskate, this was shoestring stuff. In the Service days, when he was with Section 4 of A Branch there would have been one to watch in the car and one to drive, and at the far end of the road, also tucked in at a side street, there would have been the back-up car and two more. In the bloody Service days there would have been bodies committed on the ground to cope with target surveillance, those who would stay with the cars and those who could duck out and dive for the Underground if that was how the target chose to move . . . But there was no point bitching, nothing gained from moaning. Dreaming of the Service days was crap and pointless. He was on his own and just bloody lucky to have found a parking space off the double yellows in the side street, and he would be going well if the target came out of the target house and used a car, and he would be going bad if the target came out from the target house and ignored the target car and walked four hundred yards right to the Piccadilly line

Underground or two hundred yards left to the Central line.

The big decision for Penn: to have another cigarette or to unwrap another peppermint. There was a cigarette packet's cellophane on the carpet by his feet, and silver paper from the peppermint tube. He sat in the passenger seat of the Sierra, pondered, made up his mind, and lit another cigarette. He sat in the passenger seat because that was the drill, because then the locals would imagine that he was waiting for the driver and be less suspicious of a stranger in their street. What they had said on the training course, before he had gone to Section 4 of A Branch, the watchers, was that personnel should be 'nondescript'. A good laugh that had raised and Penn had the starter to win the bonus because he was reckoned good and proper 'nondescript', like it was going out of fashion. He was the man who did not stand out. Penn was the guy in the crowd who made up the numbers and was not noticed. Funny old business, the chemistry of charisma . . . at the first course he had actually been called out of the crowd by the instructor and held up, grinning and sheepish, as the example of what a watcher should be like. Penn was *ordinary*. He was average height, average build, naturally wore average clothes. His hair was average brown, not dark and not light, and average length, not long and not short. His walking stride was average, not clipped and mincing, not busy and athletic. His accent was average, not smart and privileged, not lazy and careless with the consonants. Penn was the sort of man, damn it, who was accepted because he made few ripples . . . and wanting to make waves, wanting to be recognized, was what had pitched him out of the Service.

Dragging on the cigarette . . .

The door of the target house was opening.

Stubbing the cigarette into the filled ashtray . . .

He saw the target.

Coughing the spittle of the Silk Cut and remembering the woman from Section 4 of A Branch who had come to the garage they used under the railway arches in Wandsworth and slapped a No Smoking sticker on the door of the glove compartment and dared him, and bloody won . . .

The target had turned and carefully locked the front door of the house and was walking. The target was coming towards the parked and heated-up Sierra. He made a note on the pad, time of departure, and he eased his average weight across the gear stick and the brake handle and slid in behind the wheel. Naughty little boy, the target, and not playing it straight with the lady, the client.

Penn was taking £300 a day, a half to the company, for ten hours a day, cooking in his car with the Silk Cut smoke up his nose so that the lady, the client, should not be conned out of her fancy salary. It was mid-morning and the car would have stunk anyway from his socks that were damp and his trousers that were still wet from the rain when he had walked round the back of the target house to check whether there was a rear exit, and a hell of a good thing that there wasn't because this was solo surveillance. The target was the fourth male out of the house that morning. The target had followed a West Indian in building site overalls, and an Asian, and a student with an armful of notebooks and college books.

The target wore old jeans and a loose sweater, and a baseball cap back to front, and the target came past him whistling. A miserable morning with more rain in the air did not faze him. Enjoy it, sunshine, because it won't be lasting. Bit late, sunshine, to be heading off for the office. Good and modern sense of dress in that office, sunshine. The target went on down the road, and it was kid's play because the target had no suspicion that he was watched and took no evasive precautions. The target didn't swivel, didn't cross the road fast, didn't grab a taxi, didn't dive for the Underground.

Penn followed him down the road, crawling the car, watched him cross at the lights, and it was pretty obvious where he was heading on a Thursday morning. Too easy for a man trained in surveillance to the standards of Section 4 of A Branch. The target was a Turkish Cypriot, tall and good-looking and with a rakish step, and hadn't a job and was living in bedsit land, and the gravy time was just about up. The target had milked a good number until the client had walked into Alpha Security, SW19, and been allocated the new boy on the staff. The client was a plain woman, thirty-six years old, with a high-quality brain and a low threshold of loneliness, who earned a salary of £60,000 plus a year by flipping gilts and bonds in an investment team. The client had fallen hard for the target and now wanted to know whether the love of her life was all he cracked himself up to be. It was bad luck for the client that she had chosen the target to fall for because sure as hell the target was living a little lie and the claimed job in property development was economical, skinflint, with the truth.

Bad luck, Miss Client.

He parked up.

Tough shit, Mr Target.

He locked his Sierra.

Penn sauntered along the pavement to the Department of Social Security office. He went inside and found a place on the bench near the door and he watched the slow shuffling queue that was edging towards the counter where a bleak-faced girl stamped the books and doled out the money. He watched the target going forward in the queue. He lit a cigarette and his hand shook as he held the flaming match. It was where Penn had so nearly been. If it had not been for Alpha Security and the partners, three tired guys looking for a fresh pair of legs to take on the dross of the donkey trade, then Penn might just have been in that queue, going forward slowly. He sat it out, and he went through two more cigarettes. He waited until the target had reached the security screen at the counter and given the sour face a winning smile and won something back from her, and she had pushed the money through the hatch to him. The target scooped the money and slid it into a thin wallet. The target was whistling again when he left the DSS office.

Penn made his way back to the Sierra.

In his mind, as he drove south across London, he mapped out the report that he would make for the client.

When he gave the client the report, she might weep and she might mess the little make-up that she wore on her plain face.

Back at the office above the launderette in the road behind the High Street in Wimbledon, Deirdre gave him the note.

'Just gave his name as Arnold. That's his number. Said you should call him . . .'

★   ★   ★

She would not cry, not where her tears could be seen.

Mary walked from the church door, and she had the offer of Charles's arm and declined it.

The undertakers' men were immediately ahead of her and they carefully manoeuvred the steel frame trolley that carried the coffin over the loose chippings of the path.

It had been a good service. Alastair walked beside her. Alastair usually came up to scratch when it was required of him, damned hopeless when it was taking the Confirmation classes for the village kids, useless when it came to counselling the pregnant teenage girls, but always good at taking a service when the grief was heavy in the air. Alastair had been vicar to the village on the Surrey/Sussex border for seven years, had come from an industrial parish in the West Midlands, and liked to say that he had been hardened to misery. He had been taught to say the right things, and say them briefly. Mary thought he had made a useful job of the address, highlighted the positive points, which must have taken him some soul searching, of a young life taken. He had said that only the superficial side of human character is displayed and it was arrogance for the living to dismiss unshown quality in the dead . . . Well done, Alastair. She stopped. Charles stumbled because the halt was sudden. His wretched mind would have been absorbed with the Seoul contract and he had let her know, and no mistake, that the funeral of his step-daughter did not come convenient. She stopped and Charles stumbled because the undertakers had halted to get a strong grip on the trolley that carried the coffin. They lifted the trolley from the path, onto the grass. The coffin was heavy, expensive, the last gesture of throwing money at a problem, and the wheels of the trolley sank deep into the wet grass. They moved forward again, slow because of the sodden ground. Justin, her first husband and Dorrie's father, coughed behind her, it might have been a snivel. The reptile had a cheek being there and it was rotten of him to have paraded his second wife, the little shrew. It had been Justin's going, running off with the little shrew, that had been the kick-start of the problem. An open and pleasant child had become a moody and awkward and bloody-minded horror story, and hadn't grown better. She hated herself for it, for thinking

33

of those times, but they lined up in her memory, the times when her daughter had driven her beyond distraction point . . . The autopsy report said that her daughter had suffered a knife wound at the throat and a compressed fracture of the lower front skull as with a blow from a blunt instrument, and a gunshot wound (entry) above the right ear. She despised herself for thinking the bad memories of her child, her daughter, who had been knifed and bludgeoned and shot to death.

She knew nothing.

She followed the trolley and the coffin as they skirted the old stones and the trolley wheels squealed as the burden was directed around the plots. They were old stones and old plots and they belonged to the village. Mary and Charles Braddock were the newcomers, new money, in the Manor House. There was a good turn-out; it was respectful of the old villagers to come to the funeral of the troubled daughter of the new wealth. She had seen them in the church: the woman who helped in the house and the man who helped in the garden, and the woman from the shop and the man from the post office, and the woman who came in two days a week to type the letters for the charities that Mary involved herself with, and the women from the committee of the Institute, and the man who captained the cricket side who was there because Charles had bought the team's pads and stumps and bats at the start of the last season. Oh, yes, most certainly, her Dorrie would have given them something to whisper about and titter over, bloody little rich girl.

God, the poor kid . . . the kid had a knife wound and a bludgeon wound and a bullet wound . . .

They had reached the freshly dug grave. She noticed the sweat running on the back of the neck of the largest of the undertakers. She tried to picture her Dorrie, an image without the wounds. Slight build but the shoulders thrown back in perpetual challenge, a sparky little mouth pouted in bitter defiance, crop-cut hair that was a statement, messy and crumpled clothes so that when they had dragged her to Sunday morning drinks there were arguments at home and apologies to hosts afterwards. Her honeymoon with Charles . . . Christ . . . and not a relation that she owned who would have the girl, Dorrie, and certainly not

her damned father, and the child accompanying them, disaster
. . . She hated herself for remembering. A dinner party for
Charles's clients and the music battering through the Manor
House from her room and down the panelled staircase, and
Charles going upstairs, and the clients hearing the obscenities
shouted back at him, catastrophe . . . The memories queued for
her attention. She felt herself shamed for remembering. The
village boys were at the funeral. The village boys, work clothes
and casual clothes and trainer shoes and earrings, had come
and parked their beaten-up cars and their motorcycles at the
churchyard gate, and hung their heads as if they cared. The
coffin went down, Alastair recited the last prayer.

Mary took off her glove and took the wet earth in her hand
and threw it to splatter over the coffin lid.

She stood beside Charles at the gate to the churchyard.

She shook the hands that were offered and smiled automati-
cally as the mourners mouthed lies of condolence. The woman
who helped in the house . . . Charles glanced down at his watch.
The man who helped with the garden . . . Charles bit at his lip,
impatient. The woman from the shop and the man from the post
office . . . Charles had made the arrangements for as early in the
morning as Alastair would do it. The woman who typed her
correspondence . . . Charles had a London meeting at noon. The
women from the committee of the Institute . . . Charles was
fidgeting to be off and he had a floral tie in his pocket that would
be exchanged for the black tie as soon as he was in his Jaguar.

The village boys walked past her, like she was no part of their
loss.

Arnold was the last in the line. Solid and lovely and depend-
able Arnold, who did 'something in Whitehall', and she never
asked what he did and she was never told, only that it was
'something in Whitehall'. Charles kissed her cheek, murmured
about being back late, squeezed her hand, and was off and
hurrying for his car.

He had a calm voice. Arnold said, 'I thought it went well.'

'Yes.'

'And nice of those young fellows to show.'

Mary said, 'I used to tell her that it was unsuitable for her to liaise with boys from the council estate – Charles used to call them "moronic louts". Won't you be late up to London?'

'Won't be missed, not these days. Someone who might be of help to you, I've a number . . .'

She heard the slam of the Jaguar's door.

The gravedigger had reached the earth mound, and there was a wisp of smoke from his mouth and he leaned for a moment on his spade. She wondered if, when he had finished his cigarette, before he started to shovel back the earth, he would drop the filter tip into the grave.

'Thanks, but it's about time the Foreign Office did something. The embassy was precious little help in Zagreb, all the time she was missing, and last week. Frankly, they didn't want to know . . . So, you've sorted me out with some red-hot little civil servant who's going to beaver, at last . . .' She heard her own sarcasm. She smiled, small, weak. '. . . Sorry, I'm grateful to you for digging someone out. I mean, she was a British citizen. I want to know, very badly, what happened to her. It's because, I think, Dorrie loathed me. I can recognize it, obsession . . . However awful she was, I have to know. Do I come to him, the Foreign Office man, or will he come down here? I suppose it's all about war crimes, isn't it? What that American said, last year, "You can run, but you can't hide." I suppose it's all about gathering evidence and preparing a case against the guilty, who- ever they are.'

Arnold said, and there was sympathy on his dried and thin lips, 'Don't be disappointed, never helps to set the sights too high. I'm afraid it is the best I can do . . .'

He passed her a small piece of paper. She read a name and the address of Alpha Security, and a telephone number.

'. . . I'm sorry that I can do so little.'

He was walking away. She said after him, soft, 'And women with obsessions are always tiresome, correct?'

'God, what's happened to you?'

Deirdre stared up at him from her desk behind the typewriter. Not that he had interrupted her typing, and her magazine of knitting patterns lay across the keys.

Penn said, 'Just, the chummy didn't want to take it . . .'

He tried to grin, and that hurt his lower lip, but his pride was hurt more than his lower lip. He was learning the business of 'skip-tracing', the trade's vernacular for the locating of debtors, and learning also that not everyone enjoyed being pitched out of bed at dawn and greeted at the front door with the Service of Legal Process. Chummy was a little taller than average, a little heavier than Penn, and had stood in his doorway, his belly bulging his singlet, and swung a mean right jab from nowhere. The pride was hurt because Penn was trained to hit where it mattered and to hit so that a man stayed down, but to hit now was to invite a counter charge of assault. So he had dropped the Legal Process on the front mat and beetled it back to his car. The split lower lip was not bad enough for stitches in casualty, but blood had run down onto his shirt front.

'You look a right mess, Mr Penn . . .'

And he felt a right mess . . . and he felt a right wimp . . . and a toerag who was behind on the payments to the finance company for a four-year-old Vauxhall had stuck one on him.

'Does it show?'

Deirdre was secretary to Alpha Security. She ruled the outer office, and she probably had a thing going with Basil, one-time CID, who had founded the private investigation agency nineteen years back along with Jim, one-time Fraud Squad, and Henry who had once been with Telecom as an engineer. He definitely thought she was an item with Basil, and that anything that crossed her laser vision would go back, pretty damned fast, to Basil. It would go back to Basil that the new boy, young Penn, had come back from Service of Legal Process with a split lower lip . . . Good for his battle honours, another medal to set alongside the kick down the flight of stairs from the boot of the man who was wanted as a defence witness, filling up the trophy cabinet. Deirdre snorted, not necessary for her to tell him that his split lip was viewable at a hundred paces.

'Your client's here.'

He had his handkerchief out and he dabbed the wound, and that hurt hard. He looked through the glass and into the waiting room, into the drab little room that hadn't enough light, nor enough comfortable chairs, nor any recent magazines. She was half an hour early. It was because she was coming that he had hurried the Service of Legal Process, blundered in, and caught the right fist to the lower lip. She was a tall woman, almost beautiful, and she wore clothes of a cut that wasn't seen every day in the office of Alpha Security above the launderette. She had her head down and there was a tissue in her hands that she squashed, pulled, squashed, in a nervous rhythm. She wore a good suede coat and a long black skirt, and there was a bright outsize scarf looped over her shoulders. He thought it was the first time for her, first time in the office of a private investigation company. She had quality diamond stud earrings and he could see the pearls at her throat.

Penn accused, 'Didn't you offer her a coffee?'

Deirdre bridled. 'Stupid fart, Henry, didn't put the milk back in the fridge last night, milk's off. I can't just swan off and leave the phones . . .'

'I want some coffee and I want it now.'

'You're not much of a sight, Mr Penn, not for a new client.'

'Bugger the phones,' he said. 'Coffee, now . . .'

And that would go back to Basil, soon as he trooped in, mid-morning. A sledging from dear Deirdre, that Mr Bill Penn, quite aggressive, quite rude, and no call . . . but she was collecting her handbag. He had a split lower lip and blood on his shirt and he strode to the door of the waiting room. Never explain, never apologize, a good creed. She must have heard him coming and as he opened the door she was looking up and for a moment there was the startled rabbit stare, and then the forced composure. And what he had to do was remember, and hard, that Alpha Security now paid the mortgage and the gas bill and the electricity and the food, and put the clothes on his back and on Jane's and the nappies on Tom's backside, and split lips and kicks down tower-block steps and solo surveillance were part of the game for a guy heaved out of Five and he had better remember it . . . She had a public face on. The composure was set as if the nerves and the fear had never been. He closed the door behind him. She was looking at his mouth but she was too polite to remark on the split lower lip and the blood on his shirt.

'Mrs Mary Braddock? I'm Bill Penn . . .'

'I'm early, the traffic was less than I'd expected . . .'

'It's not a problem,' Penn said. 'What can I do for you?'

'I expect you're a busy man . . .'

'Sometimes.'

'. . . So I won't waste your time. My daughter was in Yugoslavia. She was there when the fighting was in Croatia. She disappeared at the end of 1991, she was listed as missing. Last week I was informed that her body had been identified from the exhumation of a mass grave, in that part of Croatia that is now under Serb control. She had been dead for fifteen months, buried and hidden. I want to know what happened to her. I want to know how she died and why she died. She was my only daughter, Mr Penn.'

He interrupted, 'Isn't this a job for . . . ?'

'You should let me finish, Mr Penn . . . But since you raise it . . . Shouldn't this be a job for the Foreign Office? Of course it should. Do you know anything about government departments, Mr Penn? They're useless. That's a generalization and a true one. Good at cups of tea in a First Secretary's office, good at booking a hotel room, good at platitudes, and they don't give a damn, just some silly woman using up their day. I have been to Zagreb, Mr Penn, I was there when Dorrie, my daughter, was missing, and I was there to bring her body home. I thought it was their job to help people like me, and I was wrong. Arnold is a good friend. Arnold gave me your name . . .'

High excitement coursing, yesterday, when he had been told by Deirdre that Arnold Browne had left the message for him to call, immediately. He had sat in the cubbyhole area where Basil had given him the desk, and savoured the moments before he had picked up the telephone. All some mistake, a mistake to have let him go, and of course they wanted him back . . . or . . . pretty bad cock-up, losing him, but the Service had plenty of scope for work by outsiders who were trusted and proven, nice little one for him, and of course he was not forgotten. And what brutal disappointment crushing him, yesterday, when he had dialled the direct-line number, spoken to Arnold bloody Browne, been told that a neighbour had a problem, needed a bit of uncomplicated ferreting, needed a good plodder was what the bloody man meant . . . He ran his tongue over his lower lip.

'What was it you wanted of me?'

She had her handbag open and she had taken the ointment tube out. She didn't ask his permission. She squeezed the ointment onto her forefinger and reached forward and, casual, gentle, she smeared the salve onto the split of his lower lip.

'I want you to go to Zagreb for me. I want to know how my Dorrie died, and why.'

He thought her so bloody vulnerable, she shouldn't have been there. She shouldn't have been in the waiting room that doubled as clients' interview room in a shabby, God-awful, dreary little office. He told her that he would think on it overnight, that if he took it he would come down in the morning, if . . . She gave him an address. He would think on it and consider it. He walked her out of the office and they passed Basil on the stairs, and the one-time CID man gave her the look-over of a bloody farmer evaluating livestock. They stood on the pavement outside the launderette.

'Would you tell me . . . ?'

'What?' he rasped.

'Would you tell me what state he is in, the man who hit you this morning?'

He saw the mischief dance in her eyes.

Penn said, 'I would have been done for assault. No, if I'd hit him like I know, then I'd have been done for murder. What state is he in? Probably pretty good, probably he's looking forward to getting pissed up in the pub this lunch time and telling the rest of the select lounge how he put one on me. I served the Process, but that's a small-beer victory . . .'

Then the mischief was gone and she was serious. 'I like winning, Mr Penn, I expect to win . . . I want to know how my daughter died, I want to know who killed her, I want to know why she was killed. I want to know.'

They had been at the roadblock an hour. They had sat in the jeep and smoked and talked together for an hour before they heard the coughing approach of the truck. The engine would go on the truck if it went on burning the bad diesel that the sanction busters brought in.

No point in trying to reach Rosenovici from the Vrginmost road, because there was always a block by the Territorial Defence Force on that route. The last week, when they had been there and digging, they had used the turning to Bović off the Glina road, then taken the plank bridge short of the village of Salika to get themselves to Rosenovici.

The roadblock was at the bridge. There were four TM-46 mines laid out on the bridge. Nasty little bastards, and the Canadian knew that each held a bit over five kilos of explosive. It was the first time that he had tried, in the company of his Kenyan colleague, to get to Rosenovici since the digging, the taking away of the bodies. He had hoped to get back to the village and leave a little food for the old woman, and a little love, to have been discreet. Now there would be no food dropped off, and no love, because they were held at the roadblock . . . It was what the Kenyan called 'another peace-advancing day in Sector North'. They would not get the food to the old woman, but that was not good enough reason to back off. Push, *smile*, probe, *smile*, negotiate, *smile*, step by fucking step and half of them backwards, and *smile* . . . always goddamn smile. The Canadian police sergeant had been stationed at the Petrinja base for 209 days and could tell anyone who asked that his posting had 156 days to run. When he made it back to Toronto, when his colleague made it back to Mombasa, then both of them, bet your life, would never forget how to smile.

They were kids, they weren't out of their teens, but the TDF shit at the roadblock had shiny Kalashnikovs, and they had four TM-46 mines to play with, and they were drunk. The Canadian police sergeant reckoned that drunk teenagers with automatic rifles and mines should be smiled at . . . It would have been easy to have given up and reversed the jeep away from the bridge, away from the scarred village of Rosenovici, and driven back to Petrinja – easy, but the abandonment of the old woman would have come hard. It was worth smiling, to keep the road open to the village that was wrecked . . . Rule 1 of Sector North, and Rule 10 and Rule 100, don't argue, *don't*, at kids with high-velocity hardware and mines and booze in their guts. It was a full hour since he had smiled and asked the first time for the responsible official, please, to be allowed to contact that senior and responsible official, and he would appreciate their courtesy if that senior and responsible and important official had the time to spare, just shit . . . They could barely walk upright, the TDF kids, and every few minutes they'd go move the mines, shove them or kick them, and every few minutes they'd go drink some more.

The truck came.

The Kenyan grinned. 'You happy now, man?'

The truck stopped behind their jeep.

'As a hog in dung . . .'

The Canadian smiled. He looked out through the front windscreen of the jeep. He knew the man. He had met Milan Stanković on the third day of his posting to Sector North; he had known Milan Stanković for 206 days. And Milan Stanković had only himself to blame. The big mouth of Salika, the big boasting militia boss. It was the big mouth and the big boast that accounted, the Canadian thought, for the shit-sour face of Milan Stanković. The kids were trying to stand tall, and the kids were telling it to the shit-sour face of Milan Stanković that they had obeyed the orders and stopped the UNCIVPOL jeep from reaching Rosenovici. The Canadian smiled big, and he knew they would not be going over the bridge, and there would be no food for the old woman, and he held the smile.

The shit-sour face was at the window of the jeep.

'You cannot go over.'

The Kenyan said, pleasantly, 'It is part of our patrol area, sir.'

'It is forbidden for you to go.'

The Canadian said, friendly, 'We have never had a problem in the past, sir.'

'If you do not leave, immediately, you will be shot.'

'We are only doing our job, a neutral job, sir.'

'One minute, and it will be me that shoots you.'

'Perhaps another day, perhaps we can go over another day, sir.'

'Get the fuck out.'

The Canadian was still smiling as he reversed the jeep away from the bridge, away from the track that led to the ruin of Rosenovici, away from where they had dug the previous week. He smiled all the time that they were watched by the drunk kids and Milan Stanković. The jeep lurched back onto the Bović road, and he lost the smile and cursed quietly to himself. He had never seen the old woman, but he had heard she was there, in the woods above the village, and he had three times left food for her and the food had been taken. Perhaps it was just a story, that the old woman was there, perhaps it was the stray and abandoned dogs that took the food.

The Kenyan said, 'Maybe he has a problem with his bowel movement. Our good friend did not seem happy . . .'

'Not as happy as a hog in dung.'

The Canadian knew. It was the big mouth. The big mouth had said, 'There have been no atrocities here. We Serbs have always treated our Croat enemies correctly and with care.' It was the big boast that said, 'There are no hidden graves here. We have nothing to be ashamed of.' The big mouth and the big boast in the grimy dining hall of the administration building at the TDF camp in Salika, and all the guys around him to hear it. The Canadian had put in his report, and he had heard that Milan Stanković was called to the summit chat in Belgrade, and the village was a headless chicken, and the Professor had been dragged off the Ovcara dig for the day . . . The Canadian could smile when he remembered how they had been, the mothers in the village, the old men and the kids, when the jeeps had shown up in the week before, and not been able to deny that he had the permission of old shit-sour face to go hunting a mass grave. The Canadian could smile when he imagined old shit-sour face coming back from the Belgrade knees-up to find a nice corner of a dug field, empty . . .

'Mister, do you think we could have given him something for his bowel movement, a pill, something to make him happy . . . ?'

The Canadian said, 'A stone turned, under the stone was a secret, and the secret's abroad and public knowledge, that might just have stopped his bowel movement.'

43

'But, mister, you're not talking evidence.'

The Canadian police sergeant, far from Toronto and Yonge Street, and far from the whores and the pushers of home, had not caught a good night's sleep since they had prised the black-grey earth from a young woman's face. No, he was not talking evidence . . . It was that sort of place, Sector North, the sort of place where evidence did not come easy.

It was rare for Arnold Browne to lose his temper.

'. . . Don't ever do that to me again, Penn, or you're lost, forgotten. Just remember what you are, and you are *ex*, Penn. You are ex-Five, you are ex-A Branch. You may once have, stupidly, harboured the illusion that there is a way back – let me tell you, Penn, that the way back is not via spitting in my face. You don't *think* on it, you don't *consider* it, you damn well jump to it, and I was doing you a favour . . . I can get a score of ex-Herefords who would give the right cheek of their arses for a job like this, and I gave your name . . . Got me?'

'Yes, Mr Browne.'

'You don't patronize by *thinking* and *considering*, you bloody well get on with it.'

'Yes, Mr Browne. Thank you, Mr Browne.'

He slapped down the telephone. Yes, rare for him to lose his temper, and he felt no better for it. His anger was because of his memory of Dorrie Mowat, and God alone knew what a pain the child had been . . .

He had left home early.

He had left home while Jane was still feeding Tom. He had called once from the front door, and she must have been distracted because she hadn't called back to him from upstairs. She was too damned often distracted.

He had driven down through the countryside to the Surrey/Sussex border.

Penn was thirty-five minutes early for his appointment at the Manor House.

He parked up the Sierra in the space beside the shop. There were old half-casks outside the shop filled with bright pansies, and there was a notice congratulating the community on a runners-up prize in the Tidy Village competition. Bill Penn and Jane and baby Tom, in the maisonette, lived in Raynes Park, near the railway station, and there were no Tidy Village competitions where he lived.

Time to kill, and he went walking.

Away from the Manor House, away from the shop, past the village cricket pitch where the outfield grass was wet and the square was thick with worm casts, towards the church. Below the church was the graveyard. He saw her in the graveyard. Penn felt a shiver. She was sitting on the grass and her weight was taken by an arm braced to the ground. She was beside the heaped earth on which was the bright carpet of flowers. Her head was ducked and her lips might have moved, as if in quiet conversation, and the two dogs were close to her. The two dogs, cream-white retrievers, were on their sides and chewing at each other's ears and pawing each other's faces. She wore old jeans and a baggy sweater and sat on her anorak; he wondered if Mary Braddock would have gone home and changed and presented the controlled appearance to him if he had arrived at the time given him. He went through the church gate and his heels crunched the gravel path. Because she had still not seen him, he paused for a moment to check that his tie was straight, to check there was no dandruff on his blazer, to check that his shoes had not been scuffed. When he came up off the path and onto the grass, the dogs were alerted. They bounded away from her, and from the grave, and their leads trailed crazily behind them, and their hackles were up. He knew the basics of dogs; Penn stood still and talked gently to them as they circled him, and he kept his hands still. She looked up at him, seemed to mutter something to the flowers, then pushed herself up. He knew what he would say, and he had rehearsed it in the car, just as he had rehearsed it in bed while Jane had slept beside him . . . 'I said, Mrs Braddock, that I would think on the assignment, that I would consider it. I am a free agent, Mrs Braddock, I am not owned by anyone, most certainly not by the Security Service who sacked me, most definitely not by Arnold bloody Browne who did not stand in my corner. What I do not need, Mrs Braddock, is you ringing

45

Arnold bloody Browne, so that I get a quite unwarranted bollocking down the phone, when I am thinking and considering taking an assignment . . .' It was the same as when he had spied on her in the waiting room of Alpha Security. She shed her sadness, summoned up her composure. What he had rehearsed was gone from his mind.

'Good morning, Mrs Braddock.'

'Thank you for coming, Mr Penn.'

She walked well, tall, out of the churchyard, and he followed a half-pace behind her. The dogs looked back at the grave and the flowers, whined once together, then trailed after her.

It didn't seem to matter that he had left his car beside the shop.

She led him back through the village.

She walked him up the wide tarmacadam drive of the Manor House. The climbing roses on the brickwork were drooped dead, and the honeysuckle was ragged, not yet in leaf. The sort of house that was photographed, For Sale, in the magazines left in his dentist's reception. She took him into the hall, and there was furniture that he would have noticed through the windows of showrooms when he was doing central London surveillance. She did not tell him where she was taking him.

Up the stairs, wide, polished oak. Along a corridor, dark and panelled. Through a small door.

A bright and airy room. A child's room. A neat and cleaned child's room.

She waved him to a chair, and he carefully moved the soft bears and made himself the space to sit. She was on the bed. Bill Penn had been brought to the shrine . . .

She said briskly, 'My daughter, Dorothy, was a *horrid* young woman. She could be quite foul, and enjoy it. My husband, her stepfather, he says she was "rubbish", he's usually right about things. I am a spoiled woman, Mr Penn, I have everything that I could possibly want, except a loving daughter. She was a messer, a waster, and costly. I think she took a pleasure in hurting me . . . and, Mr Penn, she was my daughter . . . and, Mr Penn, her throat was slit and her skull was bludgeoned and she was finished off with a close-range shot . . . and, Mr

Penn, not even a rabid dog should be put to death with the cruelty shown to my Dorrie. Do I carry you with me, Mr Penn?'

He nodded.

'We'll go down to the kitchen, Mr Penn, I'll make us some coffee . . . I called her "horrid", and when we have some coffee I'll give you examples – I don't believe in putting dirt under stones, Mr Penn . . . By the by, this isn't the room she left when she went away. I had it redecorated. I made the room the way it should have been. The room is a fraud. New curtains, new duvet, new carpet. I went out and bought new books and new toys. A stupid woman trying to believe she could start again . . . We'd taken her up to London and put her on a plane to Brisbane. The last we saw of her was her going through the departure lounge, and she didn't even bother to look back and wave, and we were so damned relieved to see her gone that when we were back here, home, my husband split open a bottle of champagne. Am I boring you, Mr Penn? The morning after she'd gone I rang the decorators. I come in here each morning, Mr Penn, while my husband is dressing, and I cry. Do you know anything about Yugoslavia, Mr Penn?'

He shook his head.

'Somebody else's problem, isn't it? Somebody else's war, correct? My trouble is that "somebody else" is me . . . I didn't even know she was there, I thought she was still in Australia . . . Will you go there, please, Mr Penn?'

'If we sort out my fee, my expenses, yes, I think I would consider it.' It was boorish of him.

'You were in the Security Service, that's correct, isn't it?'

He said, sharply, 'That's not an area I can discuss.'

She looked at him, direct. 'I just wondered why you left. If I'm to employ you . . . I just wondered why an officer of the Security Service ended up where you've ended.'

'Wonder away, but it's not your business.'

Not her business . . . Not anyone's business but his and Jane's. His and Jane's business, and all the bastards that he had looked to for support. No, there hadn't been written commendations that would lie in his personal file. Yes, there had been

47

congratulations, back-slapping, snake words, but nothing to lie in his file. He had gone to his team leader, to his section leader, and to his branch leader, all graduates. He had requested their support for his application to be accepted into the inner core of the Service, General Intelligence Group . . . and he had gone to Gary Brennard in Personnel. It was not her business . . . In the new-style Service the men of the Transit van teams were dinosaur history. The new style was squatting in front of a computer screen. The Middle East squad was being wound up. The trades union squad was being cut back. The Campaign for Nuclear Disarmament squad was being phased out. The future, without a degree, was being stuck, tied, trapped in front of a computer screen with the other middle-aged, passed-over no-hopers. The future was scanning the surveillance photographs from the hidden cameras in railway stations and shopping precincts and over busy pavements. The future was searching for men with scarves across their faces, women with their coat collars turned up, carrying bags and dropping them into rubbish bins, to hurry away before the bloody Semtex detonated . . . It was not her business that he had tried for Belfast, not told Jane, and been rejected, told it wasn't for 'marrieds', not at his level. Dougal Gray, best mate, divorced, had won the Belfast appointment . . . Not her business that he had believed in his work, reckoned he protected his society, taken a pleasure that the great bloody ignorant unwashed snored in their beds at night, safe, because he sat in the damn Transit van with a piss bottle for company and a Leica . . . Not her business that in the last two years there had been bloody kids, graduates, set in charge of him and lecturing him on procedures, and running up the bloody ladder that was denied him . . . Not her business.

He felt no warmth towards her, no gentleness. Another rich woman at war with another rich child . . . But there was just a flicker, in her weakness. Just a moment, in her pleading . . . His mother and father lived in a tied cottage, his father was a farm labourer who most days drove a tractor, his mother went out most mornings and dusted and cleaned in the big house on the estate. He hadn't much time for the rich. And she took him downstairs to the kitchen and heated the old iron kettle on the

Aga and made him instant coffee, and told him horror stories of the behaviour of Dorrie Mowat.

An hour later he said, 'I'll work out what it would cost, how many days I estimate it will take. Goodbye, Mrs Braddock. You'll hear from me.'

3

The pub was down the road from the launderette, and round the corner.

'You know what you are, Penn? You are a jammy bastard.'

The pub, Basil's 'watering hole', was mean and dirty and dark. There was a table beyond the bar that was his, out of danger from the darts board. Basil, one-time detective sergeant, had made the table his own since retirement from the Metropolitan Police nineteen years back. Most lunch times, Basil was at the table with Deirdre.

'You milk that one, my son, because it's cream for the cat. You spin it out, my son.'

Jim didn't use the pub at lunch time, left Basil clear with Deirdre, but he came by at five most evenings. Jim, one-time detective constable in the Fraud Squad, liked a game of pool in the bar and a swift pint, or three, with Basil. It was where the hard business of Alpha Security was talked through.

'They don't come on trees, young fellow, they're gifts from heaven. You fell on your feet, young fellow.'

Henry, one-time Telecom engineer, came to the pub only at Christmas, birthday, or celebration time, and nursed orange juice. Henry was valuable, always sober, and spent his drinks money on bug equipment and the gear for tapping hard lines, and the new pride and joy was a UHF room transmitter built into a thirteen-amp wall socket.

'Milk it . . .'

'Run it . . .'

'Enjoy it . . .'

It wasn't talked about, but Penn assumed that Basil and Jim and Henry did odd-job work for Five. Work that was boring

and work that was illegal would be farmed out, Penn assumed. It had to be a good assumption because when he had been working out his notice at Gower Street, when he was getting all the flak from Jane as to where the mortgage money was going to come from, there had been the quiet call from the fourth floor and the request that he attend the office of Senior Executive Officer Arnold Browne. A soft word of sympathy, a frowned nod of understanding, and a *suggestion* that Alpha Security, SW19, might be looking for an able man. He guessed a little empire had been built, the tentacles spread, and Henry never seemed short of gear that cost, and plenty more than he saved by drinking only orange juice. They were a good little team: give Basil three phone calls, he could find a burglar, a mugger, a safe-breaker; give Jim half a day, he could get an Inland Revenue annual statement print-out; Henry could fix, in twenty-four hours, best quality audio and visual surveillance. They were a good little team, but needing young legs and young eyes and a guy prepared to sit through the bread-and-butter crap . . . But it wasn't bread-and-butter crap they were celebrating in the pub, with Penn buying the drinks, it was a hell of a good overseas contract, with money going half share to the partners . . . Penn felt quiet satisfaction, because Basil was almost jealous, and Jim couldn't quite hide the envy, and Henry didn't seem too cheerful.

Penn was reaching for their glasses, and none of them was shouting that it was his round.

Penn said, 'Actually, she's quite a decent woman . . .'

'Bollocks, she's a punter.'

'Daily rate, plus per diem expenses, plus Club-class flights.'

'Half the daily rate up front, per diem expenses in your greasy hand for a clear week before you go, and that doesn't include the hotel of your choice.'

Penn said, 'Pity is that her daughter was a right little tosser . . .'

He scooped up the glasses and headed for the bar.

Two pints of best bitter, an orange juice, and Penn was taking low alcohol because when he was shot of them he would be going back to the office over the launderette and he would be typing up the finances and faxing them down to the Manor House on the Surrey/Sussex border, and then he would be going home to Jane, and hoping to God, some hope, that the baby slept hard . . . and hoping to God, some hope, that Jane wasn't flat on her back with exhaustion . . . It was going sour with Jane, not solicitors and courts stage, just going stale, and he did not know what to do about it, nor whether it mattered if he did nothing about it.

He brought the drinks back, shouldered his way through the shop people and the mechanics in their overalls and the building site workers who were all on the 'black'. Wouldn't have been seen in there, not seen dead in there, when he had been at Gower Street. It still seared him, and it would do so for a goddamn long time, the memory of when he had come back home to Raynes Park off the train from Waterloo, and told Jane that he was washed up, working out his notice, gone. Jane, seven months pregnant, and hysterical, and him not able to staunch the screaming. She'd done it, Jane, she had wound him up when she had packed her job in because the baby was coming. She had done the sums of the household accounts, told him they couldn't survive, not with the baby coming, not without her money, unless he had himself promoted. She had told him he should have been made up from executive officer to higher executive officer, and like a bloody fool . . .

Basil took his drink. 'Cheers . . . I'm going to give you advice, you jammy bastard. Don't go sentimental on it, don't get yourself *involved.*'

Jim grasped the pint glass and nodded his agreement.

Henry sipped at the orange juice. 'Good trip . . . Just pile the paper up, reports, analysis, interview transcripts, like you've been a busy boy.'

'I hear you.'

He made his excuses and left them still talking, debating, arguing, what the rate of per diem expenses should be.

He walked out onto the street.

They were closing the shutters down on the fruit and vegetable shop, and locking up the jeans and denim store, and the launderette was packed full. Gary bloody Brennard, Personnel, wouldn't be unlocking a paint-peeled door beside a launderette and going

52

back to work at 6.33pm, and Gary bloody Brennard, Personnel, wouldn't even remember his little talk with Bill Penn, executive officer. His own fault, because he had not copped on to the new scene at Five. Too dumb, too stupid, to have evaluated the new mood at Five. Entry to General Intelligence Group was restricted to higher executive officers, new scene, didn't he know? Entry to General Intelligence Group was restricted to university graduates, there was a new mood, didn't he know? They didn't want watchers, nor leg-men, nor ditch-men . . . they wanted analysts and information control management, and they wanted graduates. 'Don't have a degree, do you, Bill?' Gary Brennard's sneer. 'Didn't make university, did you, Bill?' His feet hammered the linoleum above the launderette. He snatched the cover off the typewriter. 'Without a degree, without a university education, you've reached your plateau, haven't you, Bill?' He began to type. He accepted the assignment. He listed the daily rate and a half to be paid in advance, and the per diem expenses rate . . . He pounded the keys of the typewriter. 'If that's the way you feel then you should consider transferring your talents to the private sector. We wouldn't want disaffected *junior* officers, would we, Bill?' He read through the paper.

No, he wouldn't be sentimental. No, he wouldn't get himself *involved*.

He dialled the number. He watched the fax sheet go.

There was not enough light for him to make a clean job of the sewing. He did it as best he could, and it was poor work because he could barely see where he pushed the thick needle, and his hands shook. His hands shook in fear. Ham sewed strips of black elastic onto the arms and the body of the tunic. The others watched him and waited their turn with the one needle and the reel of heavy cotton.

He tried hard to hide the shaking because each of the other five men who would go across with him believed in his professionalism. It was what he was paid for, what he was there for, to communicate professionalism. There were eight lengths of black elastic now on his tunic, and he had already sewn five lengths onto his combat fatigue trousers, and when they were down at the river, when they were ready to slip into the inflatable, then they would collect old grass and they would tuck the grass lengths in behind the elastic straps. They were important, Shape and Silhouette. He passed on the needle and the cotton reel and the roll of black elastic tape. He set himself to work on Shine. He spat into the palms of his hands and then scooped the cream from the jar and worried the mess together, and made the sweeping smears across his eyebrows and nose and cheeks and chin, and his ears and throat and wrists and hands. He handed the jar to those who were waiting to use the needle and the cotton roll. He had told them about Smell, and he had bloody lectured them that there should have been no smoking since the middle of the day, and he had checked that the tinfoil was in his own battle pack for their shit and the burying of it. He had lectured them about Sound, and he had shaken each of the webbing harnesses they would wear for the rattle of loose ammunition magazines, and he had made them all walk round him in a circle until he was certain that their boots were quiet.

Ham had learned Shape, Silhouette, Shine, Smell, and Sound at the Aldershot depot, and none of the others, the dozy buggers, cared . . . They needed it, too fucking right they needed Shape and Silhouette and Shine and Smell and Sound, where they were going . . . the others were from 2nd Bn, 110 (Karlovac) Brigade, and they had been pissed up since morning and Ham was stone sober and his hands shook and his gut was tight. They were dumb bastards to be spending the night with, across the Kupa river, behind the lines. On down his checklist . . . ammunition magazines for the Kalashnikov, knife, gloves, the radio that thank Christ he wouldn't be bent under, cold rations, the balaclava, the water bottle that wasn't full of bloody brandy or the usual slivovitz piss, map and compass, field dressings . . . The big fear, what tightened Ham's gut, shook his hands, was of being wounded, of being left. It was better in the old days, better when there were Internationals on the ground like flies on meat, because then there was the promise that the Internationals, the 'mercs', would look after their own if one was wounded. You wouldn't know with this lot, wouldn't know if they'd fuck off and get the hell out in a stampede back towards the river from behind the lines. They were chuckling at him, the others, and it was because they laughed at his care and his thoroughness that Ham felt the fear.

They were dumb bastards to be with, but there was no one else who would have Sidney Ernest Hamilton, late of 3 Para, late of east London, late of the Internationals attached to the Croatian army. His fingers found the twin dog tags hanging from the dulled chain at his neck. The tags were bound in sellotape to keep them quiet. The tags gave his number from 3 Para, his name, and his blood group, and his number and name and blood group from the Croatian army. He knew it would be bad bloody news for any of them if they were wounded, captured, across the river, and double bad bloody news for a mercenary.

Ham didn't eat any of the bread that was offered him, and he turned down the alcohol, and he thought the Croatians must have known that he was shit stiff scared.

It would be late evening when they moved off down towards the Kupa river where the inflatable was hidden.

Under the new scene, the new mood, there were little chores for a senior executive officer.

The little chores were adequate to remind Arnold Browne that he was outside the mainframe of Service operations. Once a week, a little chore, he met with a senior executive officer from Six, and they talked platitudes, nothings, for an hour before going to lunch on expenses. A little chore because it was unthinkable that the Service would offer valuable information to Six, and inconceivable that Six would volunteer worthy information to the Security Service. Valuable information, worthy information, was power and would not be squandered on the sister organization . . . So, Arnold Browne who was old guard and old time would parry and probe for a straight sixty minutes with a man who was also without a future, and then go take a damn good lunch. The probing and parrying that morning had involved the tedious matter of Ukrainian nuclear warheads and he had extracted nothing that was worthy or valuable. It was ludicrous, of course, that Six should not share their information from the Ukraine so that Five could follow and monitor the Kiev

55

government's attempts to get the hardware of the former Soviet Union operational, bloody pathetic – but, then, Arnold Browne was not sharing with Six what Five had learned of PIRA arms acquisition on the Continent. He did not apportion blame. It was the way of the sisters to squabble, bicker, hold their cards close.

But lunch was good, and at a personal level he enjoyed the company of Georgie Simpson.

A bowl of pasta, a bottle from the Friuli region, a plate of liver and spinach, a second bottle called for, and the talk twisting to Croatia. Safe ground because Georgie Simpson never set foot outside inner London, and would have no secrets to guard.

A belch from Arnold's lunch guest. '. . . I'm like the rest of the great British herd, I'm bored out of my mind with the place. Victoria won't even have it on the television now, switches it straight off. She did the jumble bit last year, getting parcels together, then she read that the stuff she collected was all sitting in a warehouse; she does parcels for Somalia now. I mean, they're just animals, aren't they? They're animals, all of them, not a peck of difference between the lot of them. What gets up my nose is that people here, in their ignorance, seem surprised by the bestiality of the place. I've had the place drilled into me from birth, by my father. Back in the war, he was on gunboat escorts that ran weapons down to the Dalmatian coast for the partisans, Tito's crowd. Two or three times my father went ashore and had to go up into the mountains to meet the Serbs, and he saw a bit of what was done to them by the Croats . . . small wonder they're all A grade for cruelty. Don't want to put you off your food, Arnold, but the Croats, the fascists in their Ustaše movement, used to gouge the eyes out of their Serb friends' faces, sack them up and send them back to their hero leader in Zagreb . . . My father says the Ustaše could make the SS blush. I mean, it wasn't just genocide, it was good fun thrown in. My father said that it wasn't just a matter of killing people, they enjoyed it, most of all they enjoyed causing pain. Incredible people, barbarians. Should leave the blighters to it . . .'

It might have been the wine, could have been the company, but Arnold offered a confidence. He spoke quietly, without restraint, of his neighbour and his neighbour's second wife, and his neighbour's stepdaughter.

'. . . who must have been a right bloody fool to have let herself get caught up in that lot. What I'd call a self-inflicted wound.'

'And a wound for everyone else,' Arnold said. He waved to the waiter for more coffee, and the bill.

'And, she, the mother, wants to know what happened? If you want my opinion, she should let it rest. It's like scratching a bite, yes? You end up with blood and pain. It's different values there, their values and ours don't mix . . .'

'Not the sort of woman to let it rest. Sad, really, but she won't let it go until she's got the full picture . . . Actually, I put her in touch with a private detective . . .'

'What on earth for?'

Arnold was brought the bill. He paid cash, and it would be a month before the money was reimbursed by Accounts. 'I thought that if she had something on paper, some evidence, then she might just be able to detach herself, disengage, rejoin the living.'

'Where did it happen?'

Accounts would not wear gratuities. Arnold scooped the change from the saucer. 'The daughter was killed near Glina, the territory is now occupied by the Serbs. I believe it's called Sector North . . .'

Georgie Simpson laughed out loud, a real good belly laugh. 'It'll be a pretty thin volume then, this joker's report . . . Nice meal, thanks, puts me on my mettle, where to go next week . . . That would be a pretty bloody place to be sniffing.'

'It's only a bromide job, of course; it's not sharp-end work . . .'

They had their coats on, they were out on the pavement, their voices drifted.

'Come on, Arnold, what would you have ever known about sharp-end work . . . ?'

Arnold Browne sniggered. 'Same as you, Georgie, damn all of nothing . . .'

It was the late afternoon, and a thin sun was through the cloud, and the garden grass was drying.

The child played between the apple trees that spread above the vegetable patch. Marko had the plastic pistol. It had not been out of his sight since his father had brought it to him, taken to school, laid on the pillow of his bed. He weaved among the old tree trunks and saw the old Ustaše enemy, and fired on them and killed them. It was the game he played every day, with a wooden stick that made the shape of a rifle before his father had brought him the plastic pistol from Belgrade, killing the Ustaše enemy. He played alone.

In the village there was the scream of a car horn, sounded like an alarm, and Marko heard the shouts of men.

He played alone, because his friend, the one friend of his life, was gone. It was as if he no longer trusted that he could find a good friend again. He was six years old, and his birthday would be the next week, and although it was many months since his friend had gone he could still remember, so clearly, the knowledge that his friend had betrayed him, his friend had been a part of the Ustaše enemy. Where Marko played, ducking, running, throwing himself down onto the grass to find shooting cover beside the apple trees, he could see across the field, and across the narrow stream, and across more fields, to the village where his friend had lived. He could see the house in the village across the stream, and there was no roof on the house, and where the side wall of the house had collapsed he could see the bright cream and red of the wallpaper of the room that had been his friend's. Most days in summer he had waded the ford in the stream or his friend had come the same way to him, and most days in winter when the stream was high he had gone across the plank bridge or his friend had come that way to him. And now he knew that his friend was an Ustaše enemy, and he knew that the parents of his friend and all in the village across the stream had planned to slit the throats of their Serb neighbours . . . He knew it because he had been told it by his father. He had wondered, often, if his friend would have come in the night with all the other Ustaše enemies, and carried a knife, and cut his throat. It was too much of a betrayal for him to care to find another friend.

Marko's game died.

A car screamed down the lane towards their house.

The car braked and scattered mud in front of the house, and his father was jumping from the car while it still moved and was running towards the big door.

The dog was barking and running after his father and into the house.

Marko came from the orchard, hurrying.

He whistled for the dog to come to him. The dog had no name now, but it came to the whistle. There were five men in the car and they were crashing magazines into their weapons. The dog was his. He had saved the life of his dog. The dog had belonged to the family of his friend who was now an Ustaše enemy. It had been before the battle for the village across the stream that his friend had gone with his family, all packed with cases and bedding into the Yugo car. He had watched it from behind the apple trees. He had been behind the apple trees because for a week the snipers had fired across the narrow stream, and his mother would have beaten him if she had known he was at the back of the house. They had left the dog. He had seen how the dog had run after the weighed-down Yugo car, and he had heard his friend's father curse the dog for running beside the wheels, and the dog had run after the car until they were gone from his sight. It had been a week after the battle that he had heard the dog barking in the night from beside his friend's house, and his father had said that he would go shoot the dog in the morning, and he had cried for the dog in a way that he had not cried for his friend . . . His father had crossed the stream and brought the dog home, and his father had said that there was no point in giving the dog a new name because it would not respond, and they could not use the old name of the dog because it was an Ustaše name.

He had hold of the dog's collar when his father exploded from the big door of the house.

His father carried his army pack and a small radio and his rifle.

There was the roar of the car leaving. Marko ran to the gate onto the lane. Up the lane, in the square of the village, he saw more cars gathered, and he heard more shouting.

His mother had hold of his shoulder.

He should be inside the house.

He should not be out of the house.

His mother told him that his father had gone to lead the search for Ustaše spies, who had crossed over the Kupa river, who were in the forest and the hills above Rosenovici village.

All the rest of the afternoon Marko stood at the window of his bedroom and he gazed across the narrow stream into the curtain of trees that covered the hillside.

She paid the taxi off fast, thrust the note at the driver and did not wait for the change. The drizzle was back, and the wet clung to Charles's shoulder.

Typical of him to wait on the pavement for her. She reeled off her excuses, the weather, late train, no taxis . . . She saw his expression, set hard and annoyed.

'Sorry, sorry . . .'

He marched up the wide office steps. 'I saw your *Mister* Penn. I told him his figures were ludicrous . . .'

'And . . . ?'

'. . . I told him they were extortionate.'

'And . . . ?'

'He said that was his rate.'

'And . . . ?'

'He said that if I didn't like it, I could shove it up my . . .'

'And . . . ?'

'He was pretty damn lucky to catch me happy. He won.' Charles Braddock grinned, sourly. 'He said that he would be leaving for Zagreb in the morning. But don't think you'll be getting anything more than a load of paper . . . He was pretty damn lucky.'

She kissed her husband's cheek. 'Thank you. I rather liked him. What I liked about him was that he told me to mind my own business. Doesn't grovel too much, not to you, not to me . . .'

'Come on.'

They were going to the lift. The commissionaire had the doors open for them, wore his medals proudly, and ducked his head

60

in respect to them. Penn had told her husband that if he didn't like the terms he could shove the assignment, and he had told her to mind her own business . . . quite amusing.

The lift doors closed.

Mary said, 'My guess is he's been badly used. He's rather sweet but so naïve . . .'

'If we could, please, just enjoy a normal evening . . .'

It was the usual type of gathering for which Mary Braddock hiked to London, her husband's senior colleagues and the design team and the clients. She thought that her *Mister* Penn would not have stood a cat in hell's chance, would have been kicked away down the lift shaft if it hadn't been that the clients had put ink on the contracts that very day. She wafted through the salon, she meandered into and out of conversations. Her mind was away, away with the man who would be travelling to Zagreb, away with her daughter who was dead, buried, gone . . . A thin little weed of a man approached, her husband's financial controller, and he had caught her.

'Sincerest condolences, dear Mary, such a dreadful time for you . . .'

Sincerity, he wouldn't know what the word meant.

'Heartfelt apologies, Mary, that I couldn't make the funeral, just not enough hours in the day . . .'

No, he wouldn't have taken time off for a funeral from the small type of a contract.

'Still, she was so difficult, wasn't she? We have to hope, at last, that she lies in peace. Your Dorothy, she was such a trial to you.'

She did it expertly, and fast. She tipped her cointreau and ice against the left side of his pale-grey suit jacket. She thought it would be a lasting stain, hoped it would defeat the dry cleaner. The amber ran on the grey.

'Dorrie, she was mine, damn you, she was *mine* . . .'

She was sitting in the chair by the door and watching him. She didn't help him to pack.

'How long are you going to be there?'

His suitcase was on the bed. His clothes were stacked close

61

to the case and he tried to make a mental note of what he would need.

'Where are you going to be staying?'

She had the baby, Tom, on her shoulder and she gripped him tight. Her statements came like machine-gun bullets, hurting him, wounding.

'What's the point of it all?'

His shoes went into the bottom of the case with his bag for washing kit and toothpaste and razors, and a guidebook of former Yugoslavia, and around their bulk went his socks and his under-clothes. Penn told his wife, quiet voice, that he thought he would be away for a minimum of a week and he told her the name of the hotel where he was booked and he told her about Mary Braddock. On top of his socks and underclothes he laid two pairs of slacks, charcoal-grey.

'So, I'm just supposed to sit here and wait for you to show up again?'

All his shirts were white. It was like a uniform to him, that he wore charcoal-grey trousers and white shirts and quiet ties. He had always worn the uniform when he had gone to work at Gower Street. The jeans and the sweaters and the casual shirts that were right for Section 4 of A Branch had been kept in a locker.

'If you hadn't made such a fool of yourself then you wouldn't be running round with that deadbeat outfit, would you?'

Their home, two bedrooms, one floor, had cost £82,750. Their mortgage was £60,000. They could not have bought the house and furnished it without the help of her father, digging into his building society savings. They were not quite 'negative equity', but damn near. They could not sell the house without slashing into what her father had loaned them, or what the building society had advanced them. They were trapped in the bloody place. And it was not a home any more, but a little brightly painted prison. He thought there was enough in the case for a week, and something to spare.

'What you do now, it's grubby, isn't it? It's prying into people's lives. How do you hold your head up?'

Well, he held his head up because there was a cheque coming

into the bank each month, and that should have been a good enough reason to hold his bloody head up. He would wear his blazer on the aircraft, not fold it away in the case. He did not take Jane home any more to his parents and the tied cottage, and they had not yet seen their grandson, Tom. Nothing said, but understood amongst them all, that he did not take Jane home. If his mother rang and Jane answered the telephone then his mother just rang off. The maisonette was a brightly painted prison and the marriage was a locked cell door, but he hadn't the time to be thinking about solicitors and he hadn't the money to be thinking about new rent to go with the old mortgage. He closed the case and fastened the lock, and put the case on the floor at the end of the bed.

'And what's the point of you going there, what's anyone to gain from it?'

It was the way of her, to goad him. He looked into the frightened small eyes of her face, and they were reddened from crying from before he had come home. She was looking at his lip, which was better now, but still ugly.

Penn said softly, 'I am not going into a war zone, the war zone is Bosnia. I am going to Croatia, the war finished in Croatia more than a year ago, the war's gone on by to Bosnia . . . I am going to trawl round the embassy, I am going to see the ministries there, I am going to interview and get transcripts from a few refugees, I am going to write a report. That's what they're going to get, a nice little typed-up report. I am going to get a good fee from it, and they're going to get a good typed-up report . . .'

The tears had come again. 'You'll be sucked in.'

'No chance.'

He couldn't talk it through with her. Never had been able to, but it was worse now. It was his habit with her, to hide behind the denials. He could have talked it through with Dougal, his best mate in the Transit team, but Dougal Gray was in Belfast, had extended his tour, and the postcards with the dry tourists' messages didn't come any more. It was only with Dougal that he had ever talked through work problems and Jane problems . . . and had a few laughs . . . and once substituted white paint thinner for milk in the silver tops of an old misery's house . . .

and once . . . the best times in the Transit were with Dougal, and then Dougal hadn't been around to talk through his being dumped by the Service. And Dougal had been long gone when he had spent the worst, foul, hour of his life, going home on the train, walking from the station to the front door, preparing to tell Jane that the job was finished.

'You'll be sucked in, because you always want to belong.'

'No way.'

'Won't you? You'll be stupid . . .'

Penn knelt beside the chair. He had so little to say to her. He did not have to offer a checklist of their social arrangements that he would not now be able to meet, because they had no social life. Men from PO Box 500 were not a part of any outside community, and the pariah status remained for a reject. There was no amateur dramatics society to be told he would miss a rehearsal. There was no pub skittles team to be told that he was missing the next league outing. There was no evening education class because he could never guarantee his attendance. There was no dinner party or meal out with friends, because Five men, ex-Five men, avoided the great unwashed. He would be gone for a week and no one in their block of maisonettes, in their street, would know or notice. Might just be the story of his goddamn life . . . He put his hands on her arms and she flinched from him, and was holding tight to their baby. Wouldn't she just understand, couldn't she try to understand, that he might just *want* to go . . . ?

'I promise that I won't be stupid. It's just a report, Jane, it's not Rambo nonsense. It's just a report that will put some poor woman's torment to rest. It's nothing special.'

'Don't think, if you play the hero, they'll have you back.'

'If you'd met her . . .'

He remembered the woman, in torment, sitting with her dogs beside the grave, and he remembered that the flowers on the grave had lost their brightness. He thought it a pity that the daughter, Dorrie, had been just a 'messer' and a 'tosser'. He thought that the work would have been more interesting, more fulfilling, if the girl had been worthwhile. There was nothing worthwhile that he had been told about the girl when he had sat beside the Aga in the kitchen and drunk the instant coffee.

'I won't even be able to get close to it, not even if I wanted to. The people who did it, killed the girl, are beyond reach, they're behind the lines . . . it's only to write a report.'

4

He started to write after lunch.

Henry Carter had clear handwriting, and much to be thankful for to a schoolmistress who had presided with an iron fist over a primary class more than fifty years before. He had never lost the art of legible copperplate handwriting.

When he had completed the text, when the supervisor had gone for her mid-afternoon rest break, he would slip the sheet to Penny, a nice girl and respectful, and Penny would type it for him. The typed sheet would go with the file when he was ready to present it for transfer to the disk. It was always necessary, Henry Carter believed, to have background. One couldn't say when the file would be called for, when the material would be summoned up. It might be next year, but then it might not be for a decade. It might be that the person, young man or young woman, who would call up the file was now in short trousers or ankle socks. The war might be just history when the file was called for. He brushed the crumbs from his table, and he swirled his tongue round his mouth to try to lose the tang of the cheese and pickle. What surprised him . . . oh, yes, he could still sometimes surprise himself . . . was that he had stayed with the file right through the statutory one hour of lunch break, he had not even taken the RSPB magazine from its postal wrapping.

Onto clean paper, with a sharpened pencil, he wrote briskly.

It would be good to have the background, helpful . . .

OUTLINE: Following the collapse of the Soviet Union, amidst a wave of optimism for the future, the ethnic groups of the empire demanded again the nationhood that had been suppressed since the establishment of communist regimes after WW2. Communist centralism had failed significantly to blunt such demands.

YUGOSLAVIA: Always artificial, originally dominated in part by the Ottoman empire and in part by the Austro-Hungarian empire. Achieved a bogus national identity between 1918 and 1941 which fractured on the German invasion.

WW2: Pro and anti-Axis feelings polarized the principal ethnic groupings. Croats (RC and Europe-orientated) took Nazi side. Serbs (Orthodox and Slav) formed principal resistance (Chetniks and Partisans). Muslims (obvious) tended to regard this as others' quarrel and engendered both factions' hostility. Characteristic of Serb resistance v Croat fascism was horrific cruelty – ? 700,000 Serbs killed by the Croatians.

TITO: Main resistance leader, communist Josip Broz Tito, by charisma and ruthless rule, bound the infant Yugoslavia together. The Serb majority were over-rewarded with bureaucracy jobs, plus internal security and military. Tito's death, can of worms unlidded again.

POST TITO: Problems of different cultures, different ambitions, are not solved, nor much effort made in that direction; the adhesive is communist discipline.

POST COMMUNIST COLLAPSE: Slovenes (less important) and Croats (critical) are anxious to achieve statehood. Croats are encouraged by Germans (sticky finger in the pie again), and name a date. No thought given to the fears of the several hundred thousand Serbs living within the area claimed for new republic of Croatia. Inside Serb-Croat population were strong memories of WW2 atrocities, also the knowledge that privileged status would end. Bosnia problem not dealt with, irrelevant to this file.

THE WAR: Serb-Croat population formed Territorial Defence Force (ragtag militia) and was aided by Serb-controlled JNA (regular army). Principal Serb-Croat population areas were taken in military action, followed by 'ethnic cleansing' (removal or killing of Croat population in captured areas). Main effort of the war lasted 5 months, cease-fire in January 1992, when 22 per cent of new Croatia had been lost to Serbs. (NB: DOROTHY MOWAT killed in December 1991 when Serb militia and JNA overran the Croat village of Rosenovici, Glina Municipality.)

SITUATION AT TIME OF PENN'S VISIT TO CROATIA: (NB: PENN arrived Zagreb 18 April 1993.) The indigenous Serbs occupying parts of former Croatia had declared a 'Republic of Krajina'. Under the UN-brokered cease-fire agreement the territory was to be policed by a United Nations Protection Force (UNPROFOR), but increasing Serb hostility to the international community severely handicapped UNPROFOR's ability to carry out its mandate. UNPROFOR designated four areas of responsibility as Sector South, Sector North, Sector West and Sector East (Glina Municipality in Sector North). Cease-fire line maintained by both combatants in high state of alert, with Serb advantage in numbers and quality of armour, artillery. In the Sectors ongoing brutality towards few Croats left behind in general flight. (NB: DOROTHY MOWAT's body recovered 3 April 1993.)

He read the paper back. A little wordy, his background material, but he did not think it possible for the events of that spring two years ago to be appreciated if the context were not known.

He was thirty-four years old, and it was something he had wanted to do since he was a child.

Penn gazed from the window of the great train.

He could justify it because one of the senior instructors had remarked over a canteen dinner at the Training School, fifteen years back, that in the days of quality field operations it was always best to cross Europe by train. The instructor had said that border checks at night, sleepy frontier guards thumbing their thick books of the names of 'illegals', were never as sharp as at the airport immigration desks. The instructor had said that if an operative wanted to get unnoticed, unhindered, into eastern Europe, then the operative always stood a better than average chance if he took a rocking and winding and slow-hauling train. That was the justification, slight enough, but the hard reason was that Penn had always wished on the chance to take a great train through the mountains of central Europe. He gazed from the window into the night, and the mountains were dark shadows except where they climbed sufficiently for the spring snow to have lasted, and the steepling forests beside the track were a mass of black, and the rivers tumbled silver in the light thrown down from the carriages.

The joy of the journey was gone with the coming of the evening. The joy had been the afternoon crawl through Austria, and the images stayed with him of the tall-towered and ruined castles that perched on crags, of the farms of toy-town neatness that were in the valleys below the track, and the miniature tractors that were out in the handkerchief fields pulling the manure carts from the wood-built cattle barns. It was not his style to think the clever thoughts, that he was traversing the no man's land between the civility of old Europe and the barbarity of new Europe. His style was to inhale the beauty, the majesty, of high mountains and sharp valleys and thick forest and brutal outcrops of rock, take the beauty and majesty into his mind and imagine the delight of walking there. He wondered if there would be the same deer, the same foxes, the same badgers, as there had been in the fields and woods and hills around the tied cottage of his childhood. A place for a man to be alone. So he had taken the chance to ride the great train. He had flown in the morning from Heathrow to Munich, crossed Munich by the airport bus, and bought his ticket at the Hauptbahnhof, and eaten a sandwich, and climbed onto the Mimara Express – Salzburg, Villach, Ljubljana – to Zagreb. It was his dream, it was a collection of postcard prints, and the dusk and then the evening had come; and he doubted that he would tell Jane when he made it back to Heathrow and Raynes Park and 57B the Cedars, that he had taken a great train over a track that cut a route through Austria.

His briefcase was on the seat beside him. He reached for it . . . It was the briefcase that he had purchased, second hand, from the store in Gower Street, bought with pride thirteen years back. The briefcase had been black but long usage by a previous owner had frayed the flap and scuffed the edges and scratched the surface. The briefcase might once have belonged to a higher executive officer, even to a senior executive officer, but it had been purchased by a B Grade clerk, and it was his symbol that he belonged at the heart of the Security Service. The EIIR symbol, once gold, was worn, and it had been one of the games played by the B Grade clerk to imagine what secrets had been held in the briefcase . . . There were no damn secrets now.

He took his notes from the briefcase. He was already in the vernacular of his client. They were the notes that he had scribbled fast on the table beside the Aga of the *horrid* young woman, Dorrie. How the *horrid* young woman, Dorrie, had killed her mother's honeymoon; how she had made a quality scene when the guest for dinner had been the local Master of Foxhounds and she had poured tomato purée over the man's tuxedo jacket; how she had made a quality exhibition with the strip dance that went to full frontal at her sixteenth birthday party; how she had taken her mother's Visa, forged the signature, and bought the current 'liaison' from the council houses a 500-cc Yamaha, new; how she swore at her stepfather where the world could hear her; how she stole, screwed . . .

They had pulled clear of Ljubljana. They had lurched to an uneven stop at a halt station. There was the slamming of doors, and the scream of whistles. The train headed on in the night.

. . . How she was gone, dead, buried. He thought that his own father would have taken a strap to the *horrid* young woman, and his own mother would have locked her in a bedroom to scream, starve, do what she cared. There were two photographs in the briefcase. There was the photograph of her hanging back and half hidden behind the posed pair, her mother and stepfather, with her face pinched in aggression. It was the second photograph that interested Penn more, the girl laughing, and a prettiness on her face, and three of the 'liaisons' from the council houses with their arms on her, as if they knew each corner of her. This photograph had been hidden in her room and found by her mother. Perhaps he would find which of the photographs was real, perhaps not . . . A man towered above him.

It was as the instructor had said. A man in a uniform of cheap cloth, and with a cheap leather belt with a cheap leather holster slung from it, and a cheap cigarette in his mouth, waited over him, smelling of cheap lotion. His passport was checked, handed back to him. No record was taken of his passport number. He was into Croatia. Maybe it was important that no record had been taken, maybe not. He settled back to the photographs, and back to his notes.

It certainly would have been easier for him if the client's daughter, Dorrie, had been more than just a *horrid* young woman.

She knew the sound of the Jaguar. And she knew to take his moods from the sound of the Jaguar braking.

The braking was sharp, noisy.

God . . . she set her face, the smile of the little woman back home and waiting on an angry breadwinner returning from commercial warfare, with his damned nose tweaked or his damned ego bruised. She could usually massage his temper, turn anger to a sullen acceptance.

Mary opened the front door.

'Poor dear, what's the crisis?'

The door slammed behind Charles Braddock, kicked shut with his heel . . . Fine for him to kick the door shut with his iron-tipped shoe heel, but heaven preserve a village boy who as much as brushed a leaning elbow on the paintwork . . .

'The *crisis* is those bloody Koreans, the crisis is that they are, twenty-four hours after ink on paper, requiring re-negotiation of penalty clauses. Bloody impossible . . .'

'Poor dear. Gin's waiting.'

Routine time. Into the small living room. Into his chair. Four cubes of ice, two fingers of gin, half-slice of lemon, to the top with tonic, and let him blather it out. Mary sat on the arm of the chair and her fingers made patterns at his neck, and the gin level lowered as if the anger was gulping down his throat. Curses, obscenities, giving way to resentment, self-pity, nothing changed. After their supper, when she was putting the dishes away, she might just push him down the garden towards his 'snug', and she might just ring next door and get Arnold to report for duty across the stile.

'I mean, how can you do business with people, agree everything, have those bloody lawyers sift through it, have them sign it, then the little buggers want to start haggling again? It is just not possible . . .'

Her fingers soothed him. 'Poor dear . . .'

Resigned. 'How's your day been?'

'He rang,' she said brightly. 'He rang from the airport . . .'

'I should think he bloody did, and bloody cheerful he should have been, with the bloody money we're paying him.'

'Not, actually, cheerful. Sort of distant . . .'

She knew she shouldn't have said it. It was like another flint in a walking shoe.

She saw the frown burrow at his forehead and tried to escape. 'I don't know . . . I'll get supper.'

'Hold, hold, what do you mean, distant?'

'Well, it was the airport. He was just flying out. Nobody's communicative when they ring from the airport . . .'

'Give it me.'

She took a breath. 'It was as though he was uninvolved, of course he's not involved. It was as though it was just another job, of course it's just another job. Why should he be involved . . . ?'

And she felt the tiredness, and she didn't want to talk about it, and she didn't want to think about it, and she had sat all the afternoon in Dorrie's room. She was tired and the anger in his face lowered at her and his voice beat over her.

'His problem, Penn's problem, is he's second-rate. He's not what Arnold cracked him up to be. He's offensive and second-rate. If it hadn't been for you, I tell you, I would not have tolerated his rudeness to me. He caught me, and he's a bloody second-rater. He's taking me, you, us, for a bloody ride.'

The snap. She was trying to call it back, the face of a small

72

child, happy. The weight of a footfall on a dried branch. She had the body of the child and the clothes of the child. She went for the kitchen. The face was old, mature, not a child's, and screwed in dislike. She was shouting back at him. Always the image was of the screwed face of a young woman, never of a happy child. Her voice, shrill, 'He should join the club. Right? Should join the club because we're all second-rate to you. Right? Starting with my daughter.'

The lights were dim over the platform, the electricity supply had been reduced to save power. Penn's carriage between Ljubljana and Zagreb had been empty. He took his suitcase down from the rack and he checked that his briefcase was fastened and he went to the door. He stepped down onto the platform, into the gloom of the place. A pair of Germans, suits, businessmen, jostled past him, and Penn thought they might have been cursing that they hadn't flown. Down the platform he saw two military policemen questioning a young man against the grimed brick wall, and one of them held back a Rottweiler dog on a short leash, and Penn guessed they would be checking for army deserters. He followed the Germans through the exit arch and down the corridors past the closed ticket windows. There were men, women, sleeping on the hard floor in corners, and Penn was reminded that somewhere out in the darkness, out beyond the city, there was war.

He hurried.

He knew where he would go because he had memorized the guidebook map. There was a mist on Zagreb. He stumbled on the cobblestones of the street. A bell rang fiercely and he looked up, startled, as a tram loomed towards him. He skipped forward and tripped on a tram line. He saw the neon sign of the hotel.

Tired staff waited on him at the reception.

He walked past the entrance to the bar, closed. He looked into the casino, deserted but for the croupiers. He went by the dining room, shut.

A slow lift took him up.

He gave the porter a pound sterling coin, and the porter

grimaced as if it were dirt. He wanted German marks or American dollars, and Penn thought he could go stuff himself.

There was a siren in the darkness.

All around him, in the night, a hostility. A foreign place, this, not Penn's place. And just thirty-five miles down the road was the cease-fire line and the start of the war zone, and it was not Penn's war. He would have said that he was good at being alone, but in the hotel room he felt his loneliness. Not his place and not his war . . . He threw off his clothes. He washed. He unpacked his suitcase.

There would have been other men in the hotel, far from home, nit-picking through their lives, behind their locked doors. He chose to scratch unhappily at his marriage, as if with grubby fingernails. Alone in the room he could summon the honesty to say it was not Jane's fault, he was to blame. Five years back, making small talk at a railway station waiting for a fog-delayed train, and going for a drink when the train was finally cancelled, and sharing a taxi. She was so different to the women, the girls, in Gower Street. She was pretty, fluffy, and her skirt was always halfway up her thighs and climbing, and he was the quiet one with the *secret* of his job to hide behind. She must have felt an excitement at being with a man who did secret work for the government, something that could not be talked about, and the excitement had lasted through to marriage, and then gone sour. Gone sour because she would come home from the estate agent's, and maybe he would be just going out for a night shift with the Transit van team of watchers, or maybe he had been up all night and half the day and gone to bed and expected her to tiptoe round the maisonette as if she was a dormouse, and maybe he would snarl because she'd woken him with the telly and the soaps, or maybe it had been a bad damn awful day that couldn't be talked through because that was the lore of the Service. Maybe it was him snapping at her friends because he couldn't answer their so bloody simple questions about his work. Maybe it was him refusing, point blank, to permit her to ask her father for more money for another house deposit, digging in his heels, bloody-minded. Maybe it was him, suggesting, almost shyly that the way forward was for him to take three years out and go to college and get a bloody degree. And maybe she was right to jeer back that no way was she going to live for three years carrying him, paying all the bills, and she hadn't passed an exam since school and Wayne who managed the estate agent's drove a fifth-hand Porsche and had never passed an exam in his life . . . Maybe . . . The baby should have helped, but it hadn't. The baby, Tom, should have bonded them. The baby had cut out her money . . . It was Penn's belief that a husband should provide. A father should go to work, a mother should stay home with a baby. Old-fashioned Penn, boring Penn, and he'd said that no way was she going back to work with a minder to watch his baby . . . She'd told him, full of tears, that she hadn't listened to him, had gone back with the pram to the estate agent's, made it as far as the plate-glass window with the bright photographs of properties, and seen Wayne bending over the new girl, and a hand on the shoulder of the new girl's blouse, and she'd turned around and pushed the pram back to the maisonette. And the day after that he had gone to those he thought he believed in, on the high floors of Gower Street, and requested the chance to work on General Intelligence Group . . . and been betrayed.

He lay in the bed. From the street below he sensed the burgeoning quiet of the night of a foreign city . . . but it had been Dorrie's place and Dorrie's war.

The ant column had found his hand, a barrier, and busily crossed it. He could feel their unstoppable progress, and he did not dare to move his hand to shake them off.

He felt as if he was dead . . .

Ham didn't reckon he could have run another yard, crawled another foot, climbed another inch. The tree line had been the first target and the rock escarpment had been the second, and the final aim had been to reach, running, crawling, climbing, the summit of the escarpment.

He felt as if he was dead . . . he would have been dead if they had had a good dog, or if they had had organization and discipline. He could see them from where he lay. They were below, quartering the field that was beyond the escarpment, down from

75

the tree line of spring-green birches. Ham could hear their shouts and the whistle blasts, but they had no dogs. It was because of the wounded that they had broken off the pace of the search. It was the wounded that had saved him and the three others who had stampeded with him away from the ambush.

The light caught the grass of the field, and the sun feathered down through the upper trees and dappled onto the summit of the rock escarpment.

They had been hit at first light when the grey smear was settling on the fields and the trees. They had been caught, bunched and too close, on a track that, if the intelligence had been accurate, would have brought them to the rear side of the artillery position. If the ambush had been done properly, as an ambush was taught at Aldershot or out on the ranges above Brecon, then there would have been no survivors, but the ambush had been crap and there hadn't been fire control, and they had made it out and running. All of them running, and hearing the shouting and the chaotic chase behind them, and they had hit the open ground of the field without warning. Shit, bloody bad luck, the open field. It was there that the two of them had been shot. And he had run, too fucking right, and the others who hadn't been shot had run.

Looking down, through the thin early foliage, Ham saw the line that advanced, crouching then scurrying, towards the two wounded men.

The ants came on across his hand, and he would not move his hand and he would not twist his head.

He whispered from the side of his mouth, as if he thought he hazarded his hiding place should his lips move.

'Move once, you bastards, move once at all, and I'll break your goddamn necks.'

He could hear the three of them behind him, all trying to suppress the panting, all sobered by the ambush and by the charge out and by the climb onto the summit of the escarpment, and by the sight of the cordon line closing on the two who were wounded. Shit, no, they hadn't listened to Ham when they had crossed the Kupa river in the inflatable, and they hadn't listened to him when he had told them, swearing, that they should lay off the booze in their water bottles and they hadn't listened to him when they had moved out to get close to the artillery position under the night cover that was now gone. Shit, yes, they listened to him now . . . And if it hadn't been that the ambush was crap then they would, all six of them, have been on the ground, beyond help, as the cordon line closed. They listened, and struggled to control their breathing, and they were watching as Ham watched.

'Nothing you can do, so don't fucking think there is anything.'

He knew that the brother of one of them behind him was wounded, lying in the field.

It was the worst it had ever been for Ham. His throat was dry dust. His gut was knotted tight. His arms, legs, would have been stiffened, clumsy, if he had tried to move. There were tears welling heavy . . .

Too bloody unfair . . .

He had known guys who had been killed in close-quarters fire, and guys who had been wasted when an armoured personnel carrier had been rattled and brewed, and guys who had been mutilated when caught without cover as the rockets from the Organj launcher had come down. He had known guys from the International Brigade who had been in Osijek, in Turanj, outside Sisak, and shipped home in boxes by the embassy but that had been more than a year back, more than a year and a half. He had known guys who had said it was too goddamn dull in Croatia after the cease-fire, and who had hitched on down to Bosnia, but that was a crazy bloody place to get killed . . .

Too bloody unfair . . .

In the days with the Internationals Ham had been classified sniper first class, using the long-barrelled Dragunov, stationary target three shots out of four at 1000 metres. In the days after the Internationals had drifted off scene, or been booted, he had bullshitted expertise in ordnance. No home to go back to, had to bullshit to stay. Big bullshit if he wasn't to be on the trail down to Bosnia and the crazy bloody war . . .

Too bloody unfair . . .

They had wanted an ordnance man to get across the Kupa river and spy out the artillery position on the high ground, and their own ordnance men would have been too precious . . . As an ordnance man he would have been able to identify the type and calibre of the artillery pieces in the position, their stockpiles of ammunition, their threat . . . Big bloody bullshit, and the bullshit had put him where it was worse than it had ever been for Ham.

He did not reckon it safe to use his binoculars. Could have been flash or shine from the lenses against the low-rising sun. He could see enough without the binoculars.

He knew what he would see. He knew it because he had dreamed it in the temporary sleeping quarters behind the old police station in Karlovac town. The dream was Ham's agony.

Ham knew that the wounded, struggling to keep up with those who were not wounded, would have thrown away their weapons as they had lumbered, hobbled, after those who had run. If they had had their weapons then, sure as Christ, they would have used them. Sure as Christ they would have used their weapons and kept one back for the last.

There was no firing.

The cordon line reached that part of the field, near to the tree line, where the wounded lay. He could see it clear enough, without binoculars. He should have looked away, and he could not. The stuff of Ham's dreams, the stuff that made him sweat, toss, sometimes scream in the night. There was a bearded man, big and well set, in the centre of the cordon line, and he had a whistle in his mouth, and his was the voice of command. Ham could not see the wounded, lying in the thick spring grass of the field, but he knew where they were because he saw the bearded man kick hard into the grass and the moan carried up from the field and through the trees and reached the summit of the rock escarpment. He saw the bearded man swivel, casually, like he played kids' football, and kick again. There was a moment of confusion, men around the bearded man and bending down and two small scrimmages of bodies. He heard the orders from the bearded man, curt in the sunshine. The two wounded were held upright in front of the bearded man, and he punched them, one in the face and one in the pit of the stomach and because they were

78

held they could not fall. Then bandannas from the heads of two of the men who held them were used to blindfold the wounded. The knife flashed at the waist of the bearded man. The knife went low, quick, to the groin of the wounded man who had the bloodstains at his knee and down his right leg. Ham turned, his first movement, and he broke the column of the ants, and he slapped the palm of his hand across the eyes of the brother of the wounded man. He heard the howl of pain, sobbing . . . The tears were running on his face, and the vomit was coming. He watched it, each instruction from the bearded man, each thrust of the knife. It was worse than the dream . . . When it was over, when the sport was gone, then the bearded man wiped his knife on the grass and replaced it in the sheath at his belt, and all of them sat in the field, close to where the bodies lay, and they drank and they laughed.

They had no organization and no discipline.

After they had drunk and told their jokes, they moved off again towards the tree line, but the heart had gone from the search. They did not go far into the birch trees that covered the hillside and they did not come near to the rock escarpment.

They went back the way they had come and there were the marks of their boots in the wet grass and the trails where the two bodies were dragged.

Ham watched. He wiped his face, furtive, and his tears smeared the camouflage cream. His eyes, all the time, held the broad and powerful back of the bearded man, who walked easily, walked without care. Piece of cake, if he had had the Dragunov SVD 7.62mm, not the Kalashnikov, piece of cake for a sniper first class.

Ham murmured, 'That's a right bastard . . .'

The brother of the man who had been castrated whispered, calmly, 'That is Milan Stanković.'

'That right bastard needs sorting . . .'

'He is Milan Stanković, he commands the TDF unit at the village of Salika. He has grown the beard now because he would think that makes him more of the Serb soldier. It is, perhaps, ten kilometres from here, his village. He was a clerk. He was a junior clerk in the administration of the co-operative at Turanj. All the farmers in the region came to the co-operative with their produce, and it was marketed from there. We came, my brother and I, to the co-operative each week in the summer. It was the job of Milan Stanković to check the paper we brought, to see that we did not cheat, and then to stamp the paper. To check paper and to stamp it, now he is an important man. He would have recognized immediately the face of my brother. Often we used to bring him the best cabbages, or carrots, or a side of meat, some cheese, because then he would check our paper and stamp it more quickly. We would always look after Milan Stanković. He *knew* my brother . . . and he killed him. That is Milan Stanković . . .'

They were gone into the trees on the far side of the field.

Ham sat. He understood enough of the war to believe that if the brothers, one dead and one living, had captured the bearded man who they *knew*, then another knife would have flashed, another knife would have gouged.

He said, 'Nothing we could have done, if anyone had fired we'd all have been gone . . . It's called SERE, guys, that's Survive, Evade, Resist, Escape . . .'

They would lie up the rest of the day. At dusk they would move for the Kupa river.

The streets were cheerful, the shops had good stock, the gutters were clean. The bars were full and the *espresso* machines rumbled, and the chairs of the pavement cafés were taken. The sun shone, warm enough for Penn to have turned on his heel after a hundred-yard walk, collected his room key again, and dumped his coat and his scarf and his gloves. A fine morning to walk, and for the second time he passed the taxi line in the road outside the hotel. It was all a culture shock for Bill Penn, and he had the guidebook to tell him that this was an old city, historic and finely preserved, and he could not square the city with what he had seen in his hotel room on the television from the satellite news. On the news, across country, was Srebrenica where a town was being shelled and starved to surrender, and on the same bulletin had been clear colour pictures of British squaddies handling charred bodies, and a young officer had said his men would need counselling if they were not to be scarred for the rest of their lives. And there had been film of an American aircraft carrier, across the water, taking off with the bomb loads in place for practice runs. A war in Bosnia across country, and nothing of it to be seen by Penn as he viewed, for the first time, the capital city of Zagreb. He walked quickly. He was not a tourist. He was on assignment. He had polished his black shoes in his room, he wore his charcoal-grey trousers and his blazer and he had brushed the flecks from the shoulders. He had his white shirt and a quiet tie, and he carried his old briefcase, and it was difficult for him to realize that the months had passed by, that it was not a 'government' assignment. He had a starting place but not yet a programme. He went up Haulikova and across Andrije Hebranga and up Preradovićeva and came to a wide square. He felt comfortable; he liked the feel of the place; he would write a good fast report; he thought that Jane would have liked the feel of the city . . . On Ilica, looking left, jumping out of the path of a damned tram, he saw the flag. Red and white and blue, and looking as if it needed a full wash and tumble, and hanging limp. It was an old building and there was an arched entrance to the inner courtyard, and a brass plaque at the side door. Of course the embassy was Penn's start point. He saw the posters on the stair walls. Edinburgh Castle, British butterflies, a Cotswold village, badgers outside a sett, Buckingham Palace, it was the world to which he had once belonged . . .

Inside a small lobby, and the Englishwoman at the desk smiling and asking him with studied politeness, 'Can I help?'

'My name's Penn, Bill Penn. I'd like to see one of your diplomats, please. It's in connection with Miss Mowat. It's about the late Miss Dorothy Mowat.'

It was as if he had sworn, or unzipped his flies, because the smile was suddenly gone from her. She gestured for him to wait, and her face was cold. He wondered if she had been here, Dorrie, turning the faces cold. He thought that Mary Braddock would have been here, sitting on the hard chairs in the small lobby and turning the pages of the English magazines, killing the smiles.

He could see the Englishwoman blurred through the frosted glass of the adjacent office. He wondered if anyone had jumped when Mary Braddock had come the first time to start a search for her daughter and failed. The blurred shapes meandered across the face of the glass and towards the door. He thought the papers would have been sorted here, stamped here, duplicated here, for the repatriation of the corpse. The Englishwoman stood in the door and gestured Penn forward, and stepped aside.

The room had been large once, perhaps the salon of a well-proportioned apartment, but it was now sub-divided into rabbit hutches.

There was a tall man, in shirtsleeves and braces, rather young. He didn't offer a handshake. Cigarette smoke curled from an ashtray. He didn't give his name. The desk was a confusion of paper. He stood.

'I'm the First Secretary. Who do you represent, Mr Penn?'

'I represent Miss Mowat's mother. I've been hired by Mrs Mary Braddock.'

'And what are you, Mr Penn?'

Pederast, no . . . pusher, no . . . pimp, no . . . private investigator, yes . . . 'I am a private investigator, I have been employed by Mrs Braddock to examine the circumstances of her daughter's murder.'

'Why do you come here?'

Penn bridled. 'As a starting point. She was British, I'm British, natural enough to attend Her Britannic Majesty's talking shop . . .'

'We gave Mrs Braddock every possible help, she left here knowing as much as it was humanly possible to know.'

'Can't accept that. She wrote a note, Mrs Braddock, of what she had been told, which I read. She had been told *nothing*. If she hadn't been told nothing, then I wouldn't be here. Because . . .'

It was a sharp little voice, reedy. 'We have a full load of work and about half the staff necessary to accomplish it . . . No, don't interrupt, listen. Mrs Braddock was told everything about her daughter's death that it was possible to discover, everything. I wouldn't imagine that private investigators have too much time to read newspapers. If you read a newspaper regularly then you would know that there was a pretty horrible war going on down here, and facts, truths, tend to be rather a long way down the order of priorities. Where Miss Mowat died only a lunatic would have been. She died because she was a fool. As regards facts, in that dirty little war some 20,000 Croatians lost their lives, more than 30,000 were wounded, 7,000 are missing presumed dead, 250,000 have fled their former homes . . . Do I make myself clear? There has been an earthquake here of human misery, and against the reality of that destruction the demands of a mother for a fuller investigation into the death of one young lunatic woman is quite unreasonable. First day here, is it? Well, get yourself a map, Mr Penn, learn a bit of geography. Where she died is behind Serb lines, where she was killed is closed territory. I wouldn't want to see you or hear of you again, Mr Penn, because if I see you or hear of you again then it will mean you have caused *trouble*. I've enough to concern me without freelancers interfering in sensitive areas and making trouble . . .'

He had torn a sheet of paper from a notepad. He wrote fast on it, passed the paper to Penn.

'. . . I imagine you have to justify an inflated fee. I don't suppose you speak fluent Serbo-Croat, no? That's an interpreter. Second is the name of the man who runs the Croatian war crimes unit, he won't know anything, but he'll be impressive on your report. By the by, do you know how Mrs Braddock came to know that her daughter was here? A demand for money. Do you know how she came to know her daughter was missing? The money wasn't collected, it was sent back. Didn't she tell you? We're not talking about a very caring young woman, you know . . . Go away, Mr Penn, and I suggest you allow the dead to sleep.'

He walked to the door and opened it for Penn. Penn took himself past the Englishwoman to the main door.

He went out onto the street, numbed.

It was as if a cold wind had come.

The hunger strike was spreading on the third floor. Men were smoking more in the sleeping rooms and she had shouted and threatened. She had more families coming from Bosnia in the morning and the accommodation area was already saturated. She had received, smiling and cheerful and a sham, a delegation that afternoon from the Swedish Red Cross. It was close to midnight and she was exhausted. She had had the police in, accusing the children of stealing in the town. Men from Prijedor, on the second floor, had been close, almost, to a riot at the counter for 'Onward Movement'.

Another day ending for Ulrike Schmidt as she slipped, dead on her feet, out from the high heavy doors of the Transit Centre. She went to her car, parked in the square, and she did not look back at the old barracks building that was the Transit Centre for Bosnian Muslim refugees. The end of another eighteen-hour day and she had no need to look back on the building. The building consumed her attention, eighteen hours a day.

She slumped behind the wheel of the little Volkswagen Beetle, bit at her lip, turned the ignition key. Ahead of her was a cold supper in the fridge of her apartment, a night's heavy and unrewarding sleep, the clamour of an alarm clock. That was the life of Ulrike Schmidt, paid by the United Nations High Commission for Refugees to administer the Transit Centre at Karlovac. The men were on hunger strike because they had been promised entry with their families to Austria, the papers were in place, but the visas were delayed. The members of the delegation of the Swedish Red Cross were disarming and friendly, but adamant that they could offer only medicines, not entry permits. If the men smoked in the rooms of the barracks where the floors were covered with mattresses, where each family made personal boxes from hanging blankets, then the fire risk was just appalling. If the police came in and demanded the right to search, and if the police took away children for thieving, then there would be fighting. And if more families came in the morning, and the resident families had to be pushed into making room for them . . . if more entry permits were not available at the 'Onward Movement' counter . . . She drove away.

She left it behind her, for six hours, the misery of 2,400 refugees who were her charge.

84

Ulrike Schmidt had told the delegation of the Swedish Red Cross that the Bosnian Muslim refugees were the most traumatized people in the world. She had told them that where they stood, grasping their fact-sheets, was the most traumatized place in the world. How did she cope? she was asked by a severe-faced woman from Gothenburg. 'When you fall over you have to pick yourself up, wipe off the dirt, start again.' And she had smiled, and they had all laughed, and they did not understand what was her life for eighteen hours of the day.

She drove through the deserted streets of the frontline town towards her apartment. It was the day a letter usually came from her mother in Munich. Her life, her emotions, were shared only with her parents who wrote to her once every week. She allowed no one else access to her emotions. The jeep passed her.

Her headlights caught the open back of the jeep, and then the vehicle, arrogantly driven, cut across her. She braked.

She slowed.

There were four men in the back of the jeep. Her headlights snatched at their faces that were indistinct from the dirt and the camouflage cream.

The jeep stopped hard outside the sandbagged entrance to the old police station.

She was at crawl speed.

Three men out of the back of the jeep, jumping down, pulling after them their weapons and their backpacks. One man left in the jeep. As she went by him she looked into his face. The man sat in the open back of the jeep and his hands were locked onto the barrel of his rifle. He was older than the others and he had weight at the jowls and the cheeks of his face. The eyes were full of fear and shock. She saw the trembling of the body of the man and he blinked into the headlights of her car, and he had made no movement to climb down from the jeep. She saw the filthy uniform that was mud-covered and soaked wet. Ulrike Schmidt understood. She drove on. The fear and the shock and the trembling belonged to those who came from behind the lines, across the Kupa river. After her six hours, after the alarm had gone in the morning, she would be at the crossing point at Turanj and she would meet the new party of refugees, for whom she

85

had no space at the Transit Centre, and she would see the same fear and shock and trembling in those who had come from behind the lines.

She speeded her car.

A silent little prayer played at her lips that the letter from her mother would be waiting at her apartment.

5

Sitting upright, uncomfortable, Jović was waiting.

Penn had learned to use the staircase rather than wait for the interminable lift. He paused at the angle of the stairs, and saw the young man immediately. The hotel lobby was filled for the gathering, before the first session, of the Congress (International) of Croatian Physicians. A blend of accents and languages filtered up to him, but he saw the young man immediately. What he had imagined, somehow, was a retired schoolteacher. What he saw was a student-aged young man with a gaunt and pale face and blond hair cropped short and a pair of jeans that were ragged at the ankles and a heavy leather jacket. The doctors, surgeons, anaesthetists flowed around the young man, who seemed not to notice them but sat rigid. It had been an abrupt exchange on the telephone. Yes, he was an interpreter. Yes, he was available. Yes, he would be at the hotel in the morning. There was an aggression about the young man, Jović, that Penn noted . . . it was not possible for him to be without an interpreter.

Sharp introductions, an exchange of names. Penn had the ability to look a man in the face. Because he had looked into the eyes, the face of Jović, because they had not shaken hands, it was a moment before he realized that the right arm of Jović was taken off at the elbow. The right sleeve of the leather jacket, from below the elbow, hung loose and useless. The circle closed. An amputation accounted for the gaunt and fleshless face, and for the ravaged pallor of the cheeks, and for the blunt aggression. There were reunion greetings around them, the accents of America and Australia, the languages of Swedish and German and Swiss French.

Jović looked back into Penn's face. 'Patronizing bastards . . .'

His accent was schoolroom English.

'. . . coming here to parade their success for the mother country to see, and to write cheques, and wring their hands and play their ego, and get the hell out in the morning.'

His voice was snarled.

Would he like coffee? The young man, Jović, looked around him and there was contempt at his mouth. He led the way out of the hotel lobby, and he shouldered his way past the uniformed day porter and the bellboy, and Penn followed him out across the street.

They walked in the sunshine towards the square with the open cafés. Jović took a table and he shouted in his own language for a waiter and he ordered espressos without asking Penn if that was what he wanted, and he sat in silence until they were brought, and then he pushed the bill slip towards Penn for paying. He could lay his right elbow on the table, awkwardly, and he could flick a cigarette from the packet and strike a match, laboriously.

'How did it happen?'

'Have you been in a war, Mr Penn? No? Then you would not understand how it happened.'

'Where did it happen?'

'Do you know Sisak, Mr Penn? No? Then you would not know where it happened.'

'When did it happen?'

'When you were safe in your own country, Mr Penn. Eighteen months ago, Mr Penn, did you care about the freedom struggle of Croatian independence? No? That was when it happened.'

Penn went on, 'Right, young man . . . OK, Jović . . . If you don't want the job, so be it. I don't have to take shit from anybody. I suggest you go back to whatever corner you came out of, and moan on your own.'

A big smile that cracked the pale edges of Jović's mouth. Penn glowered at him. He said that he was an artist. He said that he studied at the School of Art. He said that he had learned of Constable and Turner, but that most he admired Hockney. He said, in a new mood and shy, that he was learning to paint with his left hand. He said, more boldly, that his rate was eighty US dollars a day. He pushed his left hand, twisted, towards Penn for the handshake and there was oil paint on his fingers and grime dirt under the nails . . . it was Charles Braddock's money . . . A powered grip crushed Penn's fist. He added, quickly, while their hands were still together that if a car was needed then he could get one, and that his rate with the car would be one hundred and twenty US dollars a day. Penn seemed to see the arm, bleeding and hanging loose, and he seemed to see the stampede from a frontline position and the bumped ride to a casualty clearing station, and he seemed to see the fresh bandaged stump, and he seemed to see the first tentative strokes of the brush that was guided by a left hand. He nodded, the money was no problem.

'Thank you, Mr Penn, so what is your work in Croatia?'

It was why he had hoped that he would not have to trail around with an interpreter, and he started, hesitantly, to talk through what he knew of Dorrie Mowat. Without an interpreter he might as well sit in his hotel room, but it was the sharing that was difficult. The story was personal. It was the story of a woman sitting at a fresh grave with her dogs and with the scent of newly cut flowers. Jović did not interrupt. He leaned back and he swirled the coffee dregs in the cup, and his mouth had curled, as if the story was a bad joke. Perhaps he tried to impress the young man, perhaps he thought that the young man would be better able to do his work if he knew it all. He was reciting the *crimes* of Dorrie Mowat, and he felt a sense of shame as he pushed through the litany, and as he talked he looked into the hard eyes that flickered, dulled, back at him. He was dead without an interpreter, and he had tried three times the day before to ring the number given him at the embassy and taken back the gabble of local language and not been understood. Penn wondered what it would be like to try to paint with a left hand. He felt that he had betrayed a trust in the telling to a stranger. He pushed across the table the telephone number given him at the embassy.

'. . . She wants to know. I've been hired to write a report. Her mother wants to know how her daughter died. It's why I've come.'

He watched Jović's back. Jović was at the telephone on the

bar. When he came back to the table his face was a mask. He picked up his cigarettes and gestured, coolly, for Penn to follow.

Penn felt himself an innocent.

'Choked me, but nothing we could do. I took responsibility, I said we had to leave them. I'll remember that bastard, that Stanković, if I ever get him in my sights. But Special Forces can't hang about . . . It really choked me to leave them.'

Ham was rested, and it was good patter. The patter had been laced with what 3 Para would have done, and he gave the cocktail body by telling the major and the captain in the first-floor room of the old police station that not even the RLI, nor the SADF's Recce Commandos nor their 44 Para Brigade, would have done it different. He had learned the patter when he had been with the Internationals and there had been jokers from the Rhodesian Light Infantry and guys who had fought with the South African Defence Force. There had been jokers and guys then who had done the rounds, done time as *Warriors of Principle* and *Soldiers of Conscience*, and Ham had learned enough from them to give good patter.

Ham said, 'We couldn't have moved better. The "Black Hawks" wouldn't have done it different. I don't know how they got to jump us. Never saw anything before we were jumped. Goddamn shame, because we weren't that far from the position, but once they'd jumped us then it was like the place was heaving with them. If we'd tried to shoot it out then we were all stiffed. We did what we could, and you can't ask more than that.'

That was great patter to have thrown in the Black Hawks, because they were 'claimed' as the elite of the Croat army, and he had seen the major take a note with his pencil. Ham thought they would all get called in, the survivors from Sector North, but he was happy to have been called in the first. It had been a crazy dumb idea to send six jerks pushing across the Kupa river and beyond the lines into Sector North of occupied territory, and it was good that the major and the captain should understand that, too right.

'I wouldn't want you to think, major, that it was wasted effort. I'll have it for you tonight, my appraisal of the route in and the route out, total detail of minefield location, what strongpoints we saw, general movement of TDF, location of hull-down armour . . . You'll have it on your desk tonight, major . . . Major, what I'd like to say, it's rough over there. We'd done really well to get as far as we had got. No, I don't know how we got jumped, but they were heavy on the ground . . . Major, that's a bad place.'

He thought he had the patter right. Wouldn't be good to show fear, would be good to show thoroughness. All officers shunned fear and adulated keenness. The major was a bureaucrat, seconded at the start of the war from the Finance Ministry, and knew sweet nothing. The major was nodding. The major would get a paper of the route they had taken and the location of the mine-fields, and of the tanks and the strongpoints, and the major would take it to his colonel. He was useful with bullshit patter.

Ham said, in sincere tones, 'I'm really sorry we couldn't do more for those brave lads, I'm really cut up about that. If the objective's important enough then of course we should go back – you won't mind me saying it, but if I have to go back I'd request more experienced troops alongside me . . .'

He had rehearsed that line. The last was said looking straight into the major's eyes, good sincerity stuff. They hadn't more experienced troops in 2nd Bn, 110 (Karlovac) Brigade. If the major reported that to the colonel, if the advice was taken, then the Black Hawks would be tasked for the next recce of the artillery guns and the munitions stores, and no way that the super shit Black Hawks would take along a bloody mercenary.

If it had just been the major to debrief him then Ham would have reckoned he had done well, but the captain, cold bastard, had said nothing. The captain stared him out, never took a note, looked at him like he was shit. The captain was an intelligence officer, fronting as liaison.

'In conclusion, sir, I'd like to say that I feel privileged to have served with those young men who didn't make it back . . .'

Ham saluted. Best salute. It was the salute he would have given his company commander at the training camp on the Brecons or the operational base at Crossmaglen in South Armagh or at Palace Barracks east of Belfast centre. Bullshit salute.

He hoped, dear God, he would never be sent again across that bloody river, into that bloody hell.

Later, when it was evening, when he could slip away and the evening darkness came to the Karlovac streets, he would go to the bar where the telephone was in shadow and behind the screen.

The major said, 'Thank you, Hamilton, thank you for good and resourceful work.'

'For nothing, sir . . .'

He had woken foul-mouthed and bad-tempered.

Her man had sworn at her while she had dressed, and when little Marko had come into their room to play in the bed he had cursed the child.

For Evica, her husband was a new man.

She had made breakfast, given them bread she had baked the evening before and jam she had bottled in the autumn, and she had tried to accept that her husband was a new man. She had dressed her Marko and they had gone to the school where she taught the third year, and where Marko sat in the second-year class. She had come back to her home at the end of the lane, at lunch time, to make a small light meal for the middle of the day, and she had found Milan still foul-mouthed and bad-tempered. He sat at the table in the kitchen and he had papers spread around him and he made no effort to clear them. She had little time in the middle of the day when she took the hour from the school, little time to waste in clearing the table, and she must waste that little time . . . There was never a point in arguing with him but the moods, black and foul-mouthed and bad-tempered, were more frequent. Marko sat at the table close to his father, and held the plastic pistol that had been brought from Belgrade, and was old enough, sensible enough, to stay silent. Her former man, the clerk in the co-operative at Turanj, had never been home in the middle of the day and expecting to be fed; it was the new way of the new man . . . Because she loved him, had loved him since she was a child in the village, the new man that was her husband hurt her. Only the beard changed him, outwardly. Inwardly, everything was changed. He no longer played basketball in Glina, he no longer followed the big matches in the football league that were played in Belgrade, he no longer worked through quiet evenings in the vegetable garden at the back of the house, he no longer talked gently with her. The war had made her Milan a new man.

The war suffocated Evica Stanković.

She thought the war was her enemy and she would not have dared to say it. The war was his life in the waking hours and the war was with him when he slept because now there was a shined and cleaned automatic rifle on the rug over the floor at his side of the bed. Those meetings in all the waking hours, and her kitchen often filled, when she came back from the school in the afternoon, with men from the village who were ignorant and stupid and who talked a babble of fire positions and patrol patterns, and her kitchen in the evenings was a stinking place from the smoke of their cigarettes and the scent of their brandy. She did not complain, would not have dared to. In the sleeping hours, her new man sometimes rolled in the bed and cried out . . . She was an intelligent woman, she had been trained as a teacher at the college in Zagreb and she could read books in German as well as Italian, and in English, but it was not possible now for her to get books because of the war, and she did not complain. And she was intelligent enough to realize that the respect now shown to her in the village owed nothing to love, nor to friendship, everything to the position of her new man. Her new man dispensed gasoline, and tractor parts, and decided who could enlist in the militia and therefore be paid, had control over the quotas of agricultural seed. They all fawned in the village to her new man, and they all gave the show of respect to his wife . . . She hated the war.

They were on the floor, heaped loose, where he had thrown them. His back was to them as he sat hunched at the table. With her toe she nudged the pile of uniform fatigues. They had been left for her to wash. There were dark bloodstains on them. Milan had not told her, Milan had kept his silence since he had come back, drunk, quiet, the evening before. She had been told it that morning by the woman who cleaned at the school, by the wife of Stevo who was the village gravedigger. She had been told that

93

her new man, Milan, had slit the throats of two Ustaše who were captured. And his fatigues, on which were the bloodstains of the two Ustaše, were left now on the floor for her to wash. On the wall above the stove, hung by thread from the nail he had hammered into the plaster, was the bayonet. It was near to a year and a half since he had brought the bayonet down from the loft. The bayonet was rusted and the handle grip had rotted. It was German army issue, had been taken from the belt of a Wehrmacht trooper and had been used by the cousin of the father of Milan Stanković to stab the trooper to death. He had brought the bayonet down from the loft where it had lain undisturbed for forty years, and he had hammered the nail in the wall and tied the thread on the handle of the bayonet and hung it. The next morning her new man had led the militia in the attack on Rosenovici.

The sunlight played on the window of her kitchen.

She was hurrying and time was against her. In her sink she was sluicing the earth from carrots from the vegetable patch. She could see across to Rosenovici, to the ruined church, to the broken houses, to the disturbed earth in the corner of the field at the end of the lane.

The sight across the stream, the devastated village, was as a pillow that was pressed down onto her face, over her nose, blocking her mouth. The sight was always with her. When she looked from the window of her kitchen, from the window of her bedroom, when she went to get wood from the heaped pile against the shed wall, when she went to the vegetable patch, when she went to the orchard to pick windfalls, when she went to hang her washing on the line, then the pillow was across her nose and her mouth. There was no escape from the sight of Rosenovici.

She had had friends, good friends, in the village of Rosenovici, and she did not dare to talk of them. She scoured the skins of the carrots. It was since he had come home from Belgrade, since she had told him of the digging in the corner of the field that he had been, all the time, foul-mouthed and bad-tempered.

Evica had not told him, would not have dared to, of the change these last two weeks in the attitude of the school's Headmaster

94

to her. There was a slyness from the school's Headmaster, a smugness, a distancing from her, since the digging. And he would have heard, as she had heard, the broadcast on the radio. He would have listened, as she had listened, to the radio in English, on the short wave, because that was the small window they could climb through each day, when each was alone. Denied books, the radio was her freedom and the Headmaster's freedom also. It had been the voice of an American on the radio.

'. . . Be identified and put on trial these perpetrators of crimes against humanity . . .' She saw from her kitchen window the dug earth in the corner of the field. '. . . Be treated exactly as were Hitler's associates at Nuremberg . . .' She had not been with those who had crossed the bridge over the swollen river and who had gone to watch the lifting of the bodies from the wet grey-black earth. '. . . Name some names, let them understand that over the long run, they may be able to run but they can't hide . . .' She had seen from her kitchen window the bodies in bags lifted into the jeeps.

She cut the carrots, dropped them into the saucepan.

The war suffocated Evica Stanković.

The bus was three hours behind schedule when it came through. There were Nigerian soldiers around her, and there were two men from the UNHCR office in Zagreb who strutted impatiently and carried a print-out of the list of names. The bus came slow, tucked in behind the white-painted personnel carrier, towards the Nigerians' checkpoint. Ulrike Schmidt always felt a numbed despair when she came to the checkpoint at Turanj to welcome in a bus from behind the lines. Her father, of course, had known total war and refugee status, and her father's first wife had been killed when the bombers had come to Magdeburg. One of the men from the United Nations High Commission for Refugees office in Zagreb, smart and smelling of body lotion, made a joke to her, as if it were clever to laugh as the bus came through, as if it were adult, and she ignored him, indeed she barely heard him. The bus neared the checkpoint and there were Serbs standing at the far side of the sandbagged position that the Nigerians manned, and the Serbs would check the print-out list of names against the papers of those on the bus. She had never, and she had written to her father and mother in Munich of this, never ever seen *shame* on the faces of the Serbs when they checked through the new batch of refugees. She knew from the print-out that the refugees represented the population of the last village in the Prijedor area to be cleansed. There would be a village, small houses and a mosque and a shop and once neat fields and a car repair yard, that would now be flattened, and the population of the village were moving away from homes that no longer existed, and they would not know if a future was left to them. Their village was the bus, and after the bus their village would be in the corners of the sleeping rooms of the Transit Centre at Karlovac. And the wretched fool, the young man from the UNHCR in Zagreb, was still laughing at his joke and she could not remember what he had said . . . She saw the broken windows of the bus. The front windscreen, to the right of the driver's vision, was a skein of cracks that radiated from the stone's impact point, and three of the left side windows behind the driver had caved in. She saw the faces of the refugees. The young man was talking at her again and she did not hear him. So quiet and so cowed, the faces of the refugees, without expression. The stoning might have been by the Serbs in Prijedor, or it might have been later in the journey, or it might have been when they were in the last Serb village before the final checkpoint. She had never travelled beyond the checkpoint, never been behind the lines, and she found it close to impossible to understand the ethnic hatred that had driven Serb people to expel their Muslim neighbours, and there was no shame.

She was a small woman. Her tight waist was held close by the belt of her denims. Her hair was mahogany but flecked now with grey that had not been there before she had come to administer the Transit Centre. She wore a pressed white blouse, open at the throat. She used no make-up, because cosmetics might seem to offer an insult to the refugees who came from the villages of Bosnia, and who had nothing. She set a smile on her face. She was dwarfed by the men around her. She was smiling briskly and going towards the door of the bus. Later, she would hear the atrocity stories. She would hear who had been raped and who had been tortured and who had been beaten . . . She saw herself as the symbol that the past, rape and torture and beatings, was finished. The young man was beside her, towering over her and talking fast, like a cockerel parading for a hen, and he would, because they always did, offer her his telephone number for when she could next get to the city and there would be a promise of dinner, and she would ignore him as she always did.

She paused at the door of the bus. There were Serbs on the steps and she stared them out defiantly until the first weakened his resolve and made room for her. They came down off the bus's steps and made a point of brushing their bodies against hers, and behind them were the faces, expressionless, of the refugees. There was no shame. The history of her own country had been only academic to her before her posting to Croatia. Something taught in secondary-level school by defensive teachers. The Nazi years, the arrogance of men in uniform, the brutality of men with guns, the fear of dispossessed refugees, had no reality for her until she had come to Croatia. Before Croatia she had been among the thousands of young persons living the comfortable existence of the aid agencies . . . Now it was all changed. The culture of the agencies was to turn the cheek, smile, deflect the insult, and that had been possible for her until she had come to Croatia. There had been little to pre-pare her for what she would find. A flight to Geneva, a job interview, a three-day course, and she had been pitched into Karlovac. She had learned on her feet . . . She had learned to hate the men in uniform and their guns. Because there was no shame, Ulrike Schmidt yearned to see them stamped down and humiliated. She cried inside for a reckoning day to be delivered to those who felt no shame. One day . . . Her father had told her, and he had known because he had been employed as a junior interpreter by the British prosecutor, that the guards at the camps in the Neuengamme Ring had taken photographs of the naked Jewish women running past them towards medical inspection, and felt no shame. She thought that the young Serbs who pushed against her breasts in the doorway of the bus felt no shame and thought themselves safe, safe from retribution. The chief guards at the Neuengamme Ring of camps had been

97

hanged by the British, but they had not thought they would be hanged when they took their photographs.

She prayed each morning, after the clamour of the alarm, for strength.

She made warmth in her smile.

'What motivates me is my belief that if war criminals are found to be beyond justice then we are entering a new age of barbarism . . .' The man chain-smoked.

They had been on the hard chairs in the corridor for an hour.

'Bringing men to trial, to a court of law, will be difficult, it will take many years, but it is the most important thing . . .' The man rested his elbows on the filled desk.

They had come through heavy sets of old doors, climbed dark wide staircases, nudged their way past heaped and cobwebbed files.

'Revenge killing is useless. It is necessary to find truth, then justice . . .' The man coughed thick phlegm to his lips.

Penn had been told by Jović that it was the ministry office for accumulating evidence on war crimes. They had sat a long hour before they were ushered from the corridor and into an office. He had tried conversation to kill the time and failed. 'It is necessary to have meticulous preparation of evidence. I am determined we will not move outside legality. If, when, it comes to trials, it would be catastrophe for a prosecution to collapse on technicality . . .' The man talked as if to an audience and the smoke eddied in the wisps of his beard.

An hour in the corridor, and now half an hour as the working of the office was portrayed. Penn wrote his notes carefully. He could not complain at Jović's translation, steady and at a good pace. He had the name of the man, and his title and the notes made good reading. The pity was that the notes were rubbish, they didn't matter. He had tried to steer the conversation, twice, and twice had been ignored because this was prepared speech time for visitors, and visitors were supposed to duck their heads in respect. A secretary had put her head round the door, grimaced at the man. Penn knew the form. The speech would end.

Handshakes, farewells, and the man would be sweeping out of the office to a new appointment.

'I work in conjunction with the United Nations Human Rights Committee and Amnesty International . . .'

'Rosenovici, in the Municipality of Glina.' Penn said it loud.

'I receive no money from my own government . . .'

'There was a battle in December of 1991 for the village of Rosenovici, in the Municipality of Glina.' Penn battered on.

'The material I gather will go to the United Nations Commission for the Prosecution of War Criminals . . .'

'You are a busy man, I am a busy man . . .' Penn saw that Jović queried him and his eyebrow was lifted in trifled amusement. '. . . I am not interested in war crimes. I am not concerned with the prosecution, or freedom, of war criminals. I want to know what happened in Rosenovici in December of 1991 when Miss Dorothy Mowat was murdered. I apologize, but that is all I am interested in.'

He saw the annoyance furrow the head of the man. 'The greatest human rights abuse in Europe for fifty years, you are not concerned?'

'I want to know what happened in Rosenovici in December in 1991 when Miss Dorothy Mowat died. Point . . .'

He saw the sneer creep over the man's mouth. 'You cross the great continent of Europe. You visit our poor and humble country. You arrive *late* after the war in which my poor and humble country has fought for its very survival. You come when the finest of our young people have made the ultimate sacrifice of their lives, after our old men have been tortured, disembowelled, after our old women have been beaten, raped, after our children have been slaughtered . . . But you want only to know how a young Englishwoman was killed . . . You are not concerned with law and justice, but with making a report . . .'

Penn said evenly, 'I have been paid to make a report on the circumstances of Miss Dorothy Mowat's death.'

The sneer played wide. 'And she was precious, and the thousands who have died were without value? To make her so precious, was she a queen?'

There was the scrape of Jović's chair beside him. It was the

99

end of the interview. Penn stood. He felt so damned tired. It had been time wasted, as time had been wasted at the embassy.

Penn said, 'From what I heard, what I was told, she was a pig of a woman.'

'There's no goddamn hot water . . .' Marty stood in the door and shouted in frustration. The towel was loose at his waist. '. . . I want goddamn hot water.'

'There is no hot water.'

'Heh, smart man, I am not a fool. I know there is no hot water. I want my shower, I want hot water. I pay for hot water . . .'

'There is no hot water. There will be hot water for your shower in the morning.'

The doctor sat at the bare wood table and his study books were in front of him. The evening had come and the light was poor in the room, but the doctor had not switched on the electricity nor had he switched on the immersion that heated water for the shower.

The American yelled, 'Damn it, I pay for hot water. It's part of the rental that I can go take a shower, and not in the morning. I want . . .'

And Marty let it go. He let it go for his own survival. If he did not let it go, if he kept shouting about the need for hot water for his shower then he would get the big story, again. The big story was Vukovar. Not that Marty Jones did not think the story should be told, just that he knew the story of each day, each night, each hour, of Vukovar, because the doctor had told him it. The doctor had been in the hospital through the siege of Vukovar. Marty paid $175 a week, $700 each calendar month, for his room and for the shared use of the sitting room and the kitchen and the bathroom, and the rental was supposed to include hot water, each evening, for a shower. He let it go . . . and the doctor should not have been studying close print without the electricity, and he let that go. The doctor was paying his way through the college for surgeons and he was keeping his mother, widowed in Vukovar, and his nephews, orphaned in Vukovar, and he was keeping the family of his close friend, killed in the hospital at Vukovar when the 250kg cluster bombs fell. He knew it all because he had been told it.

It was not easy for an American, employed out of Geneva by the United Nations Human Rights Committee, to find good accommodation in Zagreb. It was damn near impossible, on the allowances paid him, to find anything that was a personal apartment with its own front door. He lodged with the doctor, it was the best he could get. And if Marty Jones complained that, again, there was no hot water for his shower then he would get the story of the amputations carried out with a firewood saw, and the casualty wounds cleaned with boiled rainwater, and the surgery patients kept warm by a woman's hair dryer, and the fatals stacked in the yard because it was too dangerous to go bury them and there were no coffins left and the pigs and dogs running wild and going for them . . . He didn't need the stories, not when he was scratchy and hot and at the end of his day.

'Right, no shower. No shower and no problem . . .'

He went back to the bathroom. He turned the water tap and sponged soap under his armpits.

The doctor called to him, 'Marty, did you have a good day . . . ?'

He shuddered under the cold water. It was hard to have a good day in the converted freight container that had been dumped on the corner of the parade square of the barracks on Ilica, his work place. It would be a good day tomorrow when he drove the jeep down to Karlovac and got to talk with the new arrivals from some village in the Prijedor Municipality. But the best days for Marty Jones were indeed when he sat in the converted freight container, where the sun cooked the interior, where he had his computer. The best days were when he scanned the memory of the computer through what he called his 'snapshots'. These were his interviews with refugees, now from Bosnia, earlier from Croatia. The pick of the best days was when he scanned the memory with the trace, when he hacked through to a recurring name. The name might be that of an officer in the former JNA, or it might be the name of a local policeman, or a mayor's name, or the name of a man who had come through from civilian life to take a position of command in the militia, or the name of a warlord like Arkan or Seselj. The interviews in the memory were always recorded either by audio or video tape, and because he was a lawyer by training, Marty knew what was necessary as *evidence*. The best days were when he found the traces, when a name recurred, when a name gathered evidence. It was what he was paid to do, to prepare cases and accumulate evidence. The close friend of the doctor had been butchered after the fall of Vukovar when the wounded had been given by the regular army to the militia, when the grave had been dug at Ovcara, when the wounded had been shot. There was a named man, there were good traces, there was evidence of the order being given for a war crime.

'Getting there, not too bad a day . . .'

He tore the message pages into many pieces.

Two message pages, telephoned from England, from Mrs Mary Braddock, requiring him to call back.

He tore them up, dropped them into the rubbish bin in the bathroom, and let himself out of the hotel room.

No way that he was going to jump to her, no bloody way that he was going to be on the end of her string. She would wait until he was ready to report, and she could sweat, fret, whatever, until he was ready . . . And he had little to report. He could have reported a failed meeting with a First Secretary at the embassy, and a failed meeting with an official from an out-of-reality office believing that the cavalry would come, one sweet day, and take the bad guys off to the thorn bush tree where the rope hung . . . Jović had said that he would fix something for the morning. What would he fix for the morning? It was not often that Penn felt loneliness, but he felt it here after two wasted days, which was why he had snatched the offer of a few drinks with some friends of the interpreter.

Jović was waiting outside, as if the hotel was dross. They walked in the darkness away from the hotel.

'I don't know yet, but something, I have to make some more calls. You worry too much, and there will be something . . .'

'Now, see here . . .'

'You want to do it yourself? You're free. You make your own

programme, just tell me what time, what place, and you arrange it . . .'

But then Bill Penn was not a *graduate*, didn't have the bloody intellect, and had been heaved. Bill Penn was not material for General Intelligence Group. Bill Penn was clerk grade, executive officer grade, pathetic grade, with need of a nanny to hold his hand tight. Bill Penn was the 'jammy bastard' who had landed the big fat one, and who was out of his depth, and who should have stayed on debt collection and rummaging through dustbins and Service of Legal Process and surveillance tailing of a jerk who didn't know he was watched. Two days had been wasted, and he had nothing to report.

'Do what you can,' Penn said.

The streets were bright and full. The windows lit the young faces gazing at the heaped goods from old Europe. The best of London and Paris and Rome and Frankfurt brazened in front of the wide teenage eyes. Cameras and computers, furs and fridges, Scotch and silks, all there and piled high in the windows on Trg Bana Jelačića. Perhaps Jović read him.

'An illusion,' the artist said. 'We have nothing but *independence*. Old men say that independence is important. Myself, I prefer to have two arms, no war, and I prefer to paint rather than trail round with an innocent. You are goddamn patronizing, Mr Penn . . . Surprise, surprise, they have *nice* goods in their shops. They are affluent . . . Innocence to me is shit. Innocence means that you did not bother to find out before you came . . . Right, Mr Penn, understand our truth. We have no work, we have inflation, we have no factory production, but our shops are full and so you congratulate us. Who has money, Mr Penn, to go to the shops? Profiteers? Black marketeers? Pimps, spivs, crooks? Anything can now be bought in our *independent* nation state . . . What do you want, Mr Penn? If you want a woman, you can buy her. If you want a gun, you can buy it. If you want a life, Mr Penn, you can buy it. You would be surprised, in your innocence, at how cheap comes a woman or a gun or a life . . .'

They had reached the club. The music battered out onto the pavement. And the lights strobed from the doorway and fell on the anger of Jović's face, and he thrust the stump of his arm into Penn's face.

'. . . But you would not be interested in the price of a woman or a gun or a life. I apologize for forgetting your interests . . . Would you feel everyone who died here was a pig? Was it only Miss Dorothy Mowat who was a pig?'

They were inside, they had a table. Penn wore his uniform, his charcoal-grey slacks and his white shirt and his quiet tie and his brushed blazer. They ignored him. He bought the beers for Jović and Jović's friends and they ignored him. The hash smoke played at his nose. He wondered if Dorrie had been here; it was her kind of place and not Penn's. They talked, excited, laughing, in their own language and he bought more beers and the bottles crowded the table, and Penn felt a fool and a failure, and one of the girls leaned her head against his shoulder as if he were a pillar or a wall. The music of a band, New Orleans Creole jazz, punished him. He was a failure because it had slipped beyond his control.

'Jović, the morning . . .' Penn was shouting, and the head of the girl was leaden against him. 'What do we do in the morning?'

Jović was banging his empty glass among the empty bottles, and there was a sneer in his face. 'Was she really a *pig* of a woman . . . ?'

6

'Yes, Mr Penn, it was me that exhumed the cadaver . . .'

Penn felt a small tremor, excitement, masked it because that was his training.

Jović had collected him from the hotel. Jović had been morose and wrapped within himself. They had queued for a tram, squeezed on and strap-hung with the morning crowd. Jović had played his own game, no talk, led him as if on a string, and taken him to the hospital. Jović had abandoned him in a hallway of chaos in the hospital, and argued with a reception woman, and then with a manager, and then with a doctor. Jović had led him through corridors and through swing doors and past wards, finally down concrete steps to a basement.

'I heard that Mrs Braddock was in town, two weeks ago? When I heard she was in town I was stuck away up in Sector East. We've a big dig there, the Vukovar hospital people. I just hadn't the opportunity to break away. My problem now is, I've a plane to get myself from Zagreb to Frankfurt, and I've Frankfurt to Los Angeles tonight. Fifteen minutes is my maximum . . .'

Penn's hand was gouging into the briefcase, for his notebook, for his pencil, but not too fast because it was his training to hide rich and raw relief.

The Professor of Pathology from Los Angeles was a big man. He was well preserved, but Penn reckoned him over seventy years of age. The white hair was thin on his scalp and the skin beneath was dappled and discoloured. He had not shaved that morning and had white stubble for a beard. A scrawny neck, and hands with prominent veins. He seemed a man who cared.

'I can tell you when she died, that was early December in 1991. I can tell you where she died, in a field where a grave had been dug with an excavator outside Rosenovici village in Glina Municipality. I can tell you how she died, not with full technical detail, but knife wounds at the throat, blunt instrument blows to the lower forward skull, then a close-quarters killing gunshot above the right ear. I regret, and you have to believe me, that I cannot tell you *who* killed Dorothy . . .'

Penn was writing fast.

They were in an outer office and a woman brought the Professor a plastic cup of coffee. There was a vigour in the growling voice of the American, but a tiredness in his body and he drank deep on the coffee.

'It's a hell of a place there, the village that was Rosenovici. It's a place of foul death, it's where murder was done. Those responsible for the killing, they would have come from across the valley, from the sister village, it's Salika. We had the one chance to get in there and took it. They watched us, the people from Salika, and because of their guilt they hated us. They won't talk . . . And they were careful, those sort of people always are careful, there were no survivors that I got to hear about, no eyewitnesses . . . To know who killed those men, and Dorothy, then you would have to cordon that village and find every knife, every hammer or jemmy or engineering spanner, every Makharov PM 9mm-calibre pistol. The knife would, probably, still carry blood traces. The hammer or jemmy or spanner would still hold tissue that could be matched. The pistol, that's straight . . .'

Penn looked up.

The American had heaved himself up from the table and gone heavily to a filing cabinet. He was ripping the drawers back on their runners, jerking up files, discarding them, searching. Beside the filing cabinet was an open doorway. In the next area was a mortuary slab and there was a skeleton body on the slab. The bone sections were marked with tie-on labels and at the far end of the body was the skull and there was an adhesive red arrow on it, and the arrow pointed to the dark pencil diameter hole. On the floor beside the mortuary table were three bags that

Penn could see, unzipped, holding a mess of bones. The filing cabinet was slammed shut. The Professor laid in front of Penn a see-through plastic file cover which contained a crudely drawn sketch map, and another file which held black and white photographs. The photographs were tipped out, where he could see them, and the Professor's fingers shuffled them. He saw her face. Not the face of the photograph with her mother and stepfather, not the face posed with the village boys. He forced himself to look at the face of death, swollen, wounded. He closed his eyes momentarily. There was a rattle on the table. The bullet, misshapen, in a tiny plastic sack, bounced in front of him, rolled, was steady. The bullet was dull grey.

'Find the Makharov PM 9mm pistol, match the rifling, and you have a case. Find the pistol and you have evidence. You with me, Mr Penn?'

'With you.'

'Maybe not in my lifetime, but some time . . . In the Hague, in Geneva, here, maybe in London . . . I am an old man, Mr Penn, maybe not in my lifetime, but I believe in the long arm of law. I believe in cold and unemotional justice. I believe in the humbling of the guilty by due process. I want to believe it will be in my lifetime. I have only scraps to work from, but I see a picture. She was a fine young woman . . .'

Penn's voice was small in his throat. 'Tell me.'

He was looking down at his watch. The woman who had brought his coffee was grimacing at him, and pointing to the clock on the wall. His bags were beside his chair. He slapped his finger on a photograph, two shapes that were just recognizable as corpses, locked, legs and arms together, torsos together, skulls together. Penn stared back into the opaque watering eyes.

'I have only scraps . . . She was a fine young woman because she did not have to be there. The scraps give you a jumble of a mosaic, and you have to put the mosaic back together. She didn't have to be there. They were all wounded, all the men. They all had old wounds, mostly artillery or mortar shrapnel. They were the guys who had fought for the village, and they had been hurt bad, and everyone who was fit enough to quit had run out on them before the village fell. They were left behind to the *mercy* of the attack force. She was a fine young woman because she stayed with the wounded . . .'

He thought that he could hear Mary's voice. The stealing of a Visa card, taken from her mother's handbag, and the forging of her mother's signature.

'She didn't have an old wound. She could have gotten out, but none of the men could, they would have been, each last one of them, stretcher cases. She stayed with them. It would have been her decision, to stay with them. That makes for me a fine young woman . . .'

He thought he could see Mary moving easily in her kitchen, and pouring his coffee and bringing it to him.

'There must have been one boy that she loved. It has to be love, Mr Penn, to stay with those who are doomed when, yourself, you can be saved. Think on it, Mr Penn, think on it like I've told it. It's my best shot at the truth. I'm an old man, I've seen about everything in this life that you wouldn't want to see. She makes my eyes, Mr Penn, go wet. At the end, she was trying, Dorothy was trying to shield her young man from the knives and the blows and from the gunshot. The scraps tell me that, from the way they lay . . .'

He heard Mary and he saw her.

'A fine young woman, a young woman to be proud of . . .'

The room had filled. There was a director and there were managers, and there were staff from the mortuary. No more time for Dorrie Mowat. The Professor smiled at Penn, as if it wasn't his fault aircraft didn't wait. The director and the managers were pumping the Professor's hand and embracing him, and the women on the staff were kissing him, and one had brought flowers for him. Penn had screwed up the farewells to two months of unpaid work. He heard it said that the car was waiting, and they were running late for the flight. The crocodile swept up the stairs from the basement mortuary and along the corridors and through the swing doors, and cut a swathe across the lobby. Penn followed and Jović was silent behind him.

From the open door of the car, the Professor caught his eye, called through the crowd, and held the flowers against his chest, awkwardly.

'Good luck, Mr Penn. Build a case, stack the evidence. I'd like to think we'll meet again, in court . . . good luck.'

He didn't say it, that he was just there to write a report. He waved as the car pulled away.

The Botanical Gardens were always his choice for a rendezvous. It was where the First Secretary chose to take his informants. The Botanical Gardens on Mihanovićeva, a little tatty now compared with the time before independence, still gave good cover; there were sufficient evergreen shrubs and conifer trees to offer discreet privacy before the main summer blooms. It was his second posting, and it was the fourth month of his final year as field officer in the Croatian capital, and he had known *Hamilton, Sidney Ernest* for most of that time. The file on *Hamilton, Sidney Ernest*, designated Freefall, was fat, which meant that the First Secretary, as he had told his desk chief on the last London visit, knew about as much of the repellent little man as it was possible to know. So the business was done behind trees and shrubs presented to the city of Zagreb in the cheerful days of non-alignment. The map of a route taken across the Kupa river, across the territory of Sector North, was paid for with American dollars. The First Secretary checked that the map was of some small value with minefields marked and strongpoints identified. He was brusque to the point of rudeness as he discussed the map and the action behind the lines. Of all his informants in Zagreb he believed that he disliked the man, Freefall, more than any other. He strode away. The map would lie in the fat file.

The mortuary office was a colder place with the Professor gone.

Without his presence, without his passion and his caring, it was a colder and a darker place. Penn thought the work would slip more slowly. He was an interloper, and he was not offered coffee. But they gave him what he wanted. He left with photocopies of the sketch map of the grave site at Rosenovici, and of the Professor's notes on the exhumed bodies, and of the photographs of the dead, and of the written-out detail of the killing bullet that had finished the life of Dorrie Mowat. Penn followed Jović out of the hospital lobby. He felt a sense of

109

bewilderment. He reckoned that he knew right from wrong, that his mother and his father had taught from the time he could remember that there was good and there was bad. Too damned simple, wasn't he? Too damned simple to understand how the wounded could have been bludgeoned and knifed and shot. It was beyond his comprehension how a man could have looked into Dorrie Mowat's face and killed her. The photocopies were in his briefcase. The spring sunshine caught at his eyes, the freshness of the air surged to his lungs.

It was good to be gone from that place of cold and darkness.

She found him in a corridor leading off the main walkway that skirted the second floor of the Transit Centre. The walkway looked down onto the inner square, but he had made his hiding place in a shadowed corner of the corridor where the daylight could not reach him.

Ulrike dropped down, squatted beside the old refugee. He stank. She put her arms around his shoulder. He shook with his tears. It was a worn, time-abused face, and the suffering lines ploughed through the white stubble of his cheeks, and the tears ran across the lines and dribbled in the stubble. She did not know him, assumed he would have come the day before on the bus.

She did not know him, and so she did not know his story, but she could anticipate it, because she had heard the story too often. When she sat in her office with a delegation from the Swedish Red Cross or the Austrian Red Cross or the German Red Cross, when she blinked into the lights behind the television cameras of RAI or ZDF or the BBC, when she wrote her letters home she always said it was worst for the old men who were brought out from behind the lines. He cried. She took his hands, frail and thin and gnarled from work in the fields, and she felt the bones hard in her fingers. She thought, from his hands, that he had worked all of his life in fields, that he would have gone into the woods with a bowsaw in the autumn for the winter's fuel, that he would have struggled down a ladder each morning of each winter with the fodder for his few cattle, that he would have been a man of pride. She held tight to his hands, tried to give the old man strength. His home, his father's home, would have been flattened by an explosive charge. His barn would have been burned. His cattle would have been stolen, and his pigs. He might know that his son, the favourite, had been killed. It was worst for the old men who had lost everything, and hope. The children always searched for Ulrike in the Transit Centre, and they had discovered her now. The children stood in the corridor and they watched her as she squatted beside the old man who cried. She could not begin to say how the children would be affected by the sight of their flattened homes and their burning barns and their family's livestock being driven away, and by the fighting. She could see it in the old man, feel the wet of his tears on her face.

She understood the dialect of the village in Prijedor Municipality. His voice was a croak of anguish. It hurt her that the children watched. The children should not have seen an old man who had lost hope, forsaken pride.

'Our neighbours, our friends, who we worked with. How could they do it to us? Our neighbours, our friends, all of our lives, their lives, how could they destroy us? Is there no *punishment* for what they have done . . . ?'

When she had found him she had been going from a top-floor sleeping room, where she believed, maybe, that marijuana was smoked, down to the kitchens. She was behind her schedule. She could not sit any longer with the old man and hold his hand while he cried. She could offer him sedation tablets. Very good, magnificent, brilliant, a bottle of sedation tablets. Pride, no. Respect, no. Sedation tablets, of course.

'. . . Is there no one who will punish them?'

She could not answer. She took his name. The chief guards of the camps of the Neuengamme Ring had been punished, with the noose, for what they had done. The chief guards had been the defeated, the victors were never punished. She took his name so that she could leave a message at the dispensary, on her way down to the kitchens, for sedation tablets for the old man. Later, the young American would be at the Transit Centre. Perhaps the quiet and earnest young man from Alaska would find time to talk to the old man of *punishment*. She would push him towards the American, therapy to go with sedation. She kissed his fore-head. She patted the arm of his overcoat that smelled of his body and his animals' bodies.

He walked with Jović, following.

Jane would have liked the city. He tried to turn again in his mind each word that the Professor had told him, but Jane usurped. As if she were with him, as if she tugged him back to look into the bright shop fronts, as if she pulled him towards the cafés in the sunshine, as if she demanded of him that he should buy her flowers to hold as they meandered in the squares and along the ochre-walled streets. Jane would not have listened to the words, the *evidence*, of the Professor but she would have danced to the band with Jović and Jović's friends. Loving Jane for her prettiness, loathing her because now she found him bor-ing, slow, played out . . . Jane coming down to the tied cottage to meet his parents . . . Jane wearing a brief skirt and a gossamer blouse . . . Jane not helping his mother with the dishes in the sink after the tense lunch, because she had spent an hour on her nails . . . Jane not walking with her father in the fields after lunch because it was raining . . . He hadn't warned her, hadn't told her, it wasn't her fault. Jane had reckoned them dirty, they had reckoned her tacky. Two camps at the wedding . . .

All his own bloody fault.

'Where are we going?'

'You wanted to see people who were in Rosenovici, did you not?'

The cable fault between sound and camera delayed Marty.

He worked methodically in the freight container to locate the fault, step by step, then repair it.

He could not do the work outside, he needed the desk surface, and the sweat ran on his body and across his fingers.

The freight container, he reckoned, had been parked as far across the parade square of the Ilica barracks from the administra-tion block as was possible. From the open door of his freight container he could see across the parade square, past the drilling Swedish troops, past the bank of big satellite dishes, to the administration block. He was treated as if he had the plague, as if those in contact with him, up alongside him, risked contamination. He had been told to his face on his first day that the preparation of prosecutions was an 'irrelevance'. It had been given him straight in the first week, 'All you achieve, winding people up in your naïveté, is to further reduce UNPROFOR's credibility.' What they said, those who thought he had the plague, was, 'Of course there can never be trials, because the biggest criminals are those we need to sort out the mess', and they said it often. Those who thought he had contamination spat it at him, 'What you're doing, Jones, it's just a cosmetic gesture to massage a few bruised consciences away across the borders.'

Alone in his converted freight container, hot as a cook in a kitchen, he ignored what they said in the big offices of the administration block. He could cope . . . He was reared in Anchorage. He knew what it was to be thrown down, have the optimism belted out of him. Anchorage was 'false springs' when the depression of the snow hanging on until late April had to be hacked. Anchorage was the collapse of oil prices and the good men, his father's friends, heaved out of work. Anchorage was where they bred the philosophy of goddamn-minded obstinacy, pig stubbornness. And, to back his obstinacy, he had a degree in International Law from the University of Alaska, and a PhD from the University of California, Santa Barbara. His mind, methodical when repairing the sound cable from the camera, was well suited to the work of gathering evidence.

What they thought of him in the administration block caused no loss of sleep. It never had mattered to him, an Anchorage boy, what the men in suits thought. They were from his past, the men who came in by helicopter, the men who rode in the limousines to their oil company offices, the men who went out in the private jets when they had sorted the balance sheets and screwed up a few lives, like they'd screwed up his father's life. Marty Jones hated money and privilege and arrogance, and the hate was deep from his childhood. He reckoned, had reckoned from the first day he showed up on campus, that the due process of law was the one, the only, weapon that could cut down the money, privilege, arrogance of men in suits. The hate had translated to the power and the cruelty of the butchers. The hate made him a good investigator.

He would not take her anything, too demonstrative, not his way, but he looked forward to driving down the highway to Karlovac, and meeting the woman who administered the Transit Centre. He thought the German woman in the Transit Centre to be the finest human being he knew . . . But he would not tell her, did not know how to express that feeling.

Marty wiped the sweat again from his forehead and there was mist on the heavy lenses of his spectacles. The camera worked, the audio level light fluttered . . . But there was no smile of achievement; Marty seldom risked a smile.

'She called herself Dorrie. I would not forget her . . .'

Jović said that it had been the camp for officer cadets.

Still taciturn, the artist had explained nothing. Penn did not ask, he assumed that Jović had gone back to the ministry office, and perhaps he had apologized for Penn's rudeness, and maybe he had made a joke about Penn's ignorance, and it could have been that he had just said that the Englishman was a crap fool.

Jović translated, flat, no emotion nor expression.

'Yes, I remember her. She had come to Rosenovici about one month before the attack from the Partizans. I remember her . . .'

They had taken the tram to the camp for officer cadets. Out to the west of the city, in what would have been the quarter for skilled industry, but drab and smoke-grimed. The officer cadets had been well provided for. Jović went forward and talked quickly to the guards. There was an unmarked van parked up beside the small guardhouse and the guards had come from the van where they had been talking to the driver. Looking over the barrier blocking the entrance into the camp, Penn had seen the driver of the van. The face of the van driver was rounder, fuller, than what Penn had learned to see around him, and there was a tattoo at the neck of the van driver, couldn't place the tattoo, and the table in the guardhouse was stacked with cartons of Marlboro cigarettes. The guards at the barrier had wanted Jović gone. Fast instructions. Penn guessed the cigarettes were black market, and knew it was not his business.

'The front line was already north of our village. It was not possible to go by road. We were isolated in Rosenovici. The fighting was all around our village and at night we could hear the guns, and in the days we could see the tanks of the Partizans moving forward on the main road, but the war had not yet come to Rosenovici. We felt some safety because we had always had good relations with the Serb people in Salika. We put our trust in those good relations. They were our friends, they were our neighbours, they were our work colleagues. We felt that they would speak up for us. We were no military threat to the Serb people in Salika, there were very few guns in our village, we could have done nothing to intervene in the war . . .'

Her name was Maria. She shared a room with her sister that would have been small for the occupancy of an officer cadet. She said her sister was in the city that day, searching for work. She said that she had been secretary to the export manager of a furniture factory in Glina. She said that she was divorced. The room was spotlessly clean. Penn thought she had little to do, a refugee, but clean the room. As he listened, his eyes roved over the room, and he saw there were no ornaments, nothing of the past of a woman he estimated to be in her mid-forties, no bric-a-brac, nothing to sustain memories.

'She came with a boy from Australia. She came because he returned to his home. When the war started there were many boys who came back to their country. I suppose they wanted to help, wanted to fight. They were not soldiers, this boy was not a fighter. We believed we would be safe, and when we found that we were not safe, then all the roads to the north were blocked. It was a Tuesday night when the artillery guns and the tank guns were turned on Rosenovici. Some people tried to flee that night, they went into the woods and they said they would try to walk in the woods and the hills until they reached the lines of the Croatian army. I don't know what happened to them. The rest of us, we thought that it was a mistake by the regular army to fire on our village, we thought that there would be liaison with Salika, with our friends and neighbours and work colleagues. We thought they would tell the Partizan officers that they should not fire on us. They fired on our village all through the

Wednesday. There were only rifles in the village to shoot back at them. It was on the afternoon of the Wednesday that her boy was wounded . . .'

Seeing Mary Braddock in the kitchen, drinking the coffee, feeling the warmth of the Aga, listening to the calm telling. The sixteenth birthday party, and Charles away on business, and Mary trying to do the right thing, and inviting in the teenagers of her friends in the village on the Surrey/Sussex border, and buying a new dress for Dorrie, and Dorrie not wearing it, and the village boys from the council houses crashing the evening, and Dorrie dancing.

'Across the lane from the church was a big farmhouse, Franjo's and Ivana's farmhouse. It was the oldest building in the village, it had the best and the biggest cellar. It was where the wounded fighters were taken. It was the fighters who were hurt because they tried to hold a defence line, they could not hide in buildings. Some were hurt, dead, some were hurt, wounded. She brought him back from the defence line to the cellar in the farmhouse of Franjo and Ivana. She was so small and he was a heavy boy and he could not help himself. She carried him back across the fields from the defence line and the snipers were shooting at her, and we could hear their voices, the snipers, and they were shouting to each other and making bets as to which would hit her. She brought him to the cellar and she went again across the fields to the defence line to bring another back . . .'

Dorrie dancing. Dorrie in her jeans and black T-shirt. The boys, her friends, smoking their marijuana and passing the pills, and the teenage kids of Mary's friends drifting away and frightened. Mary coming from the kitchen, helpless and control lost, and Dorrie on the oval walnut-veneer table that had cost Charles £2,800 at auction and stripping out of her jeans and the T-shirt and her pants as she danced. Mary standing in the doorway, stunned, silent, seeing Dorrie's shallow breasts and seeing the straggle of the coming hair, hearing the splintering of the antique table.

'She was alone with the wounded fighters all through the Wednesday night. By the time the darkness came on the Wednesday night, the Partizan snipers had come so close that the farmhouse of Franjo and Ivana was cut off from the rest of the village. We could not reach the cellar and the boys there were too hurt to make their own way out. She could have come. In the darkness she, alone, might have managed to come. I think she chose to stay . . .'

The council house boys clapping their hands, speeding the dance, the white flashes of Dorrie's body. The dance finished when the table had collapsed and splintered. Dorrie drunk, Dorrie smoking, Dorrie popping the pills, Dorrie swearing abuse at her as she stood stunned, silent, in the doorway. Mary had told it calmly. Mary had said that it was done to hurt her.

'It was on the Thursday afternoon that the village fell. On the morning of the Thursday, before it was light, many people had left the village, gone with what they could carry into the woods. I and my sister, we could not go, our home where we had sheltered was close to the store in Rosenovici and that is on the east of the village and it was open to the shooting from Salika.

'There were very few of us left in the village when it fell. I had thought that it would be the regular troops who would come into the village when the flag was raised. There was a sheet tied to a stick and it was held out from a window of the store. It was people from Salika who came into the village, it was our friends and neighbours and work colleagues. They came across the bridge from Salika. They all wore uniforms, but I knew them as the carpenter who had made the table for my kitchen, and the gravedigger who had made the grave for my father when our own gravedigger was ill, and the postman who brought the letters to our village, and others that I knew, and commanding them was the man who was a junior clerk in the co-operative at Turanj. They took everything that we had, our wristwatches and our earrings and our necklaces and our money. They put us onto a lorry and they took us to a camp at Glina, what had been the prison there. I urinate blood because of what was done at Glina . . .'

'And Dorrie, what happened to Dorrie?'

'She was with the wounded in the cellar of Franjo's and Ivana's farmhouse when the village was taken . . .'

'What happened to her?'

The tears streamed on the woman Maria's face.

Jović said, 'She doesn't know. She has told you everything that she could know . . .'

Penn had been hunched forward on a small hard chair, and he had been writing hard. He sat back. He saw the face in the doorway, and the shabby washed-through uniform. He did not know how long the van driver had been listening, the man with the full and round face and the cropped skull and the tattoo on his neck. The woman, Maria, was speaking, and she had taken Penn's hand with urgency. She was choking the words. When he looked back to the door the face of the van driver was gone. He realized what the tattoo was, the wings and the parachute. Gone.

Jović translated, without emotion, without expression. 'She was an angel. She stayed with them when no one else stayed with them. She was an angel in her prettiness, and an angel in her courage . . .'

Penn squeezed the woman's hand. He followed Jović out into the sunlight. There were children playing, kicking a ball, there were women hanging out washing on lines slung from the trees that were in first blossom.

Jović asked, cool, 'It will be good for your report, yes?'

The potential reader had to know the man. If the man were not a composite, not a picture, then quite impossible for any future reader of the file to comprehend. Not easy, damn difficult, to make the picture. Henry Carter, sweating now because Library was so damned hot, tried to make a shape of the morsels available.

NAME:	Penn, William Frederick.
DOB:	27 May 1958.
POB:	Cirencester, Gloucs.
PARENTS:	George Wilberforce Penn (farm labourer) and Mavis Emily (née Gordon). 4, the Farm Cottages, Ampney Crucis, Nr Cirencester, Gloucs.
EDUCATED:	Driffield Primary, and Cirencester Comprehensive (name unlisted), 5 O levels, A levels in Geography and History.

EMPLOYMENT:	Home Office 1978–1980, clerk grade. Security Service 1980–1992 (resigned). Worked in F Branch (Subversives) and A4 (Surveillance). 'Capable officer in area of field work, but limited in ability to analyse complex material.' . . . (Join the club, young man!) . . . Resigned after being informed by Personnel that progress into General Intelligence Group was restricted to academic graduates.
SUBSEQUENT EMPLOYMENT:	Alpha Security Ltd, Wimbledon, SW19, as private investigator.
MARRIED:	Jane Felicity (née Perkins) 1989. 1 son, Thomas Henry, DOB 9 January 1993.
MARITAL ADDRESS:	57B the Cedars, Raynes Park, Surrey.
HOBBIES:	None listed.
RECREATION:	None listed.
INTERESTS:	None listed.
SUMMARY:	Had reached a plateau at Security Service. Was unwise to challenge promotion system. Could have continued at existing level. Perhaps believed he would be persuaded to stay, to withdraw his resignation. 'Deeply wounded' that no such persuasion was offered? (my note – HC).

Not much there, damn all there, the old desk warrior thought, and absolutely nothing there to give prior warning as to how the young man would react when confronted with that bloody awful place, with that surfeit of bloody awful misery.

More for Penny to type up when the dragon, the day shift supervisor, went for her rest-break and canteen tea.

He had a great bank of experience, seldom mined and seldom tapped, and it was a lesson he had learned . . . The dull men who were without hobbies, the ordinary men who were without recreations, without interests, usually managed to confound with surprise . . . God save the dull and the ordinary and the boring. God protect the human species from exciting and unique and fascinating men . . . that was a lesson Henry Carter had learned.

★   ★   ★

If it had not been for the war he would have been the mayor.

The Headmaster stood at the back of the hall of his school.

There was an order in these things, and the appointment to office of mayor would have come, that year, to the Headmaster, if it had not been for the war.

All of the village had gathered in the hall. A meeting was held in the school every month. He had never spoken out before, he had never stood up before to be counted, but he thought that as Headmaster he would be listened to. His was a position of importance in the village community of Salika, he believed it his responsibility to speak.

Because of the war, Milan Stanković, nothing more than a clerk, was mayor. And not mayor for a year, but now in his second term, and there would be a third. Milan Stanković, nothing more than a clerk, was mayor because he commanded the Territorial Defence Force, because he controlled the black market, because he could provide gasoline or diesel or spare parts or crop seed, because he killed. And the bodies had been dug up and taken away, and the Headmaster felt the confidence to speak.

He was at the back of the hall and standing alone. He would have to crane on tiptoe, when he spoke, if Milan Stanković were to see him. Nothing more than a clerk, and sitting in a fraud's uniform at the table facing the audience of villagers, and beside him were the carpenter and the gravedigger and the one who had delivered post when there were letters to be delivered, before the war had come. The carpenter and the gravedigger and the postman also wore the uniform of soldiers, they were the new elite of the village. He had not talked to the Priest, had not confided that he would speak at the meeting, he had no trust in the Priest.

The Headmaster believed a new age of darkness had come to the village. It was his duty to speak. He was a small man with sparse greying hair above a short beak nose that held his iron-rimmed glasses. When he stood on his toes, when he could see Milan Stanković, the image was blurred. His glasses should have been changed, but it was not possible now to get the replacement, because of the war. He had taught many of those who sat between where he stood and the table, and they followed, like sheep, a false deity. He thought it his duty to denounce Milan Stanković.

He felt no fear . . .

The Priest should have been beside him. Of the men in the village, only he and the Priest had known higher education. He felt the Priest slipped from the responsibility of duty. He had a text, as the Priest had a text each Sunday. The text had been taken from an anthology of quotations, in the English language, that had been a treasured companion since his graduation from the university. Mr Edmund Burke, 1729–1797, political theorist: 'It is necessary only for the good man to do nothing for evil to triumph.' He had been across the bridge two weeks before when Milan Stanković, who was a clerk, had been to the junket in Belgrade, he had seen the digging and seen the bodies lifted from the grey-black earth and seen them bagged. He had felt the disgrace of his village. That sense of disgrace was the keener because he had looked into the face of the elderly American who had supervised the exhumation, and seen contempt. He was sixty-two years old. He was respected throughout the village.

He was not afraid . . .

They sat in front of him, they stood in front of him, the sheep. They agreed to everything proposed by Milan Stanković. Hands rose in acceptance of what was proposed. They needed leadership, the sheep. The man who had been a clerk was beaming a smile and gathering together his papers, and there was a pistol at his belt, and his uniform was washed clean. The chairs were scraping. Little knots of villagers were sliding forward to beg favours. He did not understand how a good woman, Evica Stanković, could share a life and a bed with such a man. He loathed the man, he loathed the power of the pistol at the man's belt.

It was the moment the Headmaster chose.

'Before we go, before we leave, there are matters that should be discussed . . .'

Shoulders swivelled, heads turned towards him, and behind the table the smile faded. He spoke out loud, and he stood on his toes that he might be seen by all.

'Not one matter, several matters . . . Your children go to the school, my school. At the school we have insufficient books. For children to learn it is necessary they have books. I had discussed the shortage of books with the UNCIVPOL officers from Petrinja, and the UNCIVPOL officers had promised me they would raise the matter with UNHCR, attempt to get more books, but those UNCIVPOL officers were harassed, sworn at, blocked, threatened by the militia of this village. It was the grossest stupidity to block the UNCIVPOL officers, and I will get no books for our children to learn from . . .'

The silence was around him. When he ranged his eyes across the sheep, when he caught their eyes, they looked away. Evica Stanković, she had looked away.

'We should not be led, my friends, by men of the grossest stupidity. Nor should we be led by men who stain the name of our village. We should elect our leader, to speak for all of us, by a vote that is private and not by the vote of the bullet . . .'

He looked far ahead. Milan Stanković stared back at him. He could not see the detail of Milan Stanković's face, but he believed he saw surprise.

'We are a people who know suffering. Close to here is the great forest of Petrova Gora where our glorious Partizans fought with such courage against the fascist Ustaše of the Great Patriotic War. Close to here, in Glina town, is the church where our grandparents were burned alive by the Ustaše. Close to here, near to Petrinja, is the site of the concentration camp where the Ustaše slaughtered the children of our grandparents. And we have here, amongst us, a new group of Ustaše who stain the name of the Serb people . . .'

The Headmaster saw the movement at the table. The table was pushed back. Milan Stanković advanced on him. The sheep scattered their chairs and moved aside to make a space for Milan Stanković to reach him. Evica Stanković was among those who moved their chairs aside. He had come to make a denunciation and now his voice rose.

'I saw, you saw, the old American who came to Rosenovici. There was a report about him on the foreign radio. He is a professor of pathology, he is an investigator of the dead. Because of what he searched for, what he found, and took away, the name of our village is shamed . . .'

The fist of Milan Stanković, standing in front of him, blocking his view of the sheep, was clenched on the handle of the pistol worn in the opened holster.

'We are disgraced, all of us, because of the wounded at Rosenovici . . .'

The pistol whipped into the face of the Headmaster. He felt the stinging pain, and the blackness blurred in front of his eyes. He fell. There was no hand among the sheep to halt his fall. He was on his knees. There was wetness in his eyes. He saw the blood splatter below him. He groped his hand for his spectacles that lay close to the shined boots.

'We are all criminals because of the wounded at Rosenovici . . .'

He saw the sole of the shined boots cover the lenses of his spectacles. He heard the crunching of the broken glass.

'What they promise on the foreign radio is that acts of criminality will never be forgotten . . .'

The shined boot hacking into his ribs.

The Headmaster gasped, 'Wherever we run . . .'

The shined boot belting into his chin.

A whispered voice, 'Wherever we hide . . .'

A fist in the collar of his jacket, lifting him, and the tightness of his tie around his throat, and the punching starting, and the kicking.

'Never forgotten . . . our shame . . .'

The death of the Headmaster's voice. They let him drop, and when he had fallen they kicked him some more. He saw above him the gravedigger, the carpenter and the postman, and he saw Milan Stanković bend and wipe blood from the toes of his boots. And behind them the hall of the Headmaster's school was emptied. The chairs were scattered without formation, abandoned. None had spoken for him, the sheep. He lay a long time on the floor, after they had gone, and he did not know for how long because the watch on his wrist was broken . . . He held, clutched, his secret, the secret was the location where a survivor of the destruction of Rosenovici still lived. The telling of the secret to the Canadian of UNCIVPOL had been the payment for the promise of school books . . . He lay a long time on the floor until he had the strength to push himself up to his knees and his elbows, and he gathered together the cracked shards of the lenses for his spectacles.

The Headmaster crawled to the doorway of the school hall. He saw no movement in the road. The lamplight from the houses came indistinctly to his eyes. All gone, the sheep. All barricaded in their homes, afraid. It was difficult for him to lock the door of the hall. He felt no fear, he felt only a loathing of the man who had been a clerk . . . He, alone in the village, held the secret.

He could not be certain, but it was his training to know when a tail was on him. The late afternoon and the early evening were spent in his hotel room making sense of the note form of the interviews, and then supper and a beer in the old town. It was when he had stepped off the pavement to give room to a whore negotiating her rate with a client that he had thought he was followed. He had swung, amused, to see better the face of the whore, and her dressed like a housewife, a cardigan and a floral skirt, and there was a shadow moving behind the whore, and the shadow froze when Penn turned full face.

7

'I saw her, when the Partizans came into the village . . .'

The smells were close to Penn's childhood. Eight years old,
twelve years old, at harvest time, when the men were in the
fields taking in the barley, wheat, maize, and going to the hedge-
row and squatting down and wiping between their cheeks with
yesterday's newspaper, and the sun settling with the flies on their
mess, and the smell. Six years old, ten years old, and the milking
cattle in the parlour and the shit running out below their lifted
tails, and splattering, and the shut-in heat trapped inside the
walls and the low asbestos-sheeted roof. Penn, the boy brought
up on the farm, was close to the smells of the Transit Centre.

'It was only chance that I was in the village. You see, I am
Bosnian. I am a Muslim of Bosnia. I was trying to take the bus
from Banja Luka to Zagreb. I have the cataracts in my eyes.
The doctor in Banja Luka said I should go to the hospital in
Zagreb. I thought it was possible for a Muslim to travel through
the lines of the Serbs and the Croats, stupid of me. The bus was
stopped on the Glina to Vrginmost road. The Serbs were very
hard on me. I went where I thought I was safe, to the village of
Rosenovici. There was a madness around there, but I did not
think the madness could last. I thought I would stay in safety
in Rosenovici until the madness passed. When it became too
dangerous to stay many of the village left, at night, to go through
the woods and the hills. Because of my sight I could not go. No
one was prepared to delay their flight to help a woman who could
not see, it was necessary for me to stay. Men, women, lose charity
when they are in flight for their lives. I was there through the
fighting for the village, and I was there when it fell . . .'

Penn thought he had started to understand the village where

Dorrie Mowat had died. The village life and the farm life had gone away from him and he had taken the exams at the comprehensive school in Cirencester, and the exams had turned his back on his parents and on the farm and on the fields and hedgerows and woods, and on the smells. But he was learning, and the farm life and the village life seeped back to him.

'It was on the third day after the attack had started that the village fell. I think it was the Thursday. It was the second week in December. The village had been preparing for Christmas, their festival. The people had no presents for their children but they had cut branches of green leaves from the holly trees. They had tried to make a joy of their festival . . .'

Penn prompted gently. What had she seen, of Dorrie, when the village fell? Jović translated.

'I had been in the church. It was the first time I had been in the church of Catholics. They called the place the crypt, and the walls there were thick, of heavy-cut stone. The girl came on the night before the village fell. She came to ask the women who were in the church if they could tear up some of their clothes, their clothes that were most clean, for bandages. I could not see her well, because of the cataracts in my eyes, but there were other women afterwards who said that she was beautiful. She took the clothes that had been torn and cut into strips and she went back to where the wounded men were hidden. She had to cross the front of the church and then go across the lane and then she had to go through the garden of a farmhouse. It was all open, and when she went back there was much shooting, as if they had seen her, the Partizans, and tried to kill her. I know she had a great courage, and she was not afraid when she had the bandages and was about to go back into the open. I could not see her, but I heard her laugh. It was a sweet and happy laugh. You know why she laughed? Some of the women in the church, they had put on all the underpants they possessed and the cleanest were the third or fourth pair from their skin, and she was going to make dressings for the wounded from the third pairs or fourth pairs of the underpants, and some of the women were shy to take off their underpants. She laughed . . . I did not see her again until it was over . . .'

126

Remembering Mary's story. The story told in the comfort of the kitchen with warm coffee. Mary speaking without hatred, but from the depths of pain. The dinner party in the Manor House, black tie. The celebration of the elevation of a neighbour to the lofty eminence of Master of Foxhounds, North Sussex Hunt. Banter, silly but cheerful, spilling round the room that was panelled with old oak. Dorrie coming into the dining room, bitter face and holed jeans and a T-shirt too dirty to have been used as a rag for cleaning a floor.

'It was the irregulars, their militia, that came into the church. We knew that a white flag had been raised at the store, and we knew that most of the fighters, those who were not hurt, had already gone. We were taken out into the afternoon light. I remember that it was afternoon because the sun was low above the hills and it was into my eyes. We were made to form a line.

'We were standing in front of the church and they took anything that was of value from the women, and from me. We had nothing that was special, only sentimental, but they took it. I heard her voice. She is only a small girl, but she had so big a voice and she was shouting from inside the farmhouse that was across the lane from the church. They had their guns, and she was shouting as if she had no fear of them . . .'

Hearing the story, Mary's pain. Dorrie coming into the dining room and holding the jar of tomato purée. The quiet falling on the dining room and the cheerful joking killed. Dorrie marching to the Master of Foxhounds and shaking the jar and unfastening the lid. Dorrie pouring the rich red of the jar onto the head of the Master of Foxhounds. The tomato purée dripping from the bald scarred scalp and down to the white of his tuxedo jacket.

'She was brought out of the farmhouse. All the time she was shouting at the Partizans. And she had her arm around the waist of one of the wounded fighters, and she had the arm of another of the fighters around her shoulder to give him support. It was near enough for me to see. Not easily, but I saw . . . I saw her hit. He was a big man, and he had a beard, long, dark. I saw that man hit her and she could not protect herself because she had the wounded fighters to help . . .'

There was the noise of the Transit Centre around Penn. Crying voices and the clattering of metal pots, the beating of hammers, and the wail of radios. The name of the woman was Alija. Her eyes watered, but he had the feeling it was from medical drops and not tears. He thought she was a flotsam of war, that she would be far down any list of patients requiring a cataract operation. She held a ragged handkerchief in her hands and pulled and tugged at the edges.

He heard the hoarseness of his voice, as if his throat was blocked. 'What happened to her, what happened to Dorrie Mowat?'

She shrugged. She looked away. She murmured. She shrugged again.

Jović said, 'She has told you all she knows. The women who had been in the church, they were taken away. She does not know anything more.'

Penn stood. It was a reflex, done without thinking. He bent forward and he took the head of the woman in his hands and he kissed her forehead. The hands that had held the handkerchief were dug now into the material of his blazer. She was gabbling at him. There was the foulness of her breath close to his nose, and the smell of her clothes. He thought he might vomit and he dragged her fingers clear.

'The women who were with me, they said she was so brave. The women said she was an angel . . . It was what they said . . .'

He was away from his chair. He reeled, as if drunk, from the room with the damp peeled plaster.

He was out in the corridor. He leaned against the wall of the corridor.

There was the grin, sardonic, cold, from Jović. It had been Jović's style to hire a car and have him drive, without explanation, down the wide road from Zagreb to Karlovac, and to direct him to the Transit Centre where the Muslim refugees waited for onward passage to the safe havens and the new lives in 'civilized' Europe. Jović, he thought, played him like a marionette.

Jović said, 'Good stuff, yes? Good stuff for your report, yes?'

Penn snarled, 'Just shut your bloody mouth.'

Doubt crawled in Penn. He thought himself so insignificant. Once, two and a half years back, maybe three, he had been shuffled for a morning to a ministry to do a positive vetting on an architect who would be working on RAF station bunkers, and the architect had been in a wheelchair and so damned cheerful. The architect had said that the best thing about spending time in Stoke Mandeville spinal unit was getting to know that however bad his situation was there was always someone, in the next bed, who had it worse . . . Penn was the little bureaucrat, the little man whining about a job and a mortgage and a marriage. He thought of the scale where his problems stacked against those of the woman, Alija . . . Penn thought of what Dorrie had done, and how she had achieved love. The feeling of insignificance, it hurt.

The German woman was in the doorway of the room. She smiled, friendly, at him. She was slightly built and her face was washed clean and there were sharp lines of tiredness at her eyes. The German woman had led him and Jović to the room where they had found Alija.

'Right, Mr Penn, now I will show you around the Transit Centre . . .'

He was like all the others who came from abroad. He was like the men from the national delegations of the Red Cross and like the television crews. She was sure the place frightened him, the place that was her kingdom. They were all the same, the ignorant, they wanted to be gone before it was decent to leave. There was a wedding ring on his finger. He would have a wife at home, probably a child. He would live in a home that was small, safe, protected, just as were the homes in Munich. She did not think it right to make it easy for them.

'. . . Show you round the Transit Centre so that you can see our work here.'

'So sorry, but I don't think I've the time.'

'Always best to find time, Mr Penn. Too easy to ignore if we don't find the time.'

'I should be away . . .'

She thought that he looked a decent man. She said briskly,

'Won't take all day, Mr Penn. There are 2,400 people here, Mr Penn, and they have nothing, not even hope. It is important that I take visitors around the Transit Centre so that they are seen. Every visitor who is seen tells the people here that someone from outside has bothered to make the journey to visit them. It is a very little thing for you, Mr Penn, an hour of your time, but it shows these people that you have an *interest* in them. If you lived here, Mr Penn, you would be pleased to know that people from abroad showed an interest.'

'Thank you, yes, I'd like to.'

She thought he was a decent man because she thought he was ashamed that he had tried to run away . . . It was her regular tour, the same as for the delegations and the television crews. She showed him what she was proud of, the kindergarten for the small children, the little hairdresser's room, the scrubbed clean kitchens. She told him what it had been when she had started up the Transit Centre. She could not be sure what his level of interest was. She told him that in the last winter, when they had no fuel, no glass in the windows, it had been body heat that had sustained them. She told him of the drinking and the smoking and the drug abuse, and of the women whose menstrual cycle was blocked by stress, and of the children who ran wild, and of the men who had lost the reason to live. She thought she held his interest when he asked her how it was possible for her to cope, and she answered, as she always answered, that she could cope with the aloneness, but that the loneliness still hurt her.

It was at the end of the hour. She opened the door. The American was playing back a tape on the video.

'Not finished, Mr Jones?'

He flushed. Never could help himself when she spoke to him. It was the warmth and the boldness in her voice that brought the blood flush to his face.

'Just another two or three, someone's gone to find them,' Marty said.

There was a man behind Ulrike. He saw the man in the blazer and the white shirt and the tie, and he saw the creases in the man's slacks. Never could know whether she laughed at him and there was always the tinkling brightness in her voice. He was told the name and the business of the man, and he grimaced as if he was indifferent.

'What I'm dealing with here is *mass* crime. I'm not talking about little incidents. Anywhere you hit a golf ball round here it'll get to land on a clandestine grave. I'm talking about major league. If I got sidetracked into graves where there were a dozen people, I'd just be wasting everyone's time. No offence, Mr Penn.'

It was instinctive, his dislike of the Englishman with Ulrike. He stood too close to her, and it was like he had her confidence. He had put down the Englishman and Marty thought he saw, just for the moment, impatience flash in her eyes, at her mouth. Just for the moment, and Ulrike was telling him that the Englishman had been interviewing a Muslim woman, and named her. He knew of the woman, hadn't bothered to get round to interviewing her, finding whether she had a 'snapshot' of an atrocity.

'Was she raped?'

The Englishman, Penn, seemed to frown. 'I didn't ask her.'

'You always ask a woman here if she was raped. A statement on rape, sexual violation, a statement with audio or video, and the perpetrator's name, that can be evidence . . .'

'I didn't ask her.' The frown deepened. 'Wouldn't have thought so, seemed old . . .'

'Common mistake, mistake people make when they're not familiar with the ground here. They don't rape for sexual gratification, they rape to demean their enemy. Stick around and you'll get to know . . .'

The Englishman said, 'It's not relevant for me to know.'

He could have told him to go jerk himself. If Ulrike had not been there, he would have. His father, back in Anchorage and writing most months and working in the Brother Francis shelter for destitutes, didn't think Marty's work, far from home, relevant. And the grizzled old prospector, his friend Rudi, gold hunting seven hours' drive down the Pacific coast from Anchorage who wrote some months, he didn't understand what was relevant. And his tutor from the Law Faculty, University of

California at Santa Barbara, in his last letter, hadn't connected as to how a favourite former student found it relevant to ferret for *mass* crime. Marty had told them all in his return letters that in a new world order it was critical for the international rule of law to be established. Had written them all in his return letters that *ends* didn't matter, catching and trying and hanging didn't matter, but *means* mattered, the process of law mattered.

'Don't let me keep you,' Marty said. 'If you can turn your back, and you can feel good, then you're a lucky guy.'

He thought the Englishman soft shit and if Ulrike had not been there, in the doorway, he would have told him.

'I've just a report to write, then I'm gone. Nice to have met you, Mr Jones.'

He was late coming to his school because of the difficulty in shaving his bruised face.

It was a slow walk to the school because the road from his house to the school was rutted, and the young men of Salika were too busy in their uniforms and with their guns to use their muscles to repair the road. A slow walk because he had no spectacles.

His body hurt. Each place that he had been kicked and punched meant pain when he walked to the school.

His wife had told him that he should not go. His wife had said their life in the village was finished. The village was his home, he had refused her.

He had taken a new text that morning when he had started the walk from his home to his school. A Croat text, but that was not important to the Headmaster. The text, mouthed as he walked, was the command given, 326 years earlier, to Nikolica Bunic by the rulers of Dubrovnik when the man, the martyr, was sent to treat with the Pasha of Bosnia. He knew, by heart, the text. 'To violence you will reply by renunciation and sacrifice. Promise nothing, offer nothing, suffer everything. There you will meet a glorious death, here the land will be free. In case of difficulty, delay. Be united, reply that we are free men, that this tyranny and God will judge them.' Just to whisper the text to himself was hardship. The carpenter, Milo, watched him walk from the door of his home. The postman, Branko, watched him past the militia camp. The gravedigger, Stevo, leaned on his spade at the back of the church and could see him as he passed. Milan Stanković went by him in his car, forced him to stumble to the side of the road where the weeds grew. The Headmaster went to his school.

He was late for the start of the day at his school. The children were gathered in the hall. He heard the singing, he knew the song. The children sang of the decision of Prince Lazar to commit the Serb army against the Turk, and fight at Kosovo . . .

> There flew a falcon a grey bird,
> From the holy city, from Jerusalem
> And carried in its beak a swallow.

. . . 28 June 1389, and the lie of Serbian nobility. The anthem would not have been sung at school assembly if he had been present. The day, 28 June 1389, was captured by the extremists, the barbarians of the new order, by the killers and the murderers. The day, the nobility of defeat, was taken by the new order in Belgrade as an excuse for cruelty, for violence. There was glass in the upper part of the swing doors into the hall of his school. He could see her. She stood where he should have stood. He felt the betrayal . . .

> But that was not a grey falcon,
> That was the holy man, Elijah:
> And he does not carry a swallow,

. . . He saw that Evica Stanković stood in his place. Her arms were raised, swung to lead the heaven of his children's voices.

> But a letter from the Mother of God . . .

'Stop.'

The Headmaster stood in the open doorway, sticking plaster across his face.

'Stop.'

The children turned to him. He saw her defiance. She dared him to step forward. He saw his children despised him. He saw the children of the carpenter and the gravedigger and the postman. He saw the grandchildren of the Priest. He saw the child of Milan Stanković. He saw the freshness of the faces and their contempt. He turned in the doorway. He heard the shout behind him, forty children's voices, unbroken, in unison.

'It is better to die honest than to live in disgrace.'

The Headmaster began the slow walk home.

He had only his secret to sustain him, the knowledge of Katica Dubelj existing as an animal in the ruins of Rosenovici . . . He knew no longer how to use it.

It had been done easily and smoothly, and Penn had recognized it.

'So, what are your future plans, Mr Penn?'

Jović had introduced the officer as liaison. Jović had said that he was a captain and liaised between the Croatian army, 2nd Bn, 110 (Karlovac) Brigade, and the UNPROFOR troops across in Sector North. Jović claimed him as a friend.

'Just to pick up what help I can, captain, and to write a report,' Penn said.

Jović had said that the captain was his friend and had been with him at Sisak, when he had lost his arm.

Only a report into the death of Miss Dorothy Mowat? 'Only her death, yes.'

Not the specific situation in that part of Sector North where she died? 'How it happened, when it happened, pretty bland.'

Why was the death of Miss Dorothy Mowat, when so many had died, so important? 'Rich mother, reckons she can buy anything.'

A sensitive area, a sensitive situation, did he not know that? 'Just a report, just to let her mother sleep the better at night.'

And who else would read his report? 'Shouldn't think anyone will, just her mother.'

It was the gentle probing of an intelligence officer. Penn recognized it. He hoped his answers were ignorant, facile. He reckoned the Intelligence Officer was poorly trained. He would have done

134

it differently himself, bored harder. He knew about digging into the recesses of a man's life because he had worked in the positive vetting team that cleared personnel for work at the Atomic Weapons Establishment, Aldermaston. Trust no one, believe in no one, that was any intelligence officer's maxim, and he guessed that Jović would have telephoned ahead and engineered the meeting so that Penn, enigma, would be checked over.

And his report would not be used as a start point for a war crime investigation? 'Good God, no . . .'

The gentle probing of the Intelligence Officer, Liaison, was done during the tour of the cease-fire line. The village of Turanj was across the Korana river near to where it joined with the Kupa river east of Karlovac. Not a house undamaged, every building hit by multiple machine-gun bullets and by tank fire, and artillery shells. The officer said, for the benefit of his visitor, that it was where the Serbs had been held, where their advance had been stopped. He was told of the battle, close-quarters fighting. He listened and looked around him. An old woman was picking at burned roof timbers in the yard behind what had been her home. They were past the defensive machine-gun nests. They walked in the village of Turanj as if it were a museum, but the old woman searching in her yard told him of present reality. The front wall was off the food shop. The roof was off the scorched interior of the repair garage. Flowers grew in overgrown front gardens, and the blossom was on the magnolia and the apple trees. He was shown the co-operative building, and he was told not to go past it because he would then be in the field of vision of the snipers, and the cease-fire was variable. A cold place and quiet.

The officer said, 'In war itself there is an excitement, in combat there is an elation. Most men, you ask them, and if they give their secret answer, tell you that war, combat, should not be missed . . . But the war goes by. I know nothing more degrading than a former battlefield where there are no bodies, where there is no noise. The war passes by and the excitement is quickly forgotten. Only the vandalism of the war is left. It is the worst place you can be, Mr Penn, an old fighting ground, with just the ghosts.'

135

A cat saw him, was bent low and scurrying, but took the time to turn and spit at him. The poles that had carried the telephone wires were down.

'Would it be the same in Rosenovici?'

'Why do you ask?'

'Just trying to get the picture . . .'

'It would not be the same,' the officer said. 'Here the buildings are destroyed by war. In Rosenovici a few buildings would have been destroyed by war, the rest would have been destroyed by placed explosives. Here there is a chance to rebuild, one day. In Rosenovici there would be no chance to rebuild because nothing is left. In Rosenovici, villages like it, they went as far as bulldozing the graveyard. Here, there is still feeble life. In Rosenovici there is only the memory of death . . .'

Penn thought he was being tested. He looked away. He stared up and beyond the jagged and broken roofs of Turanj and he could see the first line of trees.

The officer anticipated him. '. . . It is where their guns are. They will be following you, through telescopic sights, maybe if they are bored they will shoot at you.'

'I am just here to make a report.'

He played ignorant. Penn walked back down the road, like getting his head shot off was no part of making a report. They drove away in the officer's car. They went back past the machine-gun positions and the soldiers waved to them, they went across the bridge over the Korana river and Penn saw, moored at the bank, two grey-coloured inflatables. He didn't like to look hard because frequently the officer slung a fast glance at him to see whether it was a trained eye or a rubbernecker's eye that examined the front line. There were tank obstacle teeth beside the road into Karlovac, and more defence positions, and there was the emptiness. They drove on, past the officer's headquarters in a new building where all the windows were taped against artillery blast. They climbed a winding road. They were above the town. On the summit of the hill was a fortress tower. They left the car. They walked along a path and in the grass beside the path were teenagers, cuddling and messing about and smoking. They looked out.

The town was in front of them.

Beyond the town were the rivers, winding to their meeting point.

Beyond the meeting point of the Korana and the Kupa rivers was the green carpet of the forest.

Beyond the forest was the blue haze line of the high ground.

The officer said, 'The high ground is the Petrova Gora, dense woodland, rock cliffs, sheer valleys. It is special to the Serb people because it was in the Petrova Gora that Tito had a field hospital for his Partizans, in the war with the Germans. The German army made many incursions into the Petrova Gora but they were never able to find the hospital. The failure was a source of frustration, that is why the Germans killed many of the people in the villages at the edge of the Petrova Gora. If you were to be there, Mr Penn, which is *impossible*, then they would lie and tell you that it was Croatian people, fascists fighting alongside the Germans, who were responsible for the killings. Through the lies they justify what they have done, now, to villages such as Rosenovici . . .'

Penn had his hand across his forehead. He shaded his eyes. He thought he could see twenty miles, maybe more. Such peace. It was where Dorrie had been, Dorrie's place. It was like the place of his childhood, where he had been before the exams and the application forms, and work in London. Peace and beauty. He strained to see better.

The officer said, 'I am correct, you see nothing that threatens? The front line between here and Sisak is the Kupa river. It is seventy kilometres in length. Across there, on their side, where you see nothing, are minefields and strongpoints and defended villages. Across there, they have 300 guns that can flatten Karlovac and Sisak in a day. Across there, aimed at Zagreb are medium-range missile launchers. One day, I hope, we can take our territory back, but not today and not tomorrow. You see, Mr Penn, it is important to us that, today and tomorrow, we do not anger them, across there. It is of strategic importance for the future of Croatia, military and economic, that the bastards, across there, are not antagonized . . .'

'Who did it?'

'Did what?'

'Who killed Dorrie Mowat?'

'It is important?'

'For my report, yes.'

The officer smiled. Jović was behind them, silent. Penn and the officer stood together and stared out across the Kupa river and the forest and towards the high ground. The sun beat at Penn.

'They do not scatter evidence, they do not leave eyewitnesses. I do not know.'

'Who would have given the order?'

'Probably the commander of the militia. Perhaps the commander of the militia in the village close to Rosenovici . . .'

'What is his name?'

'I used to know him, not as a friend, but I knew him. My wife is a teacher and knew his wife. Why do you need the name?'

'For my report?'

'You can make up a name, take a telephone directory. Just for a report, for a mother who lost a daughter, you can invent a name. Why not?'

He had been led, subtly, to the trap. He had underestimated the quality of the Intelligence Officer. Perhaps a *graduate* would not have sprung the trap, not one of the young bloody graduates of the General Intelligence Group. He stumbled.

'Pick a name out of the air, why not?'

A light murmur of laughter from the officer. 'He is Milan Stanković. I see him at my liaison meetings, I used to play basketball against him. The militia in the attack on Rosenovici was commanded by Milan Stanković.'

'What will happen to him?'

'I saw him last month, at the liaison meeting. We talked about the electricity supply. They have our territory but they do not have power. We have lost our territory but we have power. Last month, he did not seem like a man afraid, but then the liaison meeting is always behind their lines. Today, tomorrow, nothing will happen to Milan Stanković.'

Penn said, 'I will put that in my report.'

*　　　*　　　*

On that night of the week it would have been usual for the Priest to have gone to the Headmaster's house and, by candlelight, played chess.

He had not made apologies, he had not given notice of his absence to the Headmaster, he had gone instead to the home of Milan Stanković.

He was a quiet man and through the adult part of his seventy-four years he had seldom offered an opinion that he had not first known would fall on approving ears. Capable of intrigue but incapable of confrontation, he lived out the last years of his life in the intellectual backwater that was the village of Salika. He knew every man and every woman and every child in the village of Salika, but his only friend was the Headmaster with whom on that night he should have played chess and taken a glass of brandy weakened with water that would have lasted him through the game . . . and he had gone instead to the home of Milan Stanković.

He could justify his abandoning of the game of chess.

They were coming in the village to the day when the population of Salika travelled to the church at Glina where so many had died. It was an important anniversary, the fiftieth. All of the village would travel to the site where the people had been herded by the Ustaše fascists, where the fire had been lit, where a thousand had died. If the Priest had not been young, not been fit enough to survive, emaciated, in the Petrova Gora, if he had been inside the cordon, then he could believe that he would have been taken to the church and burned alive. But, to go to the church at Glina, it was necessary for the people of Salika to take two buses. The buses were in a barn near to the school. To take the buses there must be diesel fuel. To get diesel fuel he must have the help of Milan Stanković. The gaining of diesel fuel was his justification for abandoning his appointment with his friend.

He had known Milan's grandparents, Zoran and Milica, and both had died in the fire at the church in Glina.

He had known Evica's grandparents, Dragon and Gospava, and both had been burned alive at the church in Glina.

He understood what he called, when he talked with his friend as they pondered the board, 'the curse of history'. There was not, in the village of Salika, a man, woman or child, who had not been fed, since the dawn of understanding, the story of what had been done by the Ustaše fascists.

They sat in the kitchen, and he understood.

They were around the table and he had been given bitter coffee and juice, and he understood.

The Priest had baptized Milan Stanković, just as he had baptized Evica Adamovic, and he had baptized little Marko who slept now above them. The bayonet was on the wall. Against the leg of the table, on Milan's side, was the automatic rifle. All of their lives, Milan and Evica and Marko, would have been battered by the curse of history. He thought himself a pragmatist, thought himself a realist. It was impossible that the curse of history should not fall upon the big shoulders, upon the wide face, upon the big heart of Milan Stanković. The Priest thought it was the curse of history that had made inevitable the attack on Rosenovici, the fall of Rosenovici, the butchering at Rosenovici. The Priest did not apportion blame . . . But he had not gone across the stream, when many had gone, to watch the digging up of the grave and the recovery of the bodies. Perhaps, he had not wished to take the gaze of the old American, near his own age, who had come and directed the digging . . . Milan agreed with no dispute to allocate the diesel for the buses.

He considered Milan the best of the younger men in the village. The best basketball player, but he no longer had time for sport. The best organizer, such as the time he had led the other men in the village in the flattening of a football pitch, but he no longer had time for triviality. The best husband, but Evica walked around him as though a wall rose between them. Milan sat morose opposite him, his back to the window and the last light. The Priest thought that the curse of history made a treadmill for the best of men, and the drive of the treadmill was faster. Milan sat subdued opposite him, and never turned to look out across the stream to the corner of the field in the dusk distance. Walking briskly on the treadmill, elected by acclamation to head the village militia. Jogging, and the visit to the village of the barbarian Arkan who was a criminal from Belgrade and who had raised his own force of gaol filth and who had posed in front of the War Memorial with Milan. Running, when the attack, supported by the tanks and artillery, had been directed on the Croat neighbours of Rosenovici. Sprinting, when the wounded were taken from the cellar of Franjo and Ivana, and he had played chess with Franjo, when the wounded were taken out and the girl. Pounding, when they had come with their spades and zipped bags and dug. Careering, when the Ustaše spies had been captured . . . The Priest did not know how Milan could go faster, and he did not know what would happen to him if he fell from the speeding treadmill.

The Priest offered his thanks for Milan's time, for the promise of the diesel and Evica let him out.

He walked up the lane from Milan Stanković's house, going slowly, but he speeded his frail stride where a wax lamp threw light across his path.

He did not wish to see the opened window, to see if his friend sat alone in front of the board.

It was like a bad pick-up in a bad bar.

He had written up his notes of the day, good material. He had walked up into the old city and bought a good meal. He had come back to the hotel, striding and wondering what Jović would pull on him the next day. He had taken his key at the reception, been handed the telephone message – would he, *please, please,* call Mrs Mary Braddock – crumpled it and handed it back to reception to dispose of. Earlier, he had made his own telephone call, international, and no answer. He had gone into the bar for a last drink. He had ordered a beer, local, good, and cheap. He hadn't seen the man at first. His eye caught the clutch of journalists whose table was covered with filled ashtrays and emptied bottles. He was eavesdropping on them, they were back from Sarajevo and noisy. He was halfway down his beer when the man came off his stool and the movement caught Penn's attention. He saw the van driver from the camp for officer cadets, he saw the shadow shape from when he had stepped off the pavement to give the arguing hooker better space for her negotiation. A round full face, darting sharp eyes, close-cut fair hair, old acne scars on the cheeks and the chin, a bulging neck above an open white shirt and on the neck was the tattoo. A rolling swagger walk, a small man's walk, coming from his stool with his glass in his hand.

'Evening, squire – bit far from the old smoke . . .'

'Evening.' Penn offered him nothing.

'Don't see a lot of English here – mind if I join you . . . ?'

'Please yourself,' Penn said coldly.

'Nice to talk English – better than all this foreign jabber . . .'

Like a bad pick-up in a bad bar. He thought of when he had been in Curzon Street, early days in the Service, close to Shepherds Market where the girls were, when he had gone out for a sandwich at lunch time, and he didn't think there would have been a hooker who would not have been ashamed at such a bad pick-up. The tattoo, close to him, was of the Parachute Regiment's wings. Penn didn't feel curious, only tired. He finished his beer, but the man was in fast.

'You'll have another? 'Course you will . . .' The man was leaning across the bar and flicking his fingers at the barman. 'Two more local piss. Move it, my boy . . . Dozy buggers, right? . . . I'm Sidney Hamilton. I get called "Ham" – So, what brings you to this shit hole, squire?'

'Just a bit of work,' Penn said.

'Out from UK, are we, squire? I packed it in there, no future. It's all niggers there, and slit eyes, and fucking Irish . . .'

'Why were you following me?' Penn said, quietly.

'Beg pardon . . .'

'Why were you following me? Why were you listening yesterday to my conversation?'

The darting bright eyes had narrowed, focused. The new beers were in front of them.

'Smartarse, eh?'

'Straight question, shouldn't be too difficult to manufacture a straight answer,' Penn said.

But a diverted answer. 'Just heard a word, the word triggered. You know how it is, squire? You hear a word said and you get to listen. It's not a crime . . .'

'What was the word?'

'Rosenovici, the Croat village in Sector North, you were talking to that hag about Rosenovici . . .'

'You know Rosenovici?' Penn tried to stay casual, didn't know whether he succeeded.

The confidence was flowing again. 'I know Rosenovici, hell of a battle there, big fight. *Warrior of Principle*, squire, that's me. Bad fire fight there . . .'

'You were in Rosenovici?'

'The village was cut off. They'd brought tanks up, T-54s, wicked bloody things. They'd got the old Stalin's organ, that's the multiple rocket launcher . . .'

'Were you in the village?'

'They had artillery up there, howitzers. There was right shit going in there . . .'

'You were there?'

'Well, I wasn't actually . . .'

'Where were you?'

The eyes darted away. 'I wasn't actually *there*, would have been minced if I was there. We were close up. We'd been sent in to make contact with our guys who'd legged it into the woods. We had a corridor open for them to get out through. We had it on the radio. We had it on the radio when they signed off, put the flag up. I was near there . . .'

'Not actually there?'

'*Near* there, last week . . .'

'Walked into Sector North?'

'Didn't take the bloody Central line. 'Course I bloody walked. Recce job. It's bad shit in there. We lost two guys . . . These fuckers, they've no bottle. We had two guys wounded but the other fuckers wouldn't stop for them, bottled out. No lie, I saw them killed. Their throats were slit. They used knives on them. I couldn't do anything because the other fuckers had bottled out . . .'

'You can walk into Sector North?'

The man was drinking faster, and flicking his fingers for the barman, and shovelling the banknotes onto the bar.

'If you know what you're at, which I do. Know where to cross the Kupa river, know where the mines are, which I do, and the strongpoints . . . He's a bad bastard in there, he's the commander of the militia. He's at the village across the stream from Rosenovici. He's Milan Stanković. He did it himself, used the knife. I could have dropped hiɯ, if the other fuckers hadn't bottled out . . .'

Penn felt the pinch in his stomach. He swayed, slightly, on his stool. He held tight to his glass.

'. . . Say, squire, you know where Nagorno Karabakh is? Where the hell is that fucking place?'

Penn said, 'It's a bit left of here. You know those little globes that kiddies have, where you put a pencil in the top to sharpen it, well on one of those it's about a half-inch to the left.'

'You pissing on me, squire . . . ?'

'It's the other side of Turkey.'

'I heard there was a good little war there. I heard they wanted good men. Could be South Africa, security, but there's all those niggers. This is just fucked up here . . .'

'Why did you follow me, Ham?'

'Who said I bloody . . .'

Penn cut him. 'An answer to my question, Ham – why did you follow me?'

Like a ball being punctured. The bombast of the man went flat. He was standing, off the stool, and he was pulling a thin wallet from his hip. The photograph in the pouch of the wallet was of a skinny little woman, brunette, and the woman was holding a child in a party frock.

'It's Karen, and that's Dawn, my little one.'

'Why me?'

'You're a bloody gumshoe, you're a dick. That's what you are, a private detective.'

Then the story rolled. An old photograph, yes. She'd done a runner, yes. She'd taken the kiddie, yes. No contact and letters sent back 'Not Known at this Address', yes. And he was far from home and when the bullshit was turned off then he wanted the love of his woman and his kiddie, yes. A lonely boring little man, yes. He wanted them found, his Karen and his Dawn, yes . . . Penn would not have known the answers before he had gone to work at Alpha Security. He had had his share already,

144

bombastic men coming up the stairs to the office above the launderette, showing a photograph of a woman and a kiddie, and wanting them found . . . Basil had told him that looking for a woman who had quit with a child was a 'Go Careful Area'. Basil had said it was necessary to go carefully or the woman might end up in the casualty section . . . He looked into the woman's face, knotted, and the child's face, strained. He took an address, a police station in Karlovac, he wrote down a telephone number. He was told to ask for 2nd Bn, 110 (Karlovac) Brigade, then for 'Ham', everybody would know Ham. He looked a last time at the photograph, then gave it back.

'You didn't tell me your name, squire . . .'

Penn eased off his stool. 'I'll be in touch, maybe.'

8

'Yes, I saw her . . .'

It was Jović's success. The tram ride out to the west of Zagreb, through the old quarter, then out amongst the apartment blocks of the capital's new suburbs. Jović's success had brought them to the end of the tram route, to where the track ended. Jović had said that the wood huts used by the construction workers of the last block to be built were now a refugee camp. To Penn it was a desperate place. There had been rain in the night and the puddles glistened in the first sunlight of the morning. The road to the camp would have been gouged out by heavy plant equipment. He stepped carefully, but the mud gathered at the caps of his cleaned shoes. There were children here, but too beaten to play with a football, there were men standing listless and watching their coming. The place had its own aggression. He had seen small gardens carved out of the rubble at the edge of the camp, and thin thorn bushes had been planted round the plots, pitiful little efforts to make a home in a refugee camp. The huts were for communal living. They walked inside, carried more rainwater and mud inside, as others had done before, then into the gloom of a corridor. A line of men waited to use the basins of the wash house, a queue of women waited to use the lavatories. Jović had given a name, waited, and they had been led by a sullen guide to a bleak and small room.

'I had taken food to the cellar in Franjo and Ivana's farmhouse, in the early morning. There had been a halt in the shelling and I was able to go with food. We had only bread to give to the wounded, and the bread was old. It was when I was there, in the cellar, that the firing started again, and I could not leave.

146

I was in the cellar when the village fell, when the Partizans came . . .'

Her name was Sylvia. She shared her wood-walled room with her husband, and he lay on the bed with dead eyes, and Sylvia said he was now diabetic. There were two boys, who she said were aged ten years and seven years, and the older boy twitched all the time and the younger sat across his mother's lap and would not be separated from her. Penn judged her close to nervous collapse, and he wondered whether it was worse now, or had been worse when the village was fought for. She chain-smoked cigarettes.

'She had come with the boy from Australia, and she would not leave him. Everyone told her that it was not safe to stay in Rosenovici, and she ignored everyone. Perhaps I understood her, because my eldest son was with the fighters, and I would not leave the village. I cannot say whether she realized properly the extent of the danger but she refused to go. It was early on the Thursday morning that I reached the cellar with the bread. My son was in the cellar . . .'

Quietly, Jović told him what she said. Penn wrote the words fast in his notebook. He was humbled. She had lost her home, and she had lost her future, and her mind was turned, and she dragged hard on the filters of the cigarettes and threw half-smoked ends into an old tin. She said that she had been the secretary to the director of the railway station at Karlovac.

'She had come, herself, the previous evening, when there was still shooting, to the church where we were hiding and she had taken clothes that had been torn up for bandages and for dressings, and we had told her then that it was dangerous for her to be with the wounded. She never listened, in the month that I knew her, that she was in the village, it was never her way to *listen*. When I came into the cellar she was bandaging the wound of my son. I can see it. It is never away from me. I see it each night, and it is near to a year and a half ago. I will never forget it. My son had hold of her wrist. She was trying to bandage the wound at his stomach, but he could not be still because of his pain and it was difficult for her to make the bandage stay. I can see it because there was a small candle lighting the cellar. My

147

son held her wrist as she tried to make the bandage and I saw his love for her. They all watched her, where they lay, they all watched her and they all loved her . . .'

He thought of what Mary had told him, stories and pain.

'I knew the village could not fight on for much longer, and there was too much firing for me to go back again to the church. I thought that I would be useful if I stayed in the cellar, and I thought I could help the Partizan soldiers to move the wounded after the village fell. I thought they would want help to move the wounded boys to the ambulances to take them to the hospital in Glina. It was in the afternoon on the Thursday that they came into the cellar, but it was not soldiers. The men who came were from Salika, that is the Serb village across the stream from Rosenovici. I knew all of them. The first who came in was the postman from Salika, and quickly after him was the gravedigger, and there was a carpenter who had made the chairs for our kitchen. They were fierce with us. Most of the wounded were kicked. They were shouting at them to stand up, and none of them could stand and they were kicked because they could not stand. She shouted back at them, I do not think they understood her language, but I saw her punch the postman when he kicked one of the fighters. I thought they had a fear of her, I thought they did not know what to do with her. We were taken up the steps from the cellar and she made the postman, Branko, and the carpenter, Milo, and the gravedigger, Stevo, help to lift the fighters up the steps. He was in the garden of Franjo and Ivana's farmhouse . . .'

Tasting the coffee, feeling the warmth of Mary's kitchen, hearing the pain stories. He shut them out . . .

'I have shame because I did not have the strength that she had. They threatened me with a gun, they told me I could not help. I was the last out of the cellar. He was in the garden. They did not know what to do, it was for him to decide what to do. Some of our fighters were kneeling and some were on the grass in the garden, and she held two of them upright, and all the time she shouted at him, and he went to her and he hit her with the end of the barrel of his rifle and she was still shouting at him. I would not say he was a friend, but I knew him well

148

enough, and there were days when I used to accept a ride from him as far as Turanj where he worked and then I would take a bus into Karlovac. She was not shouting at him, pleading, she was shouting at him in anger. I should have called to her, told her not to shout at him, but she would not have listened . . . They made a line of them. There were some who could walk, just, and there were some who were carried, and she helped two of them. They took them along the little road in the village to the square where there was the café and the store and the school. They took them past the school and away along the lane that goes to the fields. He gave the instructions, they took them away down the lane because that is what was ordered by Milan Stanković . . .'

'What happened to Dorrie Mowat?'

He watched her. The tears streamed on her face. Her fists were clenched and he thought she might hit him. He knew he reopened the wound. He understood why the shame held her. She had been allowed to stay in the garden of the farmhouse. She would have seen the back of her son, walking or carried or supported, and she would have seen the bobbing head of Dorrie between the two young men that she held upright, and she would have seen the guns and the knives, and she would have known. Her words were a torrent breaking on Penn.

'I saw them until they were at Katica's house. The lane bends after Katica's house. I could not see them after they went past Katica's house.'

He said, flat, 'Who killed them, your son and her boy and Dorrie Mowat?'

Jović said, 'She told you, she saw them taken as far as the old lady's house. She does not know what happened after they had passed the house. She told you that Milan Stanković gave the order for them to be taken along the lane, past the old lady's house, towards the fields. She told you what she knew . . .'

'But it is correct that she did not see them killed?'

A bitter flare in Jović's face. 'She buried her son four days ago. Can you not comprehend what these people have suffered, what you make them endure again for your *report*? She did not see them killed, correct.'

A quiet in the room. The husband had not spoken, lay on his back, defeated. The children held their mother. The woman, Sylvia, looked with bruised eyes, into Penn's face.

Jović said, 'She does not understand why it is important, who shot them, who beat them, who knifed them. She says that Katica was in her house when the village fell. She knows that on the previous day Katica's husband went out to the yard to get wood and was shot by a sniper. She knows that Katica was in her house, with the body of her husband. She knows that Katica was not brought out of the village with the others who survived. She has not seen Katica since . . . Does anybody care what happened to them or who did it, she says, does *anybody*?'

He said, grimly, 'Would you thank her for her time . . .'

'She says that she has only time left to her. She says, and she says it is what they all said, she says that the young woman was an angel . . .'

He blundered out of the room and away down the corridor. He shoved his way through the queue of men and women lined up for the wash house. There was a cockroach crawling amongst the feet, going slow because it was already damaged by kicks, and then it was stamped upon by a bare foot. He saw the slime of the destroyed creature. The cockroach was forgotten, the feet tripped past it. He saw himself as the creature, insignificant, gone from memory . . . but Dorrie was remembered . . . He could write his report, embellish it for effect, take the money, be a creature squashed and slimed. Perhaps, in life, there was just one chance . . . Penn felt humbled . . . He walked fast out of the camp, and Jović had to scurry to keep at his shoulder, towards the waiting tram at the end of the track.

She came in from her shopping.

She played back the answerphone, and there was a message advising the date of the next meeting of the south-eastern branch of the Save the Children Fund, and a query on the availability of the marquees for the garden party at Whitsun in support of leukaemia research, and the secretary who did two days a week would not be coming in the morning because of influenza. She let the tape run. She did not hear the voice. The voice, crisp, competent, was absent from the tape.

The dogs were scratching at the kitchen door.

She let them out and they jumped at her, happy.

Maybe it was just a folly. Maybe she had no right to know. Maybe the dead should sleep. Four times now she had telephoned the number of the hotel in Zagreb, four times in growing annoyance she had left her message and four times in increasing loneliness the message had not been answered.

She left her shopping on the kitchen table. She took the leashes from behind the door.

Mary walked her dogs through the village.

She walked on the drying grass. Next week they would take the flowers away from the grave. She laid her coat on the grass and sat on it. Next week she would bring more flowers. The dogs hunted out fallen wood and lay beside her and chewed and spat the morsels clear. She heard herself, her own words, saying, calmly, that she enjoyed *winning*, and she wondered what he thought of such stupidity. She heard herself, her own voice, saying that her daughter was *a horrid young woman*, and she wondered how he had taken such betrayal.

Shared her secrets with him, given her secrets to Penn, wretched little private detective, opened herself to him, stupidity and betrayal.

'For nothing, Dorrie, should have allowed your rest . . .'

He walked with Jović.

Jović showed him the big German cars speeding on the cobbles and said they belonged to the new elite of racketeers. Jović said that the country was rotten and that the profiteers fed from the carcass . . . And every few minutes Jović would stop, hold out his hand for telephone money and be gone into a bar, and then be back, and not offer any explanation . . .

Each time he was left on the pavement he gazed around him. The city was at ease. The war was forgotten, tucked and hidden behind the cease-fire line that was thirty minutes' drive away.

He had never seen a tram before Zagreb, clanking and swaying monsters with raucous hooters to announce their coming, with the passengers clinging inside to the straps, and the lines running polished amongst the worn and smoothed cobbles.

He watched a flower seller.

. . . Jović showed him the great circular plaza. It had been the Square of the Victims of Fascism, now it was the Square of Croatian Celebrities . . . Jović showed him the Historical Museum, closed for reconstruction, indefinitely . . . Jović took him into a yard behind a building and in the yard weeds grew amongst the mighty toppled statues of the former regime in Stalinist bronze, and Jović said the statues would be cut up and melted down, destroyed as historically incorrect . . . Jović said that it was necessary for history to be rewritten in new nationhood, said it and grinned sardonically. Jović took him to the Tourist Bureau and there were no new guidebooks of the city; the old ones were all recalled for pulping, and the new ones would carry no reference to the Ustaše fascists . . .

A new bar, more money for the telephone, Penn waited outside.

The rain had started again.

The artist said, 'There is no record of her coming out. There is a database for refugees who have left the occupied territory, and she is not listed. She is classified a missing person. The detail is small. She is Katica Dubelj, she is eighty-four years old. She was in her eighty-third year when Rosenovici fell. If she had died between then and now, it is the sort of matter that is discussed at the liaison meetings, if her body were returned for burial here then it would have come through the Turanj crossing point, escorted by UNHCR. I cannot help it, but she does not appear on the database . . . There are a few old people who still live across there, perhaps in the woods, perhaps they are tolerated. She is beyond your reach, alive or dead. It is the end of the road, Mr Penn. I think you should be satisfied. You know the last weeks and the last days and the last hours of the life of Miss Mowat. Only a few minutes have escaped you . . . Satisfactory, yes? Do you want me to book the flight for you?'

Penn said he wanted to be alone.

'Shall I come tonight for my money, or in the morning before you fly?'

Penn took out his wallet. He counted out the notes, American dollars. He took the scribbled receipt written on the ripped paper from Jović's notebook.

'I think we did well, I think you will write a good report.'

Penn shook his hand.

'I think that by next week you will have forgotten us, Mr Penn. We are easy, with our problems, to forget . . .'

Penn had no pleasantries for Jović, and he saw the surprise of the man. For the moment he believed he had, at last, unsettled the artist. No banter, no chat, no laughing, and no thanks, as if he had no time for them. There was a confusion on Jović's face, but he was proud. Jović, Penn thought, would not have known how to grovel, and was gone, skipping away across the road through the cars, lost in the pedestrians on the far side, never looking back.

He had finished, or he had not begun. Finished, not begun, it was Penn's decision . . . A light rain fell and it brought a dust with it that lay on the cars, and it settled on the shoulders of his blazer. He made room on the pavement for two young men who swung their weight on crutches, war amputees. He was the intruder. He prised himself into their lives, into the life of the city, into the lives of the camps. It was Penn's decision on whether he had finished, or whether he had not begun. She had had everything and he had had nothing. She had had privilege and advantage and abused them. She could have walked into college but she declined to. He would have called her, to her face, if he had met her, 'selfish little bitch'. Had had everything while he had had nothing, had been *free*, and he had never been. It was as if he should have been warned away, kept safe distance. And he had prised, beaten, kicked his way into the life of Dorrie Mowat.

'I told you, and you cared not to hear me . . .'

Charles barking and the gin spilling from the glass rim.

'. . . I told you that you were wasting money, but you cared not to listen.'

'I just wanted to bloody know . . .'

Mary walking the lounge, spinning, like a caged creature, and smoking which was new for her.

'. . . Don't I have the right to know?'

'It's obsession, and obsession will break you.'

'I tell you, he wasn't flash. He was well-mannered and he was considerate . . .'

'Mr bloody Penn, he's taken my money and he's taken you for a damn great ride. When he's ready he'll be back. When he's back there will be his bill, and there will be a report that is bullshit. They're grubby people and you chose to involve them.'

'Sorry – what sort of day was it?'

'A bloody awful day.'

'He could have rung me back, could have talked to me. Sorry . . .'

She went to her kitchen, started the supper. What hurt was that she had thought Mr Penn cared.

The media had hit the hotel.

Penn, rueful, sat in the bar and nursed the fourth beer, might have been the fifth.

The circus had hit the hotel.

Penn listened, and he watched.

It was reunion time for those from Sarajevo and those from Vitez and those from Mostar. There was embracing and kissing and bellboys bent under the weight of equipment boxes. He sat apart from them, listened, and his hand twitched to his tie; no ties on show in the circus, no blazers, no pressed slacks, no shined shoes.

Penn listened because the talk was of staying alive.

Staying alive was paying the welding company in Sarajevo to fit the shrapnel-proof sides onto the reinforced Land-Rover chassis: 'I'd have bought it, too bloody right, 81-mm chunks coming in.' Staying alive was not going to Srebrenica across country on foot: 'Crazy place, place to get killed, not worth the hassle.' Staying alive was laughing for the wild man in Sarajevo who had brought a cow across the airport runway, under the snipers' guns: 'Best bloody milk in the city.' Staying alive was getting down to the mortuary in Mostar after the shelling: 'He was about twelve, he'd got new trainers on, sticking out under the blanket, the trainers made it front page, and it syndicated.'

To Penn, listening, they made staying alive just about possible.

They were in town for a wedding. They were going back to Sarajevo and Vitez and Mostar in thirty-six hours.

It was his decision, whether he had finished, or not begun. It was as if her freedom laughed at him, as if the laugh was recklessly loud in a cavern of silence. As if she danced in front of him, feral, a creature of his childhood woodland, challenging him to follow where she led. He had never been *free*, had he? Bloody structured, bloody trapped. Duty, stability, discipline, commitment, Penn's gods. It was as if she had never been defeated, not even in death . . . as if he had never succeeded, not even in life. He had not known freedom, would never know it unless he followed . . . It was like a pain in him. He finished his beer.

Penn went out of the hotel, to walk, think.

He sat in his kitchen and he fastened the belt that held the holster at his waist.

The carpenter, Milo, bent beside the table and eased off his shoes, then dragged on his old boots, and he heard the intake of breath from his wife because the boots shed dried mud onto the floor that she had washed.

He went to the refrigerator and took an apple and put it into the pocket of his heavy coat. It was a good refrigerator, the best that could have been bought in Zagreb, but the door was always open because he had learned that to close the door meant the gathering of mildew on the inner walls. There was no power in Salika. It was near to a year and a half since the carpenter had made the two journeys, with the wheelbarrow, across the river and come back with the refrigerator from Franjo and Ivana's kitchen and the television from the house behind Rosenovici's store. They both looked well in the carpenter's home and he spat back at his wife each time that she declared them useless because there was no power.

With the holster at his belt, with the apple in his pocket, he took the hurricane lamp down from the shelf above the sink. He could no longer use the big flashlight because the batteries were exhausted. He lit the lamp and clumped in his old boots across

155

the kitchen floor, and left more mud. He went out into the night. He went to his store shed and he took from the nail the sharp bowsaw and his big jemmy and the lump hammer.

He went past the house of the Headmaster, where a small light burned, and he groped down and found a stone in the road and threw it hard so that it rattled the upper planking of his house. He went past the house of the Priest, the old fool, and past the house of the gravedigger, Stevo, and called out to him, and past the house of the postman, Branko.

Short of the bridge, he shouted forward. There would be young men on the bridge, guarding, and it was best to call forward. He yelled his name into the night. The light swirled around him and beyond the light was blackness. No moon that night and he could not see the ruin of the village nor the trees beyond it, nor the outline against the skies of the higher ground. It was to please Milan Stanković that he went with his pistol and his apple and his bowsaw and tools out into the night. They were good boys on the bridge, good laughter when he came to them, and they pulled aside the frame that was laced with barbed wire so that he could go onto the bridge . . . He considered Milan Stanković the finest man in the village of Salika. He hated to see it, what he saw every day now, the sullen and hostile and bleak face of the best man he knew. Milan had said, that morning, that Evica had complained of the table in the kitchen. It was too old, and the glue was dried out, and the surface was too scratched to scrub clean. There were fine timbers to be had in the ruins . . . The wind was around him as he walked up the lane towards the village of Rosenovici, and there was light rain, and once he stumbled and nearly fell because he had been looking ahead to the edge of light thrown by the hurricane lamp and he had not seen the deeper hole left by the jeeps that had come for the digging . . . He did not understand the recent mood of Milan Stanković. The carpenter thought that he could bring the life smile back to the face of Milan when he presented him with a new kitchen table. At the edge of his light, he saw a cat sprinting away, stomach down, and he kicked a stone fiercely towards its starved ribcage . . . There were none in the village who would come with the carpenter to Rosenovici at night, the scared farts,

156

but he would gather up sufficient seasoned wood from the timbers and haul it back that evening and work through the small hours, catch some sleep, then work again through the day, and have the table ready for the next evening.

The carpenter would have said that he was afraid of nothing.

He reached the village.

There was an owl in a tree up the hill.

He had been back to the village many times, never with Milan. The timbers would not be at the square, not at the store nor the café, because the headquarters of the Ustaše had been there, and the greatest concentration of tank fire had been there. He had been back for the refrigerator and for the television, and to help others round up the cattle left there, and back for the shooting of the dogs that had been abandoned there, and back to look and to search among the homes for hidden jewellery, and he had been back to stand in the group that had watched the digging. Milan had never been back. There was fine wood in the roof of the church but what had been burned had fallen, and the rest of the roof spars were too high for him to retrieve. The farmhouse with the *cellar* had not been burned, but it had been dynamited, destroyed, the timbers would lie under plaster and stone rubble. Milan always found an excuse for not returning to Rosenovici.

He stood in the square. The wind played at his face, coming from the east and cold. The light caught at the houses that had been destroyed. The carpenter could see up the *road* along which they had marched as escort to the wounded. He was not frightened of darkness. He thought he knew in which house he would find seasoned timber. Out of the square and along the *lane*. He had brought up the rear, pushed them, driven them. It was the lane up which the bulldozer had been directed, following them. He was not frightened of darkness but the silence around him was broken by the wheeze of his breathing and the stamp of his boots, and the carpenter shivered, felt the cold of the wind. Ahead of him, at the edge of the light, was the collapsed gate, then the black expanse of the *field*. It was through the gate that they had taken them, and then the bulldozer had followed, and the bulldozer had clipped the gatepost, collapsed the gate. Short of the field, where the lane bent, was the small house

157

which had not been destroyed. It might have been the postman, Branko, or it might have been the gravedigger, Stevo, but both had claimed to have shot the old bastard Ustaše. He could remember it, seeing the flash of her face at the window, the old bitch Ustaše, as he cursed them to go faster, and he could remember the face of the girl. It was only a hovel. The carpenter reckoned he would not have put pigs in the house of the old bastard and the old bitch, but the hovel had been there since the time he was born and the timber would be good, seasoned. In his mind, they were both together, the face of the old bitch at her window, and the face of the girl . . . The door groaned as he pushed it.

The hurricane lamp threw its light inside the one room. He smelled the damp of the room. It was close and small and he saw the sacking in the corner, as if it was used for a couch bed. Not a place for a pig, not for cattle. He had to work quickly because the oil was poor quality in the hurricane lamp and burned faster than good oil, but good oil was no longer available. He began to rip the wide panel strips from the wall, the best wood and seasoned. He used the jemmy, and then the lump hammer to hack away at the last holding nails. The noise was around him and the dust of the plaster lathe. He often thought of the girl. It need not have happened to the girl. She could have gone, with the other women. The postman, Branko, had tried to pull her away from the two wounded men, tried to save her, and she had fought the postman, had hurt him. The dust clogged at his nose. And when the wide panel strips were free, he reached up and belted with the lump hammer at the ceiling plaster that cascaded on him. The beams were good. He wanted two lengths of beam, each his own height, for the legs of the table he would present to Milan. Making room with the jemmy and the lump hammer for his bowsaw . . .

The blow caught him.

He was turning in the grey white of the dust storm.

The shrivelled figure, black, and the hurricane lamp guttering, and the stick raised as a club.

His eyes watering from the blow, his vision hazed.

He clung to the stick, the club, wrestled it away.

Claws in his face. Feeling the drag of the nails, razor lines of pain, on his face. Clutching at thin wrists, seeing the bony fingers reaching for his eyes.

The shrivelled figure, black, gone in the mist of grey white, gone into the darkness of the door.

He staggered to the door. He had his pistol out from the holster. There was only silence around the carpenter. He fired the pistol up the lane and down the lane and the crash of the shots burgeoned at his ears. He had no target. He did not know where to fire. He emptied the magazine of the pistol, and he ran. He left behind him his bowsaw and the jemmy and his lump hammer, and the failing light of the hurricane lamp. He ran down the lane, he splattered the potholes of rainwater, and he ran through the square. He was panting hard when he reached the bridge and he shouted out his name that the guards should not shoot him. He found them scared, cringing, hiding down behind the sandbags, and they had their own light which they shone in his face. He wiped his cheeks. He did not know what he could tell the young men who guarded the bridge across the stream. His own blood stained the palm of his hand.

Finished, or not begun.

Penn sat on a bench in the park, the darkness around him. Penn thought he had made the decision.

To go to the end, that was his father's code. Doing it properly, that was his mother's code. On a bench in Zagreb, with noisy basketball played open air under floodlights beyond the darkness, he thought of them. His father, looking at him direct, pipe clamped in his teeth, would have said that he had taken the money and that if he hadn't wanted shit in his face then he should not, first, have taken the money. His mother, averted head and pursed lips and wiping her hands, would have told him that he was under obligation, but that he should go carefully.

When he had swotted for the exams that had lifted him from the countryside, prompted by his history master who had helped with the forms, he had sent off an application for work as a clerk in government. He was going back into the rock of previous years, now, chiselling for guidance. Taken on at the Home

159

Office. He wondered how they would have reacted, at the Home Office, to his query as to whether he had finished or whether he had not begun. Working with paper, pushing paper, annotating paper, moving paper, discarding paper, for the Prison Service department of the Home Office. They would have said, the ones who had worked with him in the clerks' pool, who were still there working in the clerks' pool, that he had *finished*. Five o'clock, old chummy, time to be gone, always finished at five o'clock, old chummy. One late night and there was a panic meeting between the Home Office and Security Service and an assistant under secretary stamping empty corridors, searching for a file fetcher, finding Bill Penn, clerk. He had run half the night down to the basement and back up to the third floor with the files they had needed. He had brought the coffee. He had gone out for sandwiches. He had kept the files coming, and the coffee and the sandwiches, when their heads were on their bloody knees in tiredness, and a week later the job offer had come through, clerk grade in Library at Curzon Street, then at Gower Street. In Five's Library they would have said he had *finished*. Into F Branch, pushing paper on 'subversives'. Into A Branch, working with the 'watchers'. The guys in F Branch and the guys in A Branch, they would have said, too damned right, he had *finished*. The guys in F Branch and A Branch would have been quoting training courses, evaluating back-up, querying days in lieu for extra days worked.

But there was no training, there would be no back-up . . . It was Penn's decision.

He had the obligation, and he would go carefully.

It would be for her, Dorrie . . . Not for Mary Braddock in the Manor House, not for Basil and the creeps at Alpha Security, not for Arnold bloody Browne who had not lifted a finger when he'd needed help, not for his Jane and his Tom and the paying of the mortgage for the roof over their heads, but for the love of Dorrie . . . He had the photographs of her. The photographs were in the inside pocket of his blazer, dry, safe, close to him. He thought that what he wanted, wanted most in the world, was to share in the love of Dorrie. He saw the face that was loved, the face of mischief, sparkle, hatred, bloody-mindedness, courage, the face that was putrefied and drawn from the ground and wounded with cuts and blows and a pistol shot . . .

And all the rest was shit . . .

It was as if she called. It was as if he should follow. He knew that he wanted her love, certainty, more than anything he had wanted in his life. He craved the freedom that had been hers. As if he heard her loud laughter, daring him.

Not *finished*, because it was not begun.

Ham saw him come through the door. Then he was looking round, checking the tables, searching for a face.

'Hello, squire, funny seeing you in this shit heap . . .'

Most evenings Ham ate alone. Couldn't abide the crap they served up in the old police station. Most evenings he asked the guys if they'd come down the town and join him, and most evenings they had a reason not to, fuck them. He ate alone in the café on Križanićeva inside the walls of the old city. He pushed out the chair opposite him.

'. . . So what brings you down the sharp end, what brings you to sunny Karlovac?'

'You wanted a bit of tracing done. You wanted to know where your wife was, and your kiddie. I'll do that.'

Ham said quickly, 'Can't pay a fancy fee . . .'

'No fee, no charge.'

Ham said, suddenly doubtful, 'Not for fucking charity. What's the game, squire?'

'For a favour.'

'You tell me, what's the favour?'

'You said you'd walked into Sector North. I want a route. I want to know where to go, where not to go. That's my fee for the trace.'

Wide-eyed, Ham said, 'That's fucking dumb talk . . .'

'No charge for the trace, but you give me a route so as I can walk to Rosenovici.'

Ham said, 'You don't get me to go . . .'

'I want a route, to go on my own.'

9

There was the same message on each of the boxes, different languages. The boxes were stacked high to the ceiling cross struts. Baby Food (Nutritional) – Gift of the People of Germany. Pasta (Shapes various) – Gift of the People of Italy. Medicines (Antenatal/Postnatal) – Gift of the People of Holland. Rice – Gift of the People of the United States of America. Tents (with blankets) – Gift of the People of the United Kingdom. The biggest section of boxes was labelled as a mobile operating theatre – Gift of the People of Sweden – and there were cigarettes in boxes, and alcohol, and soya, and hospital drugs. Penn was walked down the corridor between the boxes that filled the shed. He read each label. He thought of the advertisements he saw in the papers back home, and those on the commercial radio stations. He thought of the kids standing in the High Street where he lived and rattling collection tins, and he thought of the women who knitted warm clothes for refugees, and he thought the business was dirty. He had not been brought to the shed for food, medicines, drugs, nor for cigarettes nor alcohol. The mercenary had brought him to the shed because that was where he could buy a gun.

Anything could be bought, that was what Penn had been told.

Anything he had the money to pay for he could buy in the shed.

Ham had brought him out from the old quarter of Karlovac, out through the modern city, and he had seen the scar marks of the shelling, and they had crossed over the Kupa river and headed into the industrial estate. It was a dead city. No smoke from the chimneys, no lorries carrying away finished products. The city had died because the city sat astride the front line.

There had been two 5-series BMWs parked outside the shed, and an Alfa. A giant man had come quickly through the door of the shed and his gaze had been hostile, intimidating, before he had seen Ham.

There was an office space at the far end of the corridor between the cardboard and wooden crates. Ham had said he should take a gun. Ham had said that walking into Sector North without a gun was about the same as going in bare-arsed. Ham had said that he should pack a gun before he packed his toothpaste. Three men were in the partitioned office at the end of the shed. They lolled back in easy chairs and there was a haze of cigar smoke, and one listened at a telephone and one was talking local language into a mobile, and each wore designer jeans and a loose-fitting designer leather jacket as if for uniform. They were all under thirty years of age. Penn stood distant in the doorway and each casually shook Ham's hand, but the enthusiasm was the mercenary's, and they seemed to Penn to regard Ham as dog shit on the pavement.

What sort of gun did he want? Penn shrugged, like they should tell him what was on offer, and there was a big peal of laughter from the heavy man who was not listening on the telephone. Good English spoken. He could have a T-54 tank (Soviet), he could have a 120mm howitzer (American), he could have an RPG-7 rocket launcher (Soviet), he could have a Stinger ground-to-air (American), if he could pay . . . The mocking laughter subsided . . . He could have a Heckler & Koch machine pistol, or an Uzi high-fire-rate sub-machine gun, if he could pay . . . The eyes were locked on him . . . Ham had said to him, where he was going, every male understood the workings of firearms, their culture, cradle-to-grave stuff. Penn felt like stale piss. He knew how to strip down and clean and reassemble a .410 shotgun because that was what he had used around the hedges and fields and woods of the farm where his father drove a tractor. Now he felt inadequate. Penn knew how to strip and clean and reassemble a Browning 9mm automatic pistol because that was what he had been shown on the two-day firearms course organized for newcomers into A Branch. It was fourteen years since he had downed a pigeon with the shotgun, and it was seven years since

163

the two-day firearms course. He asked if they had a Browning 9mm automatic pistol. The heavy man swivelled his chair. The telephone was down and the mobile was switched off. They seemed to strip him with their eyes. The heavy man dragged the keys from his pocket that were held to his waist belt by a thin chain, reached forward and unlocked the tall wall safe. He was spilling handguns onto the desk, pistols and revolvers, short-barrelled and long-barrelled, with or without silencer attachment, old and new. When it came, Penn recognized the Browning 9mm automatic pistol, no silencer. It was pushed towards him, like a toy. He lifted it from the table, held it. It felt strange in his hand, unfamiliar, and he tried to hide that. How many rounds of ammunition? He had fired four magazines on the two-day course. He said that he would like to take fifty rounds. Again the mocking.

Two hundred US dollars for the Browning 9mm automatic pistol, one hundred US dollars for the magazines and the ammunition.

And twenty-five US dollars each for four RG-42 fragmentation grenades that Ham said he should have.

And fifteen US dollars for the olive-green backpack that was pulled off the floor, from among the rubbish.

And ten US dollars for webbing and for a canteen and for a knife.

And five US dollars for the boots.

Penn peeled the American dollars off the wad in his wallet. The heavy man said that he liked to offer a discount, and the discount was five dollars. Penn didn't smile. Penn handed him the four hundred and twenty-five dollars. He stood his ground, waited on his receipt. He hitched one strap of the backpack over his blazer shoulder so that it hung loose against him. He stood in the doorway.

'Thank you, gentlemen. I hope you'll give me a good price when I bring them back.'

Penn was halfway down the corridor between the boxes and crates before their laughter subsided.

The nice girl, Penny, who showed some respect for him, brought back the backgrounder sheet she had typed for him. Henry Carter looked up, smiled at her the way that he thought young people liked to be smiled at. He thought she was a nice girl because he had worked with her father, a considerably long time ago, but he always made the point of asking after her father's health, just to remind her that he had pedigree.

'Still hard at it then, Mr Carter?'

He rested from his writing. 'Yes, it's rather an interesting one.'

'Very interesting, what I've just typed up for you. Will there be more for me to type up?'

'Tomorrow . . .' He grinned, then whispered, 'Dragon alert . . .'

He could see over her shoulder, the return from tea break of the supervisor. The nice girl, Penny, scuttled away from him. The file was taking shape now, and he placed her typed work where he thought it relevant, near to the start. Good background, notwithstanding the arguable advantages of hindsight, he thought always useful, and the thin biography. Always useful to improve the understanding of a file. Well, if a future reader of the file did not comprehend the situation on the ground, and the prime player's personality, then it would not be easy to appreciate the quite dreadful hazard into which this young fellow proposed to walk. He read back what he had written.

SECTOR NORTH
(Situation as of April/May 1993.)

Sources: Newspapers, Field Station (Zagreb), Field Station (Belgrade), United Nations Monitors (SIS personnel), FCO digest.

Sector North represents that area closest to Zagreb, administered by local paramilitary Serb forces. An armed camp. All aspects of civilian life are governed by Territorial Defence Force (TDF). No central government, power rests with local warlords. Local warlords exercise power of life and death over few remaining Croat civilians (elderly), and over their own people.

Male population has been mobilized into TDF. Patrols and roadblocks manned at night. Large areas of afforestation have been mined. High state of alert amongst all sections of population fed by local radio (Petrinja and Knin), constant reports of vigilance required against Croat spies and saboteurs. Croat SF (Special Forces) efforts at penetration for intelligence gathering have most generally ended in failure, even when utilizing personnel formerly familiar with topography. Use of high ground with visibility for defence positions and strongpoints.

In addition to TDF forces there is a major commitment by former JNA (Yugoslav National Army) on the ground. Under forest cover there are sufficient armoured vehicles to punch through to Zagreb, also substantive artillery and missile positions.

Location of JNA and TDF forces made next to impossible by restrictions on UNPROFOR movement inside Sector North. Both paranoid that UNPROFOR provides intelligence to Croats, hence severe curtailment on movement. That movement restricted to a few main roads; all access to frontline area is denied. Security Council tasking cannot be fulfilled by UNPROFOR units.

UNPROFOR HQ logistics officer (Canadian): 'Our operations in Sector North have virtually ceased to have any meaning. No respect now exists for the blue flag. It is impossible to function.' TDF personnel frequently drunk, always hostile.

No dissent in Sector North to authority of warlords. To complain is to be beaten, killed, expelled. Local population characterized by extreme brutality and hardness, a historical legacy. Were buffer population implanted by Hapsburg empire to block Ottoman expansion – succeeded.

Topography is rolling hills, heavily wooded, small villages surrounded by farms, few roads. Offers potential for incursion by trained SF, but difficulties as listed above mitigate severely against non-skilled personnel.

Summary: A mantrap for the uninitiated. Area of extreme danger.

He had the words of the file, and the photographs, and in the morning he would have the large-scale map. The light was slackening outside. He understood. He would not have claimed any particular credit for his understanding, but he felt the events were within his experience. Been there, done it, seen it, hadn't he? No, not to this squalid little corner, not to this exact place, but he had been to other armed and fortified front lines, and he had pushed young men, with quite a firm shove, into such mantraps of suspicion and hostility. It was because he understood that the memories seeped back. So many years before . . . He did not think these young men, dull and ordinary and boring, went because they were brave. He thought they went because of their fear of personal failure . . . Old men such as Henry Carter, senior men, experienced men, men who had never done it themselves, went to these front lines that were armed and fortified and gave a young chap a pretty firm shove, then went back to a hotel or a safe house villa to hang around, stooge around, wait to see if they made it out of Iraq or East Germany or Czechoslovakia or Iran . . . An awfully long time ago. But they were all sharp in his mind, all the young men. All of them dragged to the cliff edge. Extraordinary, but they all seemed to go willingly.

He stood, stretched. He took the fax message that he had written earlier to the supervisor. He asked for it to be sent, and he believed that his smile was gracious.

The memories came close. Too often the memories that would be carried to the grave hustled into the mind of the old desk warrior. Standing on the safe side of the fence with the minefields and the tripwires and the self-firing guns, and hearing the explosions and the shrill German shouts, seeing Johnny Donoghue leave the young woman who was living and her father who was dead, watching Johnny climb the bucking bloody wire. The memories, standing and seeing and watching, were not erased. Sharpest of the memories, neatly condensed for an addendum to his file, was the late supper of cold cuts of meat and spiced cheese and gassy beer, served by an impatient landlord in the Helmstedt hotel. Johnny, lovely young man, bottling his emotion in silence. Such dignity . . . and he had been on the safe side and did not know how to communicate with Johnny, and the two of them toying with the food . . . he felt so humble. In the morning they had caught the flight from Hanover back to Heathrow, parted with a limp handshake. Before the next Christmas he had sent a card to Johnny, but it was not replied to. He had never again seen Johnny, lovely young man. He had used him, and the memories, damn them, did not mist.

Back at his desk, he thought of the place, Sector North, as a mantrap.

They were in a wood. It was the middle of the day and the sun dappled down through the early leaves on the birches. Ham had quit the bullshit. Penn asked questions about his Karen and his

167

Dawn. There was a softness in Ham's voice and he'd lost the obscenities and the swagger. It was later that Ham had gotten round to talking about the rudiments, what could be told in a couple of hours, of survival movement behind enemy lines.

There was a cordon around the village, as tight a line as the men from Salika could draw. Eighteen of them made the line, covering with their guns the open fields around the village. It was like a rabbit shoot. Eighteen men to watch the fields between Rosenovici and the stream and the road and the woods on the higher ground.

They had whistles, and each man in the cordon line, when he was in the position given him, blasted his arrival. Some had the new AK47 assault rifles and some had the hunting rifles with the long accuracy barrels that had been handed down from their fathers, and some had shotguns. Branko, the postman, waited on the road that led to Rosenovici from the bridge for all the whistle blasts. With him were his constant companions: the gravedigger, Stevo, and the carpenter, Milo. They were the dogs that would go in and flush the rabbit, and the postman chuckled, some goddamn rabbit, some goddamn claws on that rabbit, and he looked slyly across at the carpenter and the raw lines on the carpenter's cheeks. It was a bright morning, good for sport.

He heard Milan's shout. Milan was on the high ground above the village.

They went forward, three of them, with the dog bounding ahead. He could see Milan, past the tower of the church that was broken, and Branko waved his handkerchief to show that he had heard, that they were moving. Milan should have been with them. It had been the postman's idea to ask Milan to bring the dog. He'd thought the idea clever, because he had reckoned that if Milan brought the dog then Milan would be with them among the ruins of Rosenovici. Something had to shake the man out of his morose misery. And the dog would know where to look, the postman reckoned.

Milan had said that they could take the dog, that he would control the cordon line.

The dog led them into each building. They watched each

house, put the dog in, then followed the dog, always the dog went first. They searched each building. It was necessary to be careful because the fire and the dynamite had weakened the floor boards and brought down the rafter beams. He had known those who had lived in each house because he had come there each day, way back, with the letters from the kids who were away at the colleges in Belgrade and Zagreb, and the letters with the stamps of Australia and America. The postman felt nothing bad, because they had been, all of them, goddamn Ustaše. They were the people who would have come into Salika at night, with knives, and with fire, no doubting. They would have done what their grandparents, the original goddamn Ustaše, had done, killed and burned. He felt nothing bad, and did not understand why Milan, the best, felt something bad.

They had cleared the homes leading into the square.

They cleared the church and the store and the home that had been used as the HQ. They put the dog into the cellar of Franjo and Ivana's farmhouse, and while the dog was down in the cellar he had stood on the stone flags of the kitchen. Most times that he came to the farmhouse, Branko had been given a slash of brandy in the kitchen while they opened the letters from Franjo's nephew who was in Australia or Ivana's aunt who was on the West Coast in America. No concern to him, the brandy, because Franjo and Ivana were the same as the others, goddamn Ustaše. If it was no concern to him then he did not understand why it concerned Milan.

They cleared the school.

They shouted their progress across the village, across the fields, up to the tree line on the hill where Milan controlled the cordon.

Branko watched the dog. It would have been the first time that the dog had been taken back to Rosenovici since its family had gone, left it, let it run beside the wheels until it could run no more. The first time that the dog had been back since Milan had gone to the edge of the village and called the dog and brought it home to his son. And the goddamn Ustaše dog was remembering. The dog whined at a heap of collapsed rubble. The dog whimpered beside the wall section with the green flowers on a yellow base of interior wallpaper. The dog curved its tail over its privates, sniffed, crawled on its belly over the wall section with the wallpaper. The postman was not concerned that the old American had come with the UNCIVPOL and dug for the bodies . . . They could dig where they goddamn wanted, they could cart the bodies, stinking, back to Zagreb, and then they could do goddamn nothing . . . And he did not understand why Milan had such morose misery. What could they goddamn do, nothing? He shouted for the dog and it came back to his side. They were going up the lane.

A small shed. A stone shed with a roof of rusted corrugated iron. Precious dynamite would have been wasted on the shed, fire would have had little to burn. In the shed the dog found a plastic bag. The bag was white, and inside the bag were dried crumbs of bread. The shed was forty paces short of what had been the home of the Dubelj pair, goddamn Ustaše. Between the shed and the home of the Dubelj couple was a small paddock, thick with weeds. A cow had been kept in the paddock and a goat and two pigs. Stevo had the cow, and Milo had the pigs. The postman had taken the goat, but had killed and eaten it. He had felt strong until they reached the house of Katica Dubelj.

The door hung open, held only by the lower hinge. It was dark inside. The dog held back. The postman kicked the dog through the door. The carpenter was behind him and there were the raw scratch scars on the cheeks of his face, he was not hurrying to push past him. He went inside, into the goddamn smell and the darkness. He held tight to his gun. He had to stand, very still, and wait for his eyes to work for him. The dog was in the corner. The image cleared. The dog scratched in a heap of rags, maybe sacks, in the corner. He saw the hurricane lamp that had died and the bowsaw and the jemmy and the lump hammer dropped on the old linoleum. There was another bag, white, and he lifted the bag and crumbs of bread crust fell from it. The dog had come from the corner and sniffed at a chewed apple core.

The dog held a scent down the lane from the house and through the entrance to the field where the bulldozer had crushed the wooden gate.

The dog followed a scent that skirted the low wall of grey-black mud around the pit, went over the tyre marks of the jeeps. There had been heavy rain in the night and Branko slipped and fell in the field as he tried to keep pace with the dog. He could see Milan above him, close to the tree line. The dog went past the grave.

The dog reached the small ditch that came down the field and, at the ditch, the dog lost the scent.

They tried the dog up the ditch, right side and left side, but the dog had lost it.

The postman trudged up the field, sliding, cursing, until he reached Milan. He showed Milan the plastic bags in which they had found the crumbs, and the chewed apple core. He told Milan that *someone* had been there, recently, had eaten there, slept there, the scar scratches on the carpenter's face proved it. He asked Milan to come down into Rosenovici so that he could see for himself where they had found the plastic bags and the apple core. Milan refused him.

Milan was the postman's leader, he would never criticize him. He watched Milan walk away. He had taught Milan, boy and man, everything he knew of the game of basketball and he had been superb. Milan walked away along the edge of the tree line, took the long route so that he would not have to cross the village. He could remember when Milan, in attack, brilliant in the dribble, fantastic jumping for the net, had led Glina Municipality to victory against Karlovac Municipality, taken the cup, a player without doubts. Milan was going the long way round the village towards the bridge.

The postman did not understand the goddamn problem.

Ham had slung a white T-shirt, filthy as if it had been used to clean the plugs of a car engine, across a low bush of thorn. They sat a dozen paces back from where the T-shirt was draped and Ham talked Penn through the maintenance and cleaning of the Browning 9mm automatic pistol, and then made Penn do it, and then tied a handkerchief round the front of Penn's face and made him do it again, and he made Penn load a magazine with the blindfold still in place. It was seven years since the two-day firearms course and it was more forgotten than he had realized.

Later Ham would show him what he had also damn near forgotten: how to crouch, lock his legs, extend his arms, find the target, aim and hold it, how to fire the pistol. Ham talked low and keen, as if firing the pistol was of importance.

In the grip on the back seat of the Cherokee jeep were seven video tapes, nine hours of audio recording, thirty-seven pages of handwritten notes.

Marty drove along the wide highway, back to Zagreb.

They were good 'snapshots', the video and the audio and the notes from the stories of the latest refugees from the village outside the Bosnian town of Prijedor. He drove steadily, did not exceed the speed limit, although the road ahead was empty. EWT 19, traumatized but coherent, had said that he had seen seven pairs of fathers forced to have oral sex with their sons, before the fathers and sons were shot – *evidence*. EWT 12, thirteen years old but with a visage going on sixty, had said that he had seen prisoners ordered to castrate fellow prisoners with their teeth – *evidence*. And plenty more . . . eyewitnesses telling his microphone of rape and beating and killing, telling it like it was – *evidence*. The evidence would go from his notes onto disk. The disks and the video tapes and the audio would go on the courier flight back to the second-floor office in Geneva. But it was just damned ridiculous . . . It had hurt him that he had not seen the German lady when he had pulled out from the Transit Centre. He had wanted to see her, wanted to be with her, had checked her office, actually gone up the staircase and through each of the third- and the second-floor rooms, and the dispensary, and the kindergarten and the kitchens, been told she wasn't there, anywhere, and kept looking for her. It had been a long time since he had last gone looking for a woman, and wanted to be with that woman . . . It was just damned ridiculous that his work, work of this importance, should be dumped off in a damned converted container.

He was coming into Zagreb, picking up the traffic.

Had he looked at himself, which he did not, Marty Jones might not have liked what he saw. His mind did not acknowledge the ravages of stress. The videos that he filmed were of rape, the audios he recorded were of torture, the notes that he wrote were of foul cruelty. The woman he reported to in Geneva, three weeks back when she was down in Zagreb, had said to him, 'Don't you get sick of it, Marty? Why don't they *just* kill each other? What does it do to you, Marty? Why do they have to cut out eyes, cut off noses, cut off heads – why can't they just kill each other. How do you stay sane, Marty?' He had not known how to answer her.

But he never looked in the mirror. He had a dream, and the dream was a prepared case . . . It was just damned ridiculous that he had to make the dream in a converted freight container.

He drove into Ilica barracks. The parking lot available to him was up by the A block, where the big shots were. There were workmen carrying prefabricated partitioning and timbers in through the main doors. The big shots were extending their office space, reaching into the roof area. The big shots had space, and he had the damned converted freight container.

For the rest of the day he would get his notes onto disk, and get the package off, and then he might just raise some damned noise.

He unlocked the door of his container, pulled it open, and the wall of heat hit him.

The crows above them had scattered with the first shot. The quiet came again to the woodland of birches. The magazine was exhausted. Four hits on the T-shirt, two hits for every three misses. Ham didn't criticize. Back on the training course the instructor had given him hell with three hits for every five misses. Penn guessed that Ham didn't criticize because it was too late to rubbish him. Quite relaxed he had been on the training course, but time was not running then . . . When he had cleaned the pistol, he sat with Ham and they went over the maps. They had a tourist map that Ham had bought in Karlovac, and they had the sketch map that Ham had drawn. The sketch map would take him to within six miles of Rosenovici. There were minefields marked on Ham's hand-drawn map, and strongpoints and villages where there would be patrols and roadblocks. And all the time Ham seemed to watch him, in a manner open but sly. Ham watched him as if he were meat hanging from the hook in a butcher's window, evaluated his quality. Penn thought Ham was making a reckoning on whether he would get himself back to go for the hunting of Karen and Dawn, and he thought also that Ham judged him capable of bringing back intelligence bullshit that the mercenary would present to his officers . . . He was a rotten little man but he had taken the one chance and perhaps would be remembered. Dorrie was a *horrid* young woman but she had taken the one chance and was loved. Jović was a prickly bastard who learned to paint with his left hand, and might succeed . . . It was about winning his own respect, about walking his own path, taking the one chance . . . And the afternoon was slipping.

'Of course we'll have another . . . Well, how's the self-inflicted wound? . . . It'll have to be a cheaper one.'

Georgie Simpson had his arm raised for the attention of the wine waiter. The food wasn't good. The monkfish didn't taste as if it had been swimming too recently. Best to kill another bottle. Arnold Browne didn't believe he cared too much about the freshness of the fish; he wiped his mouth with the napkin.

'Not a lot moving on that front.'

Which was economical with the truth. The truth, and it rankled, was that he had been summoned, the last evening, to the snug at the bottom of the neighbour's garden at about the time he was looking to his bed and his book. Given a token whisky, not generous, and berated. Hammered. Penn did not respond to telephone messages. Penn had been away nearly a week and not a squeak from him. Penn was on the gravy train. Penn was a bloody waste of money . . . No shortage of money, Arnold wouldn't have thought it was small change to Charles bloody Braddock . . . Penn was the wrong man.

'What sort of chap?'

'I beg your pardon . . .'

'The private detective – you told me last week you'd arranged for a private detective to travel.'

'I did, yes . . . He's a good fellow. Not bright, but dogged . . .' Arnold had hold of his glass and his fingers shook and what was left of the wine spilled onto the crumbs on the cloth.

'You all right, Arnold?'

'Not bright enough for Five, not bright enough to have been taken into General Intelligence Group, not bright enough to have a future. But *dogged*.'

Georgie had the wine waiter, muttered to him. Within his price stricture, anything. 'In my slow mind there is the grind of cogs meshing. You recommended a Five reject?'

'He's a very good investigator.'

'Go to the end?'

'Do you have something I could smoke, Georgie, a cigarette or a cigarella? Bless you . . . Yes, he'd go as far as was possible, maybe further.'

Georgie lit the cigarette for him. Arnold coughed hard.

Georgie said, quietly, 'Going to the end is where the evidence is.'

'If there's evidence to be had I'd back him to get it.'

The bottle was on the table, uncorked. Arnold poured for himself, and his hand still shook.

'Are my friends at Five playing funny little games, Arnold?'

'Depends on your perspective, whether they're funny . . .' And he wanted to talk, talk to anyone, talk even to Georgie Simpson, and it was a hanging offence in Gower Street to talk to personnel from Babylon on Thames. 'Evidence is leverage, right? Leverage is pressure, right?'

'You're a bit ahead of me.'

'I usually am, Georgie.'

'So stop pissing on me.'

'Words of one syllable . . . What I'm told is that we require the means for pressure. We wish to pressure those moronic hooligans in Belgrade. We wish to pressure the Serbs . . . Too fast for you, Georgie? . . . Evidence is pressure in the world of public relations, the spin merchants, the image men. The Serbs, bloodthirsty mob, want to appear virgin clean, but good evidence tends to stain the snow. It's all part of the pressure game to get those morons to the conference table.'

'You didn't tell me that, last week.'

'Blame the monkfish.'

'Congratulations. You have an uptight reject . . . ?'

'Yes.'

'Told about a half of the truth . . . ?'

'Could be a quarter.'

'Straightforward sort of chap, not too much intelligence . . . ?'

'Fatal to be intelligent.'

'Who will predictably go to the end of the road for evidence . . . ?'

'Something like that.'

'Arnold, do you have the faintest idea of what the end of the road might be like . . . ?'

'Please, don't patronize me.'

'Was this your idea . . . ?'

'We all bend the knee when we have to; of course it was not.'

'Does it end up with handcuffs and things . . . ?'

'God, no. He'll just make a report.'

'Sorry if I'm slow, haven't you hazarded him . . . ?'

'George, get the bill, there's a dear thing. Your Gavin, he went to university in London, didn't he? My Caroline, she went to Hull, Social Sciences. My man, my reject, he wanted rather badly to go to college, it didn't work out, doesn't matter why. You know what I can't abide about Caroline's friends, probably the same with your Gavin? They're so cynical . . . so scheming . . . they seem to believe enthusiasm is a vice. It's as if my reject was spared that cynicism. One of those people that are ambitious but don't know how to get themselves promoted, think promotion derives from merit . . . God, my Caroline could tell him. My Caroline would walk over our throats if the main chance was in view . . . There's something rather attractive about a man who hasn't cynicism in his backpack, but it tends to leave him so very naked . . . Sorry, been talking too much, haven't I? Should be getting back to the shop.'

He pushed himself up from the table.

Georgie looked up, staring. He thought Georgie, happy and ponderous and cheerful Georgie, was frightened. 'Haven't you hazarded him . . . ?'

'Perhaps . . .'

★   ★   ★

He sat on the bed beside her. The sheet of paper was supported by a book. Ulrike was in the doorway behind him and she prompted the translation. The woman, Alija, held the book and the paper high in front of her eyes and drew the road and the square and the lanes of the village, and she would make a mark on the map as it formed, and Ulrike would say that the mark was the school or the church or the store or the farmhouse with the cellar, and each time Penn took from her hands the sheet of paper and the book and wrote the designation word himself. The noise of the sleeping room in the Transit Centre was around them, but shut from his mind. She drew the line for the river, and she marked with a crude circle the second village that was across the stream. Ulrike told her of his thanks. They walked out of the sleeping room and down the stone stairs. Evening was rushing forward. They were at the main doors of the Transit Centre and across in the square Ham had seen him and started up the engine of the car, a small Yugo. He could sense that Ulrike was unusually serious. He thought she understood why he had come back to the Transit Centre to speak with Alija. Would he come to dinner? The smile, sorry but no can do, the shrug. Was he going back to Zagreb? The smile, the shaken head, again the shrug. She knew why he had asked for the map to be drawn. What he thought so fine about her was that there was no interrogation, no questioning, no requirement for lies. She looked into his face. He saw her tiredness and the clean skin and the strength of her chin and the power of her eyes. No questions . . . Her hand was for a moment on the sleeve of his blazer. He understood what it would be like for her, working from dawn and through the day and past dusk in the Transit Centre, alongside the misery. He thought she recognized that he made a small gesture against a wrong. He felt a marginal pride, and it was a long time since he had stood tall with himself. Her fingers squeezed, for a moment, at his arm as if to transmit comfort . . . She was gone, and the doors closed behind her. He walked in the dusk to Ham's car.

Almost dark outside, he reckoned. Hard to be certain because the windows were on the far side of the Library area, and so thick and

177

tinted. The girls were hurrying for their coats and there was a babble of talk from them, and Penny smiled at him as she loaded her bag, and the one who sat nearest his table scowled at him and she'd have a plenty big enough problem scrubbing chocolate off her blouse.

The supervisor challenged him. 'Working late, Mr Carter?'

He smiled, sweetly. 'Never was one for watching a clock.'

'You're not supposed to be here with the night shift.'

'Only once in a while. I doubt I'll attack them . . .'

What was damnable was that he had finished his sandwiches and emptied his thermos dry.

'It shouldn't be a habit, Mr Carter . . . Oh, this came for you.'

The supervisor handed him a fax message.

'Thank you.'

It was always the same when the night shift came on. There was hardly a civil word between the day shift and the night shift, capitalism and communism, chalk and cheese, and the whitter of the night shift girls was around him, complaining about the state of the desks left for them, the state of the rubbish bins, the state of the carpets. He started to read the fax. Sometimes the bickering criticism amused him. That evening, Henry Carter found it distinctly annoying, and a hindrance to his concentration.

TO:	Carter, Library, Vauxhall Cross.
FROM:	Ministry of Defence (Personnel).
SUBJECT:	HAMILTON, SIDNEY ERNEST.
TX:	17.21, 14.3.95.
STATUS:	Biography/Assessment Classified.
BORN:	Hackney, east London, 12/8/1962.
MOTHER:	Harriet Maude Hamilton. Father: No name listed.
EDUCATION:	William Wilberforce Junior, Hackney Comprehensive – no qualifications claimed.
MARITAL STATUS:	Married Karen (née Wilkins), from Guildford, Surrey, in July 1985. 1 daughter, Dawn Elizabeth, born in January 1987. Separated December 1989. Initial allegation of Battery brought by Karen Hamilton against husband, but withdrawn.
EMPLOYMENT:	(Prior to military enlistment) Van driving/ general delivery work.

MILITARY SERVICE:	Joined Parachute Regiment, March 1982. Served with 3rd Bn. Northern Ireland tours: 1983, 1986, 1989. Marksman/First Class. Promoted Lance-Corporal 1985, demoted 1986. Dismissed 8 April 1990. (Disciplinary problems led to demotion, wrecking of bar in Cullyhanna, South Armagh, followed by verbal abuse of a commissioned officer. Dismissed from Regiment after the beating of an Irish sales representative in Aldershot.)
EMPLOYMENT:	(Post military dismissal) 4 months with Personal Security Ltd (Bodyguards), Hornchurch, Essex, in close protection. Dismissed.
CURRENT:	Self-enlisted with HVO (Republic of Croatia Defence Force). Originally with 'International Brigade'. (NB: Following death of HOWARD, BRIAN JAMES, fellow mercenary, shot dead at OSIJEK, Republic of Croatia, in March 1992, he is wanted for questioning by Strathclyde Police. Local inquest recorded Open Verdict.)
ASSESSMENT:	Unstable, unreliable. Fortunate to have served so long with Parachute Regiment.

Yes, he was right, usually was, the fear of failure drove those young men across those hideous front lines. He knew, because he had stood on the safe side and waited for them to come back. So, it was the map that mattered, the map supplied by this 'unstable, unreliable' creature . . .

He breathed hard.

'Don't fuck about on me, squire,' Ham whispered. 'Get on with it.'

He steadied himself, eased his weight forward on the side of the inflatable. The noise of the great Kupa river was an engine idling. Far away, to his right, down river, a single small light shone. The deep, dark water of the river was behind him, but

179

close was the fast sluicing sound as the current broke around the paddle manoeuvred by Ham to hold the craft steady.

Penn reached back. His fingers felt down Ham's arm to his hand. The palm of his hand wrapped over Ham's fingers on the paddle.

'And when I'm back, then I'll go find them, find them and tell them that you love them.'

'Just come back with your balls still under your belly.'

'The bloody map, Ham, it's a good map?'

'The only bloody map you'll ever get. On your way, squire.'

His boots were hung by the laces round his neck, his socks were knotted at his throat. He hesitated. If the map was no good . . . If the bastard had drawn the map wrong . . . If he could not follow the map . . . If the map . . . The fist caught him on the shoulder. The fist pushed him off the side of the inflatable. He splashed in the water. His bared toes sunk in the slime mud and the fallen weed. Panic time. He reached back for the side of the inflatable to steady himself, but the paddle was into his ribs. The drive of the paddle propelled Penn towards the bank that was the dark mass ahead of him. The backpack caught his head and landed on the bank above him. He struggled forward, stumbling through the mud. He groped for the bank, and the tree branches were in his face, and he grasped at them and they broke, and then he had a better hold. He dragged himself through the reeds and up the bank. His hands caught at the shoulder straps of the backpack. He sagged.

He could see the inflatable moving out towards the main flow of the river, a shadow shape and the quick flash of the paddles breaking water. He watched the inflatable all the time that he could see it, and when he could no longer see it, he searched for it.

Penn wiped his feet with the sleeve of the tunic. He drew on the thick wool socks. He laced the boots. He threaded his arms through the straps of the backpack.

He was in Dorrie's place. The silence and the black darkness were ahead of him. The silence was good. He was at ease in silence. He could be silent with himself, and Jane would have thought him sulking, had been able to absorb silence from the childhood days when his mother had taken him to the church in the village where she worked the swab cloth on the flagstones and tidied after the ladies had taken down the flower arrangements. Silence was safety and it nestled around him. He had come to Dorrie's war.

Penn pushed himself up, started forward.

10

It was as Ham had told him . . .

Penn had moved on his stomach up from the river bank, trying to insert himself between the reeds where they were most thick. To spread his weight, was what Ham had told him, and not to walk where it was easiest, where boot marks could be most clearly seen. He had moved up the bank and there had been the open space that he assumed was a path, and he had rolled across the space, which was difficult with the backpack, and the pistol on his waist had bruised into his stomach. Past the open space, the path, he had found, as Ham had told him he would, a single low strand of barbed wire. He had found it because the barbs on the wire had suddenly trapped him, become embedded in the material of his camouflage tunic. Ham had told him that he should not shake the wire because it would carry empty tin cans, and he should not go beyond the wire because it marked the perimeter of an area where mines were buried. He had a sort of reassurance when the barbs of the wire caught at him, proof that Ham knew. He had picked the barbs off with small and careful movements, then crawled in the darkness along the length of the wire, threading the wire through the circle he had made with his thumb and forefinger until his hand was a mess of blood from the barbs. He led himself, on his stomach, along the length of wire until his hand felt the post and then the twine binding the wire to the post. From the post the wire twisted in direction and headed back and away from the river behind him.

It was as Ham had told him . . . another path, going away from the river, and he had searched for a small stick, as he had been told to do, and he had held the stick loose in front of him as he had walked at the side of the path. Ham had said that he should be at the side of the path because the mud that would betray his boot weight would be in the centre of the path. He had held the stick loose in front of his knees because Ham had said, but didn't know, that there might be a tripwire slung across the path, at knee height, and a tripwire might rattle empty cans, or it might detonate a grenade.

It was as Ham had told him . . . Penn stopped when he reckoned he had gone a full hundred yards from the river bank. When he had stopped, he groped with his fingers and found the barbed wire that ran two strides from the path, and he followed the barbed wire deep into the birch wood.

He had sat down on the old leaf mould, and waited.

They were desperate hours to wait, especially when the rain had started. The rain dripped from his head to his chest and his shoulders. He tried to ration how often he looked down at the luminous hands of his watch. Should have rested, should have catnapped, as Ham had told him, but he could not have slept and could not have dozed. He reckoned he heard each dribble and splatter of the rain coming down from the tall birches, and each minuscule shifting of his weight where he sat seemed a confined explosion of sound. He waited for the dawn.

The dawn was late because of the low cloud. The dawn coming late meant that he would have to push faster when he moved off.

When he could see where the weight of his boots would fall, then it was the time for him to move forward. There was no going back. There was no inflatable waiting at his bank of the Kupa river. There was no alternative to moving forward. There was nothing in his mind of sentimental crap, staying alive was going forward. As Ham had told him . . . the most dangerous part of the journey for him was the first five miles, and the worst of the most dangerous ground was what he would cover in the first mile. He tried to razor his concentration. The first mile was where the minefields were most closely settled, where the tripwires were, where the military ruled. The first five miles were where the patrols would be most frequent. It was the *fucking* contradiction, was what Ham had said, that he must move most carefully in the first miles, and move fastest.

183

When he could see the path, Penn hoisted the backpack onto his shoulders and went forward.

Not running, not jogging, but going with a brisk pace. When he had gone half a mile, twelve minutes going on thirteen, he realized the futility of the map drawn by Ham. He had no detail. The farmhouse was not marked on the map.

The farmhouse was two-storey, brick-built from the ground up and then heavy-set planking for the upper floor. There was a wide balcony area at the front on the upper floor. He could see the man clearly. The man on the balcony did not bother to look out, to wonder if he were watched. The man opened the front of his trousers and urinated through the bars of the balcony and down onto the waste ground near to the front door of the farmhouse. And then Penn saw the woman, nightdress under her coat and above her black rubber boots, and she had the washing basket on the ground beside her and was starting to peg out the clothes – a bloody early start for the old house chores – and she bawled. Penn heard her voice, full of rich complaint, and was near enough then to see the man scratch, and ignore her, and yawn and stretch and belch, and still ignore the beat of her complaint, and turn to go back inside.

Penn moved on. Each time that he stopped he tried to be certain that he was against the line of a thicker birch trunk. As Ham had told him . . . never to be in Silhouette, never to be the unnatural Shape, and Sound and Smell and Shine could bloody wait, it was Silhouette and Shape that mattered. At the back of the farmhouse were outbuildings and barns, a mess of slumped roofs and corrugated iron and abandoned harvest equipment and the corrals for cattle and pigs and sheep. Parked up amongst them were three military lorries and a jeep. He could no longer see the front of the farmhouse but the woman's yelling carried to him, and there were new cries of encouragement and jeers from young troops. So young. Half asleep and paddling around in the mud, the troops, but they had their rifles slung on their half-dressed bodies. Hesitation, to move or not to move, but the light was growing all the time . . . None of the training on the Five surveillance courses seemed relevant. He had only his instincts to protect him, and the guidance that Ham had given him, and the instinct and the guidance seemed damn all of nothing. Going so carefully, tree to tree, along the track, and knowing that if the movement were seen . . . holy shit . . . going carefully. One of the troops, a fresh-faced young boy, a straggle of beard on his chin, walked purposefully from the barns and up the field towards the track. Carried his rifle and a small entrenching spade, and three dogs gambolled and chased around him. Penn had to move, because the line that the trooper had taken would cross the track ahead of where he now stood. He had to risk the movement. Going forward fast, too fast, going from tree to tree, spurt rushes. Just a boy coming up the hill behind the outbuildings, probably a shy boy, probably looking for a place where a shy boy could dig his small pit and defecate and not be watched. There was a terrier dog and a cross-collie dog and there was a big, slow, heavy-coated dog. His last surge, and the terrier had its hackles up and the cross-collie barked, and the heavy-coated dog didn't seem to know what the hell was happening. The boy was twenty paces from him. Slow hands, trembling, feeling into the flap of the backpack, twisting his arm round, finding the paper holding the sandwiches that Ham had given him. Ham had said there was cheese and beef and pickle in the sandwiches. The terrier growling as the boy dug. Slow hands, clumsy, unpeeling the newspaper from the sandwiches. The cross-collie barking as the boy lowered his trousers and the rifle was beside him. Penn put the sandwiches gently to the ground, on the wet dead leaves. The heavy-coated dog wagging its tail in vigour. Penn understood dogs because that was his childhood. Dogs had poor eyesight but had the sense of smell and the sense of hearing. They came close. It was his luck that the boy had his crouched back to him. They were close, and he looked into the sharp teeth lines of the terrier and the barking fangs of the cross-collie and the happy friendship of the heavy-coated dog. With his boot he edged the sandwiches closer to them. He went on his toes. He went in silence and behind him was the snarling for possession of his sandwiches. Penn went with his chest heaving and his legs leaden and his heart pounding. He went, and all the time that he moved he waited for the shout

185

and the metal scrape of the rifle being armed, but he heard only the dogs disputing for his sandwiches.

When he had gone past the farmhouse where the troops who guarded the front line were billeted, he looked back. The boy was walking down towards the farmhouse and with his bowels cleared the boy whistled. He wondered whether he could have knifed the boy. Just a shy boy, just a pack of farm dogs, and Penn understood what Ham had told him . . . a *fucking* dumb place to be.

He made ground, went hard, had to cover good distance before the daylight settled.

It was a response to the rejection.

The rejection was of him, not his wife, which made it wound the more. For his wife there was normality in Salika village. She was the nurse. She could still move amongst the people of the village, visit the elderly, examine the children, weigh the babies, while her husband stayed at home with his books and his loneliness. Each of the days that she had gone out, since his challenge at the school and his beating, the Headmaster had asked her what was said of him, how he was spoken of . . . She had thought she, too, would be rejected, and she was not, his wife could go into the homes of the village and talk, gossip, advise and drink coffee . . . and she answered him straight, always had spoken to him in frankness since the youth of their marriage. Simply nothing was said of him. It was as if, she had said the night before and that morning as she hurried his breakfast, he did not exist in the life of the village. His wife had gone to visit the two sisters who suffered from rheumatoid arthritis, to offer them comfort instead of drugs that were no longer available. He was alone in his house. He was with his loneliness and the books that he could read when he held them as far as his arm would stretch in front of his face and when he sat close to the light of the window.

The Headmaster believed there were two women and one man who had cared about him, and the two women and the one man had now rejected him.

Evica Stanković had taken over the running of the school and used his office as her own.

The Priest had missed another evening when he might have called by.

To counter the agony of his rejection the Headmaster determined, that morning when there was still insufficient light for him to sit in his window and read, that he should pray to the good God, if the good God was there. He did not believe that the good God was known to his former friend, the Priest who rejected him. Their bond had been intellectual, not religious. He resolved that he would struggle in his own way, to find the necessary words of prayer. He was a communist, of course, and he would not have been elevated to the Headmaster's position if he had not been a member of the Party; he did not know the way of prayer. His mother and his father, dead so long, knew of prayer and he would try to summon the memory of them. He would go in darkness to that place of evil. He would pray alone where evil had been done.

He would pray in that place of evil for guidance as to how he should utilize the secret he held.

If they had not been sitting on the track, if they had not been squabbling over cigarettes, if they had not been scuffling for the bottle, Penn would have walked into the patrol, into the arms of the five militia men. But they were sitting on the track and one yelled as he snatched the cigarettes and one shouted as he grabbed the bottle. First statue still, rock still, stone still, then retreating back along the track, cat careful, cat cautious. He edged back up the track from them, testing each footfall, looking behind him to be certain there was no dried wood that he might step on. He slunk away from the track and into the depth of the trees, and he lowered his weight down slowly and then he knelt and then he lay on his stomach and there was a thick bush of holly between himself and the track. He heard their laughter and their cursing. They were moving again, coming to that part of the track closest to where he lay. Not daring to move . . . He could have been pitching up for work at Alpha Security, first in and climbing the stairs to the office above the launderette, he could have been hearing the wail as the shutters went up on the shops beside the launderette. He could have been going to work with the smell of Jane on him, and the taste of Tom's food from the kiss on the cheek. He could have been going in to collect the Legal Process to serve, or going in from the night-time watch on a husband's cheating, or going in to meet a builder whose competition knew the contracts he was bidding for . . . Not daring to move, and seeing the young faces of the militia men. Ham hadn't told him what to do if he were bounced. Ham hadn't been through the *capture* bit. Each one of them had a knife at his belt. They went by him close enough for him to see that.

They went off down the track.

He had almost walked into them. He felt a true excitement. The excitement was an exhilaration. Truth was that he had never before known such excitement. The blood pumped in him. They wouldn't have known what he meant, about the excitement, at Alpha Security, how it coursed in him and lifted him. The excitement was danger. They wouldn't have known what he meant in A Branch. The excitement was his own. He would move for another hour, and then rest up till the dusk.

'Nothing I can do for you, Mr Jones. It's the pressure of space . . .' The Danish woman in Administration (Property) deflected him.

'We all have our little crosses, Mr Jones. Better we learn to accept them and live with them . . .' The Libyan man in Administration (Headquarters) put him down.

'Can't help you, Mr Jones. My good fortune, I don't have a dog in that fight . . .' The Canadian man in Administration (Finance) moved him on.

'It's sardine time here, Mr Jones. You're lucky to have what's been allocated you without sharing . . .' The Swiss woman in the Civilian Affairs Office (Central Directorate) dismissed him.

'The question is one of protocol, Mr Jones. Protocol dictates container accommodation as suitable for your work . . .' The Ethiopian man in the Civilian Affairs Office (Deputy Director) was contemptuous.

'You people, your job, your endgame, it pisses me off, Mr Jones. If I put it bluntly then perhaps you'll understand me better . . .' The Irish man in the Civilian Affairs Office (Director) kept a pleasant smile and spat through his teeth.

It had taken Marty all morning to get that far. He had been shuffled up the ladder, and with each put-down he could have tossed in the towel and gone back to the ovenlike container on the far side of the parade ground at the Ilica barracks. But not that morning, no sir . . . There was a big photograph on the wall of the office of the Director of Civilian Affairs. The photograph was labelled as 'Co. Cork – Where God comes to Holiday'. The Director liked to show the photograph to his visitors, show them where he was reared and where his parents still lived. Marty thought the seascape of cliffs and the Atlantic was second-rate compared to the mountains and fiords of Alaska. He had not come to talk about Co. Cork, he had come to *demand* better accommodation for his work than a pressure cooker steaming goddamn freight container. He had been told outside by the willowy German secretary to the Director that there was no possibility of entry without an appointment, and when the meeting inside had broken he had simply elbowed his way inside, sat down, challenged for attention.

'. . . You, your work, Mr Jones, is an obstruction to what we attempt to achieve.'

'I want a proper room. I am integral to the United Nations' effort in former Yugoslavia. I want decent accommodation.'

While he had waited outside there had been a multinational bicker in the English language between the secretaries with German, Swiss French, Scandinavian and Indian accents, about desk space. He had filed an affidavit the last evening, from an eyewitness, who had seen prisoners of the Serbs beheaded by a chainsaw. Rome was not built in a day, that sort of crap, but sure as hell the UN empire was putting in a spirited challenge. He had transferred to disk the statement, the last evening, of an eyewitness who had seen a man castrated after a cable had been tied between a motorcycle and his scrotum, and the motorcycle had been ridden away, and the man had died from blood loss. The secretaries had air conditioning and they had window light. His work was pissed on. The goddamn secretaries were looked after and he was not.

'I am a busy man, Mr Jones, so do me the favour of bugging out of here and going back to your quite adequate work area.'

'A dog couldn't work in there.'

But he was an Anchorage boy. Anchorage bred them stubborn. What he had learned from twenty-two months in New York, turning round paper on member nations' subscription debts, and what he had learned in Zagreb had given him a deep-running hostility to the fast-created empire. They had the good apartments, and the good allowances, and the good life, while Marty Jones survived in a stinking hot goddamn oven.

'Maybe a dog would be doing something more useful than your war crimes shit. Let me tell you a few facts of life, young man. War crimes talk is just a sedative for the poor punters outside of here who've joined the "Can't We Do Something Brigade". There will be no war crimes tribunal. You may want to jerk yourself off each night at the thought of Milošević, Karadić, Mladić, Arkan or Seselj, standing in the dock without a tie or a belt or shoe laces – it won't happen. Like it or not, and don't patronize me by thinking I like it, it cannot happen because I need those bastards, and all the rest of the grubby little murderers that walk this godforsaken corner of earth. I need them to sign a peace treaty for Bosnia, then a peace treaty for occupied Croatia, and I'm not going to get them to sign if there's a sniff of handcuffs in the wind . . .'

'Then you give the world over to anarchy, intolerable anarchy.'

'I need a lesson from you? Where have you been? You have been fecking nowhere. Peace between Egypt and Israel if the Brit buggers were still hammering for Begin to be tried for terrorism, for Sadat to be tried for making war? Peace in Namibia if half the South African Defence Force were to be wheeled in front of a court on genocide charges? I know reality because I have faced reality . . .'

'Your argument is morally bankrupt.'

He faced the big, gross-set Irishman. He would screw him down, screw him down hard, if the opportunity ever came his way. Screw him down so that he screamed.

'And your office is a converted freight container, so feck off back there . . .'

Marty went back in the sunlight across the parade ground, back to his video and audio tapes and his computer disks.

The gravedigger, Stevo, had been on the expedition to the church at Glina, but it was not personal to him.

It was personal to Milan Stanković and the postman, Branko, and the carpenter, Milo, but not to him because no one from his family had died in the fire of the church.

They were ahead of the buses, it was usual for Milan to have a car when he needed it, and the fuel to go with it. Before the war, before the rise of Milan, they would all have been on the buses for the annual journey to the church at Glina. Since the war, the gravedigger had not been able to make the particular long journey that was personal to him. His own mother and father had been murdered in the Crveni Krst concentration camp that had been sited at Niš, near to Belgrade. He knew that Milan, and he was grateful that Milan had tried, had last year attempted to arrange the long journey for him, but there had been shelling on the road that week, near to Brčko, and all traffic had been halted. His father had died in the big breakout, 12 February 1942, from the camp at Niš, machine-gunned against the wall by the Croat Ustaše guards, and his mother had died at the hands of the Croat Ustaše killing squads on the hill called Bubanj that was near to Niš where a thousand were killed each day, and they were buried now, together, amongst the trees on the hill called Bubanj.

The buses would be far behind them now, and the old Mercedes with in excess of 150,000 kilometres on the clock powered them home. He knew it was not the ceremony at the ruin of the church that affected Milan. It was not the ceremony and the prayer and the singing of the anthem and the reciting of the poem of the Battle of Kosovo that left Milan sullen and quiet, because he had been that way for too many days since the digging in the field at the end of the lane in Rosenovici.

And the others in the car had taken the bastard mood from Milan Stanković.

191

And because it was not personal to him, where they had been, the gravedigger, Stevo, thought it right to break that bastard mood. He leaned forward. The radio in the car played, faint and distorted, and the singer was Simonida with the one-string *gusla* to back her. He tapped Milan's shoulder.

'Milan, I love you . . . Milan, if you were dead, I would dig the best hole for you . . . Milan, why are you now such a miserable bastard . . . ?'

The gravedigger thought he could break the mood with mischief.

'. . . Milan, you are a miserable bastard, you are a miserable bastard to be with. If you want me to, Milan, I will go and dig a hole, as deep as I can dig it, so that I have to chuck the earth up over my shoulder, and you can go and lie in the hole and I will chuck the earth back on top of you, and that might cure you of being such a miserable bastard . . .'

He had reached forward, and his fingers worked at Milan's shoulders, like he used to see the postman's fingers, Branko's, at Milan's shoulders when he loosened him before a big match of basketball.

'. . . Milan, you are a miserable bastard to be with, and you make everyone else a miserable bastard. Look at us, we are all miserable because you are a miserable bastard . . .'

And the man pulled himself forward, and broke the gravedigger's hold on his shoulders. And he thought he could play Milan because he had the sort of black humour that would make Milan laugh. The gravedigger was on the crest, and he could not see Milan's face. If he had seen it he might have sat back into the seat, let the springs tickle his arse, but he could not see it.

'You know why you are such a miserable bastard, Milan? You are a miserable bastard because you are *scared* . . .'

The gravedigger could not see Milan's face, and he could not see his hands.

'. . . You are *scared*. Have been scared since that old American came and farted over at Rosenovici. Why are you *scared*?'

Then he saw Milan's face. He saw the erupted anger. He saw the hands and he saw the pistol. The face was against his, bright red and flushed. One hand coming past his eyes and locking into his old straggled hair and pulling his head forward. One hand holding the pistol and driving it through his teeth, grating them, until the foresight ground against the roof of his mouth. And he had seen Milan kill, and he could not doubt that Milan would kill. And he had seen a bastard Ustaše killed by a bullet fired from a pistol deep in the mouth, and seen the crown of the head, where the hair was thinning, lift off. And the postman had swerved the car, gone half into a ditch and come out, and the carpenter cowered away against the far window of the back of the car.

And the anger was gone. The foresight of the pistol scraped the roof of the gravedigger's mouth and against his teeth and nicked at his lip. And the smile was there, as if Milan was saying that he was not scared.

Stevo's mouth was raw agony and he could feel, already, the wet of his trousers at the crutch. He did not tell Milan that he thought he lied with his smile. He squirmed in the wetness that he sat in.

Laughing. 'We should go get the hag in Rosenovici. Lie up for her, like it was wild pig we were lying up for. Milan, you miserable bastard, you should be with us . . .'

But the shoulders had ducked down, and he could not see the face, whether it still smiled, whether it was still angered. For the old American had come to Rosenovici, and Milan Stanković ran *scared*.

The map had shown the escarpment of high rock in the trees. It was where he had found the small torn shreds of the chewing gum wrapper, and he recognized the brand name of the wrapper, and he knew that Ham had been there, as Ham had said he had.

There was a field of winter grass below the escarpment on which he lay. He could see the trails across it and the flattened grass in the middle. He could not see blood, but Ham had said he would not be able to see the blood. It was clear in Penn's mind, and the clarity killed the excitement that had been with him through the length of the day. He looked down onto the flattened ground where two men, wounded, had been skewered with knives, and he looked down onto the trails in the field where

193

the bodies of two men had been dragged – and no point in further thinking on it, the flattened grass and the trails in the grass, and Ham had not talked of the risk of capture.

Penn moved down from the escarpment, down again into the depth of the trees.

The shadows were longer, the grey merged with the falling gold of the evening.

He had slept just, during the length of the day when he had rested up, he had eaten a pie and not yet missed his sandwiches. It was two hours back that he had left his resting place through the day, a shelter made by an uprooted oak. He had slept just, then woken at the sound of children's voices, but they had not come near him.

Penn checked the map when he had reached the base of the escarpment rock. There was a plan, a fragile plan, in his mind. A better man, a Special Forces man, would not have moved across the damned river without a solid plan locked in his head. He did not have that training. The plan grew. He would get to the village of Rosenovici, he would walk at night along the route where they had taken Dorrie, where she had been. He would walk past the house where Katica Dubelj had lived. He would look for her in her house, and only there, nowhere else that he knew to look. It would only be a gesture, to look for Katica Dubelj, because he did not think she would speak English and he knew nothing of her language. He would find the disturbed grave in the corner of the field. It would be right for his report that he had walked the road through Rosenovici, and along the lane and into the field. It would be important for his report that he had gone to seek out Katica Dubelj . . . It was not good enough for Penn that he should take a name from a telephone directory and embroider a story. Basil would have said he was a fool not to flick the pages of a directory. Jane would have said he was an idiot. Dougal Gray, who had been his friend in the Transit van, would have understood. With the plan he reckoned it possible that he could look back into the eyes of Mary Braddock, see her respect, and take her husband's money. He could tell them that he had walked where Dorrie had been. He moved away slower than before he had come to the escarpment, before he had seen the flattened grass and the trails in the grass. He thought he could move for another two hours before darkness came.

'I'm so sorry to trouble you . . . Tell me, please, is the crossing point at Turanj open?'

Ulrike Schmidt sat in her office. The Transit Centre was awash with the noise of shouting, screaming, laughing. The evening cooking smells filtered to her. Her assistant, a nice Ghanaian girl, but happily scatty, stared across from her own desk, confused. Ulrike had never before rung the liaison office with the request for information as to whether the Turanj crossing point was open, and her assistant knew it.

'Thank you, but could you, please, make certain. Yes, I'll hold.'

She was thirty-nine years old. She held the telephone like a conspirator, like a teenage girl who spoke by telephone to a teenage boy and did not wish to be heard. When she went home, every two months for a weekend, back to Munich and the apartment near the Hauptbahnhof, then her mother and father told her of their pride. And her mother, each time on the one evening that she was at home, before they went to dinner in a restaurant, would sidle into her room and ask her nervous question. It was difficult to be truthful, and more difficult not to be truthful. No, she had no plans. No, there was not a particular man. It was difficult to be truthful because her mother's face would cloud and the question would not be repeated. The answer, always, was followed by the breezy excuse that life was too hectic, work too ferocious, to share. There were flowers and there were invitations, but there was no particular man.

'Definitely, the crossing point is open. You have heard nothing about it being closed tomorrow? No . . . Thank you. It was just a rumour. I am so sorry to have troubled you. Good night.'

She put down the telephone, and her assistant was watching her, puzzled. Ulrike blushed. She gave no explanation. If she had given her assistant an explanation, truth, then the girl might just have climbed onto the central table in the office where the computer was, and danced. Her assistant was scatty enough. But

195

the truth was that a man she cared about was behind the lines, across the river, in the place where the stories came from of atrocity and bestiality and torture. She cared because he took a road that was different from the turned cheek and the fixed smile. The truth was that if a man had been captured behind the lines then the border crossing at Turanj would have been closed. The Serbs always closed the crossing point when they discovered incursion into their territory.

If the crossing was still open then he stayed free.

It was the end of the day, and the end of the map.

There was a brisk rain shower falling into the upper branches of the trees. The last of the light showed Penn where he should spend the night. No mines laid off the track because there were tractor ruts and the tread of worn trailer tyres. A small tin hut had been abandoned beside the clumsy heaps of cut wood, and Penn judged it was where the timber men sheltered from heavy rain and where they made their coffee and ate their food. The men who came to the hut would be the same as the timber men on the estate of his childhood, who had talked with him and amused him, and they would kill him if they found him. Too dark for him to move further, and the hut was the final point on Ham's map. He squatted down in the hut, then curled onto his side, closed his eyes. In six hours, three at dawn and three at dusk, he had covered twelve miles according to Ham's map. It was important that he should sleep.

Ham had said that where the map ended was six miles from Rosenovici, perhaps seven but not more. He would go forward, blind, in the first light of the morning.

She was old, and Ham could not afford a girl.

She was old enough and cheap enough to look for trade in the side streets off the square behind the big earth ramparts of Karlovac. It was usual for her trade to be with the Muslim men of the Transit Centre.

Ham did not know her, he had not been with her before. It didn't matter to him that she was old, but it was important that she was cheap. Chicken shit pay from the army, and the slimmest cut left in his pocket from selling on the imported cigarettes, she had to be cheap. He lay on the bed. He could see she was old from the single unshaded bulb, hanging down from the ceiling, and he could see the flab ridges of her waist after she had unbuttoned her blouse, and the wide weight of her buttocks after she had peeled down her knickers. She smoked while she undressed, not the imported cigarettes that he handled but the loose filled sort that came from the factory in Zagreb. He had heard a child cry out in the night, from behind a closed door, and she had shouted back at the child. When she was naked, the prostitute straddled Ham on the bed, heavy above him, and her last gesture before earning the money that she had whipped from his hand and buried in her bag was to reach across him and grind out her cigarette.

He tried to think of his Karen. It was always best when he closed his eyes and thought of Karen. But he could not find her in his mind. The pillow sunk below his head. She felt for him, opening his trousers. He could not find Karen in his mind. He saw the thin and faded wallpaper of the room on the sixth floor of the block on Mihovilića that was away from the old walls of Karlovac and near to the river and the bridge that carried the main road to Zagreb, and there was a narrow framed picture, not straight, of the crucifixion, and there were a child's plastic toys on the floor near to the chair where discarded clothes had been dumped. The bed heaved as she worked harder with her fingers. Couldn't help her, couldn't respond to her, couldn't think of Karen. Because the bed heaved, iron springs screaming, the child behind the closed door cried out again, and the woman ignored her child. Her face was above him, she had the waist of his trousers down to his knees, and his pants pulled back, and he could not respond to her. There was contempt at the woman's mouth. She had already been paid, and her interest was going.

Couldn't think of Karen.

He could only think of Penn.

He had checked at the operations centre before going out of the barracks in the old police station. Casual questions. Was it all quiet over there? Any balloons going up over there? Bored answers. It was all quiet over there, just a sniper, two rounds, near the milk factory that was across the river where they had the salient, nothing else. He was thinking of Penn, and Penn should now be at the end of the map because that was the schedule drawn for him, and Penn should now be holed up in the woodcutters' hut. The shiver came to him, and he thought of Penn who was alone, and the thought shrivelled him.

The big mouth with the thick lipstick rim hovered above Ham, and he could not turn the face and the bagged eyes and the grey-flecked hair into the face of his Karen. And the big mouth with the thick lipstick rim curled at him in disgust because he could not respond.

He hit her.

He smacked with a closed fist into the side of her face.

Faces replacing the pain in hers. The face of the barman that he had punched in the bar at Cullyhanna because the barman had back-chatted the patrol. He was hitting her with both fists, belting feverishly into the flab lines of her stomach. The face of the Irish sales representative who had jogged his arm, spilled his pint, in the pub in Aldershot, put on the floor with the fag ends and the beer puddle and kicked. She was off the bed and whimpering in the corner, crouched among the clothes she had dropped. The face of Karen, when he had belted her, when she'd cried, when she'd packed, when she'd gone out of the front door with her bag and his Dawn. All the faces, fleeting, gone . . . Penn's face stayed.

He pulled up his pants and his trousers.

Ham left the door of the bedroom open behind him, and the door of the apartment, and the woman whimpered and the child cried.

He jogged down the stairs.

Ham thought only of Penn, and his fear.

The compliment, that Benny Stein would not have recognized, was that he was the most popular, the most revered, the most talked about driver in the aid convoy team sponsored by the British Crown Agents. Going off through those bloody awful people, through their bloody awful villages, was not worth thinking of without Benny Stein to humour them along.

The Seddon Atkinson, his lorry, was loaded full, eight tons of wheat flour, yeast, sugar, and seed.

And now the damn tricky girl was playing up on transmission, the only one of fifteen Seddon Atkinsons in the lorry park that was contrary. Two engineers worked with Benny Stein to get the tricky girl roadworthy for the morning, and two more of the drivers had come back after their hotel dinner to the lorry park out by the Zagreb airport to see if the tricky girl would ride in the morning across the Turanj crossing point and down through Sector North and on into Sector South.

If it had stood up and slapped his face, Benny Stein would not have recognized a compliment, but it was one hell of a big compliment to him that two engineers were prepared to work as long as it took through the night to get the tricky girl roadworthy, and two of the other drivers had come the long drag out of the city centre to check how they were doing.

Past midnight, and the convoy manager had joined them to peer down into the exposed engine space, and leaning forward behind the convoy manager was the convoy administration manager, quite a crowd to get the tricky girl roadworthy. Not that Benny Stein, long-distance lorry driver, overweight, middle-aged, stubbed height, shiny bald head that was alive with oil smears, would have noticed. An aid convoy going down through Sector North and on into Sector South might not be safe if Benny Stein wasn't in the line, might not be fun. When the transmission was fixed, when he'd gunned the engine, when he'd driven round the lorry park lunatic fast, when he'd crashed the gears, done the emergency stops, when he'd put the tricky girl through the hoops, Benny Stein pronounced himself satisfied.

He tried not to think of the past, but to concentrate on the present.

The image of the fox was the past.

Penn's present was each footfall of ten strides, then the listening and the silence, then the moving again. He could not kill the image of the fox. The present was going forward in the dawn and he had slept too poorly to have wanted to eat before there was enough light for him to leave the timber men's hut, and he

199

counted himself lucky that the rain showers that had beaten on the tin roof of the hut had been cleared by the wind. Ham's map was finished, and the map bought in the shop in Karlovac was too small a scale to help him with much beyond the lines of the roads. He could get a rough bearing from the early movement of the sun and that was sufficient to guide him. He was deep in the woods and going well, but always there was the prickle of nervousness at his back.

The past was the image of the fox.

There had been chickens inside a walled and roofed wire cage at the bottom of the tied cottage's garden. It had been his job through his childhood, each evening, to feed the chickens and to collect the eggs. It was easy enough for a fox to approach the cage, to sniff the wire mesh of the cage. But approaching the cage, sniffing the cage, didn't fill the gut of the fox. The fox had to find a way through the wall of the cage, scratch back the loose seams of the wire, dig frantically under the wire, chew at the frame of the door, if the fox were not to go hungry. And scratching, digging, chewing, aroused the frightened screams of the chickens. It was easy enough to get close but the bloody awful bit, for the fox, was doing the business. With the cackle of the chickens came his father with the shotgun, and the dogs from the shed and the big flashlight from the shelf beside the kitchen door. Three foxes were killed near the chickens' cage during his childhood, two shot by his father when caught in the flashlight, one trapped by the dogs against the panel fence by the fruit bushes. One fox had made it in. It was the night when his father and his mother had taken him to the pantomime in Chippenham, a foul wet night, and before the expedition to Chippenham he had fed the chickens fast under the rain and not latched properly the gate frame, not hooked the chain onto the bent nail. Penn couldn't count on it, that the frame door to Rosenovici would have been left open. It was easy enough for him to get there, but when he roused the chickens . . . But he was trying not to think of the past.

Penn could hear the sounds of tractors.

He had been going along the side of a hill that was close set with trees. He had no path to guide him, no trail. He could move well and quietly on the mat of damp leaves. He was drawn forward towards the engine sounds of tractors.

Suddenly, he was looking into the valley. There had been a fine rock in front of him, weather-smoothed and lichen-coated, and the rock had blocked the valley from him. Past the rock, and he saw the valley. There was a stream going fast, well swollen, that cut the valley into halves. Two tractors worked in the grass fields on the far side of the stream from him, and both pulled old laden manure spreaders. The fields on his side of the valley were unworked and weeded up.

He saw the contrast, and he understood.

His eyes tracked the progress of the stream past a pool where the water ran slower with the white spume giving way to dark depths, and he thought it would be a place for trout. Beyond where the tractors heaved out manure there were cultivated strips and he saw women working, dark shapes in the early morning mist wrapped in thick coats against the cold and bent over hoes and forks. On his side of the stream there were no cultivated strips, no women, nothing planted.

His eyes moved on, attracted to the soft colours further down the valley. The apple trees were in blossom, there were cattle grazing across the stream and children played amongst routing pigs and a dog drove sheep along a track, and it was all on the far side of the stream.

Yes, he understood.

He saw the smoke climbing from the chimneys of the village across the stream, and when he squinted his eyes and shaded them from the low sun he could see the shape of the houses and the block of the church and the brightness of flowers. He saw a car pass another car. His gaze roved across from Salika, over a linking bridge, rested on the twin village that was his side of the stream. He saw at first the mirror image, then the reality came. The broken church, the small houses without roofs, the foliage of brambles and nettles growing high in a lane. It was difficult for him at that distance, more than a mile, to see the detail of Rosenovici. But he saw that one village lived and one village had died. And at the edge of his vision, blurred by mist coming off the dew on the grass, he thought he saw a grey-black scar in a corner of the field that was immediately before the village that had died.

A cock pheasant faced him.

He saw nothing that was danger. The valley was at gentle peace. He knew the fox would have thought the chickens' cage was a place of gentle peace until the birds screamed and the gun came and the dogs were loosed. It was where Dorrie Mowat had been . . . and where Dorrie Mowat had been knifed and bludgeoned and shot to death.

The cock pheasant rose up on its clawed feet, beat its wings, shouted the warning.

He looked again across the stream to the ruin of Rosenovici. He had taken the money, and when he had taken the money he had given his commitment. He wanted to earn his own pride . . . He sat in the shadow of the big rock, where he could see down the valley, where he would wait through the day. When he could no longer see the apple blossom, and when the tractors had driven back to the living village, and when the women had trudged home, and the children, then he would move again and work his way under the cover of coming darkness towards the village that had died . . . He wanted to make a report that would earn his own pride.

The cock pheasant careered away in noisy flight down the length of the valley at gentle peace.

11

So nearly . . .

First would have come the crows, and after the crows had taken carrion there would have come magpies and jays, and after magpies and jays there would have been rats, and after the rats there would have been crawling insects, and the worms would have come for the final feast.

The jaws seemed to laugh at Penn, the eye sockets seemed to stare at him.

He had so nearly stepped on the skull.

Two winters and a summer, he thought, had given every chance for the birds, rodents, insects and worms to strip the flesh and muscle and tissue from the face of the skull. The mouth leered, the eye sockets challenged him. Walking a pace to the side of the track in the late afternoon half-light under the tree canopy, his foot poised to drop and take his weight, he had seen the skull in the leaves and brambles. The skeleton was lying on what had been its stomach, but the head was twisted as if the final living movement had been the attempt to see the killing danger behind. The skeleton was clothed in a long dark-brown overcoat, and there were trousers that had also not rotted, but he could see the bones at the ankles, above the shoes, because the man had not worn socks, and he could see also the bones of the hands still clasping a farm sack of rough hessian. He was in the tree line, going towards Rosenovici, and he could see down through into the trees and into the quiet calm of the valley, and there was a golden light settled on the valley. He had no business with it, the knowledge could not help him, but he bent and he took the finger bones from the neck of the sack and they came away easily. Inside the sack, stuffed in, were the clothes of basic winter necessity, what a man could carry for himself and for his woman. He saw it in his mind . . . the moment when someone in the doomed village had claimed there was a window of opportunity for flight, and frightened men and women had jumped for the window, taken what they could carry, and tried to smuggle themselves through the perimeter lines of their enemy. He wondered if Dorrie Mowat had seen this man go, wondered if she had wished him well, wondered if she had kissed him or if she had hugged him, wondered if she had told him that she would stay . . . He had so nearly stepped on the skeleton of the man who had been at the head of the fleeing column.

When he went forward, edging his way, he found the others. All skeletons, all dressed against the cold. The skeletons lay in a straggled line. There were the remains of women and of children and of babies. There were bulging suitcases of rotted cardboard and decaying imitation leather that were tied shut with farm twine, there were more hessian sacks, there were the heavy plastic bags that had once held agricultural fertilizer. He counted a dozen skeletons in all. In the cases and sacks and bags he found the necessities of survival, clothes and children's favourite toys and the small framed pictures of Christ in Calvary. He supposed a machine gun had taken them, traversing. Some would have run forward at the first explosion of shooting and some would have frozen still and some would have tried to go back. Last in the line was a tall woman and he could see that her body wore three dresses, and there was a bag beside her where she had dropped it and each hand still held a small swaddled bundle and the bone of the third finger of her left hand was amputated, where her wedding ring would have been. He understood what she had carried, what in her death she had not let go of because the two small skulls were close to her boots. He wondered if Dorrie had known them, if Dorrie had kissed and hugged the babies, if Dorrie had told the mother why she would stay to the end with the wounded.

He felt no hatred, because his mind was chilled.

No fear, because his mind was numbed.

He went forward. He had walked half of the distance to the village that he must travel before darkness. Dorrie had been here, in the valley, and would have seen the tractors and the women and the animals, and Dorrie had stayed to the end . . . She pulled him forward. It was as if she had taken Penn's hand, and there was mischief in her smile, as if she taunted him, as if she dared him to come closer to Rosenovici. He did not think there was anything in his life before that had been worthwhile. She had captured him, with her taunt beckoning, with the laugh of her lips and cheeks.

That *horrid* young woman, he would have loved her. Penn wanted to be near to Rosenovici before darkness. That *angel*, he would have loved her.

He had put down the book because there was not enough light through the window for him to read more.

He was still cold. The Headmaster sat in his chair. He was hunched, bowed, with a blanket of thick wool across his shoulders, and he rubbed hard at his upper thighs to put warmth in them.

All through the day he had been cold.

His trousers, soaked from the wading of the river at the ford that was not guarded by the scum boys of the militia, could not be hung on the line to dry outside in the day's spring sunshine. It would have invited suspicion to have displayed his wet trousers for the village to see. His shoes, mud-caked, could be left, discreetly, at the kitchen door because no one from the village now came to their house, that much was guaranteed. The plague was on his house, but his trousers would have been seen from the road and his wife had not complained to him, just laid them wet and filthy over the wood frame in front of the kitchen stove.

Although he shivered, he felt a sense of true liberation.

It had been good to pray in that place of evil, kneeling in the mud, crying silently for the forgiveness of them all. He did not think it an idiocy, which was what his wife had said it was, that he had waded the ford to go to pray in that place of evil . . . He made out a movement through the window, the hurrying walk of villagers going towards the crossroads near the church. He stood up from the chair and pressed his face against the cold glass and craned to see where the villagers went, hurrying. He saw the white jeeps stopped near the church, and he saw, in a blur, the Canadian policeman who had promised to bring him books for his school in return for the sharing of his secret, and the Political Officer who was an educated man.

He felt his strength because he had prayed in that place of evil, knelt in that muddied pit that shamed them all, and he would wade the ford again that night, ask again for their forgiveness, pray again that the guilty would face harsh retribution. He knew that some, a few, had the courage to stand up because he had heard it on the foreign radio. There were some, a few, who had sheltered and hidden their neighbours, Croat or Muslim. There were some, a few, who had stood against the tide and shouted against the barbarism of the concentration camps and the killings and the digging of graves in the dark silence. It was worth praying for, harsh retribution for the guilty.

The Headmaster climbed the stairs of his house. It was right, when he went to see the UNCIVPOL Canadian and the Political Officer, that he should wear his suit.

'We have a job to do, and the job is mandated by the office of the Secretary General of the United Nations . . .'

The Political Officer was Finnish, but it was many years since he had lived in the family home at Ivalo, up north by the Arctic Circle, close to the Russian border, and many years since he had served in the offices of the Foreign Ministry, down south in Helsinki. The Political Officer was a United Nations man, had been for seventeen years. He did not know whether he had offended a particular dignitary, whether he had made waves where oil should have been poured, but following an investigation that he had led into the use of United Nations facilities by the families of diplomats accredited to New York, he had been shipped overseas. His wife's home, where she was with the children, was New Jersey. His home, where he was alone, was the spa town of Topusko. Perhaps it was his penance, for digging too deep into claimed expenses, that he was posted to Topusko in Sector North.

'When you hinder me, then you hinder the world. It is a great conceit for a little man to hinder the humanitarian efforts of the world community . . .'

The Political Officer had come to Salika to offer what he called 'moral weight' to the efforts of the Canadian and Kenyan police officers. He used big language, and he recognized that his words fell empty.

'You should know, Mr Stanković, that each obstruction of our work is logged and filed. If I were in your position, Mr Stanković, I would be *unhappy* that my actions had attracted so many reports . . .'

'Go get the shit out of here.'

He regarded the man as a brute. The Political Officer's training was in the quiet world of diplomats and bureaucrats and functionaries. He assumed that he was regarded as a dull man at cocktails and poor company at the dinner parties of the social circuit, but he believed himself to be a man of rectitude and decency. Because of what he believed himself to be, any meeting with Milan Stanković, was personal pain . . . and there were so many like men scattered among each valley of the area that he covered from the spa town of Topusko. The length of Bosnia, the width of Croatia, there had been atrocities and graves dug, through the length and the width there were thousands of old women, old men, washed-up debris on a shore, who died alone for the want of a parcel of food brought in secrecy . . . He made the point of calling this one by the title of 'Mister', little victories were hard to come by and *Mister* Stanković always wore military fatigues.

'We have the right of free access anywhere in this territory . . .'

'You go where I say, only where I say. I say you get the shit out.'

Nothing of his upbringing in Ivalo had prepared him for confrontation with the likes of Mr Milan Stanković, nor for the others similar to him who ruled over similar villages. Nothing of his short work in the Foreign Ministry in Helsinki had prepared him, nor anything in the hushed corridors beyond the Secretary General's inner sanctum. Once, a year after his posting to New York, jogging with his wife and his three children at night in Central Park, he had met such a beast, seen a knife, handed over his wallet and his credit cards from the pouch at his waist. It had been his only experience of the beasts before coming to Topusko. But that beast had gone, running for bushes and shadows and cover, had not stayed in conceit to confront the weakness of him and his family . . . He knew the Headmaster by sight, for conversation, and he saw him coming up the road behind Stanković. There was always a curious undressed look about a man without the spectacles that were habitual to him. The Headmaster had twice offered him a game of chess, but there had never been the opportunity. There were deep orange-blue bruises on the Headmaster's face, and welt scars on his cheeks, and the lower lip was split and angry.

'We have a file on you, Mr Stanković, that grows more thick each week. I promise you, from the depths of my heart, that we are not stupid men. We have the file . . .'

The hand was on the holster, fiddling for the locking button of the flap.

'We have a file. Maybe you will be an old man when the file is presented to an examining magistrate. You are one of those, Mr Stanković, who tells me loudly that Serbs and Croats can never again live together – I tell you, *never* is a long time. My experience, Mr Stanković, those who shout loudest that there can never be reconciliation are those who hide the greatest guilt . . .'

But the pistol was out of the holster. The Political Officer rated his file as a puny weapon when set against the Makharov pistol. The pistol was armed. The clatter of the metal parts seared at him. For seventeen years he had believed in the power, glory, authority, of the blue flag. The reality was a loaded pistol on a village road. There was a shout from beside the Canadian policeman's jeep, a wiry little man in camouflage fatigues trying to peer past the bulk of the Kenyan's body and into the back of the jeep. He said in his reports that went to the desk of the Director of Civilian Affairs for on-passing to the Secretariat in New York that there was so much cruelty, so much fear, and his power of intervention was so minimal. Milan Stanković was striding away towards the jeep, and the Headmaster had reached him.

'My friend, what happened to you . . . ?' The question of a fool.

The small piece of paper was put in his hand. He was told it was a prescription for the lenses of spectacles.

'We will have them made, my promise, we will bring them to you. Was it him that did that to you . . . ?' The question of an idiot.

The Headmaster shrugged, turned away.

They had the door of the jeep open, and the Canadian and the Kenyan were blocked from intervention by the rifles. He saw the bag lifted out and held high, and passed to the hands of Milan Stanković. It was because of the bag that he had come to Salika with the two policemen, and the Political Officer had believed he possessed the seniority to argue his way through the roadblocks that curtained Rosenovici. The face of Milan Stanković was in front of him, and the face was contorted in hatred. The white plastic bag was held up. The three cartons of milk were tipped out and each one in turn was stamped on. The three loaves of bread were kicked, as footballs, across the road and into the rainwater ditch, and the cheese and the ham, and the apples from the kitchens of the hotel at Topusko where he had his room.

Another failure.

Failure was the reality of the power, glory, authority, of the blue flag.

He had good control of his voice, did not raise it. 'What, Mr Stanković, is a war crime? The killing of the wounded after the finish of a battle is a war crime . . . Who, Mr Stanković, is a war criminal? The leader of the men who killed the wounded after the finish of a battle . . . Do you sleep well, Mr Stanković, in your bed? Each night I add to the file . . .'

'Get the shit out, and stay out.'

Another failure.

The Political Officer could not see in the face of Milan Stanković if there was guilt or shame or fear. He hoped they came, journeyed to the beast in the quiet of the night, gnawed at him. It was all he could hope for, that the brute's face would, one day, quiver in guilt, shame or fear, one day . . .

★   ★   ★

209

He was losing time.

With the lost time came impatience.

Penn wanted to be close up to Rosenovici before the total darkness came down on the woodland of birches.

With the impatience came arrogance.

The wire line that marked the perimeter of the minefield ran away to his left and seemed to reach as far as the edge of the tree line. If he were to skirt the mines going left then he estimated that he would have to break the cover of the trees, and he reckoned there was still sufficient light for his movement to be seen. He looked up to the right and the barbed wire stretched away to a rock wall. To go round the minefield, going right, he would have to backtrack and then climb the cliff, and that would be serious delay. He wanted to be close up to Rosenovici . . . Penn could see the evidence of the mines.

The trees were thinly spaced here, as if they had been coppiced within the last five years, and there was room for armoured personnel carriers or tracked vehicles to power between the tree stumps of the old harvesting.

The evidence of the mines was from their antennae.

It was his impatience and his arrogance that led him to step over the barbed wire line. The antennae, as far as Penn could see, were laid out in straight lines. The antennae of the mines were eighteen inches high, reaching to just below his knee cap. Penn had never been on a course, not for a weekend and not for half an hour, on mines. It was pretty obvious to an impatient and arrogant man, a man running late, that the mines with the antennae were developed to catch the undersurface of a vehicle chassis if the wheels or tracks rolled clear. He could step out briskly, and ahead of him was better light to tell him that the last of the woodland was near. There would be better light because a field was ahead, and if the map of Alija was correct, if she had drawn it with accuracy, then the village of Rosenovici was beyond that field. The minefield was no problem. There was a quiet around him because the tractors were gone now, and the harsh voices of the women, and the shouting of the children was stilled.

Penn, in sight of the break of the tree line, coming to the open greyness of the field, saw the cat.

There had always been cats at the tied cottage, semi-wild and only fed in the worst of the winter. Penn knew cats.

It was a big brute with nothing handsome about it.

The cat was black-coated but the white flash at its chest alerted Penn to its advance.

Penn stopped. The cat was a distraction. Couldn't help but watch the cat, and if he was distracted by the big brute then he might blunder in the dropping light against the fine khaki wires that were the antennae. He stopped and the antennae wires, motionless, were squared about him. The big brute came fast towards him. The throaty growl of the cat called to him. He could see its ribcage.

The cat crossed open ground, a dozen paces from him, and at the centre of the open ground was the spike of the antenna's wire. Penn reckoned the cat would have been a household pet or a farmyard ratter, and the cat had been abandoned in the flight from the village, perhaps by one of those who now lay as skeletons deep in the woods.

The big brute hesitated because Penn stood still. He could see the knots and the burrs in the cat's coat.

The throated growl had become a purring roar. Penn knew cats . . . On the carpet floor of dead leaves there were no stones for him to throw at the cat. Unless he moved past an antenna wire he would not be in reach of a dried branch to throw at the cat. He could not shout at the cat, he was too close to Salika, down through the trees and across the river, he could not shoot the cat with his Browning 9mm automatic pistol. Penn knew the way of an abandoned cat that had found a friend.

The cat arched its back. The purr riddled the wood. A cat with a friend always wanted to show its pleasure by arching its back, then finding a surface to rub against, and the surface nearest the cat was the needle-thin antenna of the mine.

Penn cooed at the cat. The back of the cat was against the antenna. Penn slipped to his knees, and stretched out his hand and he murmured his love for the cat. The antenna wavered as the vigour of the cat was arched against it. Ten pounds of high explosive in the mine below the antenna, maybe twelve pounds, enough high explosive to take the wheel off an armoured personnel carrier, enough to immobilize a tracked vehicle. Penn urged the cat, gently, to come to him. The cat left the antenna and the wire swayed like a dying metronome. Penn's heart pounded. The cat, wary, circled Penn, and there were antennae on either side of him, and an antenna wire behind him. He cooed, murmured, urged the cat to come to him. Again the high arch of the back, again the fur bedded against the wire, to his right . . .

The cat came to him.

One movement . . .

The cat was against his knee.

One chance . . .

The cat howled its pleasure.

If he missed the one moment, the one chance, Penn thought the cat would scudder out of his range and find an antenna wire to snuggle against.

Penn grabbed the cat with two hands. No friendship, no love, he held the cat tight. The cat bit at his wrists and its back claws slashed at his upper arms. Penn held the cat as if his life depended on it, as if his life rested on an antenna wire not being bent over. He tramped in the last light past the antennae, through the final trees, going towards the field with the cat hacking and spitting at him.

He was through the minefield.

Penn threw the cat hard away from him.

He stepped over the barbed wire strand.

The cat snarled, as if its friendship had been betrayed, and stayed back from him, and there were no antennae for the cat to arch against.

'All right, you old bugger, I'm sorry. Please, don't do that to me again, but I apologize.'

The cat watched him. He took a slice of ham from the paper bag in his backpack and tore it into quarters, and flipped the meat towards the cat.

The cat dived for the food.

In front of Penn was the field. He could see the small wall of earth in the corner of the field. He could make out, just, the outline of the broken roofs of the village and the jagged rise of the church's tower.

It was what she would have seen, where Dorrie had been . . .

It was warm for the late afternoon.

Benny Stein sweated.

It was hard going, getting the sacks of seed out of the back of the Seddon Atkinson lorry, but best to be in there with the local Knin 'coolies' because that way their sticky fingers couldn't pilfer so bad. Best not to make it easy for them.

A pretty little town, Knin, pity about the people, and when they'd done the unloading then he'd try to find the energy to climb the long zigzag road from the warehouse by the football pitch down on the river and get up to the old fortress above the town. He was good at photography, prided himself, but the Canon with the 125mm lens was back at the hotel in Zagreb, and if he'd pulled out a camera up by the old fortress then the guns would have been raised and they'd have been bawling. It was the people that spoiled Knin, and the people didn't seem to him to have any bloody gratitude for him hiking down their way with his lorry and fourteen others.

He sweated, he heaved a sack of seed. He brought it down from the tail of the Seddy. He carried it to the trailer. They were good guys who worked with him, good crack.

Sweating, gulping, 'Heh, wasn't that the Hun *Frau* at Turanj? Wasn't that the *Frau* there?'

A good guy, packed in stockbroking to make five hundred quid a week driving a lorry into Sector North, 'Too old, Benny, you are, for looking at skirt . . .'

'Too bony for me, the *Frau*. What was she there for?'

A good guy, a banker who had dropped out of gilts, taken a money cut to run a truck into Sector North, 'Getting fruity, Benny? Getting the hots? She was waiting for a refugee bus . . .'

'You know what? She had that look, a lot of broads give me that look. Half Hackney's broads, most of Palmers Green's, they have a sincere romantic problem 'cause of me. I take cold baths, I walk away from it, too bloody complicated for me, but she had love. You know the Argie one . . . ?'

The tickle of laughter from the one-time banker and the one-time stockbroker.

Benny recited,

> '. . . An Argentine gaucho named Bruno,
> Once said, "There is something I do know:
> A woman is fine
> And a sheep is divine,
> But a llama is Numero Uno!"

'. . . Well, you know what I mean . . . Perhaps she's got a big fellow, a big NigBatt guy, and she's pining. There's not a refugee bus scheduled through today . . . that's all.'

He knew when the refugee buses came through. Refugees were something from Benny Stein's past. He'd had his little laugh from the *Frau*, and he thought her the grandest woman he had ever met, and when they were not driving, nor doing maintenance, then he would hitch a ride down to Karlovac and head for the Transit Centre, and his last project had been carpentry for the little desks and low stools of the kindergarten . . . He understood about refugees because his grandparents had walked out of Czechoslovakia fifty-five years before and his father had walked with them, and all they had owned was stacked in an old pram that they had pushed as they had walked. He'd thought, looking at the *Frau*'s face, that it wasn't just a bus arrival she waited for.

He had walked into a gate, and he had ripped the shins of his trousers on fallen wire, and he had cracked his knee on a dropped gravestone, and he had been in the ditch.

It was black dark in the village and Penn had a little chat to himself, waspish.

It was imbecile to be padding about the ruin of the village in the black dark, and he should get a better grip of himself, slow down, stop the charge. Do it like he had done it as a child, when he had gone early in the morning into the top copse where the keeper bred the pheasant chicks in the summer, and sat under the widespread oak and waited for first light when the sow brought her badger young from the sett. Going back to the basics of his life . . . The only course where he had beaten the graduate intake into Gower Street had been the rural surveillance course and crawling up in the wood's night, so quiet, that when he had put his hand from behind over Amanda Fawcett's mouth she had squealed and wet her jeans. The only time he had won an instructor's praise, and Amanda Fawcett, stuffy bitch with a 2.1 out of Sussex, had had to wear her shirt tails outside her trousers for the rest of the morning, and a *fucking* malicious grin she'd given him on his last day, coming out of Administration when he'd given in his ID. And Amanda bloody Fawcett, graduate, General Intelligence Group, paper pusher, wouldn't have made it a hundred yards off the river bank . . . After the little chat to himself, Penn stood a long time quite still, and he allowed the night sounds of the village to play around him.

The owl's shout, the whine of a swinging door, the creak of a dislodged roof beam, the motion of the stream against the piles of the bridge, voices that were distant and brought on the wind.

He stood in what he thought had been a square and the only building clear to him by its size was the mass of the body of the church. There were lamps lit in the windows of the houses across the stream where a community lived, breathed, and he could see sometimes a wavering torch on the move. There was an occasional small beam thrown up from the bridge, and it was from the bridge that he heard the young men's voices larking their boredom at guard duty. He stood quite still. He thought that when Dorrie had crossed the road, where he was now, with the torn lengths of the women's clean clothes, she would have had flares to light her way, and there would have been buildings burning. He could not see the farmhouse outline where the cellar had been, where she had run to. He had the map in his mind.

When he had calmed himself, then he moved again.

He went slow and he had one arm outstretched in front of his face and his other arm in front of his legs. Twice his fingers brushed into low rubble and once his fingers caught at a lowered telephone wire. It was a rough lane that he took, and sometimes his lower hand flicked against the taller weeds that grew between the ruts of the lane. He tried to make each stride a measured one, and he counted each stride that he took because Alija had told him that the house of Katica Dubelj was 150 paces from the square. There was a new sound catching at him, and he could not distinguish it. A few paces from Katica Dubelj's house, where it should be, and the new sound was there again. He had counted out his strides, and he groped off the lane and his fingers found a fence set around with clinging thistles and sharp nettles. He tracked the fence and he came to the wall of the house of Katica Dubelj. He came to the door. If she were alive she would come back to her home every night, or every third night, or one night in each week, if she were alive . . . It was what Penn thought, what had brought him to the village of Rosenovici, that there was the small, minimal, chance she would come. It was past the house of Katica Dubelj that Dorrie had been marched to the field, with the wounded, to the grave. He would wait through one night for her to come, if she were alive . . . His fingers were off the stone, then into the void, then feeling the rough plank surface of the door . . .

It was the sound of a man who cried out.

Penn was drawn forward.

The words of a man with pain in his mind.

At the end of the lane was the broken strut of a gate, across the entrance to a field. He had that sense of the openness beyond the gate that his fingers rested against. He heard the words cried staccato and growing in his eyes was the failing light of the torch beam. The shapes were appearing, gathering strength. The words were of anguish. He saw the earth wall around the pit, it was what he had seen from the tree line in the dusk. Going closer, going in stealth. He saw the shape of the man who knelt in the pit. Penn looked at the grave, at the burial place of Dorrie Mowat, and a man knelt in the pit in prayer. An old man spoke the prayer of a personal agony, and knelt in the pit with his head hung. Going closer, drawn forward, he could think of no threat that would come from an old man, in prayer, kneeling in the pit where Dorrie Mowat had been buried. Going closer, as to the sett of the old badger sow. Crossing the ground where she had been stabbed, bludgeoned, shot. Going covert, as to the culvert drain where Amanda Fawcett hid. Stepping silent in the loose slither of the mud over which had been dragged the joined bodies of her lover and Dorrie Mowat. Drawn forward . . .

It was luck. His father said that men who got lucky, most times, deserved their luck.

He came at the old man from behind. He came in a sharp movement, across the small torch beam, threw an instant shadow, and was over him, and the strength of Penn's hand was across the old man's mouth. If he prayed at the grave he could be no threat, if he was no threat then he could be a friend, and Penn needed some luck.

Into the blinking, staring eyes. Did he speak English?

The head nodding. Would he shout out?

The head shaking . . . Penn needed some luck.

He took his hand from the old man's mouth, and he came around the old man and he saw the tremble in the old man's body, and he thought of what the fear had done to Amanda Fawcett. He took the old man's thin hands in his own and he held them as he had held his grandfather's hands on the night before death. He squatted in the mud in front of the old man and the small beam of the torch was beside him. The old man wore a suit and a tie knotted slimly at the collar of a white shirt, and to the thighs the suit trousers were soaked wet.

'Who are you?'

'My name is Penn . . .'

'Why do you come here to a place of evil?'

'I come to find the truth of the death of Dorrie Mowat . . .'

The old man took back his hands and he reached with his fingers for Penn's face.

'. . . I come to find how she died, and to find who was responsible . . .'

The fingers brushed in gentleness on the harshness of Penn's jaw and followed the contours of his nose and his mouth, as if to be certain that he had not discovered fantasy.

'. . . I come to find the eyewitness, if she is alive, the woman who is called Katica Dubelj.'

The old man switched off the torch. He took the sleeve of Penn's coat, and they stumbled together out of the shallow pit. Getting closer to the tart mischief of Dorrie Mowat, edging

217

nearer to her . . . The old man led Penn away across the wetness of the field.

All together, huddled in darkness, Branko and Stevo and Milo had taken a position in a ruin that was across the square from the church. They shivered and chewed on cubes of cheese and had a small corked bottle of their own home brew. Nothing, not a cat, not a man, no one could move through the village without passing them. Across the stream, the big clock in the tower of the church at Salika beat out the chimes of midnight.

The Headmaster wheezed as he climbed the track. 'I am the Headmaster of the school . . .'

Penn wished he would shut his face.

'I am the Headmaster, but I am now rejected because I have spoken out against the shame of our people . . .'

They made enough noise going up the track, without adding to the noise with talk.

'I should now have been the mayor of the village, but ignorance rules and savagery . . .'

Penn thought that Ham would have punched the old man, the Headmaster, until he stopped his talk.

'When we had only one school, before I was Headmaster, the children from Rosenovici came to our school in Salika, and Katica Dubelj was one of the women who gave the children lunch. Because I know her, I have a responsibility for her . . .'

Penn had been led, at a brisk pace, into the woods at the top of the field. The tight grasp, sharp fingers, all the time held at the sleeve of his fatigue coat. He could not see ahead of him, beyond the immediate drooped shoulders of the Headmaster, and the lowest branches whipped off the Headmaster and into his face and across his body. He guessed the path that wound up through the wood was the secret of the Headmaster and the lowest branches that cut at his face and snapped back at his body told Penn that the path was rarely used. It was a good way to go, and between the brisk pace of the climb there were rest halts when the Headmaster gasped for breath and his lowered shoulders shuddered from the exertion, and Penn heard the chime of the far-away church for the half-hour and then for the hour. Once there was a cacophony of noise rushing away from them, the stampeding flight of a wild pig or of a grown deer.

'We lived together, in the old days, we had our friendships across the prejudice of birth, until the madness came. The madness has destroyed what was a fine community, destroyed, because Rosenovici is across the stream from us but always with us. We cannot shut away the sight of Rosenovici. We look at what we have done, every hour of daylight we see what we have done. The heart has been torn from us. I help you, Penn, because you have the power to hurt the madness . . .'

It was the smell that first caught Penn. He was wondering who would believe him, Mary Braddock or Basil at Alpha Security or Arnold Browne, and the smell was of stale excreta. He was wondering whether any of them, safe at home and deep in their beds, would believe that he had trekked behind the lines, gone there because he had taken the money, and the smell was of unwashed filth. He was wondering whether Jane would believe him if he shared it, whether she would back away from him and hold little Tom clear of him, and the smell was of lingering dirt. He was wondering if it mattered, whether anyone believed him . . . What mattered to him was truth, and the *truth* was Dorrie Mowat's smiling cheek, and he had never before searched after truth. It was in his mind to think about those who rejected the truth. They were in their beds and in their chairs in front of the droning televisions and in their bars with their elbows slouched on the counter, and they were bored with the truth. They were in the other maisonettes of the Cedars, and in the roads of Raynes Park, and in the pubs, and they were hurrying with their bags of washing to the launderette before it closed, and they were the late workers in the offices of Five, and they turned their *fucking* backs on the truth. They were 900 miles from him, and they had not the space in their hearts to yearn to find truth. Bloody good, old chummies, wash your hands of it, scrub them with soap, old girls. Lucky old you, old chummies and old girls, because the truth is boring . . . The torch beam now shone ahead, and the Headmaster mouthed small cries, as if warning of their approach. Penn thought, from what the torch beam

219

showed, that in daylight he would have walked right past the mouth of the cave, but he would not have walked right past the smell.

It was as if the Headmaster called, softly, to a frightened cat, or to a dog, or to a wild crow that should come for food.

The torch beam trapped the narrow mouth of a cave set behind a rockfall.

'I used to come here with food. I used to take the food from my wife's cupboard. You take food from a woman's cupboard and she notices, she questions. She said that if I took more food, for the Ustaše bastards, then she would denounce me. Do you understand, Penn, that in the madness in which we live a wife can denounce her husband . . . ? I have my own shame, because I do not bring her food any more . . .'

The Headmaster tugged at Penn's sleeve and dragged him, hunched low, into the mouth of the cave. He could have been sick, was swallowing back the bile, coughing, the smell was like a cloud. The torch beam played faintly around the walls of the cave where the water dribbled, glistening, then wavered on deeper into the cave.

It was not often that Penn had a big thought, not in his child-hood and not with the Service and not with Alpha Security. The rag bundle was cowered in the recess of the cave. Perhaps a big thought could only come in a place such as this. It would only have been a rag bundle if there had not been the brightness of the eyes reflected back by the torch beam. Penn's big thought was that this was the one chance in his life to find *truth*. She was so small. She was wrapped in sacking rags . . . He followed the Headmaster down onto the floor of the cave, sat cross-legged.

The Headmaster talked.

Her voice cackled back.

Penn heard the clock chimes come faintly from across the distant stream.

'She saw it herself. She saw them taken past her house and into the field. They had to wait while the bulldozer dug the pit. She could see it from the window. Each of them killed one man, but she says that she saw the girl killed by Milan Stanković . . . I have to go back, across the stream. What more do you want?'

220

Penn said, 'I want her to walk me through what she saw, each place and each moment what she saw, right to the killing of Dorrie Mowat.'

The Headmaster was glancing furtively at his wristwatch, shining the torch beam onto the hands. He said that he would return the next evening. Did Penn know the risk of staying? But the intoxication of the *truth* had caught him, and he waved his hand, dismissive, to reject the risk. The Headmaster was gone.

Truth was evidence. Evidence was the naming of Milan Stanković.

Penn sat on the floor of the cave and could not see her, the eyewitness.

12

Penn woke, no dreams, deep sleep.

Could recognize nothing. Blinked to get the light into his eyes. Tried to focus. Did not know where he was . . . It came fast . . . He kicked back the blanket. He felt the damp in his hip joints and his shoulders and the ache from the rough ground, and was hell's thankful for the hotel's blanket. The smell caught at him. Penn remembered . . .

The sun threw a long shaft into the recess of the cave. He wondered if she had been there all night, if she had slept, if she had stayed in the crouched posture against the inner wall of the cave. The cave, big in the small light of the Headmaster's torch, seemed shrunken, little more than a cleft. He yawned, stretched. He smiled at her and won back no acceptance of his presence. He tried to smile warmth.

He looked hard at her.

There was little to see of her because there was a shawl of torn cloth across the crown of her head that covered also her ears and her throat. What he could see of the face was a mosaic of age lines, weathered and grimed. Small hands, without spare flesh, were clasped rigidly on her lap, and he saw the deep-set dirt as if they were painted with it. She wore a long dress of black cloth that shrouded her and the cloth had the stale dankness of the cave. Over her dress, open to the waist, was a big overcoat, too large for her sparrow size, and Penn thought it might have been her husband's, and there was a knotted string holding it to her waist. Her short legs were extended in front of her and her stockings, heavy grey wool, were shredded at the knee and her feet were in small-sized rubber boots that came half of the way up her shins. It seemed to Penn as if the shawl and the dress and the coat and the stockings and the rubber boots were moulded to her body . . . Did she have other clothes? Did she change the clothes? Did she go to a stream and strip and wash? . . . He was wondering how long it had been since she had changed her clothes, washed herself. In his mind he made small markers. Had she changed or washed since his little Tom had been born? Washed or changed since the acid session with Gary bloody Brennard (Personnel)? Changed or washed since he had last laid up rough, through a night, in the undergrowth beside the Network South-East rail track when they were watching the lock-up garage for the Irishman? Washed or changed since the battle for Rosenovici and the death by a sniper's aim of her husband, and her flight to the woods, the cave? His Jane showered in the morning and in the evening. His mother stood in the kitchen of the tied cottage and stripped to the waist, and didn't care if her kiddie had seen her, and soaped herself. He made the markers and wondered if she had ever washed or changed since she had come to the cave.

He tried to smile across the cave floor. Would she come back with him?

Katica Dubelj was the eyewitness. Would she come back to Zagreb and make the statement?

Had she the strength to go back with him, across country?

Penn smiled and he gazed into the dead animal eyes of the old woman. He did not think she had the strength . . . They had no language that was common to them. He pulled his backpack round from its pillow position and when he made the movement she cringed back against the cave wall as if seeking a cranny where she could hide from him. When the Headmaster returned then they would make a statement and the Headmaster would write the story of the eyewitness, and she would make her mark as authenticity. She did not have the strength to go back with him, across country. He had given ham for the cat and sandwiches for the dogs, he was down on his food stock. There were bread rolls in the backpack and there was cheese, and the opened packet of ham, and there was an orange . . . Penn split a roll open and he laid a piece of cheese in the roll and then peeled off a slice of the ham and laid it with the cheese. He crawled towards her across the cave floor and he held the roll of dried-out bread in front of him. She could go no further back, and he came close to her, until her hand, the bony, filthy claw, darted forward to snatch the food from him. Christ, and she had no teeth . . . She tore at the roll, broke it into pieces and wolfed the pieces. She could not chew them down, they were swallowed indigestible. When she had finished the pieces then she picked for each crumb and each fragment of the flaked bread. It was as if he fed an untamed animal. He passed the orange to her. He wondered when she had last seen an orange. Jane had orange juice on the table each morning, and it was maybe a year, maybe a year and a half, since Katica Dubelj had last seen an orange. She grabbed at the orange and her fingernails, black-coated, nicked the full flesh of his hands, and a little blood ran. She pulled the orange into pieces and stuffed them down, pith and fruit and peel, into the mouth without teeth. He saw the juice dribble from the side of her mouth and when the orange was gone she lifted the fold of her dress to her lips and licked the juice off. She had gratitude and she wanted to share. It was picked from the cave floor from amongst her bedding sacks. It was passed to him in her closed claw fist. He held out the palm of his hand and the claw fist opened . . . Christ, a bloody root. She scurried back to her far edge of the cave. A sucked bloody root . . . She watched him. It was truth, the reality of the war. He wondered how many of them there were, old people holed up in caves in the woods behind the lines, sucking roots for survival. He thought that if he sucked the bloody root then he would be sick onto the floor of the cave . . . They would have sucked bloody roots in caves in the glorious and pleasant land that was England a thousand years and more before, but this was civilized *fucking* Europe, and now . . . He would have the statement when the Headmaster returned, and her signature, her mark, as an eyewitness. He reached again into his backpack.

Penn took out the brown paper envelope.

He had the photograph of Dorrie Mowat.

Penn showed the face of Dorrie Mowat, the cheeky smiling mischief challenging face, held it up.

There was joy cracking the mouth of Katica Dubelj, as if the mouth had been touched by love, as he had been touched, and there was the cackle laugh of the old woman, a memory coming back to her that had been private and suppressed too long. She reached for the photograph and she took it and she kissed it. She babbled at him and he shook his head because he understood nothing of what she said. She took his hand in her tight claw fist and she led him as a child out into the sunlight falling through the high tops of the trees. She pointed down through the trunks of the trees towards the village and then gestured towards the sun and made with her small arm the arc of the sun falling.

Penn thought it was the promise of Katica Dubelj that she would take him to the village when the darkness came, where the truth was, and he would have her statement.

He had heard his wife's voice beyond the steel door, frightened, sent away and not arguing . . .

The Headmaster sat on the mattress on the concrete shelf.

He had heard Milan Stanković's voice, harsh, in the guard-room beyond the steel door, state that the matter would be dealt with on his return, later . . .

The Headmaster sat cramped in the cell built of concrete blocks and the light came through the meshed grille at eye level in the steel door.

He had heard the postman talking about his hands and his fingernails, and he did not know why the state of his hands or fingernails was important . . .

The Headmaster sat in his damp trousers, sat huddled in his jacket, and they had taken away his tie and his belt and the laces from his shoes. He did not know what he would say when Milan Stanković returned from his meeting, wherever he went, and his mind was too terrorized to concoct a reason for his having been alone, in darkness, soaked wet from crossing the stream's ford, in the village of Rosenovici. His mind was too confused to manufacture a story of innocence.

If he had not met the Englishman . . .

They had not brought him food, and they had not talked to him. They left him solitary to wait for the questioning of Milan Stanković. It was an aspect of the madness that so many men,

225

hundreds, thousands, had sat in cells throughout the beauty of their land and waited for questioning and torture.

If he had not stayed so long at the cave . . .

He did not know, could not know, how he would respond to the beating or to the knife or the burning by cigarettes. Did not know whether he could hold his silence against the pain. Could not know whether the pain of torture would prise from him the secret.

If he had not hurried noisily back through the village towards the stream's ford . . .

Benny flicked the 'speak' switch. He said gravely, 'We can't all be heroes, *somebody* has to sit on the kerb and clap as they go by.'

He heard the laughter, distorted, coming back over the loud-speaker in the Seddy's cab.

'That original, Benny? . . . Who'd you lift that off, Benny? . . .'

'Nothing original about me. Will Rogers and I collaborate.'

'Cut it, Benny, do me the favour.'

He obeyed. The convoy manager had cause to be stressed up, pissed off, because the rock that had come through the side window of the Land-Rover had caught his face above the collar of the flak jacket and below the rim of his helmet. The move out of Knin had been sweet enough, 0700 departure, but the shit had started in a village just up the road from Titova Korenica with ugly women and dwarf kids lobbing rocks. The convoy manager had a bandage over his face, looked a really fine hero. Rocks in that village, and four windscreens broken.

They were blocked now by mines.

They were up from Slunj, almost with the whiff of the river at the Turanj crossing point in their noses, and there were mines, and four little arseholes to negotiate with. Good stuff for the hero, the convoy manager, to negotiate with. They were blocked in between a cliff face and a river, a good place to get the old head blown off. It didn't happen on every run, but happened too often, that they were messed around on the convoy route. Benny reckoned that up the road, between Slunj and Veljun, they were moving tanks, maybe artillery, and a track had gone broken or a wheel had got holed, and they weren't having a United Nations relief convoy going by and seeing what they were moving. It was difficult for him to get the bloody great pisspot on his head out of the window, but he took the trouble. Past all the lorries, past the Land-Rover, the convoy manager was in his second hour of failing, too right, to negotiate the removal of the mines from the road. Their schedule was all shot to hell. The kids with the mines, from what he could see, were drunk, and they'd a good game going. He saw the convoy manager stride back to his Land-Rover.

The voice, tight with controlled anger, was in Benny's cab.

They were going to take a minor road over towards the Bosnia border. They were going for the scenic route . . . for the tourist run . . . going up towards Glina, then would work back through Vrginmost for the Turanj crossing – way behind schedule.

He sat in the Seddy's cab, snuggled in the flak jacket and with the weight of the helmet squat on his head, and hit the gears. The convoy took the fork road east, drove off the main drag, and away from the kids with their 'frag' mines, and he smiled down at them like it was a pleasure for him to be going the scenic route. And the kids loosed off their AKs into the air, as if they'd won a war and not just diverted an unarmed aid convoy.

They were laid out neatly on the bed, her new files. She had drawn the new curtains back, because she came into the room each evening and closed them. Mary Braddock sat beside the new files on the new duvet and she had kicked off her shoes onto the new carpet. The new soft toys, bears and rabbits, were on the new pillow of the bed, and the shop assistant, when Mary had bought them, had prattled to her as if she were a grand-mother, and she had not contradicted the shop assistant, nor told her of obsession, or the weight of guilt. Because of the new paint and the new wallpaper it was a pretty room, and a room that was correct for a child who would grow to be a climbing star, not a *horrid* young woman. It was after a spring shower that had beaten on the mullioned window, and the sun shone into the pretty room.

The size of the new file was a measure to Mary of the scale of the obsession. She had read about herself in the newspapers, different name and different address, but read about parents who shared with her the obsession to know. The newspapers printed sad photographs of fathers and mothers sitting close on settees, with the picture of the dead child, the lost loved one, in the frame behind them, those who demanded to know and who had failed. She could recall the sad photographs of the stunned parents of the 'friendly fire' boys in the Gulf, of the girl in the Kenya game park, of the young man murdered in Chile's capital, of the young woman who had died in Saudi, and the sad parents all had the same refrain of confused criticism for the help they had been given. All her friends said it was *obsession*. She shared the file with none of them, and she did not allow her secretary, two days a week, to type the letters of which the copies went into the file. There were the copies of fourteen letters written to the Foreign and Commonwealth Office; her friends said she should close her mind to an episode better forgotten. There were four letters personally addressed to the ambassador in Zagreb; there were two letters written by hand to the President of Croatia. None of the replies were curt or brusque or rude – the replies, aide-drafted, signed by the dignitaries, were bland and oozed sympathy, and were bloody useless. Her friends said that she should start again . . . The telephone stampeded her out of the newly decorated, newly furnished bedroom for a child.

She ran for the stairs.

God, please, make it the call . . . Penn's call . . .

The dogs slithered with her down the stair carpet, cannoning against her legs.

God, please, make it Penn's call.

She snatched up the telephone in the hall. The dogs barked raucously, as if her run for the telephone was a fun game.

'Charles here. Where were you? Outside? A nice morning up here in this filthy city. Sorry, darling, but it's all negative. Did I tell you, can't remember if I did . . . ? I pushed the problem of that odious detective to Frankfurt. They've a satellite office in Munich. Their people in Munich have called up Vienna. Vienna have links into Zagreb. I got a few faxes to fly . . . Someone from the associate office in Zagreb actually went to the hotel, this morning . . . I don't know what it means, but the bastard hasn't been in the hotel for four nights. He hasn't checked out, his account's still ticking up, but he hasn't used the hotel for four nights . . . They don't know where he is . . . I'm sorry, darling, but I did tell you what I thought of Mr Penn . . .'

Mary held the phone, swayed.

'Are you still there . . . ?'

Small voice. 'Yes.'

'I'll burn his bloody arse when I get to meet him, when I get his bloody bill . . . Darling, dinner tomorrow, can we manage two more? Push the chairs up a bit, can we? A quite hideously boring couple of guys from Utrecht, but it's an EC contract, and fat. Don't know how they'll mix with our crowd, but it shows willing. 'Course you can cope, darling . . . Why don't you run out to Guildford, get something nice, new? See you this evening . . .'

She went back slowly up the stairs and tidied the file on Dorrie's bed.

They were a rather more cheerful crowd for him to be with than the day shift, and they did not seem to regard him as a hostile antibody inserted into Library.

And the memories seeped again over the pages, typed and handwritten, and the photographs and the worn maps. Shaken the hand of that lovely young man, Johnny Donoghue, and watched him go tired away to the entrance tunnel of the Underground train at the end of the arrivals concourse, and gone to look for the car that would run the old desk warrior back to Century House. Walked down his corridor on the eleventh floor. 'Hello, Henry, have a good trip?' 'Well, I wouldn't say . . .' Carrying the duty free towards his corner of the office. 'Just one of those things, I hope you're not thinking it'll be your head on the block?' 'Well, we did all we could . . .' Settling down into his chair. 'Always a problem when you use an amateur, don't you think?' 'Well, you win some and you lose some . . .' Brought a beaker of coffee, and sipped it, and opened his briefcase, and started out on the arid damned report for the file of a young man's journey through the lines, a used young man.

It was long after he would normally have cleared the desk and trudged away to the station, but the night shift's supervisor had wandered, friendly, to his desk with a mug of coffee for him. A good young fellow, and chatty, and they talked desultorily about the new world that was dangerous, and nostalgically about the old world that was comfortable. The usual sort of garbage . . . He waited his moment, then asked.

Henry Carter requested the trawl. Didn't know what they would find if they trawled for him, didn't know if they would find anything.

He had the clearance.

He wouldn't have called the supervisor a chum, but there had been times back in the old Century House that he had shared a lunch table with him in the canteen.

The trawl had left in the net what he regarded as a prize catch.

A short memorandum at the top of a light pile of flimsies, and worthwhile him staying late because it was a catch that the day shift supervisor would never have searched for . . .

From: George Simpson, Security Service (Liaison), Rm C/3/47.
To: Desk Head Yugoslavia (former), Rm E/2/12.
Ref: GS/1/PENN.

Following regular weekly liaison meeting, I took lunch with Arnold Browne, Sec Serv, ranked senior executive officer. In confidence AB spoke of Sec Serv involvement in former Yug, using a reject freelancer. Involvement follows death in Dec 91 of Dorothy Mowat, Brit citizen, in Croatian village overrun by Serb irregulars in area now designated by UNPROFOR as Sector North. Following recovery of Mowat's body (April 93), AB recommended to deceased's family that PENN (William), formerly with Sec Serv and now private detective (exclaimer), should travel to Croatia to investigate circumstances of death. AB drops that PENN, 'dogged' and 'end of road man', will hopefully produce war crimes evidence for use in pressuring Belgrade towards peace talks/negotiation, which Sec Serv can onpass to FCO . . . Sounds like empire building, sounds like interference outside Sec Serv remit. Are we happy query.

Signed:
Simpson, George.

He knew Simpson, old Georgie. Simpson, old Georgie, was the
sort of man that he used to meet in the corridor, never seemed to be
in a hurry, never seemed to have anything pressing, could always
give him the latest cricket score. He could see Simpson, old Georgie,
under-achieving and passed over and frightened witless of redun-
dancy, wrestling not too hard on a matter told in confidence. Carter
thought that so much now fell into place . . . A trust betrayed? . . .
Well, Simpson's, old Georgie's, dilemma about betraying a trust
hadn't gone the distance, hadn't stopped him snitching.

It was an old maxim, but true, that confidences didn't count for
too much in the trade . . .

The Intelligence Officer fronting as Liaison had known that the
opportunity would not come until the end of the meeting. At
the break-up there would be coffee provided, and biscuits and
juice, and the opportunity.

There was a working relationship now that civilized the meetings. Stiff, formal, but a relationship . . . The meetings were
always in the police station at Tušilović that was twelve kilometres into the occupied territory from the crossing point at
Turanj. The relationship had prospered sufficiently for there to
be a hot line from his office in Karlovac to the police station at
Tušilović, and a monthly meeting across a table. They never
came to Karlovac . . . And it was usual, also, for the Intelligence
Officer to meet Milan Stanković at Tušilović . . .

The Intelligence Officer, before permanent secondment to the
military, had been chief salesman (export) for the timber factory
at Karlovac. He was trained to read body language. The Serb
was sullen, there had to be room for sport there.

More on the agenda concerning the electricity supply across
the cease-fire line: deadlock. The sort of agenda item on which
Stanković would usually have shouted his opposition, hammered
the table. The matter of the woman, Croatian-American, who
had travelled from Chicago for her mother's funeral at Topusko,
and been kept waiting three days in Zagreb with no permission
for entry into Sector North granted, until after the burial and
no explanation. The sort of matter on which Stanković would
usually have sneered contempt.

231

The Intelligence Officer anticipated sport.

They had been through the litany of cease-fire violations. A sentry, frozen and lone, looses off a single shot. A section, bored, responds with a mortar round. A platoon, angry, replies with an artillery piece. A company, furious, loads up an Organj multiple rocket launcher . . . The sort of litany on which Stanković would usually shoot his mouth off.

There had to be good sport because Stanković was sullen, head hanging.

The Intelligence Officer came round the table and he held the coffee cup in his hand. He eased himself onto the table, sitting casual, beside the big bowed shoulders of Milan Stanković.

'Hello, Milan . . . Bit quiet today . . . How's Evica? My wife always tells me to ask after her . . . Managing, is she? I heard her school was short of books, but then you're short of everything . . . Must have been shit, through the winter, without the power . . .'

He watched the hands fidgeting and the body hunched, and the Serb's eyes avoided his own.

'. . . We're quite well on with the new co-operative building, out on the Ilovac road, good position and close to the Zagreb highway . . . Your farmers happy? You built a new co-operative? No? Well, maybe next year, maybe some time . . .'

There was clearly a personal burden there for the Intelligence Officer to scratch at. He probed, and sipped his coffee.

'. . . You know what people ask me, friends who know I come to the meetings, the ones who used to know you? What they ask is this. That Milan Stanković, the clerk once but the big man now, what does he think his future is? I've an idea of the future, long-term, because nothing will be forgotten. What I tell my friends, the people who ask me, it may not happen in my lifetime nor in yours, the vengeance, but my son will come for your son because it will never be erased . . .'

He wondered if it was shame that he saw, or whether it was fear. He imagined his quiet voice as a knife between the blades of Milan Stanković's shoulders.

'. . . I nearly forgot to say. I'd have kicked myself if I'd forgotten to say it. There are questions being asked about you, your name is mentioned. I suppose if you hadn't been in Belgrade then you would have been able to prevent it, but you were in Belgrade when they dug for the bodies of our wounded that were killed after Rosenovici fell. That was a mistake, you being away in Belgrade. I'm told they're filling a file on you, Milan . . . There was a bigger mistake . . .'

The Intelligence Officer was bent over Milan Stanković. Good sport. He whispered the words into the ear of Milan Stanković.

'Time I was getting on, time I was back in Karlovac. Not too bad there because we've got power. Please tell Evica that my wife wanted to be remembered to her . . . They're asking questions, filling a file. Killing the English girl, Milan, that was a serious mistake . . .'

They talked quietly in the guardroom. They sat away from the scratched steel door of the cell.

Branko, passing his cigarettes: 'It was the same bag in the police jeep . . . the same bag, white plastic, as was in the Dubelj hag's home. The goddamn bastards brought more food.'

Milo, stubbing his own cigarette, taking another: 'It wasn't that fucker's hands. You saw his nails, I saw his nails. Wasn't his bastard nails, was a woman's.'

Stevo, striking the match: 'We go back tonight, skip the music shit, we go back tonight until we find her, until she comes back down into that pig place . . .'

They smoked, they flicked their hands of playing cards on the table, they ignored the man behind the steel door of the cell, they waited for the return of Milan Stanković.

She had come back to the crossing point at Turanj.

She had again left the Transit Centre and driven to the crossing point and parked her car, and waited. The convoy of the aid lorries, returning empty, should have been through an hour before. If the convoy had left Knin promptly and made good time, then it might have been through an hour and a half before. She stared up the road from where the Croat militia stood, and the light had started to dip. She looked up the hill, up beyond the small sangar of whitewashed sandbags where the troops of the Nigerian battalion had their machine gun, up towards the defence positions of the Serb militia, where their flag flew, and on the hill, greying in the low light, would be their trenches and their strongpoints and their mortars and artillery. Each time she glanced down at her watch and realized the convoy was delayed, then the fear tripped in her. If the convoy was late then it would be because of a security alert . . . if there was a security alert it would be because of a discovered infiltration . . . if there was a discovered infiltration it would be because Penn was hunted . . . Each time she looked at her watch the ratchet of her fear turned. If nobody did anything, if everybody just wrung their hands, if nobody acted, if everybody said that action was impossible, then the camps of the Neuengamme Ring could be built again, then the wickedness could come again. She saw the car come slowly to the far checkpoint and stop . . . If the big men of the chancelleries and ministries did nothing, then only the little men could *try* to halt the wickedness . . . The car came on from the far checkpoint and stopped again at the NigBatt sangar . . . Penn was the little man and was alone, and behind the lines, and trying . . . The car came forward, going faster, between the rubble of the fought-over village of Turanj.

She was apart from the militia checkpoint, and when the car reached them the militia men pointed to her, and there were smiles on their faces and she imagined they called her the 'silly bitch' or the 'daft whore'.

The door of the car opened. She knew the Liaison Officer. He was often at the meetings she attended at the Karlovac Municipality.

He came to her. Perhaps it was something in her face, but the smirk was wiped off him.

'You have a problem, what is the problem?'

'Why is the British convoy late?'

'A difficulty down the road . . .'

Said breathily, 'What difficulty?'

'A route interference, they have had to divert. Why do you ask?'

'What is the interference?'

'Some kids, mines, near to Slunj . . . Why do you ask?'

234

'No difficulty in the Glina area, nor near to Vrginmost?'

'It is the usual interference, and the Glina area is quieter than the grave . . .'

'You are sure . . . ?'

'I am returning, Miss Schmidt, from the liaison meeting with the people from Glina Municipality. There is no difficulty in that area, the difficulty is at Slunj. May I repeat, please, my question . . . Why do you ask?'

'It's not important.'

It was only the first beating.

Starting with a slap, then punches, then kicks.

But he had not been burned.

It was the fire that the Headmaster dreaded. The flame would be the worst.

He had known Milan Stanković through all of the young man's life, known his mother and his father before they had gone to live in Belgrade.

The Headmaster had once liked Milan, when the boy was the basketball star of the village school, when the young man had been the hero performer of the Glina Municipality team. He had always had time for Milan Stanković before the war . . .

All through that day he had lain in his cell and waited for Milan Stanković's return from the liaison meeting, and he had thought of the fire against his body . . . It had been just slapping and punching and kicking so far, and he had held the secret tight in his mind.

Only staccato questions, not an interrogation.

When the interrogation came, then there would be the fire against his skin . . . But he did not understand why Milan Stanković had shown no appetite for hurting him, and he had seen between the slaps and punches and kicks the confusion of the expressions of the postman and the carpenter and the grave-digger, as if they also had not understood.

It was important to the Headmaster to keep his secret as long as it was possible for him to survive the pain.

The music from the hall in his school beat at the meshed grille high in the door of the cell.

After the music, after they were drunk, they might come back to the cell with the fire . . . He did not know how long he could protect his secret, but by the night, by the time they were drunk, surely the young man would have turned away from the evil that was Rosenovici.

It was his hope.

'Run hard, young man,' he murmured to the walls of the cell. 'Run hard so that I do not betray you . . .'

She had offered him berries from her store that was under the rags of her bed, while they waited.

The berries were bullet-hard, dried through, and he estimated they had been picked the last autumn from the dog rose brambles in the wood, and from the branches of thorn trees.

They had waited an hour in the cave, as the shadows had fallen into darkness, for the Headmaster.

It was all in gestures because they had no language. He showed her the palms of his hands, rejecting the berries, then declining the root section that she offered.

The Headmaster had said he would come, and they had waited. And he knew as certainty that she did not have the strength to come, across country, with him to the cease-fire line, and he did not have the language to persuade her, nor to tell her that the Headmaster must record her statement. Penn would have bet, high stakes, that the Headmaster would return.

After the first trumpet call of the big owl from a high tree down towards the valley, she wrapped her shawl tighter around her face, she knotted the string more closely around her overcoat, and she replaced the berries and the root in her food store under the rags, and she stood. Penn smiled at her, to reassure her, and did not know whether she saw his smile in the cave's gloom. He had the pistol in the pocket of his coat and a spare magazine, and he checked that the pistol was armed and on 'safety'. He felt a skein of worry, that the Headmaster had not come.

It was Katica Dubelj's decision that they should wait no longer for the Headmaster.

She took his hand, as if she could reassure him. He was trained by A Branch of the Security Service, he carried a Browning 9mm automatic pistol, there were four hand grenades in his backpack, and the shrivelled-up woman, eighty plus years of life lived, reckoned he needed her reassurance . . . Christ.

She babbled words at him, and the only word that he caught was the name of 'Dorrie'.

Going back to Dorrie's place, Dorrie's death . . . and he knew her only by the words of others who held the love, and by the photograph, and nothing before in his life had mattered so much as the *truth* of Dorrie Mowat's village, Dorrie Mowat's killing. He would go from Rosenovici. He would not return to the cave. It was the best time for him to say his thanks to her. He had his hands on her light shoulders and he kissed the old woman softly, on her forehead, below the line of the stinking tight shawl, and she pecked at his cheek, stretching up, with her dried mouth that had no teeth. The humility dug into him. He hoped that he would never again feel the arrogance that was the trademark of a watcher of A Branch. He hoped that he would never again swagger in conceit . . . She laughed, guttural, and dragged him out of the cave.

They went fast down the narrowed track from the cave.

All the time she held his hand.

He scrambled to keep up with her skipping short stride.

They came nearer to the high tree where the big owl shouted.

Gaps in the tree trunks, and Penn saw the small pin lights of the village across the stream. The wind was coming into the trees, and Penn heard the murmur of music from the village across the stream.

She went quickly and pulled him clumsily after her.

It was the movement of a scavenging vixen fox. When they were out of the wood, she used the overgrown hedge at the side of the field, scurried close to the spread hazel and the thorn. Stopping and scenting and seeming to sniff for danger, and going on.

No shadows now. The gold from the sun gone grey behind the trees above Rosenovici. She never lost her grip of him . . . He grinned to himself. First she had felt the need to reassure him, now she did not trust him to move silently in darkness.

They went by the corner of the field, not stopping. A sharp

thought . . . where was the Headmaster, why was the Head-master not with them? . . . Sharp, because she hurried him past the black pit of the dug grave.

She stopped, suddenly, and he cannoned into her back, and she turned, only a slight outline in the darkness, and her finger jabbed at him, as if she criticized the child she led, as if bloody Penn knew nothing of covert movement. She waited, the vixen fox, at the broken gate at the end of the lane, and listened to the night. He heard only the bleating music and the grind of a swinging door and the creaking movement of fallen rafters.

Penn was led to her house.

He was taken into the house, through the open and hanging door.

She was miming what she had seen.

She stood at the window at the front of her house, and she pushed her head against the shards of the broken glass, identified what had been her viewpoint. Penn was not yet accustomed to the dark of the interior before he was pulled again and his feet crunched the glass and he cursed, and she hissed her complaint. She took him back out into the lane. Now she loosed his hand.

He stood in front of Katica Dubelj's house and he watched, squinting to see, the mime act of the eyewitness. She was the guards, and she seemed to kick some forward, and to beat others as with the stock of a rifle. She was the walking wounded, and she seemed to carry some, and she seemed to drag others. She spoke the name, she was Dorrie Mowat, and she seemed to support two heavy men, and her arms were out, and she seemed to buckle under the weight of the men, and she seemed to turn once and aim a kick back behind her.

She took his hand again.

She walked Penn back through the fallen gate and into the field.

They slithered together on the wet of the grass and the weeds, and across the tyre ruts left by the jeeps.

Penn was led to the edge of the pit.

She made the mime again.

She was the guards, and she moved to take their places in a half circle facing the pit, and she seemed to aim down towards the ground. She was the wounded, sitting. She was the wounded, lying. She said the name, and she was Dorrie Mowat, and she seemed to crouch down on one knee and her arms were outstretched as if she held the shoulders of two men against her small body, and her mouth moved as if she shouted a defiance. She was the bulldozer and she growled and she jerked up her arms as she walked the length of the pit, and she seemed to throw back the pit's earth.

He watched, and he would forget nothing. He would not forget that Dorrie and the wounded men had watched the bulldozer gouge out their grave.

She scrambled across the earth wall and down into the pit.

He could barely see her, the black-grey shadow shape against the black-grey earth of the pit.

The music, across the stream, was a frenzy.

She lay in the mud at the bottom of the pit. She was the wounded and waiting. She stood. She made the knife thrust and she made the chopping blow of a hammer . . . She moved, a pace. She seemed to stand above the next of the wounded, waiting, and she thrust with the knife and chopped with the hammer . . . another pace . . . another . . . Penn forced himself to watch. Dorrie had been the last in the line, Dorrie and the boy that she loved. He had to watch Katica Dubelj, because it was what he had come for. She was a guard, she was a man from the village where the music played across the stream. She seemed to try to pull them apart, Dorrie and her boy, and she recoiled back and held her eyes as if extended fingers had been punched into them.

She spoke the name.

The whisper. 'Milan Stanković.'

She went crab fast to the near end of the pit, and her hand was first at her face to show the length of the beard.

'Milan Stanković.'

She was Milan Stanković, and she seemed to hold a pistol in her hand. Stopping, aiming, the pistol hand kicking, a pace . . . stopping, aiming, the pistol hand kicking, a pace . . . This was hard for Penn to watch, Milan Stanković working methodically down the line and fetching the last life from the wounded who had been stabbed and bludgeoned . . . Stopping, aiming, the

239

pistol hand kicking, a pace . . . She did not hurry herself, she made each movement as she had seen it, she was the eyewitness . . . Stopping, aiming, the pistol hand kicking, a pace . . . Going closer to Dorrie Mowat and her boy. She seemed to stand above them, then reach down as if to break the hold, and then she seemed to double away and clutch her hands at her groin as if that was where the kick had gone. She was reeling back. She was reaching for the knife and slashing. She was reaching for the hammer and crashing it down. She was aiming the pistol. The pistol hand kicked twice. She whispered the name, 'Milan Stanković.'

He turned away.

It was what he had come to find . . .

The power of the light seared into Penn's face.

13

His eyes saw only the white brightness of the light.

There were excited shouts from in front of him and then all around.

The light stripped him bare. He stood in the white brightness. He dared not move. If the fear, the panic, had not been frozen into him in that moment when the light caught him, then he might have tried to duck away or throw himself to the edge of the light, but the fear was in him and with the fear was blindness.

The old woman had been behind him.

She had been in the pit behind him when he had turned away.

With the shouts, with the click of the safety catches, there was a sudden stifled scream, a man's hoarse pain. The light never left Penn. It was what he himself would have done, or what his instructors from far back would have told him to do. 'Put the light down, sonny boy. Be close to the light but not on it, sonny boy. 'Cause if they're going to put suppressive fire down, sonny boy, it'll be the light they go for . . .' That is what an instructor would have said, and he realized the angle of the light was low, as if it was on the ground. There was a hammer of shots behind him, semi-automatic on a rifle, and after the shots and the scream there was the sound, briefly, of ripping cloth.

Penn did not dare to turn to see whether Katica Dubelj, old woman gone animal, old woman gone eighty years of her life, old woman who had never been on a surveillance or an evasion course, old woman not strong enough to go cross country, had made it clear through the thorn and wire in the hedge beyond the pit.

There was a loaded pistol weighting the pocket of his coat. There were four grenades in his backpack. Penn did not dare to reach for either. Very slowly, so carefully that the movement should not be misunderstood, he stretched out his arms, kept his hands open, raised his arms.

He thought he was the prize. He heard behind him, after the bullet volley, nothing of pursuit. Fear seemed to numb the movement of his legs so that they were rigid scarecrow stilts, and to loosen the hold of his guts so that he wanted to piss, crap. The fear trembled the movement of his arms, up high and into surrender. His eyes blinked, uncontrolled, and the water from his eyes distorted the glare of the cone of light.

There was still shouting, but coming closer to him, moving closer and slowly because they could not know the fear that shackled him, as if he was still dangerous to them.

Only his mind was not frozen. In his mind the thoughts raced . . .

Ham hadn't talked of escape and evasion. The fat-faced little bastard hadn't talked about what to do . . . He had once been at a Territorial Army depot in Warrington, a marksman's rifle gone missing, a suspicion that it might have been sold to Protestant paramilitaries from Ulster which was enough to bring in Security Service involvement, and an Escape and Evasion pamphlet picked up off a book shelf. He had been waiting for them to wheel in the armourer, and he had flicked the pamphlet's pages, just from interest. He had read . . . the first moments of capture offered the maximum opportunity of escape, also offered the maximum opportunity of getting the old head blown off because of the high state of adrenaline of the captors . . . He had read that it took real guts, big bravery, to antagonize captors by going runabout. His hands were high above his head.

In his mind the thoughts cavorted . . .

He was shit scared, frightened, and Dorrie Mowat had been here. Dorrie Mowat, the *horrid* young woman, had kicked one man in the privates, punched one man in the eyes, spat at the whole goddamn lot of them. Dorrie, the one that all who had touched had loved, had sat in the wet grass where he now stood in surrender, and her arms had been round the wounded man that she had chosen, and she had sat and waited while the bulldozer dug out the pit. She hadn't had the fear. A shape loomed at the edge of the cone of light.

In his mind the thoughts raced . . .

Jane in the small room, little Tom on her lap, with the television on: 'And what's the point of you going there, what's anyone to gain from it?' Failed her. Mary in the kitchen and making the coffee: 'I think she took a pleasure in hurting me . . . and, Mr Penn, she was my daughter . . . and, Mr Penn, her throat was slit and her skull was bludgeoned and she was finished off with a close-range shot . . . and, Mr Penn, not even a rabid dog should be put to death with the cruelty shown to my Dorrie.' Failed her. Basil holding court to Jim and Henry in the darts bar of the pub round the corner from the launderette: 'You know what you are, Penn? You are a jammy bastard.' Failed them. The old American Professor of Pathology: 'Build a case, stack the evidence' . . . Maria who was a refugee: 'She was an angel in her courage' . . . Alija who needed the operation to her eyes: 'She could not protect herself because she had the wounded fighters to help' . . . Sylvia who was cloaked in the nervous collapse: 'Does anybody care what happened to them, who did it, anybody?' . . . Failed them.

The blow was at the back of the neck.

Failed them all . . .

The blow was with the stock of a rifle, short swing.

And failed Jović who had interpreted for him, and Ulrike who had touched his arm to make a talisman for him, and Ham who had given him the map . . . And failed himself.

He was pitched forward by the blow. They were all around him and the shadows of their bodies masked the cone of white light. He wondered if they would shoot him there, or whether they would take him some place else to kill him, and felt he did not have Dorrie's courage. He tried to cry out, beg mercy of them, but his voice was suffocated. The fear consumed him. When they had hit him some more times, when he had seen the grinning of cold faces, when he had smelled the foul close breath of them, then they searched him and found the pistol and they skewered his arms back and pulled the backpack off him, then they hit him with the rifle stocks some more.

243

Penn was pulled to his feet. He could hear the music from across the stream.

Penn (William), Five reject, failure . . . He was held tight and dragged towards the pin lights of the village across the stream.

They were through Glina.

The convoy was belting. It was not usual for the convoy manager in his Land-Rover to let the fifteen Seddys behind him sniff the wind and belt, but they were all pissed off and Benny who was driving three from the back supposed that the wound on the convoy manager's face had lost its numbness and would now hurt like hell.

Benny wasn't fussed. It did not matter to him that they had been off the main roads, into the ditches, up bloody awful rutted lanes. He'd done the runs into northern Iraq out of Turkey to resupply the Kurds in winter, grinding in low gear down tracks that had never seen a loaded Seddon Atkinson before. He made it his business to know the land, read up on his guidebooks and he wrote twice every week to his wife, Becky, to tell her where he had been and what he had seen. There wouldn't be much to write to Becky about Glina because they had belted through the pretty little town, but he'd think of something to say. He only wrote to Becky about the towns being pretty, never about the people being shit. It was not his way to frighten her, to tell her that most days he wore a pisspot on his head and a flak jacket of kevlar plates front and back across his body, and he didn't tell her that the doors of the cab were armour-reinforced, nor that he had sandbags under his seat as protection from mine blasts. On the main road and belting, perhaps forty-five minutes if they weren't messed again from the Turanj crossing, and the voice crackled on the radio in his cab.

'Guys, there's usually a roadblock between Glina and Vrgin-most. I don't want to spend half the night yammering with some defective on a roadblock. There's a right a few miles ahead, up to a village called Salika, I reckon we can get round the block, then back onto the main heave . . . OK, guys?'

They didn't have call signs, the drivers didn't like to play at military games. If they'd had call signs then all of them would have been Foxtrot Something, all F-word stuff. Call signs were for kids playing soldiers . . . The answers tripped over each other, and not many of them polite. And Benny's next letter to Becky would not tell her that his nerves were hacked jagged by driving in darkness on stone tracks through these shit awful villages, through these shit awful people.

Bad news that there would be another shit block to divert round . . .

He flicked the 'speak' switch. It was important to get a laugh because the nerves of all the drivers and the convoy manager would be as hacked jagged as his own.

'You know what Lily Tomlin said: "Things are going to get a lot worse before they get worse" . . .'

They brought him down to the bridge.

They had tied his wrists together, cutting hard, behind his back, and his ankles so that the bones chafed each other, and they had to drag him.

They came down to the bridge and they pitched him onto the planks and he fell onto his stomach and was trying to twist his head away so that his nose did not take the force of his fall. There was a rusted old hurricane lamp on the bridge that threw a good light from beside the sandbag position of the guards. It was then he saw for the first time the three men who had taken him. The one was thin and big, another had a heavy body and was taller, the last was slight and shallow in his build. They'd thrown him down, dropped him like the dead roebuck that a stalker and the keeper had shot in the long copse behind the tied cottage, and they had the same excitement of the stalker and the keeper, and all three had the weathered faces of the country, aged, and Penn knew the country was cruel . . . He was a specimen to be boasted of, and he heard words that were similar to 'English' and to 'spy', and the old bastards were showing the young guards of the bridge his passport and the Browning 9mm automatic pistol and the spare magazines and the grenades. He did not see any more at the bridge. Penn tried to tuck down his head when the young guards at the bridge took their turn.

She hadn't flinched from the kicking . . .

Dorrie had faced up . . .

She had kicked them back, punched them back, shouted back . . .

She had kept her pride, her goddamn courage. Dorrie Mowat, a *horrid* young woman, hadn't let them see her fear.

He forced his eyes open. He looked into their faces as she had looked into their faces, into their boots, into their eyes. He didn't see Jane, he didn't see Mary . . . He saw Dorrie Mowat. He wondered if she watched him and laughed at him, wondered if she knew the love . . . God, and he had failed her.

They picked him up with rough hands under his armpits, and they dragged him on over the bridge, and he heard the beat sound of the music from among the pin lights of the village.

The sergeant came to her with his thermos of coffee. A good hour gone now since the sergeant had last tried to play the kind uncle, and get Ulrike on her way.

She took the coffee, thanked him.

She sipped the warmth of the coffee. The sergeant was defeated, knew it and did not seem to care. She was not moving. She was staying until the aid convoy came through. The convoy was eight hours late . . . She did not believe the sweet talk of the Liaison Officer who was long gone.

Sweet talk seldom convinced Ulrike Schmidt.

Sweet talk of happiness and friendship had lured her to the job with the organizing committee for her city's Olympic Games. Nineteen years old, waiting to go to university, taking the job of helping to get out the results for the swimming and the judo and the archery, joining the weeping girls with her own tears when the shadow stain of violence cut down the Israeli athletes.

Sweet talk of progress in ending human misery had trapped her into United Nations work, the university discarded, and service in Lebanon and Cambodia, becoming a part of the cynical company that realized nothing changed through their efforts, little was made better.

Sweet talk of love and marriage had brought her to the bed of an Australian army major in Phnom Penh, and there was the letter left casually on the dressing table of his quarters, and the photograph of the major's wife and four children in the drawer, under his uniform shirts.

Sweet talk in Geneva had told her that the refugees from Bosnia would be cleared through the Transit Centre inside four weeks because there were promises of resettlement from the governments of Europe. She dealt each day with hunger strikes, protests, trauma, because the governments lied.

Ulrike drained the beaker of coffee.

When the convoy came through then she would know, forget the sweet talk, that there was no alert up the broken road from Turanj, up beyond the machine-gun post, up behind the lines.

Silent prayer was not sweet talk.

He was the king, it was the court of Milan Stanković.

He was back from the liaison meeting, back from the cell block at the headquarters of the TDF unit of his village. He had survived Evica's carped complaint. In his home, coming sullen to his kitchen, and facing the barb of Evica. Would he get himself together, because now he was shit . . . Would he hike himself up, because now he was pathetic . . . Listened to Evica. Heard her call him shit, rubbish, pathetic. Held out his arms for her and she had come to him, closed his arms on her and their little Marko had clung to his legs and the dog had bounded happily against his back. He was the king, the chief man, and he had held the warmth of Evica against him and felt the warmth of his little Marko against his thigh and his hip . . . It was the Canadian policeman who was shit, and the Political Officer, and the liaison man from Karlovac.

He was amongst his own and was loved.

He could not be touched. He had kissed the eyes and ears and mouth of Evica, and the head of his little Marko. He was beyond their reach, those who were shit, pathetic, rubbish. The king danced. The music was heat around him. The chief man drank. The shouts were about him. It had been the strength of his Evica that had liberated him, and the spit of her tongue.

He danced and he drank as if the death shroud was taken from him.

The king danced with the queen. Space was made for them

247

in the centre of the hall of the school. There were shrill shouting faces around them, and the clapping of a hundred hands about them. She was so lovely, his queen, and dancing wild with him and her full skirt sweeping high on her thighs as he led her. The loveliest girl in the village, now the loveliest woman in Salika. As he danced, wild, the folk dance of the Serb people, so the hands of the men who acknowledged him as king reached out with glasses of brandy. As he danced, he drank. He felt he had found freedom. He was the power of his people, the glory of his village. Spinning with the dance, the skirt of Evica climbing, the music faster, the clapping louder, the brandy spilling from his lips, Milan knew he was the king.

Coming to the climax of the music and his feet were stamping and Evica's feet were gliding, and the clapping hammering in him. He was free . . . and when the music had climaxed, and when he had drunk again, then he would sing. He was the king . . .

They came through the door of the hall. They were dragging the man. They brought the man to him, through the parted crowd around him that had gone to silence. And the music died.

Milan stared down at the man who lay prone on the floor. He saw a man who was trussed at the wrists and ankles. The man was dressed in filthy wet fatigues, mud-smeared. The man gazed back up at him. The face of the man was blood-spattered. Branko was dropping onto the floor, noisy clatter, a heavy pistol and then four grenades, rolling loud. Milo was shaking out onto the boards of the floor a backpack, socks and underpants and a thick sweater and spare magazines for the pistol, and old bread, and an envelope of brown paper. Stevo threw the passport down onto the floor. The postman and the carpenter and the gravedigger smiled their pride. Around him were the people of the village, all watching him. He bent down. He looked at the passport. The passport was British, United Kingdom of Great Britain and Northern Ireland. He reached for the envelope. He stood and took a sheaf of photographs from the envelope. The man with the blood on his face gazed up at him. Evica was beside him . . .

Like a blow hitting him, Milan saw the face.

The face that he had known, and the knife wound.

The gasp of Evica beside him.

The face swollen in putrefaction, but with the bludgeon wound on the forehead.

The face that he recognized, and the bullet wound above the ear.

And they were all watching him because he was their king, and the fear twisted in him and could not be shown. The freedom was gone, the liberty was lost, and the brandy was beating in him. Trying to focus on the face on the floor and the face in the photographs. The face of the man on the floor gazing back at him, and the face of the woman in the photograph, and blood on the faces that merged. He unhooked the clasp knife from his belt, threw it to the carpenter. The twine at the ankles and at the wrists was cut . . . *she* had not been bound. Evica held the photographs and shivered. It was what was expected of the king. Branko and Stevo lifted the man up, and he stood in front of Milan and swayed. Milan should not show fear, not in front of those who admired and worshipped the king, and *she* had not shown fear . . .

A short arm blow, as hard as he could punch, he hit the stomach of the man.

The man staggered, went down, was on his knees.

The man stood again. Milan did not see the fear, and *she* had not shown fear . . .

He threw the man into the crowd around him, for their pleasure.

They were crawling into the village.

Benny reckoned they were going slowly because they had missed the turn. He reckoned they should have taken the left turn before they were into the village. He knew it was a Serb village because the roofs were on the houses and the church had a tower and what looked like the school wasn't a burned shell.

The convoy manager, Benny reckoned, had screwed up and was crawling because he knew it, and it was long odds against tiptoeing away when they had to turn round and back up, a Land-Rover and fifteen Seddon Atkinson lorries.

249

It was strange, Benny thought, that they could pitch up in this lost forgotten corner of pretend civilization and not have half a hundred people coming out the woodwork to know their business. Peculiar . . . The convoy manager, up ahead, had started the turn and back-up routine . . . It looked, dark quiet, a hell of a bad place to be lost, a hell of a good place to be shot of. The lorries were manoeuvring, like leviathans, and at present no bugger with an AK's safety off and armed coming out of the houses to ask their business.

Benny waited his turn to manoeuvre.

Penn heard, just, the shout. The shout was an order.

The last of the kicks went into him, into the small of his back, and the last of the women's nails clawed at his face, and the last of the punches went to his unprotected stomach.

The pain ran rivers in his body. The shout was a command. He tried, hard, to keep his eyes open because that seemed important. He lay on the floor and the boards were wet with his blood and his spittle and his urine. Six would have done courses on Resistance to Interrogation, Five didn't . . . any rate, not for his level of A Branch non-graduate. In a circle around him were the heavy laced shoes of the men and the light slide-on shoes of the women and on some of the shoes were dulled stains . . . not a course for his level of A Branch non-graduate, but maybe for the top grade, super *fucking* experts who went to Belfast. It was a hallucination for Penn, kicked, clawed, punched, to be thinking of courses for Resistance to Interrogation for top-graders who went to Belfast, but the hallucination swamped him . . . There was a woman in Gower Street and he'd been down a queue for the coffee machines when she'd been at the head, she'd been pointed to and he'd been told that the Provos had trapped her in some God-awful pub, no back-up present, and she'd fought her way out, just a slip of a woman with rusted gold hair and a flat chest and rounded shoulders, who had taken her coffee and walked slowly back to her office like she was a bored woman, not a top-grader . . .

The big man, the voice of command, the one who had swayed when he had seen the photograph, the one who had hit him first, broke the cordon circle. The big man came towering towards him.

Penn blinked up and tried to retain the focus of his vision . . . couldn't break the hallucination. There were two women in his mind. Both top-graders . . . The woman with the rust-gold hair, bored in London, in the coffee queue, who had the courage to fight clear of a killer enemy . . . and the woman with the cropped hair, the mischief smile in her photograph, who had the courage to bury her fear when the killer enemy closed. He was so wanting to be brave. Bravery might just be survival, or it might just be dignity, or it might just make the *fucking* knife and the *fucking* bludgeon and the *fucking* pistol shot *fucking* easier . . . The hallucination rode him. Talking in the open-plan office area of A Branch, chattering idly about the hostages in Lebanon, and the big mouth, graduate 2.2 Reading, claiming that he would have gone for escape; and the simpering mouth, graduate 2.1 Warwick, whining that she would have gone for a runner; and Penn, non-graduate, trying to contribute quietly that an escape attempt took more courage than anything, and being ignored . . . and just the idle chatter of a hallucination in a quiet hour of a London office because *fucking* escape was not on the reality agenda . . . The big man pulled him up.

The big man had a loose beard grown free across his face, not trimmed. Between the matt of the beard growth, the tongue of the big man wiped his full lips. Above the growth of the beard were the eyes, evasive. The face, the eyes and the mouth, as Penn saw it, were empty of passion.

The woman beside the big man held the photographs outside the envelope, as if she did not wish again to look at them. She wore a bright full skirt, flower-patterned, and an ironed white blouse that was simple, and there were sweat streaks in her hair at her forehead.

Penn stood and hoped that he would find the courage.

The question was put to him. The woman interpreted the question.

'Who are you?'

Trying to speak strongly. 'I am William Penn. I am a British citizen.'

The answer was repeated by the woman to the big man. A second question. 'Are you a mercenary from the Ustaše scum?'

Trying to stare into those evasive eyes . . . 'I have no connection with the Croatian army.'

'A lie. You wear the uniform of the Ustaše scum.'

'I bought the camouflage uniform on the black market in Karlovac.'

The big man made the question. The woman interpreted the question. She spoke formal taught English. 'What was the mission?'

Penn heard it, the revving of heavy engines behind him. No one moved around him. They hung silently on the questions put by the big man and the answers given by the woman beside him. Could not know where it would lead him, where it would take him, but knew the importance of bold talk . . .

'The village of Rosenovici, across the stream, was taken in December of 1991. There were wounded men in the village who were sheltered in a cellar during the final attack on the village . . .'

'What has that to do with a mercenary?'

'. . . The wounded men were taken from the cellar after the fall of the village. They were taken to a field, they were sat in the field, laid out in the field, while a bulldozer dug . . .'

The interruption. The woman had translated in a quiet voice while he talked, and the circle craned for her words.

'What has that to do with . . . ?'

'. . . While a bulldozer dug a grave pit. The wounded men were then killed with knives, and were bludgeoned, and were shot, and they were buried . . .'

'What has that . . . ?'

'. . . They were buried in a mass grave in the corner of the field . . .'

'What . . . ?'

'. . . Buried in the mass grave in the corner of the field was a young woman. The young woman was not wounded in the battle for the village. She had chosen to stay with the wounded. She had chosen to be with them at the end. She was not a fighter, she had no guilt. She was butchered in the pit dug by the bulldozer . . .'

'Why was she important . . . ?'

Staring all the time into the face of the big man, and the eyes above the matt of the beard darting away, and the tongue in the midst of the beard sliding on dried lips.

'. . . She was English, and that is why I came. She was not Serbian and not Croatian and not Muslim. She was not a part of the quarrel. She was English and her name was Dorrie . . .'

Staring into the face, and hearing the drip of the translation. He had spoken the name and there was a little gasp and a small murmur in the circle around him. He was trying to hold the pain and the tremble, trying to ape the mischief moments of Dorrie Mowat.

'. . . Her name was Dorrie Mowat, and there was no cause for her killing. It was cowards' work killing Dorrie Mowat.'

'Who sent you?'

'I was sent by the mother of Dorrie Mowat. I came to find how Dorrie Mowat died. I came so that I could tell her mother how she died, in a pit. And I came so that I could tell her mother who killed her, the name of the man, the man who was responsible . . .'

Penn felt the moment of power. He heard the engines of big vehicles away behind the door. No one moved in the circle around him. He didn't know where it would lead, couldn't know . . .

'Who knew her? Who knew Dorrie Mowat?'

He heard the echoing ring of his voice. The woman interpreted.

'Who met her when she lived in Rosenovici before the fight, before she was butchered?'

He turned from the shifting eyes, from the licked lips. It was all a fraud.

'Did you know her . . . ?'

It was a fraud because it was pretence that he held the high ground, when he held *fucking* nothing . . . He searched the faces. An old man, a young man, a teenage girl . . . It was a sham act.

'You, did you know her . . . ?'

253

He searched the faces, challenged them, and they would not meet him. He ranged over the faces of the circle.

'Who met her . . . ?'

He reached the woman who held the photographs, who interpreted the questions and answers. She dropped her head.

'I met her.'

Penn whispered, 'Why did you meet her?'

'I met her so that I could talk English with her. I met her before the fight for the village so that I could better my language of English.'

Penn said, 'I came so that I could tell Dorrie's mother the name of the man who killed her daughter, so that she would know the name of that man. I came to prepare a report for Dorrie's mother, I came to find the evidence against that man . . .'

He saw the fingers of the woman twisting on the photographs, tearing them and she did not notice.

'What was the name?'

The wall around him was of shame. He had won his dignity, as Dorrie had claimed hers. He had stamped his death warrant, and *fuck* them. The circle about him was of guilt. She would be laughing at him, laughing loud, from her mischief face. Dignity was won . . . Somewhere he heard the roar of lorry engines pulling away . . . *Fuck* them, because they couldn't hurt him, if he had his dignity, they could only kill him. It was Penn's moment. It was, to him, as if he were alone with the big man facing him. It was as if all else was suppressed, as if each other person in the circle held no importance. It was a handsome face, a leader's strong, good face.

'I have the evidence for my report that Dorrie Mowat was killed by . . .'

Penn heard the voice of the woman who interpreted.

'. . . Was murdered by Milan Stanković.'

And in front of him the face flushed in anger, and the fists caught at him.

Penn shouted, 'His name is Milan Stanković.'

Men around him, the circle broken, hands grabbing him. He saw the face the last time, the anger flush in the matt of the beard, and the woman who had interpreted was sobbing. He kicked and he struggled, and he was forced towards the door of the hall. He had his *fucking* dignity. He bit at the hands that held him. His *fucking* dignity, what Dorrie had had. He writhed with them as they pushed him through the door, into the night.

The lorry in the line was starting to roll. The line of the lorry lights speared the darkness of the village and the lorry was in front of him, beginning to move. The opening of the door of the hall flushed the inside light onto the Union flag on the lorry's door. Only two men were able to hold him as they came through the tight space of the doorway.

Penn saw the small round startled face.

He bit the hand on his arm. He elbowed into a stomach.

It was his chance.

He broke free. There was black darkness beyond the lorry.

Penn yelled, 'Kill your lights.'

The one chance only.

The lights died. Night darkness around him. He ran.

The darkness was his friend.

He threw himself under the moving wheels of the lorry, and rolled.

He didn't know what the hell happened, but he had killed the lights. Just the glow of the dashboard in the cab and the fluorescent buttons of his radio. He was nudging the lorry forward. The far door of the cab came open and there was a quick blast of night air. There were hands groping by his shins and ankles, and something, Benny didn't know what, was thrown from the cab floor. It hit the wooden fence across the road, clattered in the dark. There was weight across his legs and panting, wriggling movement. Something else, Benny didn't know what, was thrown from the door of the cab, and that seemed to go further and it hit glass across the width of the road, perhaps a greenhouse, perhaps a cold frame. The door closed quietly on the cab, and the weight came over him and prised into the gap behind his seat and the passenger seat. There were men running round the Seddy, going across the road towards where something had hit the wooden fence, and something else had smashed a glass surface. There was shooting, he could see the gun flashes in the big side mirror of the Seddy, could see the fireflies of the bullets going towards the fence and where the glass pane had been broken . . . and all the lorries were hammering it now, because of the shooting.

The lorries swerved, each in their turn, for the road they should have taken.

Benny was cool.

He didn't favour panic.

The radio in his cab was a jabber of voices, all calling for the convoy to get the hell out, get the distance in. There was the sharp panted breathing behind him, and Benny realized the man stank. He was in cruise gear and they were doing good speed, and the village was behind him, and the sound of shooting was fading. He was cool, no panic, and he could think well. Benny reckoned it to be about, give or take a bit, twenty-five minutes to the crossing point at Turanj . . . and he was in deep shit, deepest without a bloody bottom. Because the first rule, aid convoy driving, is don't get *involved*, but the yell had been English. The second rule is not to take *sides*, but the shout had been English and desperate. All the rules, up to one hundred and one bloody rules, said the aid convoy system went through the window if the drivers weren't, all the way, *impartial*, but the cry of 'Kill the lights' had been English. What he had done was get involved, take sides. And what he'd done, when they hit the crossing point at Turanj . . . if back in that black village they'd gotten their act together, raised the radio, lifted the telephone, sent a fast bloody pigeon . . . what he'd done was to hazard the whole of the aid convoy programme. People survived because the aid convoys went through without getting involved. People would starve if the aid convoys were banned because the drivers had taken sides. People depended on the aid convoys crossing the lines, impartial . . . Perhaps, Benny thought, before they were at the crossing point at Turanj, he'd just chuck him out, push him clear.

In the convoy queue, spearing the night with its lights, the Seddy hammered forward, going sweet.

256

Benny unhooked the pencil torch from the dashboard clip. He shone the light around his feet.

'Now then, my old cocker, you have just lost me my sandwich box, that my Becky gave me – and you have just lost me my fire extinguisher, and I am not allowed to drive without a fire extinguisher in the cab – and I'm thinking you should do the decent thing and, please, close the door after you . . .'

Benny shone the torch behind him, into the gap behind his seat and the passenger seat. He turned to look fast behind him. In the narrow beam, Benny saw the blood on the face and the cuts and the bruises. Back to the road. He thought he had seen the face of a man who was softened for death. He twisted again. Benny saw the stubble growth that dammed the blood, and the eyes that squinted between the puffed bruising, and the swollen split lips. He dragged down the switch of his torch, and again the cab was in darkness.

'You are, my old cocker, a heap of trouble . . .'

14

When the big torches came and the guns, they would have him against the stream.

Milan shouted orders among the babble of the men of the village. 'Make a line . . . Search everything, coal sheds, tool sheds, the barns . . . Search your houses . . . Keep the line . . .'

The men of the village stood in line as they had been told to, waiting for the big torches and the guns to be brought. Between shouting the orders, his eyes flicked down to his watch. Milan stood on the steps of the school building and behind him were the two swing doors into the hall. They had only their small torches, sufficient to light a way from their homes to the hall for the social evening, and they had no rifles until the firearms were brought from the locked armoury of the headquarters building . . . Five clear minutes lost . . . Five minutes lost since Branko had pushed his way back into the hall, licking at his wrist that was bitten, and Milo had followed him with his hands held across his groin. Five minutes lost since they had blurted that the bastard had gone . . . and been heard to crash through Petar's fence, and been heard to run into the greenhouse where Dragon brought on his spring lettuces. He had not seen it for himself and he must take their word on trust . . . Behind Petar's fence and Dragon's greenhouse was wire and then sodden fields, and then the stream. That was where they would get him, the bastard, when he came to the stream. The first orders he had given with his barely suppressed fury had been that they should run, shit quick, to the bridge, alert the bridge guards and get themselves across the fields on the far side of the stream. They alone had guns and a torch. They'd gone fast, scuttling in their goddamn shame. Five minutes lost and men were running back to the school steps with their torches, and Vuk was panting his way back from the armoury at the headquarters with an armful of rifles, with his pockets bulged by the magazines.

The line was formed.

It was a muddled story, it was something about the bastard breaking clear, and rolling under the lorry, and then going through Petar's fence, and then breaking Dragon's greenhouse . . . Where was the goddamn lorry? But Milan had to move the line. The torches caught at Petar's fence, and the broken glass of Dragon's greenhouse. There was the clatter in the line of rifles being loaded and cocked.

He glanced again at his watch. They should be in position now on the far side of the stream, and they would be raking the bank with their flashlights. They would drive the bastard to the bank . . . He gave the order for the line to move . . . and the minutes were crawling and lost.

Milan heard the curses from the line. The men wore their best trousers, and their best shoes, and their best sweaters or jackets. The women in their best dresses were streaming from the doorway behind him, and they carried away on plates the bread that had been baked for the evening and the fruit and the cheeses that had been taken earlier to the hall. It had been an attempt by his trapped village to throw off the mood, his own mood and everybody's, of being held prisoner, and the *bastard* had destroyed the attempt. He searched the faces of the women who carried the food home, because they had all heard his name given, and all heard the name of Dorrie Mowat, and the bastard had used the word that was *coward*. He searched the faces, and none met his, and the minutes on his watch were frittering away.

Evica was beside him, carrying in a linen cloth the food she had brought for the evening.

'Do you have him?'

The excitement of the chase, of being the king who gave the orders, slipped in him. 'No.'

Evica said, simply, 'I could not help myself, when he looked at me, when he asked who had met her. He was so . . . so *bold*.

I could not help myself when he faced me . . . What does it mean, the man coming to make a report . . . ?'

There was a shout. He did not answer her. Milan ran across the road. At the side fence in Petar's garden he was shown the plastic box. There was a single bread roll in the box, with squashed tomato and pressed cheese in the cut in the roll and half a bar of chocolate. He felt his nerves squirm in his belly. Another shout. The torches showed him the way. He climbed the fence between Petar's plot and Dragon's garden. Milan saw the broken glass pane on the roof of Dragon's greenhouse, and more torches shone inside the greenhouse. On the trays of spring lettuces was the fire extinguisher amongst the plants and the shards . . . It had been gone, it had been buried, and some nights he could even forget it, and the bastard had come to bring back for him the face of the young woman . . . He was shouting. Who saw the lorry? Was it just one lorry? What colour were the lorries? Which way did the lorries go, towards Glina or towards Vrginmost? The minutes slipping on his watch. Were the white lorries from a convoy of the United Nations?

Milan Stanković ran.

He ran like the athlete he had once been.

He ran for his life, and for the *bastard*'s life.

Hoarse, chest heaving, Milan scrambled into the office area of the headquarters.

The minutes slipping.

'. . . They all bad-mouthed her back in England. She was just a *horrid* young woman. There seemed to be a story about her for every year of her life, the stories seemed to queue up to foul-mouth her. Her mum told the stories worst, like it was something she had to get release from. The way of the release was to find out what happened to her. There was no release until her mother knew what happened to her, who killed her. They were throwing money at it because they'd cash coming out of their ears. "Just go there, Mr Penn, and write a bloody report, and then we can forget little Miss Dorrie who was an awkward bitch", it was something like that . . .'

Benny listened. Sometimes the voice behind him stopped,

when the radio came on, when the convoy manager had some crap to tell them from up front. He drove carefully, and the whole of the convoy was going fast.

'. . . And I came here, and it was all lies that had been said about her. Perhaps, at home, she had just been a bloody nuisance, perhaps she was just a bloody cuckoo child in a second marriage, perhaps she just got in the way, perhaps she didn't start to live until she was at Rosenovici . . . I came here to pocket the money and write a report, good bromide stuff, a few names and a few quotes, good money. You know how it is, Mr Stein, when you're sucked into something, it's like you're being pulled towards a cliff. Why did this one killing in one village matter? Can't answer it . . . Best I can do, it's something about that young woman. I learned about her, each time I was told about her then I was pushed closer to that bloody cliff . . .'

Grabbing for the telephone, whirring the handle of the field set that linked to the Glina military, hearing the deathly response of silence . . . Milan pushed it aside so that it fell useless to the concrete floor. He turned to the radio set that was the back-up, that sometimes functioned.

When they had powered out of that God-awful village then the cab radios had gone apeshit. Each driver, and the convoy manager, wanting to know what the fuck was going on, what was the shooting. Benny hadn't given them a laugh, hadn't given them anything until right at the end of the exchanges. He'd waited to the end, then pressed his 'speak' switch, and he just said he'd seen nothing, because they'd have kicked him half to death if they'd known.

Benny listened.

'. . . She was just brilliant. I don't think I'm just some mooning bloody sheep. She was incredible. It wasn't just that she stayed with the wounded because she loved one boy. You see, Mr Stein, Dorrie could have carried out one boy. She was a tough little thing, made of barbed wire. She could have put one boy on her shoulder and she would have stood a good to middle chance of hiking him into the woods and finding a hole in their lines, but that would have been walking out on the other boys. She was just brilliant because she gave all of them her courage. I was dragged to that cliff, dragged over that cliff . . . I looked him in the face, I looked into the face of the man who used a knife on her, the man who shot her. It was like she'd given me the courage, like she was with me, to look into his face and not be afraid . . . I don't suppose that makes much sense, Mr Stein.'

Benny said, 'I was going to chuck you out.'

'Because the shit's in the fan, because they'll be waiting at the crossing point . . . ?'

'Because I'm not supposed to get involved.'

'I reckon if I laid up for a couple of days, rested, then I reckon I could swim the river . . .'

'Like hell you could,' Benny snapped, short.

'There's a rendezvous tomorrow night, where there's going to be a boat, but I'm off line for the pick-up, I don't have a map for the location, but I reckon I could swim the river . . .'

He hadn't used his pencil torch from the dashboard, not since right at the beginning. From what Benny had seen, when he'd used the torch, the guy wouldn't make it to halfway, not against the current of the Kupa river. The rest of the drivers would kill him if they knew.

'You won't be swimming. You'll be staying bloody put . . . we'll see what's there, at the crossing point . . .'

It was so slow for Milan to make the radio link with Glina militia. The man who knew the radio was away back at the greenhouse in Dragon's garden, and the procedure for transmission was written up in scrawl on the wall above the set.

And an imbecile at the other end when he had made the contact.

'. . . And it's a spy you lost? In Salika village, you lost a spy? What would a spy want with Salika village? A *foreign* spy . . . ?'

A bored man, sitting the night watch on the radio in the Glina barracks, nursing a bottle, and at last there was amusement for him.

'A foreign spy has come to Salika village, that centre of military secrecy? Should they know in Belgrade that a foreign spy chose to visit Salika village . . . ?'

Losing the minutes. Could not tell a bored man sitting the night watch on the radio at Glina barracks about a grave, about an investigator with evidence, about a young woman who had not shown fear.

Milan shouted, 'If the crossing point is not closed, if the convoy is not searched, I will come for you, my friend, and I will flay the skin off your face . . .'

When the alarm clamoured for the Close Support platoon, Ham was on his bed in the dormitory quarters, and reading his best magazine. His mother sent it him, not often because most times the old cow forgot. Nagorno Karabakh, wherever the fuck it was, seemed the right place, and there were guys already there, but then there was also an article with photographs of guys who had made it down to Tbilisi, wherever the fuck that was . . . The alarm shifted him.

He was snatching webbing kit, going for the Dragunov marksman's rifle that was his personal weapon when Close Support platoon was on 'immediate', buttoning the flies on his camouflage trousers, running for the stairs of the old police station.

And no fucker in the lit yard taking the trouble to explain to him why the alarm had gone. He heard, among the bloody yelling, there was heavy radio traffic on the other side, there was a guy running on the other side, there was some sort of flap at the crossing point, something about a bloody convoy . . . It was all to do with their radio traffic, on the other side.

He was in the lead jeep going down sharp to Turanj. He thought about Penn, crazy guy.

They were slowing.

The convoy manager was saying, distorted, in the cab, 'I'm hooked into their radio. There's a problem, but I can't make sense of what it is, probably just that we're so delayed . . . They're saying they need to search the lorries. You know the form, guys, that we are not supposed to allow UN vehicles to be searched . . .'

He lay behind Benny Stein's seat and the passenger seat. He had a rug that covered some of his body. He heard the sharp whistle of Benny Stein's breath and heard him mutter an obscenity.

Going down through the gears, crawling.

The voice was saying, 'What I'm thinking, guys, is that the laws of the game might just get bent a bit. If the choice is between bending or sitting here for the rest of the night high on principle, and since we've not any *loose* women from Knin on board . . . OK, guys?'

Penn said, 'I'll do a runner, which door?'

The answer was very quiet, so calm. 'What I'm seeing on my side is a big jerk with an ugly machine gun. And on the other side, three jerks with rifles, and what I'm seeing further up front doesn't get better.'

Penn said, 'I'm sorry, I mean that.'

'Bit late, my old cocker . . . They've stopped ahead. We're all closing up.'

So helpless. It had all been for nothing. For nothing he had found the Headmaster praying in a grave. They were inching forward. For nothing he had found Katica Dubelj, eyewitness. He waited for the grinding of the brakes. For nothing he had found Milan Stanković, war criminal.

'What are you going to do?'

'They're opening up the cabs ahead, my top cat's letting them in. You know what Oscar Wilde said? He said, "In matters of grave importance, style, not sincerity, is the vital thing." Give it a go.'

Penn was looking into Benny Stein's face, and it was calm as if he was taking the kids out for a Sunday afternoon ride. Going very slow, and swinging the big wheel so that the lorry went out of the line that was pulling up, then straightening the wheel. Penn saw the hands go to the gear lever, then to the ignition, and the engine slurped to quiet. A silence around Penn, and the gentle rocking of the cab going forward. The pace of the lorry quickened. Benny Stein was winding down his door window.

'Time to see if old Oscar had it right . . .'

They were rolling faster. Penn heard the first yell, and Benny

Stein had his head out of his door window and was howling it into the night. The brakes . . . The brakes gone . . . No control because the goddamn brakes had gone. Going down the incline through Turanj. Penn saw the white sides of the freight lorries slipping by, quicker. All the time Benny Stein was yelling that his brakes had gone, and waving every miserable mother out of the road. Going by the Land-Rover, and Benny Stein was turning, side of his mouth, muttering about 'Shit or bust', saying they'd shoot or they'd laugh. They hit the checkpoint. The cab of the lorry clipped the corner of the sandbag wall. He had his head down and he had his hands over his head, and he would have said, and reckoned he'd not lied, that Benny Stein had twisted the wheel the necessary fraction to take out the corner of the sandbags. The cab lurched, and Penn bounced, and he thought there was a popping of tyres, as if there had been a chain with spikes on the road. They were waiting for the shooting, or the laughing. They went clean through the UN barrier, broke the pole across the road. And the cab pitched worse, and he felt the tyres shredding, and all the time Benny Stein was yelling himself hoarse that the brakes had gone. The lorry jerked and he saw the wall loom against the cab's passenger side window, and that slowed it, and Penn saw Benny Stein's hand furtively slip to the brake handle, and he saw his foot pump the brake pedal, but gently so that the ripped tyres did not scream. They came to rest.

Penn croaked, 'That, Mr Stein, was style . . .'

'Get out. You told a good story.'

'I said that I was sorry . . .'

'It was because you talked a good story. Get lost.'

Benny Stein's hand, fleshy, reached and caught at Penn's collar, and he was dragged through the gap between the seats, and shoved out of the open door.

He lay in the road beside the ribboned front tyre. The door above him was scraped. The fender in front of him was dented deep.

'Thank you,' Penn called back up at the slammed door of the cab.

He crawled to the side of the road, to the heaped rubble of a collapsed house. Benny had jumped down from the cab and was striding towards the broken pole of the United Nations block, and the wrecked sandbags of the Serb block. So tired, and all the pain was back with him. He looked past the soldiers, and the woman was running with flapping legs, towards him. She came across the road from where she had been standing beside a car. He saw in the lights of the crossing point her concern, and Ham had broken clear of the group of soldiers and was ambling towards him. There was shouting back up the hill, and he heard Benny's voice, loud. They all danced for Dorrie . . . He danced for her, and Ulrike Schmidt who gazed into his face, and Ham who walked towards him with a wide smile, and Benny Stein who was yelling hard about the failure of his brakes . . . She had touched them and they danced for her.

'You're a fucking mess, squire. How was it?'

And if Ulrike had not had hold of his arm, and if Ham had not taken him under the armpit, he would have gone down.

Evica said, 'So, he could be this side of the line, or he could have gone . . . ?'

Milan lay fully dressed, still in his suit, on the top blanket of the bed.

Evica pressed, '. . . So, he could have been in the lorry that crashed the checkpoint?'

The dirt of his suit, and his shoes, would be on the top blanket. Milan said, empty, 'I don't know.'

Evica held his hand, and on the hand was the mud of Petar's garden and Dragon's garden. 'What will happen to us, if he went through the line?'

All that he had, all that he leaned on, was the wife beside him and the child sleeping in the next room. Milan said, 'What I was told was that one day they will come for me . . . In a month, in a year, when I am old, one day. Perhaps their children will come for our child, one day . . . We have to wait, for the day they come.'

'Because we cannot run . . . ?'

'Cannot run anywhere. Because of what has happened, of course I have known there will be revenge one day. But it was vague, just in my head. But it was said to me direct, at the liaison meeting, and you know his wife, and he said that one day, direct, if it were not him that came for me then it would be his son that would come for our Marko. It would go on for ever, as long as the memory lives of what was done. Like a curse on us, and on Marko. Maybe I did not believe him, and then the Englishman came, and I was named. It had been a safe world before the Englishman came. We on our side of the line, they on theirs. They could not come across the line and reach us. They could sit in Karlovac town, they could say what the shit they wanted, but they could not touch me, and then the Englishman came to us, to me . . . I believe him, the Liaison. I believe now that they will come for me one day, or that his son will come for our Marko. If I had known I would not have . . .'

'Not have killed her, but then you thought you were safe.'

'Not have killed the girl.'

Evica said, 'He made me remember her. Two afternoons and I remember them, when she came to our shop for food because their own shop had nothing. It was three weeks before the fight . . . It was after the children had gone home . . .'

'You told me.'

'. . . And she sat in my room at the school, and we talked in English. I told her there would be no fighting between our village and her village, I told her there was no quarrel between us. She spoke of her home, and her mother, what her home was like and what her mother did . . .'

'We cannot run and we cannot hide.'

Through the gap of the curtains, Evica saw the first light of the new day.

She said, sad, 'We have to live. We have to wait, as she waited in the field, but we have to live . . .'

Soft, gentle fingers moving on the wounds . . . A woman's fingers, and tender . . . He was in the cellar, and there was only the light of a small tallow candle . . . He was the wounded, and the face of the young woman was above him, and her fingers dabbed, sweet, at the wounds with sharp iodine and salted water . . . She touched him and she had no fear . . . He loved her,

267

the young woman who cared for the wounded in the cellar . . .

Penn stirred, his eyes flickered. The fingers with the cotton wool were close to his eyes . . . God, and his face hurt. It was a woman's room, bright and alive, and the candle in the cellar was gone, and there were flowers on a table across the room from the bed.

Ham sat on the floor, his back against a neat chest, and he held the long-barrelled rifle across his knees.

Ulrike flashed her smile, nervous and short, embarrassed, and she was pushing up from beside the bed, as if she had been kneeling close to him as she had cleaned his face wounds and sterilized them.

Ham said, 'You cut it fine, squire . . . You got through before they'd organized. Their communications are piss-awful, you wouldn't have got through half an hour later . . . That driver did you well, there's not another fucker other than me and the lady knows you were up aboard . . . How much did you drop the driver, squire?'

Penn said, 'I told him why I'd gone.'

He said that he wanted to go back to Zagreb, make his report, and buy the biggest bottle of Scotch in the city, and they said that they'd share it.

It was morning.

They helped him to dress, Ulrike carefully and Ham roughly, and the pain of the kicks and the punches had stiffened to each corner of his body. He thought he would always remember, long after he had written the report and drunk the Scotch, the image of a cellar and wounded men, and a young woman without fear.

He went hunting trouble first thing.

Marty had talked it through with the doctor from Vukovar, his landlord, and the doctor had steeled him to it. He had talked it through because the long-distance telephone call had woken them both in the apartment, and half the night they had sat over coffee, and the doctor had toughened him to it.

It was raining soft, like it did in the spring in Anchorage when the snow melted, as Marty strode across the central grass towards the steps and doors of A block. He had gone hunting trouble before opening up the converted freight container. There would need to have been a GI provost on the door of the suite of the Director of Civilian Affairs to have stopped him. The goddamn phone call, in the bad half of the night, hadn't been from Geneva, but goddamn New York. Marty went past the secretaries to the door and didn't knock, he went on in.

They were round the Director's desk. Marty saw on the sleeves of their uniforms the insignia of Canada and Jordan and Argentina. They had a big map over the desk, and the Director was with them and looking at the map's detail through a magnifying glass, and a cigarette hung from his lips. And they turned, the soldiers and the Director, in annoyed surprise.

He hammered, 'I just wanted to say that I am not prepared to be treated like crap any more. And I just wanted to say that I find it incredible that one United Nations agency is active in blocking the work of another United Nations programme. I find it shameful that you have gone behind my back to sabotage my work . . .'

'What the feck are you talking about?'

'I am talking about getting pitched out of my cot in the goddamn middle of the night by New York, to tell me that my work is causing *offence*, my work is a *nuisance*. I will not tolerate that goddamn crap . . . I will not tolerate you crawling behind my back to get New York to order me to cool it. Are you with me?'

'If you go now you can go down the stairs on your feet . . . If you wait one minute, you'll go down the stairs on your face.'

'Because I am inconvenient . . . ?'

'Because . . . listen to me, you silly young man, listen hard . . . There were refugees supposed to be coming through Turanj crossing point today, but the crossing point is closed. There was an aid convoy supposed to be going through Turanj today, but its passage has been cancelled . . .'

'That's not my problem. My work is to prepare war crimes . . .'

'*Listen* . . . I'll tell you my problem. They have a maximum alert along their line, they are leaping about like they've pokers up their arses. Our movement is quite restricted. Why . . . ?

There is some garbled story about a war crimes investigator, captured and escaped . . .'

'I know nothing . . .'

'Too fecking right . . . I doubt you know the length of your dick. My job is to keep our access into Sector North. And all this is after I suggested to New York that I could do without a wet-behind-the-ears puppy giving me shit from the high moral ground.'

'Where?'

'Glina Municipality . . .'

Marty looked at the map, where the magnifying glass rested. 'Where?'

'The rumour is he was picked up in Rosenovici . . .'

He swayed. He felt the cold on him. He remembered what he had seen, the man in the Transit Centre, the man with Ulrike. He remembered the lecture he had given, goddamn patronizing, and the answer, 'I've just a report to write, then I'm gone.' He remembered the Bosnian Muslim woman that the man had talked to, and she had been in Rosenovici. He rocked.

'It's just a rumour . . . I am a busy man. Do you wish to leave on your feet or on your face?'

Marty had no more anger. He let himself out, quietly.

It was the irregulars, from Glina town, who interrogated the Headmaster.

They were the men of Arkan, who was Zeljko Raznjatović, and they called themselves the Tigers, and they were men freed from gaol cells in Belgrade. They had come at first light from Glina, and they had taken control of the headquarters building in Salika. They had come to the village because he was known to them, because Milan had once posed for a photograph in front of the War Memorial with their leader, Arkan . . . it was as if his only function that morning was to make them coffee. They had taken his room and his radio and his desk, and they stubbed out their cigarettes against the bared stomach of the Headmaster. The screaming rang in Milan's ears. It was the agonized screaming of the man who had taught him at school, of the man who had been Evica's friend. With the cigarettes, crushed and stubbed out,

Milan heard of the Englishman's journey of discovery, and of Katica Dubelj who was the journey's guide. After the screaming and the telling, the irregulars of Arkan took the Headmaster from the cell of the headquarters and out into the road that cut the village. They wore plain belted one-piece uniforms of grey-green, and when they came out into the road they had put black hoods over their faces so that only their mouths and their eyes were visible. Out in the road they did not need Milan to bring them coffee, so they sent him from house to house in the village to get the people to come and watch, and he did as he was ordered, until there was a small crowd in front of the Headmaster's home. He could not face his own people, nor could he face the Headmaster who was made to stand in front of the door of his home, nor could he face the weeping wife of the Headmaster who was held back by the irregulars. They shot him first in the legs, and then in the stomach, so that death would be slow.

When the Headmaster died, the men of the village and Milan, led by the irregulars, were climbing the track in the woods, going where the Headmaster had told them they should go.

Ulrike drove the car, and Ham talked all the way. Ham talked his bullshit, of battles and fire fights, and Ulrike drove and said nothing, and Penn lay across the back seat of the car.

He was leaving behind him Dorrie's place. He was quitting Dorrie's war.

The bootprint was sharp in the mud of the track, and the man had worn military boots when he had been brought to the school.

They had the clear tread of the boot to tell them that the Headmaster had not lied when the cigarettes had been stubbed out against his stomach, and the evidence quickened their pace up the track through the trees. There was a light rain falling in the trees and heavy cloud coming from beyond the hill, and Milan could see the rain, later, would be heavier. He was at the head of the column and walked immediately in front of the leader of the irregulars. His own people were behind him and he could not see their faces and he did not know what their enthusiasm for the work was. It was where the Headmaster had said it would be, the cave entrance between the two large rocks, and in the worn mud close to the entrance was the bootprint squashed over the lighter traces. Milan could smell her . . . There were many torches crowded into the narrow cleft of the cave's entrance, and the beams caught her. There was laughter behind Milan. The torches found her cringing back at the far wall of the cave, like a trapped rat. There was more laughter behind Milan. Milan turned. He called forward Milo who had the scratches on the cheeks of his face, and he gestured forward Stevo who had the bruised privates. There were many pressing behind him to see the trapped rat that was Katica Dubelj who had fed him and most of them with their lunches at the school . . . She was the trapped rat and her mouth seemed to snarl at the torch lights, and she had no teeth, and she was the *evidence*. He knew that the man had not been found, and he knew that a lorry with failed brakes had crashed the checkpoint at Turanj, and he knew that his name was on a file in Karlovac, and on another file made by the Political Officer at Topusko, and the trapped rat was the eyewitness. He wondered if he would tell Evica . . .

The hand of the leader of the irregulars was on his shoulder, pushing him into the cave.

'You're not telling me, in honesty, that you wrote it up . . . ?'

'Of course I wrote it up, Arnold, I wrote up what you told me.'

'Georgie, it was in confidence . . .'

Georgie Simpson didn't like to face him. Not that he would have described Arnold Browne as a friend, not really possible for Six men to be friends with Five men, but he was almost fond of the man. They had nothing in common, not hobbies, not holidays, not career paths, but he had come rather to enjoy their weekly session and weekly lunch. That would all be behind them now, the sessions and the lunches, there would be different men given the job and few enough confidences exchanged then . . . He didn't like to face him because Arnold Browne made no attempt to hide his quite positive anguish.

'I'm not proud, and I'm not a happy man. I put a memorandum in, I reported our conversation . . . This morning, Arnold, and I might face a firing squad for telling you, this morning I was summoned on high. I was instructed to telephone you, arrange an extraordinary meeting, I was to pump you, Arnold. You said your man was "dogged" . . .'

'You reported my confidences back, you should know what I said.'

Georgie Simpson ignored the sarcasm, no citations to be won here, best ignored. 'You said your man would go to the end of the road . . . We have a listening post at Zagreb airport. We monitor Serb radio traffic principally. We have 2,500 troops in Bosnia, we have to know what's planned. Please don't interrupt me, Arnold, please don't. The radios are monitored twenty-four hours, but obviously we're not wasting our time interpreting whether General Mladić wants express delivery of new loo paper, soft tissue. We have trigger words. When a trigger word comes up then the transmission gets classified Immediate for analysis. Obviously their tongue-twisted version of "British" is a trigger. It's been pretty shambolic transmission, but we picked up "British spy" and "British investigator", captured then escaped, and the transmission was coming out of a village called Salika, and there was a name . . . What I'm telling you, Arnold, in confidence, is that Salika is adjacent to Rosenovici, and the name of the spy, investigator, is Penn . . .'

He thought he might have smacked poor Arnold Browne across the bridge of the nose, to make his eyes water.

'What are you going to do?'

'Your people are out of their depth, Arnold. They are meddling in matters beyond their remit . . . Our station officer, Zagreb, if your *dogged* Mr Penn gets safe back to base, will pick him up by the scruff of his neck and throw him on the first plane to Heathrow. And your lovely lady will be told by my hairy-arsed director to cease interfering. Your Penn is a busted flush, I'm afraid, and we'll be taking his legs off at the knees . . . Sorry, Arnold, but it's a sharp game, ours, and that's the way it'll always be . . .'

Penn dictated and Ulrike typed and Ham whined away in the corner.

He was rambling, contradicting himself, coming to stand

behind her and reading what she had down on paper and changing it. It was full of errors because it was an old stand-up typewriter that she had begged from reception and the arms were forever sticking because it had been on the floor of the back office and was clogged with muck. Ham was muttering to himself, wallowing in his own pity, and they ignored him except for when he filled the glasses.

'No, I need what Alija said before I have what Sylvia said, and what Alija said should be in direct quotation, because she is the more important eyewitness. "The women who were with me, they said she was so brave. The women said she was an angel . . ." I want that in direct quote.'

'So, where then does Maria go, does she go after the American? You know what this will do, Penn, when it reaches them? It will break them, you know that . . . ? Right . . . for the top copy, Maria and then Alija and then Sylvia, and then your journey . . .'

Ham said, splashing the drink from the bottle, 'Get it down you, squire, 'cause you bloody earned it, and don't leave yourself short of credit. Take the bloody credit for what you did. We never got the bloody credit for what we did, the Internationals, when we held those fuckers at Sisak. If they'd broken us at Sisak, where Billy and Jon Jo were zapped, where Herb who was AWOL from the Guards was fragged, where the big Oz guy went, they'd have been in fucking Zagreb for tea. Didn't give us any bloody credit . . . You make double bloody certain, squire, those posh smartarses know what you did . . .'

Slow going in the hotel room, the writing of Penn's report.

And what it would do to them, that was not his problem.

Because Mrs Chadwick had the flu, Mary worked in the kitchen alone. Most times, when there was dinner for friends, Mrs Chadwick came in to help. Mary was happier alone actually . . . Other friends, of course, had daughters still at home who would flick the recipe pages and find the outrageous and get the exotic into the Aga. The sun was going down, slanting through the window and onto the wide pine table . . . She hadn't a daughter . . . She worked briskly at what she did best, boring food. She had the clock on the wall to guide her, and if she worked briskly then everything would be in place, and there would still be time for her in the last light to walk the dogs through the village to the church . . .

The report was two sheets, closely spaced typing, and there were Penn's last notes handwritten in the margin. He glanced down at the two sheets, and the words were a jumble for his eyes. There was precious little left in the bottle, and there was precious little down on two sheets of typing paper . . . precious little to tell of eleven days. They were all allocated their lines, and they had caps for the typing of their names. He should have felt an elation, should have felt proud and strutted the length of the room. But there was only an emptiness . . . He should have wanted to share his pride. He had no conceit. It did not seem significant to him that he had made the march, learned, and ultimately broken clear from the certainty of death . . . He had been close to Dorrie and he thought that he had joined the queue of those who had failed her. In his terms, her life was worth just a report. It was the measure of how she had driven him, mocked him, that his best effort was just a report. It was as if, in his mind, she had given him the one chance of his life to walk alone from the herd, to walk tall above the herd, and he had failed to take that chance. He felt a failed man, not a changed man. The old disciplines were supreme. A clear and brief report sent immediately, a fuller report to follow, just what he would have done after a week's session in the surveillance team, what he would have done for a client of Alpha Security . . . He would never forget her, and now he would turn his back on her. He would go back to the office above the launderette, and the maisonette that was too small. People liked to say there was one bloody chance in this bloody life and they were probably bloody well right. He glanced down at the sheets of paper and Ulrike looked up at him and she waited for him to nod his satisfaction.

He wondered whether the report would be read in the kitchen or taken to the old elegance of the sitting room, whether she would take it upstairs to Dorrie's bedroom. Just a mass of words now, blurred by the Scotch, but the names with the caps were

275

highlighted. Three lines for the Croatian war crimes investigator, seven lines for the American Professor of Pathology, five lines each for Maria and Alija and Sylvia, four lines for the Croatian Liaison Officer . . . Three lines for Ham who had gotten him there, four lines for Benny Stein who had taken him out of there . . . fifteen lines for the Headmaster, twenty-one lines for Katica Dubelj, and on the lower half of the second page were twenty-five lines that quoted the words and described the body and face, and the village, of Milan Stanković. Under the long paragraph concerning Milan Stanković, killer of Dorrie Mowat, there had been room for Ulrike to type his name.

Penn nodded. He was satisfied. He took the room's *gratis* biro and he scribbled his signature above his own typed name, and then he wrote the fax number with the international code at the top of the first sheet. It was his report and he was finished. He put his hand, momentarily, on Ulrike's shoulder, and he felt the hardness of her bones, and he took his hand away in shyness because he could remember the soft fingers that had dabbed the iodine into the cuts on his face. The road had turned. At the point that the road had started she had been a *horrid* young woman, and he could see, the last time that his tired eyes speed-read across the two pages, the words 'courage' and 'bravery' and 'love' and 'angel' . . . He hoped that she would read it in the bedroom, alone, where she could not be seen . . . Just bland bloody words that filled two pages of a report and they did no justice to so many, and they short-changed the Headmaster and Katica Dubelj . . . just a bloody inadequate report. No place for the fear, no space for the terror . . . Just a report, something that money could buy when it was thrown at a problem.

He hoped she would read it in the bedroom, alone, because his report might just break Mary Braddock.

'You still with us, squire?' Ham slurred.

'Still with you, Ham.'

'Let me give you my advice. Good advice from real combat . . .' Ham belched, and he was rolling across the room, and the last of the bottle was going on the desk and on the typewriter's keys. 'It's just a fucking job, squire . . . What you need, squire, is a little of the old home comfort, a lot of the old bottle . . . You need to get well pissed, have a bit of a cuddle, forget it because it was just a fucking job . . .'

He saw the kind care of Ulrike, different to the stand-off mischief love of Dorrie. Perhaps it was 'old home comfort', perhaps it promised 'a bit of a cuddle'. Probably it was getting 'well pissed' . . . He might ring Jane in the morning, and he might not. He might get a plane in the morning, and he might wait until the afternoon . . . The city moved noisily below the window of the hotel room. It would be a long time, Penn thought, before he heard again a silence like that of Rosenovici village, and the lane past Katica Dubelj's house to the field, and the grave pit in the field.

'Don't come back empty, squire.'

Penn let himself out of the room. He walked down the corridor towards the wide central staircase, and the sharpness of the pain in his body was replaced by a stiff ache that was everywhere. There was a television crew in the lobby with their boxes around them and their light meters and clipboards and their self-importance and they noticed him as he came down the stairs, and the plasters and the cuts and the bruises and the grazes seemed to amuse them.

He asked for a bottle of Scotch at the reception, soonest, charged to his room, and he gave the woman on reception the two sheets of paper for the fax.

'Yes, send it now, please . . .'

15

'Good God, didn't realize it was so late . . .'

Henry Carter had a watch on his wrist and there was the big digit clock on the wall, and it was many hours since he had looked at either. Past midnight, and time did not seem any more to matter that much, not now that he had reached the chronological moment when the fax sheets assumed relevance. The supervisor, apologetic, as if it were an intrusion to disturb him, handed him a bacon sandwich.

'. . . That's really too kind, that's very considerate. The time just seems to have run away with me.'

As it had . . . The dragon of the day shift would not have brought him a bacon sandwich, not if he had been faint with hunger, and the dragon would most certainly not have permitted the transistor radio that played jazz piano. Rather a pleasant atmosphere, if he had not had the photocopies of the fax sheets in front of him . . . He pushed them aside so that the diced onion filling would not fall on them.

It was as if they tolerated him as a harmless fool, without snap or bite, but the old desk warrior had the hard core of experience that helped him to understand only too well the compulsion that pushed men forward. One memory hurt him the worst. Mattie Furniss, running a section, revered and respected, had been held in a torture cell in the Iranian town of Tabrīz and had broken out. Mattie Furniss, given up for lost, had walked alone to the mountains on the Turkish border. Proud Mattie Furniss had declined to admit that the pain of torture had broken him . . . They'd sent for Carter, summoned the weasel. Carter, the weasel, had destroyed good old Mattie Furniss and won from him the truth. Of course there were bloody casualties in this life . . . Mattie Furniss, with the shotgun barrel in his mouth and his toe on the trigger, was a casualty. He could see as yesterday the church, hear as yesterday the hymns, recall as yesterday the shame

278

as he had sat far from the altar and the widow with her daughters. The file on the desk in front of him, taking on an ordered shape, scratched the memories.

'Totally illegal, cooking on the premises. We've had to invest in a very powerful deodorant spray, the sort for the most sweaty armpits . . . Are you going through the night, Mr Carter?'

'Looks like it. I'm hoping to get away at lunch time, mid-Wales. To tell you the truth, this isn't the sort of file that I'd want to leave over until next month . . .'

'Interesting one?'

He spoke through a mouthful of the bacon sandwich, so good, plenty of fat left on the bacon. 'Not just interesting, rather tragic, and it's a text book on interference, what happens when you shove your nose in without thinking through the endgame . . . Sorry, that's rather a heavy speech . . . If you'll excuse me . . . Oh, and thank you so much for the sustenance.'

The supervisor of the night shift drifted away and his feet glided and his hips swayed with the motion of the jazz beat. There were many triggers to what had happened, to the tragedy, but he thought the two sheets of the photocopied fax message were at the heart of the matter. The music was gentle, lulling him, but he was too old a dog to be seduced by atmosphere. Gentle music did not ameliorate a barbarity. The two sheets of paper sent from the hotel in Zagreb would have been a sledge-hammer knocking down the doors of Mary Braddock's home. He returned to them, drew the blood from them . . .

REPORT ON THE DEATH OF DOROTHY MOWAT (MISS)
by
William Penn – Alpha Security Ltd
(Prelim. report – interviews)

GOVT. CROATIA WAR CRIMES INVESTIGATOR: Is preparing evidence for future use in war crimes prosecution. No interest shown in this particular case of killing of Dorothy Mowat (DM), a foreigner.

PROFESSOR OF PATHOLOGY, UCLA: Supervised exhumation of DM. Killed with Soviet-made Makharov pistol. 'A fine young

279

woman because she did not have to be there, because she stayed with the wounded' from the battle for Rosenovici tho' she herself was not a casualty. Could have made her own escape. At the end DM was trying to shield one young wounded fighter from 'the knives and the blows and from the gunshot'.

EYEWITNESS 1/MARIA . . .

And the sledgehammer would have brought a cold wind into Mary Braddock's home.

'They get on wonderfully, but then Jocasta's such a caring girl, and Tarquin's so easy. It's such a relief . . .'

It was prawns and crab with cubes of turbot, done in a cheesy sort of sauce, for the first course. Guests didn't talk, not these recession-ridden days, about the value of their houses, nor about the cost of the school fees, nor about their Jules Verne holidays. Houses were repossessed, children had to be withdrawn from schools, holidays for some were impossible. Safe talk, talk that would not, in ignorance, wound, was about how first-marriage children tolerated second-marriage children. Charles always poured the neighbours fierce gins before bringing them into the dining room, he was good at giving the conversation a hefty kick-start, and *children* were safe talk.

'I don't know how I'd do without Emily, she wants to be a nanny, poor sweetheart. She's getting the training with Ben, don't know how I'd do without her.'

The Belgians hadn't finished eating. Mary wondered if they slept together, the big Belgian with the stomach and the little Belgian with the shaved head. They hadn't finished and they hadn't said much, as if the offspring melding of first- and second-marriage children was low down on their agenda. Well, it would be, wouldn't it, if they slept together . . . It was prattle conversation, washing over her, and when the bloody Belgians had finished she could get back to her kitchen and heave the bloody lamb out of the Aga oven.

'Tanya's become really excellent at soccer, that's because Jake is so marvellous with her. But I do worry for Jake. Jake gets more soccer with Tanya than with his father. His father's quite hopeless . . .'

Mary stood. If the bloody Belgians didn't like her crab and prawns and turbot, in a cheesy sort of sauce, then they could bloody go without. One perfunctory 'Can I lend a fist, Mary?' from Giles, the bankruptcy accountant, and a curt shake of her head. She put the bowls on the tray.

'We were allowed to have Jocasta for Christmas, but only after a solicitor's letter . . . lovely, darling, quite delicious . . . she's so much happier with us . . .'

She carried the tray out of the dining room. She left the door ajar. If the Manor House had not been listed, Grade 2, then they'd have been able to knock a hatch through from the kitchen, but Charles had said that a hatch knocked through would be an act of heritage vandalism. She toed open the door of the kitchen and clattered the tray down onto the table. She was by the Aga. She was away from them, and they could talk now freely, ditch the safe talk. She heard them.

'Do you think she's getting over it, Charles? . . . God, what a trial for you both, Charles . . . She put you both through a hell of a hoop, Charles, but Mary particularly . . . I think you showed the patience of saints . . . Don't take me wrong, Charles, but I think Dorothy was quite wicked, and God knows where that came from . . . Time's a great healer, Charles, like an open window with a smell, time will make her forget . . .'

Mary heard their voices, and she heard the low bleeping from her den room, not much more than a broom cupboard, off the kitchen. She had the lamb in the basting dish out of the Aga oven and onto the table. She was tipping her vegetables, potatoes and carrots and leeks, everything that was boring, into the serving dishes. If the bloody Belgians hadn't taken so long then the cutlets wouldn't have dried out. She tilted her head, and she could see over the back of the settee in her den room to the fax machine on the table beside the television, and she saw the paper spilling out. And Judy with her tail, silly wagging tail, had broken the plastic frame that caught the completed faxed messages, and Liz would chew anything that was paper or cardboard, and Judy and Liz were craning from their baskets on either side of the Aga, alerted by the working sounds of the machine. She left the vegetables and the lamb cutlets and the gravy and the jelly, she strode off into her den room on her mission of protection for the fax message.

She picked the first sheet off the floor, and the second sheet was rolling.

She read the address of the headed notepaper, and the title of the message, and the name of the sender.

She sat on her sofa, and the dogs came against her legs, and she read.

She heard the voices through the opened door of the kitchen, across the hall, through the opened door of the dining room.

'. . . So much love for such an undeserving child . . . I think she's coming to terms with it, the reality that Dorothy was just a shameful little minx . . . Such a dreadful place she went to, I won't read about in the newspapers, I switch the telly off when it's Sarajevo. She's got to wash it out of her mind. It's not our responsibility if they want to behave like animals there . . . I think she's on the mend . . . You should take her away, Charles, about as far away as you can go, where that dreadful girl can be forgotten . . .'

She read what she had demanded to know . . .

EYEWITNESS 1/MARIA: Refugee from Rosenovici. DM had come to the village with a Croat/Australian boy who joined village defence force, was wounded. DM carried wounded back from front line to the cellar. There when village surrendered. 'She was an angel in her prettiness, an angel in her courage.'

EYEWITNESS 2/ALIJA: Muslim Bosnian refugee, trapped in Rosenovici. DM organized collection, under fire, of dressings for wounded. After surrender DM was brought with wounded from cellar, beaten by Serb militia, but refused to be separated from the wounded. 'She was so brave . . . she was an angel.'

EYEWITNESS 3/SYLVIA: Refugee from Rosenovici. During the battle DM, alone, nursed the wounded. After the surrender, the Serbs attempted to separate DM from wounded, she fought them.

The wounded were taken down a lane, DM helped carry two of them, DM was beaten. 'The young woman was an angel.'

CROATIAN DEFENCE FORCE LIAISON OFFICER (name withheld): Rosenovici is now a 'dead' village, destroyed so that its inhabitants have nothing, ever, to return to, even the cemetery bulldozed. Names MS (see below) as local militia commander, who would believe himself safe from accountability for death of DM and wounded.

SIDNEY E. HAMILTON: Mercenary, serving with Croat Defence Force, ex-3 Para, provided necessary info, weapons and general material for my entry to Sector North, Rosenovici area.

BENJAMIN (BENNY) STEIN: Crown Agent lorry driver, Brit aid convoy, rescued me (life threatened situation) from Sector North at considerable risk to himself, his colleagues and the future shipment of aid through Serb-occupied territory.

HEADMASTER/SALIKA VILLAGE SCHOOL . . .

She had the photograph in the old silver frame on the table beside the fax machine. Because Charles never came there, she had the photograph in her den room.
She read . . .

'Well, my dear, you wanted to be told, and you have been . . .'
He said it out loud, then caught himself and smiled, and he saw that at least three of them in the quiet of Library where the jazz music played softly, were watching him and curious. Yes, like a blow from a sledgehammer . . .

HEADMASTER/SALIKA VILLAGE SCHOOL: Salika (Serb) is twin village to Rosenovici (Croat), 1 mile apart. (Capture of Rosenovici by Salika men, who were responsible for killing of wounded and DM.) Found praying at night in Rosenovici mass grave site, 'a place of evil'. He helped me because 'you have the power to hurt the madness'. Educated, intelligent, early sixties, with personal bravery to condemn the war crime killing of DM and wounded. In the past he had carried food to KD (see below), but stopped

283

after threatened denunciation by wife. A man standing alone against his own society. Recently removed from headmastership of school, now isolated in Salika, recently beaten by paramilitaries. Took me to meet KD, the only known eyewitness to the killings (other than participants). Was due to accompany me and KD into Rosenovici, following evening after meeting, but did not show. An extremely brave man.

KATICA DUBELJ: (See KD above). Aged 84. KD is only prime eyewitness to death of DM. Now lives in cave, 1 mile approx, in woodland NNW from Rosenovici. Quite appalling conditions, diet of roots and berries, no hygiene. All other former residents of Rosenovici are refugees, or dead. Speaks no English, cannot write. Because Headmaster did not return, no signed affidavit of her evidence. Unable to communicate with her except by sign, shown photograph of DM, recognized, kissed it. Took me in darkness from woods into Rosenovici village. Showed me from her house the route used by paramilitaries to take DM and wounded to mass grave site. Route passed directly in front of her window, which afforded clear view of grave site. Paramilitaries commanded by MS (see below). KD mimed action. DM carried two wounded, kicked 1 paramilitary. DM and wounded made to wait in field while bulldozer dug pit. DM and wounded forced into pit. DM, holding her boy, last in line as wounded knifed, beaten, shot. Final effort made to separate DM from her boy, unsuccessful as DM fought paramilitaries back. DM and boy killed by MS (see below) after DM kicked him. KD escaped when I was captured and taken to Salika village. My opinion, KD is a most reliable witness with total recall of events.

MILAN STANKOVIĆ . . .

Henry Carter felt so old. So old and so tired and so sad.

They were all trapped by young Dorrie Mowat, who was dead. All trapped, Mary and Penn, Benny and Ham and the eyewitnesses, and the Headmaster and this most extraordinary old woman . . . and himself. All flies in the skein web of the spider that was Dorrie Mowat.

'Would you like some more coffee, Mr Carter?' The supervisor called across the Library floor.

'They didn't have it in my day, but then that sort of music would

never have been allowed in Library in my day . . . I don't suppose you've any brandy . . . ? We all demand the truth, but we very seldom stop to consider the consequences of knowing the truth . . .'

There was brandy, cheap and Spanish, kept in a locked drawer of the supervisor's desk, hidden from the day shift, and poured for him into his coffee mug.

They were all looking at him, each young man and each young woman on the night shift, as though he were just a sad, tired, old desk warrior, trapped in nostalgia by a file.

She came very quietly down the stairs, but then she knew which step creaked, carrying her bag and her shoes.

They were still talking, still discussing her, in the dining room, as she went silently back into her kitchen.

'. . . You've got a chance now, Charles, and you'd better damn well take it. Like someone's overboard and you go into the water to get them out, double damn quick. You've got a chance now to rescue her . . . My nephew was down in Bosnia, driving Warriors, he said that standards of common decency don't exist, it's a cruel madhouse. We should all turn our backs to it until they come to their senses, and so should Mary . . . She's such a lovely woman and the strain she's been under, the stress, so many years, it's been pitiful to see . . . I tell you, Charles, each time I came here, when I left I'd say to Libby, thank God that child's not ours . . .'

Mary took the last saucepan off the Aga's hot surface, and she closed up the Aga's lids. The dogs, slavering mouths, were sitting either side of the table and the tray with the cutlets was between them. She covered up the vegetables. She took her coat from the hook behind the door, and the keys for her car.

'. . . Do you think, Charles, that Mary needs a hand? Jocasta's such a help . . . Emily's always there when I need her . . .'

Mary took a sheet from the memory pad.

She wrote, 'Gone away. Dorrie's business. Back soon. Don't ever let those bastards and bitches into our house again. Mary.'

It was Charles's business maxim, never to explain, never to apologize. She left the note under the gravy boat, where he'd see it, when he came searching . . . She wondered how long it would take them, the stupid puerile bastards and the malicious scavenging bitches, before they came to offer help, and she wondered whether Judy and Liz would have beaten them to the lamb cutlets. She was drawn back, a last time, to look at the photograph in her den room.

Mary said, 'Darling, understand me, I am so sorry . . . and I am so proud.'

She slipped out, carrying her bag and her coat, through the kitchen door, closing it carefully after her.

She would drive away through the village, leave it behind her. Behind her would be the garden of the Manor House where she had that afternoon picked spring flowers for the lounge arrangements, and behind her would be the brick cottage with the climbing wisteria where the old widow with the varicose veins lived whom she had visited that afternoon, and behind her would be the smiling greeting of the butcher where she had bought her meat that afternoon, and her neighbours and her friends who had been a part of her life that afternoon. All behind her.

There was a bitter wind on her face, a cleansing wind.

When he had no audience then he hated to be alive.

Sometimes the drink made Ham morose and self-pitying, and sometimes it made him loud and aggressive.

He sat on the floor of the hotel room and the Dragunov rifle with the big telescopic sight was on the carpet near his stretched legs, and he held loose to the bottle's neck and the bottle was going down. He felt such morose self-pity because he was alone and they ignored him. They were on the wide bed. He could see Penn's head, and he might have been sleeping, and he might just have been lying still with his eyes closed, and he could see the fingers of the German woman playing smooth patterns on the skin of Penn's face. Penn was his nightmare. When he was alone, his nightmare was capture, and capture was torture. They always tortured the foreigners. He could see Penn's face, where her fingers made the patterns, and his face was the start of the torture. There were many nightmares for Ham, when he was alone . . . Torture was the worst but the fears, when he was alone, competed with torture. The small kid in the tower block, his father long gone, with the acne, bullied and *rejected*. His Karen holding tight to his Dawn and carrying the suitcase to the door of the married quarters house and wearing the bruise he had given her with his fist, and her not looking back as she walked to the taxi, and his bawling after her because he was *rejected*. His 'Sunray', commanding officer of 3rd Battalion, Parachute Regiment, reading the riot act at the depot in Aldershot, telling him it wouldn't go to court but that his services were no longer required, *rejected*. Him being told, the bastard sneering, that he didn't fit into the scene at Personal Security Ltd (Bodyguards), wasn't smart enough with the clients, didn't keep his mouth shut enough with the clients, going at the end of the week, *rejected*. His getting pissed up in the bunker at Osijek, and the crap guy Howard needling him because he had the photograph of his Karen and his Dawn, and the gun pulled to shut the bastard up, and the shot in the bunker blasting his ears and the blood on his body, and the other Internationals chucking him out and letting him know that they didn't want him when they headed for Bosnia, *rejected*. The nightmares of rejection pushed close to the worst nightmare, when he was alone . . . And the man on the bed with the woman, he was different. The man, Penn, listened to what he said, with no shitty sneers. The man on the bed thanked him. Penn didn't shout at him, didn't rubbish him. There hadn't been officers like Penn at 3 Para, hadn't been management like Penn at Personal Security Ltd (Bodyguards), hadn't been commanders like Penn in the Internationals. Penn listened, and Penn thanked him, no other bastard did. Because he was close to Penn, Ham felt safe from the nightmares . . .

And he believed what Penn told him . . . believed that Penn would take the flight out in the afternoon, when he'd slept and sobered, and go find his Dawn and his Karen.

He thought Penn the best man he ever knew . . .

'Have you any bloody idea what the time is?'

Georgie Simpson said miserably, 'It's past one here . . .'

'And if you didn't know it, there is a time difference between London and Zagreb. I have 2.17, it is 2.17 in the morning.'

He could hear, down the telephone line, a baby crying. 'I'm sorry . . . I was told to speak to you personally. They seemed to think it urgent. I was told it wasn't to go by telex . . .'

'So damned urgent that it couldn't wait till the morning?'

He ignored sarcasm by habit. And Georgie Simpson had never been elevated to the responsibility of running a field station, and he had never ceased to wonder at the goddamn arrogance of field officers abroad, wearing a first secretary's cover. It was not the moment to let it be known that his own office, from which he had telephoned Zagreb at two-hour intervals from eleven o'clock the previous morning, had the heating off and was cold as the grave. 'You weren't in your office, and neither your secretary nor your wife knew when you were returning . . . I'm sorry . . .'

'We don't run by the clock here. I've actually been in Sector East, not that you'd know where that is. I've actually been in a quite bloody unpleasant area, not that you'd understand it . . . Well, what's so important?'

'Can we go to "secure" . . . ?'

There were clicks on the line, a sharp bleep, then the voice level from Zagreb was at reduced volume.

'Give it me . . .'

Georgie Simpson gave the name of William Penn, described the nature of his assignment, spoke of Security Service meddling . . .

'I met him. I gave him a useless start point. He came to see me. I told him to let the dead sleep. I told him to go away.'

He felt he held the high ground, felt more cheerful. 'Didn't listen to you, I'm afraid. Pity that you've been out of touch. If you'd been in touch then you'd know of events in Sector North . . . We think he'll be back in Zagreb by now . . . Get him on the first plane, will you?'

'Yes.'

And it was not Georgie Simpson's business to concern himself with Penn. Not for him to consider the effect of his telephone call, on 'secure', to Zagreb. He was just the Joe who passed on messages from an unheated office in the small hours of the night. But curiosity stirred in him.

'You said that you'd met him?'

'I did, does it matter . . . Personally, I regard it as late for conversation . . .'

'I just wondered about him . . . I mean, what on earth did he do it for?'

'I am actually rather tired . . . They're a bit pathetic, these sort of people. Dig into their lives and you'll find angst . . . are you following me? They're failures, and they're looking for a way back. Myself, if I needed to up the dose of self-respect then I hope, dear God, that I could find an easier way than trekking into Sector North. It's a bad hook to be caught with because there are likely to be tears at the end of the line . . . Don't ever bloody well ring me at this time again.'

'My apologies to your wife. Sorry I woke the baby . . .'

Ulrike thought the squat little man in the uniform that was a size too large, on the floor with the long-barrelled rifle beside his legs, was like a guard dog. Sitting without speaking, sitting and always watching. The mercenary did not matter to her.

She lay on the bed beside Penn and she stroked his face and his chest where she had unbuttoned the front of his shirt. Long enough it had taken, holy Christ, for her to follow her mother's message.

Ulrike Schmidt's mother told a story of a friend. The friend lived at Rosenheim, on the autobahn and the train route from Munich to Salzburg, so it was easy for her mother to travel to see her, and to update the story. Her mother's friend made preparations for each stage of her life . . . at chess speed. The education that would present her with maximum earning capability, the husband who would be a rock for her, the holidays that would relax and divert her, the home that would be pleasant and convenient for her. Her mother's friend could no longer find a private bank to employ her, and was locked in a loveless marriage, and had been food poisoned the last winter in Mombasa, and the home was mortgaged to the bank as collateral to her husband's failing business. And the friend, her mother said, stuck stubbornly to the principle that everything must be planned for. And it was rubbish . . . All the planning, all the preparation, that had sifted through job opportunities, weighed the young suitors, agonized over brochures to the sun, toured housing developments, was rubbish. Her mother said, coded for Ulrike each time she flew from Zagreb to Munich for the weekend, that her friend had never known the freedom of impulse.

She lay on her side. Some of the night he had been awake, but he was sleeping now. She lay on her side, her head held up by her crooked arm, and she watched over the peace of his sleep, and her fingers moved gently over the bared ribcage that showed the colouring of bruises. It was her impulse . . . Her mother's marriage had been impulse. Few would have looked at the harrowed man, her father, mourning the death of a loved one in the bombing of Magdeburg, and inconsolable, a teacher without a school. Her mother's impulse had brought long love, long happiness . . . She would tell her mother about Penn when she next flew to Munich for the weekend. She could see the two faces in the photograph frame on the bedside table, the young woman with thin lips and the baby without hair. But it was her impulse to protect the man who had walked alone into Sector North . . . not love, because she did not know love. Love was beyond her experience . . . It was attraction and it was interest and it was fascination. She wanted to protect him, lie close to him, and in the loneliness of her life his sleeping body seemed to bring a comfort to her. And by protecting him, she thought she might show him her gratitude. He deserved her gratitude. He had done what she craved to do and was not able to, he had confronted the bastards of the uniforms and the guns, a tiny gesture, maybe, but few others did it. What she wanted, what she could not have, was to make happiness for him, to take him from the bed and march him into the old city and hear the music throb and take him in her arms and dance, dance wildly, dance till the dawn came. What she wanted was to dance with him and laugh with him and wear a flower that he had given her . . . but he slept and she protected him . . . And the morning would come too soon, and the aircraft would scream from the runway, and Penn would be gone back with his cuts and bruises to the young woman with the thin lips and the baby without hair.

He had walked into Sector North just to write a report, and

the report was gone . . . And she had never met another man in her life who would have walked into Sector North just to establish the truth that was necessary for a report.

When he had woken, when he had sobered up, when he had gone on the plane, then she would return to the daily and nightly misery of the Transit Centre . . .

She sat in her car and watched the milk float judder down the street. She was parked up outside the terraced house. It was a neat street, decorated and smartened with bright window boxes of pansies and hanging ivy. When the milkman had passed, she left her car and went to the front door, and rang the bell. It was four minutes past six in the morning. She shivered. She waited. She stretched because she had been sat in her car for three and a half hours before the milk float had turned into the street. She heard slow feet coming clumsily down the stairs behind the door. She had been to his wedding, Charles was a friend of his parents. She flexed her hands, felt her nerves rasping. The door opened. Blinking eyes in the half-light, a loose dressing gown, bare feet, tousled hair.

'Good God, Mrs Braddock . . . what on earth . . . ?'

He was half her age, Charles said he was very clever. Charles had said that if her Dorrie hadn't been such a bloody messer then Jasper Williamson would have been the right sort of man.

'Please, I do apologize, I need advice.'

Eyes narrowing. 'What sort of advice?'

She stood on the step. He was the only one she could have come to, she could not have come to any of the fat cat lawyers who were Charles's friends.

She said in meekness, 'International law, I suppose that's what it's called.'

Eyes concentrating. 'What sort of international law?'

She blurted, 'Prosecution of war criminals.'

Somehow, he understood straight away. 'Because of Dorrie . . . ? You'd better come in, Mrs Braddock . . . 'Fraid it's a bit of a tip. Had people in last night. I was sorry to hear about Dorrie . . . I can only tell you the basics.'

He led her into the long living area, and he seemed not to

know where to start with the filled ashtrays and the dirtied glasses and the emptied bottles, and she told him that he shouldn't bother. She took the two sheets of fax paper from her handbag and gave them to him, and he'd groped for the mantelpiece and his spectacles. She thought that he'd probably have reckoned Dorrie to be quite awful, like everyone had, like she had . . . He sank down onto the sofa and he started to read, and she began to collect up the glasses and the ashtrays and took them through to the kitchen. Didn't know much, did she? Knew how to bloody tidy up. Didn't know much about mothering, did she? Knew how to bloody wash up . . . He was reading slowly, and he'd found a pad of paper, and he'd started to take notes. When she had all the glasses and all the ashtrays and all the bottles away into the kitchen, when she had run the hot water into the sink, Mary came and stood behind him. She could read over his shoulder, what he read . . .

MILAN STANKOVIĆ: (See MS above.) Commander of paramilitaries in Salika village. Formerly clerk to agricultural produce co-operative. Aged early to middle thirties. Tall (approx 5'11/6'1), athletic build, no facial distinguishing scars etc, beard and full hair dark brown, eyes grey-blue. Well dressed, suit for social evening, quite obviously the undisputed leader of the community.

After capture I was taken to Salika school hall. Punched by MS. Interrogated by MS through interpreter. Gave my name, confirmed my nationality to MS, told him purpose of my journey to Sector North. Told MS that he had been identified to me as the killer of DM.

My impression, MS deeply shaken by being named, through interpreter, in front of his village peers. From my kit he had seen photographs I carried of DM after exhumation, my impression was that he recognized DM's facial features. Evasive and unsettled when confronted with my accusation of guilt. After villagers beat me, he gave the order for me to be taken away, don't know intended destination, don't know whether I was to be executed immediately or later. Managed to break free in confused situation. I am not trained in Escape and Evasion – I believe my life was saved by intervention of BS (see above). I have no doubt that DM was murdered by the direct actions, stabbing and beating and shooting, of Milan Stanković of Salika village, in Glina Municipality.

Faithfully,

William Penn, Alpha Security Ltd.

'Right, Mrs Braddock, what do you want to know?'

'I want to know how I can nail that bastard to the floor.'

'Give me a few minutes.'

She went back into the kitchen. She filled the kettle for coffee, and she started to rinse through the glasses. She saw that he was reading the two faxed sheets a second time. She wondered if he still thought Dorrie to be quite awful, like everyone had, like she had.

A young woman came down the stairs, naked, so pretty, so different from the young woman in virginal wedding white, and didn't seem to notice that an intruder had usurped her sink and was making free with her coffee. The young woman picked up a packet of cigarettes and wafted away back up the stairs.

Clever young Jasper, who would have been right for Dorrie if she hadn't been 'such a bloody messer', was pulling thick books off the shelves, and he took the coffee mug without comment. Mary dried the glasses. She cleaned the ashtrays. She stacked the empty bottles outside the back door. She wiped the wood surfaces down. She found the vacuum cleaner in the cupboard and ran it over the carpet. His head was down in the books and he had torn strips of paper as markers, and his pencil writing was filling the pages of the notepad. The young woman came down the stairs, white blouse and executive blazer and discreet navy skirt, with a briefcase, and kissed clever young Jasper, and was gone out onto the street. He didn't seem to notice her. He hadn't touched the coffee she'd made him. He put the books back onto the shelves. He stapled the handwritten sheets together, with the two faxed pages.

'It's all there, Mrs Braddock. It's a bit complicated, but if you take it slowly . . . I'm in court in an hour . . . Of course it's possible to prosecute, but what it needs is the determination.

293

Without that determination then the world just rolls on. The notes are Halsbury's Laws, it's Volume 2 . . . You'll have to excuse me, Mrs Braddock, but I've got to move . . . You see it's not important whether Dorothy is now the English rose or whether she was an awkward little bitch, a crime is a crime is a crime. The British jurisdiction would be pretty complicated, what with Yugoslavia not being a country any more, and it being a civil war, but the Geneva Convention on the treatment of prisoners sews it up. There's a procedure in place now for dealing with war crimes in former Yugoslavia. It can happen, if there's the determination . . . I've got to go and dress, Mrs Braddock . . . Whether that determination exists, well, you'll find that out, it's not for me to say. Whether you can "nail that bastard to the floor", I just don't know.'

'Thank you.' She took his notes from what he called Halsbury's Laws, Volume 2, put them in her handbag. 'I want to hear him scream.'

'Only one problem, but it's cardinal. It's one thing to find the determination of the great and the glorious to prosecute, something else to have the accused man in custody . . .'

'Where are you going?'

'To walk, to be alone . . .'

'I have to open the school.'

'To be alone . . .'

He didn't think his wife had slept, and he had heard most chimes of the church clock.

They were in the kitchen, and Marko was still at the table and hanging back on his breakfast because there was crisis between his mother and his father. It was what Milan would have expected from Evica. She had to open the school, she had to make the pretence of normality. It was her strength, that life must be lived. She was chiding Marko for not eating, and she was clearing the table in the kitchen, and she was routing for the books she would need for the day in school. She had the strength and he did not. He had not told her of Katica Dubelj in the cave in the woods. He was not strong enough. She would hear it at the school in the morning, she would know it when she brought Marko home for their lunch . . .

294

He wanted to be alone. He fastened the clasp of the heavy belt over his jeans, and the weight of the holster carrying the Makharov pistol dragged at his hip.

He went out into the morning.

He had not kissed his Marko, and he had not hugged his Evica, and it was not normal for him to wear the holster with the Makharov pistol when he was about the village.

Milan Stanković was no longer the king of Salika. The throne was taken from him. He walked away down the lane, away from the village now ruled by the irregulars who followed Arkan. He did not wish to be seen, by his own people, as subordinate to the gaol scum from Belgrade.

He walked past the last houses of the lane, towards the open fields beside the stream.

He did not want to go back towards the village because his office in the headquarters was now the command centre for the irregulars, and they were without respect for him. His office would now be filled with their bottles and their guns and their sleeping bags, and their crude cold laughter. If he had walked back through the village, if he saw the people to whom he had been king, then he would have seen the fear in their eyes that the presence of the irregulars had brought. He walked away from the village. There were magnolia flowers in the gardens of the last houses of the lane, and tulips were open and the blossom was heavy on the fruit trees. It was so clear in his mind, the memory of how they had carried him on their shoulders when they had elected him as commander of the Territorial Defence Force, just as they had carried him on their shoulders when the team had come back with the cup won from Karlovac Municipality. And so clear in his mind how the men had begged him, pleaded with him, for weapons to use in the attack on the village of the Ustaše bastards across the stream. Not a man in the village who had not slapped his back in congratulation when he had walked back over the bridge from Rosenovici with the mud of the pit on his body. He had been the leader, he had issued the guns, he had brought the bulldozer to the field, he was responsible.

He walked in the watered sunlight beside the gardens of flowers.

It was like a closeness at his throat, because he was responsible . . . The weight of the pistol chafed against his hip.

There were no tractors out that morning, and the animals were still in the barns, and the village boys who were too old for school had not shepherded out the sheep. And he was responsible for the silence and emptiness of the fields, because he had brought this fear to the village, and what was done could not be undone . . . His eyes searched the tree line. He was wondering whether they would come again, some day, in a month or a year or in his old age, and he was wondering whether his son would carry the Makharov pistol on his hip and search the same tree line for their approach.

He walked beside the stream.

It was his home, it was a place of beauty, and the tree line hemmed him in.

The sunlight played patterns on the slow movement of the deep pool, and he saw the ripples of the trout's rise . . .

A shout carried to him. He saw, distant, back at the edge of the village, the waving arms of Branko, calling him. He left behind him the stream's deep pool and the gathering spread of the ripples from the trout's rise.

The Canadian policeman watched him come.

There were no flowers on the grave. The grave was a mound of earth and at the end of it was a single stake. There was not even a cross for the grave.

He stood beside the grave and he held the spectacles in his hand.

In five months he would be back in his beloved Ontario, back in the brick house in Kingston that Melanie's father had built for them, and he did not know what he could tell Melanie and her father about the place he had been posted to . . . Couldn't tell Melanie and her father about the cruelty, nor about the bulldozed graveyards, nor about the poisoned wells, nor about the rape of grandmothers and the disembowelling of grandfathers and the bludgeoning of grandchildren, couldn't tell them that the smile which was adhesive to his face hurt far down in the pit of his soul.

296

The wet mud of the new grave cloyed at his boots . . . Nor would he tell Melanie and her father about the Headmaster of a village school who had had his spectacles broken.

A small crowd confronted him. There were the faces that he always saw when he came to Salika, weathered faces, and amongst them, scattered with them, were the cold bearded men of the Arkanovici . . . If he had not made his report, if the Professor of Pathology had not been available for one day's digging, if he had not taken the window of opportunity, then, and it hurt the Canadian, the Headmaster might, probably would, have been alive . . . Nor would he talk to Melanie and her father about the hideous price paid by those who had gotten themselves involved . . . He'd told them to go fetch Milan Stanković.

When Milan Stanković was close to him, the Canadian turned and laid the new pair of spectacles on the grave's mound. It was something he had been really most proud of, getting the new spectacles made in Zagreb from the prescription, passed to him by the Political Officer, in just twenty-four hours. He had radioed the prescription through from Petrinja to the Ilica barracks in Zagreb and he had begged for urgency and in twenty-four hours the new spectacles had been brought to the crossing point on the road north of Petrinja. The sun burnished the lenses on the grave where there were no flowers . . .

His commissioner, the big guy from Alberta, back in the Ilica barracks liked to tell a story to the new guys coming to serve with UNCIVPOL. The commissioner had been down to Sector South, a one-night stand, and on the first day had found three old Croat women whose home was wrecked and whose well was polluted and who were starving. The commissioner had given them the bread and cheese that was the next day's lunch for his team. The commissioner's gift was witnessed. Four nights later, in the story the commissioner thought worth telling the new guys, the three old Croat women were shot to death . . . It was a story about trying to help and a story about screwing up.

He was not supposed to show emotion. He was not allowed to shout and curse. He stood to attention beside the grave, above the new spectacles. He turned smartly, his heel squelching the mud. He was supposed to smile, to celebrate little victories, he was allowed to smile. He fixed his smile at Milan Stanković, then walked away from him, went to his jeep. He had made the bastard come from wherever, come running and panting, for a fucking smile.

'Good God . . .'

The supercilious grin played at the mouth of the First Secretary.

'. . . So the Warrior of Principle is pimping . . . The Soldier of Conscience is providing some home comforts . . .'

He stood in the doorway, holding the passkey that the floor maid had given him, paid for with a packet of cigarettes. The curtains were still drawn and he saw the shape of the man on the bed, bare-chested, asleep, and there was a woman crouched over him who stared back like a cat cornered with a rabbit.

'. . . And fancy finding you here, my little friend, fancy finding your little snout in the trough.'

But Hamilton, the loathsome Sidney Ernest Hamilton, codenamed 'Freefall' on the file header, was between the First Secretary and the bed, and 'Freefall' Hamilton had a damned ugly rifle across his knees. Before he'd seen the rifle, his intention had been to get across the room, shake the sleep off the bloody man, and kick him smartest out into the corridor, down the stairs, to reception for account settling, and a sharp drive to the airport . . . that was his intention, before he saw the rifle. He saw the empty bottles close to Hamilton, and he recalled the file in the safe of his room at the embassy with six pages on an incident in a bunker at Osijek, a drunken shooting. The First Secretary held back.

The growling hungover voice, 'What do you want?'

'I want him on the plane. I'm going to put him on the first plane.'

'He's going this afternoon.'

'First plane, my little friend . . . and I don't have time for a debate.' Which was truth. The First Secretary had little time. He had a meeting with the monitoring officers, and he was late for it, and they had access to useful areas of raw intelligence. And he had a session, which had taken him seven weeks to fix, with the brigadier commanding Croatian military intelligence who was a bad old bastard from Tito times and who knew his trade. But he was wary of a rifle in the hands of a man who was hungover drunk. 'So, a bit of action, please.'

'You should let him sleep.'

Hamilton, horrible little 'Freefall', crabbed his way to the window and the rifle was dragged with him. Horrible little 'Freefall' caught the curtains and pulled them apart, letting light into the hotel room. The woman, the cat cornered with a rabbit and threatened, hovered over the sleeping man.

'Christ . . . who did that to him?'

The First Secretary saw the wounds and the discoloured bruises and the scars. He felt sickness in his throat. Penn's breathing was regular and his face was at peace. The First Secretary knew enough of what happened in sunny former Yugoslavia to an enemy. He gagged the vomit back. He remembered Penn, coming to his office.

The First Secretary said, 'You will bring him to the airport, the 1500 hours flight. I'll see him onto the plane. You get him there . . .'

The curtains were pulled shut again.

'. . . He'll be there, Hamilton, or I'll break you.'

The aircraft banked.

She was reading the bones of '(2) Ambit of Criminal Jurisdiction, Paragraph 621/Extra Territorial Jurisdiction', and slipping on to 'Paragraph 622/Sources and Rationale of Territorial Jurisdiction'.

The aircraft levelled out, west from Zagreb.

She was reading for the last time the pencilled written notes under the heading of '3. Offences Against the Person, (1) Genocide, Paragraph 424', and her eyes slid across the pages to 'H. Offences Committed Abroad', and 'sub-section 4, sub-paragraph 1 – Murder (see para 431 and seq post)'.

The aircraft was losing height.

She was reading quickly, reminding herself of '(3) Geneva Red Cross Conventions, 1864'. Turning through 'The Geneva Conventions, (3) The Convention Relative to the Treatment of

299

Prisoners of War'. Riffling through '(4) The Convention Relative to the Protection of Civilians in Time of War'.

The aircraft wallowed over the end of the runway.

She was reading the last page of the young barrister's notes, learning them so they were ingrained, '(ii) Treatment of the Wounded etc, Paragraph 1869/General Protection . . . At all times, and particularly after an engagement, parties to a conflict must take measures to search for and collect the wounded, sick and shipwrecked, protect them from pillage and ensure their adequate care; and the dead must be searched for and their spoliation prevented . . . At all times the wounded, sick and shipwrecked must be treated humanely without any adverse distinction founded on race, colour, religion or faith, sex, birth, wealth or any similar criteria.'

The aircraft's wheels touched down.

She was reading, 'Paragraph 1866/Conflicts not of an International Character . . . Treat humanely persons who take no active part in the hostilities, including members of the armed forces who have laid down their arms or are rendered unable to take part by reason of wounds . . . violence to life and persons including murder . . . the passing of sentences and carrying out of executions without a proper trial upon non-combatants are prohibited. The wounded and sick must be cared . . .'

The music played cheerfully over the loudspeakers as Mary Braddock put away in her bag the notes and the two sheets of the faxed report.

16

The pain beat against the bone behind his temples, and there were needle pricks behind his eyeballs, and there was a battering throb behind his ears. It had been a hell of a long time since Penn had been this hungover. The others were still asleep. He was padding, half-naked, round the room, moving without order, stumbling round the bed where Ulrike slept, hiking his feet over Ham's outstretched body. He should have been working to a system, should have cleared the bathroom first, then been to the wardrobe and had his shoes off the floor and his shirts and underwear and socks out of the drawers and his jackets and slacks off the hangers, and then he should have been gathering up everything that belonged to him from the shelf below the mirror including the two typed sheets that had gone for the fax transmission. But there was no system, the pain dictated that there was no order in his packing. Penn blundered around, collecting, forgetting, carrying, cursing the aftermath of the alcohol. He couldn't hold his bloody concentration, not at all. He had the case on the bed, and now he was emptying the case because the shoes and the plastic bag for his toothpaste and his shaving cream and razors were out of place, should always be shoes at the bottom and washing gear, and then the dirty clothes and then the clean clothes and then the folded trousers and then the jackets, and the whole bloody lot were out of order . . . Ulrike slept hard as he skirted the bed, and Ham slept deep as he stepped over his legs and that horrible bloody rifle, because both would have been awake through the night, watching for him. They were a holiday friendship, he knew, and they would be gone, belted out, when the big bird lifted off the tarmac at Zagreb airport. Ships that pass in the night, that sort of crap. They slept now because they had stayed awake through the night and watched his own sleep, and the thought of it, through the pain and the confusion of packing out of order, made Penn feel humility. He wouldn't see her again, nor would he chase after Ham's woman who had done a runner with her kiddie. But they had watched over him while he slept, a lonely woman and a small scumbag frightened because he hadn't a friend. He might tell Mary Braddock about them, because they were each in their way a part of his finding Dorrie's truth. Or then he might not get to see Mary Braddock. When he hadn't the pain in his head he could work it through whether he would see Mary Braddock, or whether it would just be the fuller report in a week's time and the full invoice of his charges, sent in the post by Recorded Delivery . . .

He had never been drunk incapable when he was a teenager living at home in the tied cottage, because that was the example of his mother and father, his mother taking only a sherry at Christmas and his father talking of it like it was a devil. He had been drunk incapable once when a clerk at the Home Office, and taken out to a party in the Catford flat of another clerk, and thinking afterwards that it might just have been because he was so bloody boring that they had spiked the drinks and had good sport out of him reeling and crashing and throwing up in the street; and ashamed. He had been drunk incapable once when with Five, and they had worked seven weeks on a surveillance before showing out on a shift change into the derelict van with the flat tyre that was parked up opposite the safe house, and the Irish target gone and lost, and the guys going down to the pub when the operation had been called off with heavy recrimination and an assistant deputy director general level inquest, and sleeping on the floor of the taxi home; and ashamed.

Now, he had no sense of achievement. There was no elation. It was just a report that he had written, as he had written previous reports that cut into the lives of the dead and the vanished and the criminal, as he would write further reports. He wanted out and he wanted home, and he wanted to sleep out of his system too much goddamn Scotch, and he wanted the bastard place behind him, and the fear, the shit, the pain. It was only a report . . . And the one chance was gone.

He had the shoes back at the bottom of the case, and the washing gear with them, and the underpants and the socks into the space between the shoes and the washing bag, and the dirtied clothes and the ones that he hadn't used. He was starting to fold the slacks and the jackets. The fatigues that he had worn into Sector North were on the floor near to where Ham lay stretched out, holding the bloody rifle like it was a baby's toy, and the fatigues weren't going with him, nor the boots that were under them, and he heard a brisk knock at the door.

Penn went round the bed and he stepped over Ham's legs.

The knock was repeated, impatiently. He opened the door of the hotel room.

Penn rocked.

She peered into the gloom. Late morning, closing on midday, and the curtains of the room were not drawn back. Mary peered past the shadow-dark figure that rocked in front of her. Yes, she had expected surprise, but the man could hardly stand, and the light from behind her in the corridor seemed to dazzle his eyes and he could not focus on her. She came into the room and with her heel she nudged the door back shut behind her. Only the light now from the bathroom, and the shadow-dark figure was backing away from her, away from the narrow strip of light from the bathroom. She came past the door and into the room. The smell in the room was foul, quite defeating the *eau de toilette* scent that she had sprayed at her throat and wrists in the taxi from the airport. On the plane and in the taxi from the airport, she had rehearsed what she would say to him, how she would be cool but goading, and what she had rehearsed was thrown from her mind. If she had wanted to she could not have controlled it, the sharp spasm of her anger.

'Good morning, Mr Penn . . .'

No reply from him, and he was stumbling back further from the bathroom light as if to hide in the grey gloom of the room.

'. . . How are we, Mr Penn?'

Just a growl of a response.

She was going forward into the centre of the room, coming closer to the bed that he skirted when she saw his case on the bed and the shape of the woman on the bed. The blouse of the woman was unbuttoned halfway down to her navel and she could see the sexless strength of the woman's brassiere and the white skin.

'A little end-of-term party, Mr Penn? Got demob happy, did we, Mr Penn? Hit the bottle, did we, Mr Penn . . . ? The bottle and a bit of skirt, Mr Penn?'

'It's not what . . .'

'What I think? You wouldn't have the faintest idea what I think, Mr Penn. If you had had an idea then you would not have ignored my telephone calls to this hotel. You would not have bloody well *abandoned* me.'

'You wouldn't know . . .'

'What it was like? Just a silly woman, Mr Penn? A silly woman incapable of understanding? A woman to be fobbed off with a two-page fax?'

The growl spluttered in his throat. She saw the gleam of his teeth and his words came haltingly.

'She wasn't my daughter.'

'What the hell does that mean?'

'She wasn't my daughter, and if she had been my daughter then she would not have been bad-mouthed to every stranger I could get my claws on.'

She laughed, shrill. 'We make judgements now, do we, Mr Penn? We know more than a mother does about her daughter, do we, Mr Penn? Exactly what I need, wonderful . . .'

And she was following him through the grey gloom of the room, and the woman on the bed stirred.

He said to her, and the life had gone from his voice, and there was only a tiredness, 'If it was just anger then you wouldn't have come, if it had just been anger then you would have stayed away. You came because of the guilt . . .'

'Don't lecture me.'

'Because of the guilt, because of the shame, because she was your daughter and you didn't know her . . .'

She was following him. She was drawn to him. Suddenly there was a startled grunt in the darkness ahead of her and she saw the heaped clothes that stank and the sudden movement of the body in front of her, and the rifle was coming up and the muzzle caught against her stocking at the knee.

'. . . It's fine, Ham, it's Dorrie's mother. It's Dorrie's mother who's come.'

Perhaps it was the calm that had come to the voice now, perhaps it was the gentleness that tinged the voice. Perhaps it was the smell of the bodies and the damp of the clothes on the floor, perhaps it was the rifle and the emptied bottles. Perhaps it was the woman scowling from the bed and the man crouched down hostile on the floor, perhaps it was the suitcase that was packed. Perhaps it was the *guilt*. She spat it out.

'You were going home?'

'I was hired to write a report.'

'Worth two pages, was she? Two pages and that's time to come home?'

'I have written a preliminary report, I will write a fuller report when I am home.'

'And that is your idea of the end of it?'

'It's what I was hired to do, what I have done to the best of my ability.'

'Enough, is it, just to write a report . . . ?'

'It's what I was asked to do, hired to do.'

She could not see into his face. The worst for Mary was the calmness in his voice. And with the calmness was the gentleness. She could remember her tears because of what Dorrie had done to her. She could remember when she had thrown things, saucepans, books, clothes, hurled them because of what Dorrie had done to her. She could remember Charles's accusations because of what Dorrie had done to her, and how she had gone sobbing up the stairs to beat her fists on the locked door because of what Dorrie had done to her. And the guilt roved in her . . .

Her voice rose. 'So you walk out, you walk away?'

'I don't know what else I can do.'

'It was just empty words?'

'It was to write the report you requested.'

'What the politicians said, what that American said, just empty . . . ? Fine words or empty words?'

'You wanted a report, you have a report.'

305

She stood her height. 'Was it just empty words? Didn't they talk about a second Nuremberg, didn't they talk about *war crimes*? Didn't they talk about a new world order where the guilty would be punished, where they'd be locked up and the key thrown away? Didn't they talk . . . ?'

The voice calm and gentle. Not the businesslike voice from the graveyard in the village. Not the brusque voice from the kitchen of the Manor House. 'It's the sort of thing people say, politicians. It's not to be taken seriously.'

'You saw the man who killed her . . .'

'I saw him.'

'You found the evidence of an eyewitness . . .'

'I found the eyewitness.'

'You know where to go . . .'

'I know where he is, and I know where to go for the eyewitness.'

She could not see into his face. She saw the grey shadow and the dark sockets of the eyes.

'Do you think I am just a woman to be humoured? Do you think I am just a silly woman who is obsessional?'

'I wrote my report.'

She said, hard, 'If there is a will then there can be a prosecution . . . "Sources and Rationale of Territorial Jurisdiction" and "Offences Against the Person, Geneva Conventions" and "Treatment of the Wounded" and "Conflicts not of an International Character". If there is determination then there can be a prosecution . . .'

'What do you want?'

She said, brutally, 'I *want* those empty words thrown back down their bloody throats. I want them to choke on those empty words. I want that man before a court, I want to hear your evidence against him . . .'

'What can I do?'

She looked into his eyes, pitilessly. 'Go back. Take him. Bring him. Bring him to where they cannot hide behind their empty words. Go . . . take . . . bring . . . Or are you going to walk out on me?'

He turned away from her. He was at the window. His hands

reached up to the curtains. And her voice died. The silence held the grey gloom of the room. Quite suddenly, the daylight was flooding the room, and the curtains were heaved back. It was the bruises on his face and the cuts and the scarring that she saw first. She gazed at him, and she felt shame. There was a weal on his throat, and on his chest deeper bruises and wider cuts and abrasions.

'I didn't know . . .'

'I will go back behind the lines and take him and bring him out. Will you please listen to me, Mrs Braddock, will you please not interrupt me . . . I will bring him out, but not for you. You, Mrs Braddock, are owed nothing . . . I don't think listening comes easily to you, I doubt you ever listened to your daughter, but then I am sure you are a busy woman and capable and resourceful, with many demands on your time. Does life always revolve around you? For Dorrie's sake I will bring him out, and for myself . . . Don't drop your head, Mrs Braddock, and please don't offer me more money . . . And don't think the United Nations in their glory will stand and cheer, nor our embassy, nor the government here . . . I will bring him out because knowing and loving your daughter has been my privilege. I will bring him out.'

The woman came off the bed, and she was tucking her blouse into the waist of her trousers, and then she was buttoning her blouse, and she seemed to look at Penn as if to satisfy herself that he had made up his mind. She did not question him, just checked him, and she was slipping from the bed and going for the telephone on the shelf beneath the mirror.

And the small man, the man who was crouched down on the floor with his rifle, shook his head like he heard something that he could not believe, and he said, 'That, squire, is the biggest picce of *fucking* madness that I have heard. Just 'cause the cow winds you up, doesn't mean you *fucking* have to.'

The woman was dialling a number.

She looked at the scars and bruises and cuts. 'I didn't know.'

He said simply, 'We loved her, all who were touched by her came to love her. Your problem, Mrs Braddock, is you knew nothing about that love.'

★   ★   ★

His hand was laid on Evica's hand. Just for the moment she allowed his hand on her hand. She took her hand from under his.

Milan's hand lay on the kitchen table. He drummed his fingers, he looked into her face.

She did not criticize him with her eyes because the log bin beside the stove was not filled. She did not criticize him because he had sat at the table rereading old newspapers through the whole of the morning while she had been with Marko at the school. She did not criticize him because he had not risen from their bed before she had gone with Marko to the school, had not been to the store in the village to see if there was fresh bread, had not swept the floor of the kitchen. Evica pushed the last logs of the bin onto the fading fire of the stove. She did not criticize him because she had to go out into the shed behind the kitchen door to get potatoes and beetroot, and she was wearing her washed and ironed blouse and her neat skirt that were appropriate for the acting headmistress of Salika's village school, and she took the emptied log bin with her. Her face, when he had laid his hand on hers, was without expression. He could not know from looking at her face whether she was ashamed of him, whether she was frightened for him, whether she loathed him. The body of the dog was pressed against the kitchen door as if waiting for the mistress to come, as if the master were no longer of importance. They had been married more than a dozen years ago, when he was the basketball star of the Glina Municipality and she the prettiest girl in Salika village, and he did not know her.

The boy, his Marko, came to him, sat on his lap, sturdy weight on his upper thighs, and he thought that perhaps the boy had been crying as his mother had walked him home from morning school, and there were the scars of fighting on the boy's face.

She came back into the kitchen. She was carrying the log bin, filled, and a cardboard box of potatoes and beetroot, and he could see the stain of dried mud on her blouse, and the strain of her arm muscles because the logs were damp and still heavy. And he could see, near to the broadest of the smears of dried mud, the place on the waist of her blouse where she had stitched a short L-shaped rent in the material. She did not criticize him because it was impossible now to buy new clothes. She did not criticize him because she could no longer go to the shops in Karlovac and Sisak. She did not criticize him as if he were responsible, as if it were personal to him, for the war. She had dumped the bin. He held tight to his son. She was tipping potatoes and beetroot into the bowl in her sink for washing and peeling and cutting. She knew of the death of the Headmaster, and she would know of the killing of Katica Dubelj, she had translated the accusation of the stranger who had come to their village . . . and he did not know what she thought. It had rained hard in the night. Through the window he could see the cloud on the hill above the village across the river. Her back was to him. She worked methodically over the sink.

Milan said, 'Because the stream is in spate it cannot be today, and I do not think it can be tomorrow, but when the pace of the stream is settled then I will take Marko to fish. Far up the stream, up past where they graze the sheep, where they plough, there is a good pool. I saw trout there. We will dig some worms, we will bring you back a trout . . .'

He laughed out loud and he cuddled the boy who was heavy on his upper thighs, and the weight of Marko tautened the belt at his waist and dragged the bulk of the holster into the flesh of his hip and he would always wear the holster now, and she did not turn to face him, and he did not know what she thought.

He was waiting for them at the entrance to the barracks.

Marty signed them in, and the Swedish sentries issued, lazily, visitor's permits for Ulrike and the Englishman and for the mercenary and for the tall woman with them who was elegant and beautiful.

He showed Ulrike where she could park the car.

Marty walked them from the parking lot to the freight container.

He took them inside the freight container, and he apologized for the wet mud on the vinyl flooring, and he shut down his screen and he tidied away the papers on his desk, and he said he would make coffee for them. If she had given him more warning with her telephone call requesting a meeting, then he would have gone out of the Ilica barracks and bought flowers for Ulrike Schmidt. He was filling the kettle, finding the mugs, getting the milk carton from the small fridge, looking in his cupboard for sugar.

The elegant woman, the Englishwoman, came right at him. 'Mr Jones, you are a war crimes investigator . . . ?'

And Marty hadn't even gotten round to establishing who had milk and who had sugar.

'That's correct, ma'am.'

'You are here to prepare cases against war criminals with a view to eventual prosecution?'

'Correct again, ma'am.'

'What progress are you making, Mr Jones?'

'Precious little, ma'am.'

'Why are you making precious little progress?'

He grimaced. 'Do you have all day . . . ?'

'Please, Mr Jones, just explain.'

'It depends, ma'am, on why you want to know it.'

The Englishwoman took from her handbag two sheets of faxed paper, and she passed them to Marty. He began to read. The kettle was starting to blow, but Ulrike made that her job. He read the synopsis of a killing. Ulrike spooned the coffee into the five mugs and they talked among themselves about milk and about portions of sugar. He was reading the brief text of eyewitnesses and the Englishwoman's eyes never left him as he read. He was reading the material that crossed his desk each day, that was recorded on his camcorder, that was held on his audio tapes. There were photographs pinned to the interior walls of the freight container, bad atrocity photographs, and the Englishman stared at them coldly and Ulrike ignored them, and once the mercenary made a joke of them, but the Englishwoman seemed not to see them. She watched him as he shifted from the first sheet to the second, as he weighed the names, as he drank it in. He thought of telling the Englishwoman, telling her how many thousands of civilians had died in former Yugoslavia, how many of the ethnic minorities had been cleansed, how many 'concentration camps' existed, how many homes had been burned, how many acts of criminality had been perpetrated against the defenceless. When he finished his reading he could have told her that in the catalogue of bestiality the 'incident' at the village of Rosenovici was minimal. Those that trusted him, those who were the eyewitnesses and who provided his 'snapshot' experiences were hungry and tired and traumatized, they no longer possessed the spark of action. She was smartly dressed, like a big oilman's wife. She had fine skin, like a woman who was cared for with money. He supposed she believed it her right to jump to the head of any queue he made for the priorities of his catalogue of bestiality. He handed her back the two sheets of paper.

'I make little progress, ma'am, because my work is perceived to be an obstacle to eventual peace . . .'

'Please, plain language.'

'The worst bastards, excuse me, run the show. The thinking in New York, the thinking in Geneva, the thinking at UNPROFOR across the parade ground from my kennel, is that the worst bastards have to be kept sweet so as they'll put their illiterate scrawl on whatever appeasement document ends this crap session. Plain language, I'm a goddamn leper here. Plain language, I am obstructed, short-funded, blocked. Plain language, I'm pissing into the wind . . .'

'And that's good enough for you?'

But he wasn't angry. He didn't flare. She did not seem to be insulting him. 'I do what I can, ma'am.'

'Did the killing of the wounded from Rosenovici, and the murder of my daughter, constitute a war crime?'

'Yes.'

'Does the material here in abbreviated form, provided by Mr Penn, constitute evidence of a war crime?'

'Yes, but . . .'

'But what?'

'It's good to meet you, good to make you coffee, it's good to learn about your daughter, *but* . . .'

'But what, Mr Jones?'

'But it's hollow talk, it's academic, it's wasting your time and my time because the accused is not within jurisdiction. Put simply, the guy's the other side of the line.'

'And if . . .'

'It's where it stops, the line. I'm sorry.'

Suddenly feeling tired, tired because it was a dream. A dream was a man in handcuffs, a man who was confronted with *evidence*. The dream was a man who flinched when confronted with the cold paper of testimony. The dream was always with him.

'Mr Penn is going over that line. I've his promise. He's going to take him and bring him back, across that line. So in the plainest language, have you the balls to handle it . . . ?'

'You bring him, I'll screw him down. My word to you, I'll give it my best. My word, I'll not back off.'

And Marty knew that he had lost her, lost the German woman. He knew that he had lost her to Penn. He was crushed. If he had gone more often to the Transit Centre, if he had gone more often and taken flowers, if he had pushed and shoved and heaved, if . . . He thought that he had lost what he cared for the most. He searched again for confirmation.

Marty looked into Penn's face, at the bruises and the scars.

'As long as you know, ma'am, what you're asking that man to do . . .'

First he had watched the outer door of the concourse. He had sat where he could see the door, taken a magazine and relaxed.

Later he had gone to stand near to the queue waiting to have their tickets and baggage processed, and when the queue had thinned he had gone to the desk and asked, in decent local language, for a fast look at the passenger list.

Now he used a telephone from which he could still see the check-in, while the announcement of the flight's closing beat in his ears, and he rang the hotel in central Zagreb and spoke to an idiot, and the idiot confirmed that Penn, William, had checked out, paid up and gone.

The First Secretary hurried from the concourse and outside he heard the distant rumble of a jet airliner gathering speed on the runway. It was a talent of his that he could control his fury, but he trembled in the knowledge of a failure that must be reported, immediately, to London.

★   ★   ★

'I'll go because I've said I'll go.'

Ham said, 'I told you, it's just *fucking* dumb.'

'I'll do it because I've said I'll do it.'

'You never go back, not when you've been bounced. On your own, no chance, not second time at it.'

'It's what I've said I'll do.'

The German woman was driving. She was very quiet. She had her eyes on the road and her hands tight on the wheel. Ham was sitting beside her and he had the rifle down between his legs and he was twisted awkwardly so that he could face Penn who was stretched across the width of the back seat. He knew where it was going. It was 'Freefall' Hamilton's lifetime skill that he could deflect the big decision, and he thought this time round that deflection was *fucking* out the window. He squirmed because the bullshit stakes were finished.

Ham blurted, 'Don't think I'm going with you . . .'

'Hadn't asked you, wasn't going to ask you.'

'Don't think I'm going in there with you, don't think I'll be there watching your arse. I'm not going in there with you, and that means you can't *fucking* go . . .'

'I was never asking you.'

'You go back in there and you're dead meat. Just say, just suppose, that you make it in there . . . Just say that you find the bastard, just suppose you take him . . . Do you think, when the balloon goes up, and sure as hell it will, that one man can take that *fucking* bastard out. Hot pursuit, going fast cross-country, going covert with a prisoner. You've no chance . . . For Christ's sake, you know you've no *fucking* chance. Believe me, Penn, no chance . . .'

'It's not your worry.'

'Are you just thick . . . ?'

'It's not your worry because I am not asking you.'

She was driving in the falling light on the wide road back down to Karlovac. She seemed to stiffen. Her lips moved, pale and thin lips without make-up, as if she tested something she would say out loud. She glanced across at him, away from the road.

'You don't have to be ashamed, Ham, because you are

313

frightened. We are all frightened here, all of the time, not only you. You should just make available the weapons, the food, the method of crossing the river, the rendezvous on the way back . . .'

'Don't *fucking* tell me . . .'

The headlights of the Volkswagen flared over the empty road ahead.

'You speak the truth, Ham, he has no chance if he is alone.'

He knew his place in the great organization of Six. He knew his place, influence, authority, because his wife cared to remind him of it most weeks. There were occasional good days, when Georgie Simpson would let himself into his mock-Tudor semi-detached home in Carshalton, and pocket the latchkey, and sing out the news of his arrival, and be anxious to tell her of some minimal triumph achieved that day in the great organization of Six. His wife, on those evenings, would be sitting in front of the television, and she would recognize his minor elation, and diminish him. She could put him down when he was up, and she seldom bothered to try to lift him up when he was down.

He replaced the secure telephone on its cradle. The central heating, blown along ducts from a main boiler unit, was still functioning, would be for another month. Most of those around him had discarded their cardigans or jackets, and Georgie Simpson shivered.

Only little tasks were given him. If he carried out, flawlessly, those little tasks, then he could expect to hide in the corner and remain unobserved by those bloody people who now trawled through the building for dead wood that could be hacked from the body of Six. If he were to be forcibly retired, sent packing because he could not even be relied upon to fulfil the little tasks . . . He shivered. He felt the sweat cold on his body.

He unlocked the drawer of his desk, took out the notebook where his sacred telephone numbers were written. Georgie Simpson thought of going home that evening to his wife, sitting in front of the television, and if he told her of a disaster, his disaster, then she would laugh back in his face. He dialled.

'Arnold, it's Georgie here . . . No, be a good chap . . . Past's

314

past, let it go, please. Arnold, I beg you, please, listen . . . I've just had our field station, Zagreb, on . . . We have a problem, a huge problem . . .'

The memorandum was in front of him. He cast his eye over it, slowly shook his head. Henry Carter had never thought greatly of Georgie Simpson. The memorandum of Simpson (Six) concerning his telephone conversation with Browne (Five). He thought it a pathetic little document, and all the self-serving was there of a panic-laden man who was attempting to pass on the parcel.

No, Henry Carter did not think 'panic' too strong a word. He knew the way the place worked. He understood the culture of Six. It would not have changed in the years since he had left his own full-time employment in the old Century House. There was a child's grin on his face.

Yes, Henry Carter could picture panic running a limited course, early on a spring afternoon some twenty-three months before, through the corridors above him.

A man who should have been tied down, fastened tight, was free and going loose behind the lines. A man, who was a freelancer and an amateur, was behind the lines and beyond recall. A child's grin and a quiet chuckle, because panic would have been scampering down those 'corridors of inaction' above him, kicking down the doors into the 'offices of inactivity' above him. Clever men, the men who drew up clever plans, would have been cursing, swearing, twisting pencil stems, and passing on that parcel of responsibility.

There was a new cup of coffee in front of him, the last that the night duty supervisor would bring him before the day shift came on in an hour's time. He knew his socks smelled, and he could feel the rude stubble on his chin. He thought that somewhere in the vast recesses of Babylon on Thames there would be a plastic razor that he could beg, but he did not know where he would ask for replacement socks.

His chuckle was because he saw the clever men with their clever plans cursing and scampering in panic . . . He thought of the man running loose behind the lines, beyond recall. Lunatic, of course, but predictable. Too lethal and emotional a cocktail for a decent fellow to have rejected . . . It was usually the decent ones who could be inveigled to go behind the lines, beyond recall. He knew the scenario, of course he did, he had himself twisted the screw, manipulated young and decent men, and he was not proud of what he had done, and he hoped, quite fervently, as the dawn came up over the Thames, that Mrs Mary Braddock was not proud.

The night supervisor was locking away the small microwave in which the bacon for the sandwiches had been cooked, and a young woman from the shift was spraying that end of Library with an air cleanser, and the music was already gone.

Another damn morning was coming.

She was unpacking in her room.

It was a better hotel than the one she had used on her two previous visits to Zagreb. She was on a floor above the room from which she had hunted out Penn, and there was a good vista from the window that went away past the hospital with the big red cross painted on the white background over the tiles, and over the wide street that was laced with tram tracks, on towards the formidable floodlit public buildings of the Viennese style of a century before.

When the telephone rang she was ferrying her clothes from her opened case to the wardrobe. She went to the telephone with the framed photograph of her Dorrie beside it.

Her husband's voice hacked anger at her.

'. . . Do you know what you are doing? You are *interfering*, you are interfering and *meddling*. I have had Arnold bloody Browne into my house, as if I were some sort of criminal, as if I were responsible for you. You are interfering with policy, you are meddling in matters, damn it, matters beyond your pitiful understanding . . . And don't you think you owe me some sort of bloody apology? Do you know what you did to me, and my guests? You made a bloody fool of me . . . Did you stop and think what you were doing to me, humiliating me . . . You sent that man back, that's what Arnold bloody Browne is saying, always have to get your own bloody way, don't you? That man was close to getting himself killed first time around, his luck and a deal of guts from other people saved his life. But you couldn't let it go, had to send him back again . . . God, Mary, do you understand what you've done . . . ?'

316

She put the telephone down on him.

She sat in the chair. She stared at the photograph of her Dorrie, such an old photograph because the child was laughing.

He sat on his son's bed.

He was cold from the night air. There was no heating in the house outside the kitchen, and no electricity that evening. The oil lamp threw a feeble yellow light into his son's room from the timbered landing.

Milan told his Marko that the night was clear with no sign of rain.

He did not tell his son that he had walked out into the village that evening, after the darkness had come. Did not tell him that he had walked as far as the headquarters building of the TDF, and that he had gone inside and into the room that had been his office since his election by acclamation as leader. He did not tell his son that Branko was in his chair and sitting at his desk and working through a new duty roster for the sentries on the bridge to Rosenovici and on the roadblock to Vrginmost, and it was the leader who made the roster for the sentries. He did not tell his son that Stevo was deep in negotiation with the chief of the irregulars and handing over money for the supply of diesel, and it was the leader who controlled the fuel resource for the village. He did not tell his son that Milo was talking with others of the irregulars for the acquisition of more of the heavy .50-calibre machine guns and more grenades for the RPG-7s that were stored in the concrete-lined armoury, and it was the leader who had charge of the armoury. He did not tell his son that he had been ignored by the irregulars, and by the gravedigger and the postman and the carpenter.

Milan held the boy's hand. 'If there is no more rain, if the stream has gone down, then tomorrow afternoon may be good for fishing.'

Ham took them across.

She could see nothing around her beyond the white swirl of the water where he dipped the paddle. Penn was in front of her, settled across the forward angle of the inflatable, not speaking,

and Ham was behind her and grunting at the exertion of propel-
ling the craft into the strong current of the river. Ulrike thought
that she understood what was ahead . . . she should have known.
The refugees who came by bus to the Turanj crossing point had
been through what was ahead. What was ahead was enough
to traumatize and crush and terrorize. The inflatable staggered
against the current's power. Her father was in her mind. She
had been twelve years old when he had first talked of it to her,
opened the chapter of his life that was closed away before. Her
father was a pacifist teacher and had stayed silent for self-
preservation, and the tears had run thick on her father's face as
he had explained the call of survival, for he had known who
was taken to the cells and who was interrogated and who was
eliminated, he had known the evil and stayed silent. It had been
with her all through her life, from the age of twelve, that if a
man or woman stayed silent then the time would come in later
age when the tears would roll helplessly on the face, witness to
shame. Her father would have understood why she rode the
inflatable against the current into the width of the Kupa river.
She did not wish to cry when she was old. And her father had
told her, her twelve years old, and him sitting beside her and
holding her and weeping, that after the surrender he had found
work as an interpreter for the British Control Commission. It
had been part of his work to translate in the courts that arraigned
and sentenced the war criminals. The night before the execution
of a sentence, by hanging, her father had been taken to the
condemned cell of the deputy commander of a camp in the
Neuengamme Ring, and it had been her father's job that night
to interpret for the British gaolers the last letter written by the
deputy commander to his wife, and the wife would receive the
letter several hours after the hanging. And her father had said
to her, through his tears, that it was a sweet and literate letter,
not the ravings of a beast, but a letter searching for dignity from
a man who was frightened.

She leaned forward.

Her hands groped past the backpack given by Ham. Her hands
found Penn's. She held tight to his hands.

She whispered, 'There is something you must know. Perhaps

you already know it. Something that is important . . .'

He hissed for her to be quiet.

She pressed. 'To you, now, he is an animal. When you have him, when he is taken, he will be weak, he will be human. You must not soften then, Penn, when he is weak, when he pleads . . . I am sorry, Penn, but then you will have to be cruel . . .'

His hand, freed from hers, was across her mouth. The sounds were the slight splashing of the paddle and the wash of the river current against the side of the inflatable. His hand dropped from her mouth. She eased back from him.

'If you are weak then you betray so many. You walk for those who are dead, and for the dispossessed, the tortured. It will be, for you, difficult to be cruel . . .'

She could see the dark high outline of the steep bank ahead. It had seemed important to her to tell him. Behind was the greater darkness, only a single light to see, far down river from where they had launched the inflatable. Perhaps it was why she had come, to give him the edge of cruelty . . . She had seen the convoys of UNPROFOR troops going through the Turanj crossing point and heading for Bosnia in their personnel carriers, she had seen the vapour trails of the American jets as they arced in the skies for their threatening flights over Bosnia, she had seen on the satellite television the politicians talk about the sanction of war crimes tribunals for Bosnia, and *nothing* happened, the misery continued, nothing changed. The darkness was around her, the blackness of the bank was ahead of her.

Ulrike whispered, 'It is left to the small people to do something . . .'

He slapped her face, quite sharp, stinging her. Her anger surged a moment, then lapsed. He slapped her, she thought, to give her the reality. The reality was danger. She bobbed her head as if in apology, and he would not have seen it. He would believe he was responsible for her.

The front of the inflatable hit the bank, then sidled into the broken reeds. He threw the backpack up the bank, and then she felt her arm taken roughly. He dragged her forward, had firm hold of her, then pitched her off the inflatable. She was in the void. Her fingers clawed into wet mud and her feet splashed in

319

the water among the reeds, and his hands were at her hips and heaving her higher. She scrambled up the bank, fists and knees and toes. She heard the murmur of voices behind her, the time of the pick-up, and the place of the rendezvous. He jumped and he fell half onto her and his weight beat the breath from her chest. His hand scraped up across the fatigue jacket and found a grip by her armpit, and he pulled her up to the top of the bank.

She heard the soft wash of the paddle in the water, fading.

17

'Who is he?'

'Some drone from the Stone Age.'

'What's he doing here?'

'He comes in two days a month, he ferrets into files that weren't annotated at the time. He's supposed to get them into shape so they can go onto disk for Archive, only low-grade stuff. He was in Century way back, when there were carrier pigeons, one-time pads, when it was Boy Scouts time.'

Their voices murmured in Henry Carter's ears.

'God, he stinks. Look there . . . Food grease. The wretched man's been eating in here. I suppose it's a sort of charity really, finding people like that a bit of work. Nothing that can be said to be useful?'

'It's something about former Yugoslavia.'

'Out of which nothing good ever came.'

'It can't be important or they wouldn't have let him near it . . . I'm trying to remember what he did when he was here, certainly wasn't senior executive rank . . .'

'Well, he's certainly noticeable now – is it his socks? Extraordinary, really, there's a file that nobody is remotely interested in, and it gets dug out and worked all over, and then it's reburied on disk, and still nobody is remotely interested in it. Waste of time.'

Henry Carter, his head across his elbows on the desk, opened his eyes. He saw the day supervisor and a callow skinny young man that he assumed to be from In-House Management.

The woman who was the day supervisor laughed, hollow. 'Amazing, he's alive . . . Mr Carter, you do not have permission to camp in here like a dosser. You do not have permission to eat hot fat-ridden food in Library.'

'So sorry.'

The young man said, 'It's not exactly pleasant, Mr Carter, for the people who work here to have a man who smells . . .'

Most times, Henry Carter would have grovelled a further apology. But he had been dreaming . . . Because he had been dreaming he did not offer a second apology. His voice rose.

'Not important? Of course not . . . A waste of time. Of course . . . You wouldn't have the faintest idea. It shouldn't have been asked of him. No human being in their right mind would have driven Penn back across that river. That river, it's what European history is stuffed solid with. It's a barrier, it's a demarcation line, beyond that river is the sort of danger and risk that you in your smug and complacent little lives would not comprehend. It's always the people who are smug and complacent who send young men across rivers, through minefields, into the heart of danger, and in their arrogance they never pause to consider the consequences. Now, if you will please excuse me I have work to get on with . . .'

They backed off.

None of the women at their consoles lifted their heads to stare at him.

They left him at his desk.

The memory of the dream was with him. It was a damnable dream, a nightmare. What he knew of those young men who pressed forward towards the heart of danger was that they were frightened of spitting back into the faces of those who urged them further down the road. They were compelled towards the brink of the precipice, dragged towards the edge. He seemed to have seen in his dream the young man going forward as a shadow shape in darkness, and he still saw Penn, and the image of Penn shut out the languid movement around him of the personnel of Library. He coughed some phlegm from his chest into the mess of his handkerchief, he had more bronchial problems now than ever before. God, and he needed to be out of London, needed to be on the old railway line at Tregaron, needed to be alone with the big kites manoeuvring above him . . . but not before the file was prepared, the matter was settled.

The day supervisor was a few paces behind him, stood back as if she were nervous that the 'old drone' still had enough teeth in his old mouth to bite.

There was the hissing of the air freshener aerosol.

He was drawn back towards the pain of the memories. The mem-
ories were of men who had trusted him. Johnny Donoghue, school-
teacher, persuaded to travel into East Germany, had trusted him.
Mattie Furniss, pompous and decent, had trusted him . . . but the
damned job took precedence over trust . . . Almost as if he wished
that this young man, fleshing in the file, had trusted him. What they
said, the old men of Century and the new men of Vauxhall Cross,
was that there was no escape from the job, and never would be.

He smelled the fragrance that fell around him. He seemed to feel,
not just at his feet and in his shoes, but across the whole of his body,
the cold damp of the great Kupa river.

He led her up the bank. Penn held Ulrike's hand as he took her
up the bank and beyond the line of the reeds. He did not hold
her hand because he thought she was weak or because he thought
she needed comfort. He held her hand so that he could dictate
the speed of each step that she took, and so that he could communicate the need for absolute quiet. In the darkness, with the
black depth of the river behind them, it seemed to him an age
before he was satisfied and prepared to move forward. Perhaps
it was two minutes, perhaps three, but he was crouched down
and she was kneeling close to him and he held her hand and he
could hear, just, the heave of her breathing. He could not hear
the soft splash of the paddles any longer, and there was no sound
from back across the river to tell him that Ham had successfully
reached the other bank and had taken the inflatable out of the
water and had dragged it to the hiding place among the scrub
in the swamp ground . . . it was not good to think of the swamp
ground on the other side of the river. To think of safe territory
was facile, dangerous. Penn released Ulrike's hand. His fingers
ran the length of her arm and across her neck and he touched
the hair on her head and he brought her head close to him so
that her ear was against his lips. He whispered, so quietly, into
her ear that she was not to speak. On no account should she
speak. To speak was to hazard them, no bloody way should she
open her bloody mouth. Again, his hand took hers. They began
to move forward. He did not want her too close to him so that
she stumbled against him, nor so far back that she might lose

contact with him and then hurry to regain it. He went the way he had gone before, and it had to be that way because Ham knew no other route. He led her across the path that was set back from the river's bank, and he groped down with his free hand so that he could find the single strand of wire and he made the circle of his thumb and forefinger around the wire and soon he had reopened the scratches in his hand. They went faster than he had gone the last time . . . She stepped on a twig which his own boots had missed, and he jerked her arm hard as if it were a capital sin to step on and break a twig when moving in the total darkness of a night forest.

They made good time.

A lone dog barked at the farmhouse, and there was one small lamp burning in the outbuildings. All the while that they moved he held tight to her hand, controlling her. He had told Ham they would be in fast, there for the minimum time, out fast, and he should have the inflatable waiting. Ham had nodded. 'Don't you worry on it. Piece of cake, squire.'

They were past the farm, they were far behind the lines.

'Where do they come back to?'

He tried to back his head away, twist his neck away, but the interrogator's punch came too fast for his reaction. The punch caught him on the tip of his nose and his eyes watered.

They had been waiting for him at the old police station. Ham had done as he had been told to do, driven Ulrike's car to her apartment block, parked it, pushed her keys through her letter box and then walked back to the old police station, where they had been waiting.

'Where is the rendezvous on the river, when is the rendezvous?'

Her hand came up fast from beside the trouser pocket of her fatigues and took him behind the ear, jack-knifing his head forward, and as his head bucked her other hand with the clenched knuckles drove into his lips.

Two of the military police had been waiting for him when he had come back into the yard behind the old police station and they had taken his arms with no explanation, and marched him up the steps and into the room of the Intelligence Officer who fronted as Liaison.

'Don't be boring, don't be slow to help yourself, don't believe that I won't hurt you.'

The interrogator hit, as if his head was a punchball in a gymnasium, with the left-right combination, and each blow was harder and there was the first warm trickle of blood from his upper lip that ran sweet to his gums.

The two military policemen had pushed him in through the door of the Intelligence Officer's room, and he had seen the First Secretary and tried to raise something of a cheerful smile to be met only by cold hostility, and the Intelligence Officer had gazed at him like he was reptile's dirt. He had seen the chill in the eyes of the interrogator. She wore fatigue uniform, baggy because it was too large for her smallness, and she had a heavy pistol holster belted to her wasped waist. The woman had motioned him to the chair, and when he had sat on it, straight-backed, she had hit him the first time.

'You can be a very sensible man, Ham, or you can be a silly man . . . Where, when, is the rendezvous?'

She punched straight into the fullness of his mouth, and the wide dulled gold of her wedding ring clipped the cap of his front tooth and broke it.

He reckoned the interrogator was a pretty woman, but 'fanny' always looked good in uniform, always looked best with a webbing belt and a holster. She had no cosmetics and there was a great weariness at her bagged eyes, and her breasts were heavy in their fall into the fatigue tunic when she stretched her back after each blow, like they'd suckled children. He couldn't see the First Secretary because the bastard was behind him, and he couldn't see the Intelligence Officer because he was away to the right of him, and his right eye was already closing from the interrogator's blows. He could read her face, and her face was iced calm. From what he read in her face, the fanny was bloody tired, but she would go on hitting him until she dropped, and she wouldn't care if she rasped her fists, and she wouldn't care if she hurt him. He thought she was without mercy. He knew that sort of fanny, in the Defence Force, all the *fucking* same.

All the same because they'd had a man killed somewhere on the *fucking* line, some time in the war, and they'd parked the kiddies with their mothers, and they'd put on the uniform, and they hated. There was no mercy from the *fucking* women. The women were the *fucking* worst. He had his hands up, tried to cover his face.

'You don't leave here, Ham, before I have the time and the place of the rendezvous. When, where . . . ?'

Because he tried to protect his face, he did not see the short swing of the interrogator's boot. She kicked him hard, boot into his shin, toecap onto the bone of his leg. He cried out.

He didn't doubt her. He seemed to see himself bloodstained and screaming and cringing. He seemed to see the guys who had been behind in the open field amongst the trees. He seemed to see her with the knife bent over the guys who had been wounded and could not save themselves. All the goddamn same, *fucking* Serb bastards and *fucking* Croat bastards. He did not know how long it had been, whether he had been in the chair in the Intelligence Officer's room for half an hour or an hour. A goddamn awful pain in his leg. And Penn was nothing to him, goddamn *nothing*. He should come first, second, tenth, he should come ahead of goddamn Penn every fucking time. He owed Penn nothing.

'Come on, Ham, what's the time and what's the place?'

She had hold of his head. The interrogator's fingers and sharp nails seemed to be able to take a grip on the folds of the skin over his scalp, and she shook his head until he thought his mind would explode.

Dumb and stupid enough to let himself get hacked around, kicked around. He owed Penn nothing . . .

Ham told where he was to be waiting to take the inflatable across the Kupa river to collect Penn and the German woman and the eyewitness, and the prisoner.

The First Secretary said, 'That's a good boy.'

Ham told when he was to be beside the Kupa river to pick up Penn and the German woman and the eyewitness, and the prisoner.

The First Secretary said relieved, 'That's a sensible boy.'

★   ★   ★

'Will you, please, close your mouth.'

But she didn't. He thought it was excitement, adrenaline, whatever unnamed chemicals were screwing about in her bloodstream, that made her need to talk. He supposed she was a town person and had to communicate, and he knew that he was a country person able to subsist on his own company. He didn't bloody well need to talk, she did . . . They had been on the move for ten hours before he had signalled the long halt. They had gone slow through the darkness and faster in the dawn light, and quickest when the sun had started to stream down through the thickening foliage above them. The sun was up now, throwing down gold shards, picking out and spotlighting the mulch floor of the forest.

'If we don't talk then you don't know why. It should be important to you, why. You must wish to know why I have come . . .'

'What I know is that sound carries in the forest. You think you are quiet, you are like a rhino . . .'

'What is a rhino?'

'God, a rhino moves like a double-decker . . .'

'What is a double-decker?'

'A rhinoceros is a very big, very fat, noisy animal. A double-decker is a two-floor, very big, very heavy, noisy bus . . .'

'I know what is a rhinoceros and what is a bus. How can you say I am like a rhinoceros and a bus?'

'God, Ulrike . . . will you say what you have to say, and then, *please*, be quiet.'

'Don't you need to know why?'

They were off the track. He thought they might be an hour going fast, probably more than an hour, from the place where there were the bones and the cases and the bags. He felt so tired. He lay on his back and his head was crooked up against the backpack and she sat cross-legged beside him. His eyes were opening, closing, opening again, and he could see the excitement in her face, the adrenaline and the chemicals, and he thought that if he slept and she stayed awake then he would have lost control of her. He was frightened to lose control of her in case a dog came, in case a patrol came, in case a group of loggers came, in case . . . He had not told her about the skeletons of

327

the refugees and their bags and their cases, and he did not know if he could bypass the place so that she would not see them.

'It is not required for me to know why. I have told you that I am grateful that you have come. It does not help me to know. But you insist . . . So, tell me why, then be quiet.'

So serious: 'You have to know why.'

'Tell me.'

'It is about a future.'

Brutal, he said, 'Not our future. We have no future.'

She hissed, peeved, 'There is more than our future. There is the future of the principle.'

His eyes closed again, he forced them open. 'I know nothing of principles.'

'Rubbish. You are not here without principles. You are a man of principle . . .'

'Principles get people killed. That's not for me.'

'Silly, stupid man. Without principle you would have been on the aircraft, you would have been at your home. You sell yourself too cheap. You have principle, and you have anger . . .'

'The anger is because you won't shut your mouth.'

'You have anger and principle, and they ride together, that is why I came.'

'Brilliant, thank you, good night. Lights out and silence, please . . .'

And he could not push open his eyes. Eyes closed and the tiredness clinging in him. Typical of a bloody woman that there must be a bloody discussion . . . Just like at Five, just like the women graduates in General Intelligence Group. Why must the mountain be climbed? Analysis and thought and team discussion as to why the mountain must be climbed. Best to have a paper written on Aims and Objects for Climbing the Mountain, then have a subcommittee report on the paper to the full team. Penn was climbing the mountain because the bloody mountain was there. Penn was going up the bloody mountain because Mrs Mary bloody Braddock was holding a bayonet, sharp as hell, against his backside for him to impale himself on if he should bloody well stop climbing the bloody mountain. Penn was crawling up the bloody scree slope of the mountain because *she* was there, Dorrie was at the top with the wind in her hair and the rain on her face and the mist about her, bloody laughing and mocking him . . .

Ulrike was close to him. He sensed her bent over him. There was a garlic taste on her breath. Her fingers were smoothing the hair from his forehead . . . Because the bloody mountain was there, with Dorrie astride it.

She said into his ear, 'I understand that there is no future, and the future for us is not important, but the future of the principle is everything. If nobody speaks, if nobody calls out, if there is only silence, then there is a new dark age of barbarity . . .'

He murmured, 'Principles are not important. What is important, if we take Milan Stanković, when we run with Milan Stanković, then the wasps' nest is well stirred. It's shit-frightened running then, and when you're running it's not bloody principles that'll help you along. And if we try to take the eyewitness, she's old, slow, needing to be carried . . .'

Maybe it was just the movement of her lips speaking into his ear, maybe she kissed his ear, but they had no future. The future was Jane, was Tom. It was not important whether he wanted it, or what he wanted. There was no future with Ulrike.

'It is the difference between us and them, we have principle and they have only barbarism . . .'

'Christ, Ulrike, principles don't stop bullets, can't blunt knives.'

'Penn . . . ?'

'Yes.' So tired, and slipping, and her lips breathing the words to his ear.

'Penn, if you had him, if you have taken him, but you are blocked, and you cannot bring him out, would you kill him?'

'I don't know.'

'You have to make an answer. Would you kill him as justice? Would you kill him as revenge, for what he did to the wounded?'

'I don't know.'

'Kill him for what he did to Dorrie?'

'I don't know.'

'You will remember what I told you . . . if he is begging you

329

for his life, you will have to be cruel. Do you have it inside you, good and ordinary and decent man, to be cruel . . . ?'

'Please, don't talk, please.'

'I want to know what he is like. I want to see his face, hear his speech, watch him move. I want to know how he is different. He is married, he has a child, he is a leader of his people. I understand all of those things. I do not understand how he could have beaten the wounded and knifed them and shot them. I do not understand how he could have looked into the face of your Dorrie and beaten her and knifed her and shot her. I have to believe that I will find something of him that is *different*. If he is not different then we are all lost. I see only victims. I do not know those who make the victims. I see the results of their violence but I am not able to see the source of the violence. Penn, surely you don't believe that I came here only because I was afraid for you. Penn, I despise sentiment . . . There are 2,400 souls in the Transit Centre, and they do not even own hope, and their number is minimal in comparison with the greater number who have suffered. They deserve some, however small, act of retribution . . . Half a century ago it was my own country that bred the evil, and the evil was made by men and women that you would have passed in the street and thought no different from yourself. The evil must be isolated, stopped . . . If he is a good and ordinary and decent man then there is no hope for any of us, none, then it is indeed the beginning of that dark age. I have to pray that he is different . . .'

Penn slept.

'You will give me the wit to believe that you are not joking with me?'

'No, sir, I am most serious; would that it were a joke.'

It was a part of the First Secretary's upbringing that he would address a more senior man with respect. And a lesson of his teenage years at Marlborough School, well learned, that evasion of a problem came back to haunt. He sat stiffly in the chair while the Director of Civilian Affairs paced, heaving on his cigar.

'He got himself out, and now he has gone back in?'

'That's what I am saying.'

The smoke of the cigar spat from the Director's mouth. 'You appreciate the implications of what you tell me?'

'It is because I appreciate them that I have come to you.'

'I am not a highly educated man, just a fecking Paddy, I have a bad degree out of Dublin, Business Management crap, maybe I don't have the intellect for this job. Maybe a man with a greater intellect could do this job without having to spend fifteen, seventeen, hours a day stuck at this desk or sitting in on meetings with the most God-awful people Christ ever invented, maybe. I spend those hours every day trying to stamp out the nastiest brush fire Europe has seen in half a century. I hate this place, I hate its bestiality and its barbarity, its love of slitting the throats of old friends and former neighbours . . .'

'I understand, sir.'

'What I am trying to do, with my piss-poor intellect, is create some sort of cease-fire so that the killing stops. Are you following me?'

'Very clearly.'

'I have these war crimes groupies fecking about in my backyard. At the moment they are little more than a nuisance, but each day they're here, each day they dig their hole deeper, so their power of sabotage increases . . .'

'I appreciate that, sir.'

'Let me tell you something, in confidence. Right now, this week, there is a meeting in Budapest between Croat bureaucrats and Serb bureaucrats. There is a meeting scheduled tomorrow in Detroit, out of the limelight, between a Croatian constitutional lawyer and a Serb with the same education. Two days ago, in Athens, there wound up a session involving Bosnian Muslims and Serbs . . . Thank Christ, those bloody journalists down in Sarajevo and Belgrade and Zagreb are too preoccupied with getting hero medals on the front lines, they don't know the half of what's being worked . . .'

The First Secretary knew of all three meetings, and disguised his knowledge. 'Small mercies.'

'Under the fecking carpet, we are working night and day for a cease-fire, and talk of war crimes tribunals is an obstruction. Shit, the Serbs have monsters in their ranks, but so do the Croats,

331

so do the Bosnian Muslims. Everybody in this mess is *guilty*. If an alleged war criminal is kidnapped and brought out of Sector North then I can kiss goodbye to a cease-fire, most especially if they also bring out an eyewitness. Got me? For six months now I have oiled these bastards towards talking with each other . . . You know what, you should see them. Get a Croat and a Serb together in a quiet hotel with a bar, and you sure as hell wouldn't know they've been beating double shades of shit out of each other. They want a deal. They laugh together, drink together, probably go looking for tail together. They want out . . .'

'I wouldn't wish you to think that my government in any way condones the action of this freelancer, quite the opposite . . .'

'And who will believe you?'

There might have been a microphone in the room. Best to assume there were microphones recording the conversation. The First Secretary spoke softly. 'Which is why I brought you the information, which is why we will do our damnedest to make certain no alleged war criminal is brought out from Sector North. I think we are running on the same rails. It won't happen . . .'

The face of the Director lightened, as if he were now amused. 'But it was your Prime Minister who called for tribunals . . .'

'Should never pay too much attention to political ramblings.'

'And this Penn, interfering fecking nobody, he's your man . . .'

The First Secretary was smiling. 'Pity that he didn't stay home. I met him. Not very impressive, but he's been caught up in the emotion of the place. Capable in a technical sense, but not very bright. Capable enough, perhaps, to make it back to the Kupa river, but not bright enough to see the implications of his actions. If he takes his man then we'll hear about it . . . As you know better than me, the dust sheets will be coming off the artillery pieces and the cladding will be off the ground-to-ground missiles that can reach southern Zagreb. They might even get to loading up . . . I don't think they'd fire unless this wretched clerk from Salika village is actually out of their territory. Penn will not be allowed to cross the river with his prisoner, I thought you should know.'

He saw the spreading astonishment crack the Director's face. 'You'd see him go to the wall, your man?'

The First Secretary had served one tour, two years, in Dublin as a junior Six person covered by diplomatic status. He thought he knew the southern Irish. He thought they reckoned that the British were always totally devious, quite ruthless. Well . . .

'He's not our man.'

Everything of note, everything sensitive to his work, Marty had locked away in the floor safe. He was checking his shopping list and beside him as he stood was the howl of the mains-powered electric drill. They were cheerful young guys, the two Swedish soldiers with the drill, perhaps carpenters or engine mechanics back home before their turn in the armed forces. When they had made the deep screw sockets in the floor they would fix down the metal ring that he had demanded. They did not ask him why he wanted a metal ring fastened to the floor of the converted freight container, and he would not have told them the reason for it.

He checked his list, carefully typed out.

1 Bed (collapsible).
1 Sleeping bag, plus blanket.
Food: Bread, margarine, jam, sliced ham, sausage, milk
   (3 litres).
1 Hotel room reservation (KD – eyewitness).
1 Chain (4 metres).
2 Padlocks (2 keys each).
1 pair Handcuffs (2 keys).

He told the Swedish soldiers that they should close the door when they had finished fastening the ring in the floor. The ring would hold a padlock, the padlock would hold a chain, the chain would hold a second padlock, the second padlock would hold a pair of handcuffs, the pair of handcuffs would hold a war criminal. Marty Jones had told anyone who would listen since he had come to Zagreb that it was the *means* that were important, not the *end*. He reckoned himself entitled to change his mind. He said to the Swedes that he would be out for the rest of the afternoon, gone shopping.

★　　★　　★

The sun was lowering behind the trees, edging for the summit crest of the hillside. The woodland that blanketed the long valley steamed from the heat of the day, and now there was the first freshness from the coming of the evening.

They were past the skeletons, uncared for and untouched since he had last seen them, and he had watched the control settle on Ulrike's face as if the refugees shot down were not a part of her business. The way she had gone by the skeletons told him of her strength . . . So small, so fragile, so bloody strong . . . He had pointed down to the swaddled bodies of the babies and Ulrike had not flinched, and he had felt the tears welling in his eyes.

He no longer held her hand. He felt his trust for her. Down from the trees, below in the width of the valley, he could hear the drive of two tractor engines, but the tractors and the fields were still masked from them by the thickness of the trees' foliage.

When they came to the minefield, to the needle lengths of wire rising up through the leaf carpet, he broke the rule that he had made for himself. He spoke. He told her of the cat, and he swayed his hips to show the way that the cat had eased itself against the antennae of the mines, just for a moment of lightness, almost of clowning. Then he caught a grip on himself . . . This was no bloody place to go clowning. But if they didn't laugh they would cry, and if they cried they would be broken . . . They pushed on.

She went easily. She could have been on a forest ramble. Ulrike would know the reality because she took in the refugees. She would know they were moving into the eye of the storm.

The stream was silver and black between the trees.

They stopped still. They stood against a wide oak's trunk and they could see beyond the stream to the orchard blossoms and the smoke wreath above the chimneys of Salika. Gold light fell on the valley. They saw two old tractors moving in the fields across the stream. The one spread manure and the other ploughed. And across the stream they saw a man and a child walking away from the village and Penn shuddered. He did not need to tell her . . . Milan Stanković held the child's hand and he carried on his shoulder two fishing rods and a landing net.

334

Milan and the child were coming away from the village and were walking on the far bank of the stream past the silver spate water towards a dark slow pool.

They had a plan.

The plan dictated that, first, they should find the eyewitness.

He estimated the village was a mile from the pool and the tractors were half a mile from Milan Stanković and his boy.

Ulrike understood the dilemma. She said, 'You must have the eyewitness first. You must.'

'It is our opportunity.'

'The eyewitness is evidence. Evidence is necessary.

'We get the eyewitness . . .' As if she were speaking to a juvenile. 'They have not even begun . . . They will be there when we want them to be there . . . Penn, you have to be cruel.'

He was looking at the child who skipped along beside his father and he could faintly hear the excited squeals of the child who held his father's hand.

They went back into the depth of the trees, where the trunks were set closer. He looked twice into her face to see if the sight of the target man had changed her, if the sight of the child with the target man disturbed her, and he saw nothing but a chilled and steadfast determination. They pushed on. They moved now in short rushes. He would select a big tree ahead, and he would go fast to it and hug against it, and she would come to him, and they would wait, would listen, and he would choose the next tree. He recognized that he made more noise than she did, that his feet were heavier and his footfall clumsier. He could see the jagged rooftops of Rosenovici . . .

Back to Dorrie's place, back again into Dorrie's war . . . He could see through the trees the broken tower of the church, and he could see the lane that led to Katica Dubelj's hovel home. He caught at Ulrike's arm when she came light-stepped to him, and his hand was across his mouth to demand her silence and he pointed to the grey-black smear of the earth among the weeds in the corner of the field . . . and he seemed to hear again the *horrid* young woman, laughing at him, mocking him. It was a madness, and it was for her, and her laughter clamoured in his mind.

They came to the path that climbed the hill slope behind the village that had died.

He could have turned then, when he came to the path. He saw the worn mess of the path, mud stamped by boots. He remembered how the path had been, covered in fallen and undisturbed leaves. At that point he could have gone back into the wood.

He went at the side of the path.

He came to the mouth of the cave where the grass was broken, where the boots had gathered. He took the small torch from the backpack side pouch. Ulrike's hand was on his arm, holding tight to him, as if to give him courage.

He stood in the entrance of the cave.

He shone the torch beam forward and from the dark recess twin lights, amber, blazed back at him. The beam found the cat, wide-eyed, crouched on the rag bundle, snarling at the light. He saw the parchment skin of the face of Katica Dubelj and he saw the darkened slashes of the knives' work. He saw the cat was across her stomach and past the cat's tail were the spindle-thin legs of Katica Dubelj and the long black material of her dress was forced up to her waist and he saw the white death of the skin of her thighs. He swung the light away, away from the cat who guarded her. He reeled out of the cave.

Ulrike held him.

'It is what they always do. They violate old women. They rape old women. Perhaps you are responsible, Penn.'

'Don't . . .'

'Every time, for the rest of your life, that you take a woman to your bed . . . Perhaps it was you that led them to her, Penn.'

'Don't say that . . .'

'Every time you take a woman to your bed, for warmth and for love, you will remember her . . . It is what you have to live with here, Penn, your responsibility.'

'Don't let me hear you say that . . .'

'Because you are not man enough to hear it? It's not boys' games . . . It is about survival . . . It is about the code of living that you believe in . . . You do not have an eyewitness, so you

336

have to take him and you have to make him convict himself. Are you strong enough to make him convict himself?

'I have to be . . .'

'And he has the child with him . . . Are you strong enough?'

She had walked the city all of the afternoon, not shopping and not window gazing, but a restless striding, as if walking the streets was an escape from the isolation of her hotel room.

Dog-tired, her feet killing, Mary Braddock found a café on the Trg Bana Jelačića, a table to herself. A *cappuccino* was brought to her.

It was, none of it, fair.

Not fair of Charles to shout down the telephone at her, 'God, Mary, do you understand what you've done . . .'

Not fair of the earnest young American investigator to challenge her, 'As long as you know, ma'am, what you're asking that man to do . . .'

Not fair of Penn to tell her simply, 'I doubt you ever listened to your daughter . . .'

Nothing was fair. It was what any mother would have done . . . Suddenly they came around her. They were noisy, bouncing with humour. They didn't ask her if they could take the rest of the table. She sat huddled amongst the young students. They ignored her. They were squashed close to her and they had their study books on the table and one tried to read what she thought was poetry and there was happy mocking from her friends. She drank the dregs of her coffee. And amongst them there was a pale and gaunt-faced young man with cropped blond hair, and the young man was struggling to lift an unmounted canvas from a wide bag. She saw that he struggled because he used his left hand only, and she saw the way that the right sleeve of his jacket hung empty. The work on the canvas, violent and bold and crude, showed a young woman crucified, and the cross had fallen in filth. And their laughter was around her, and she was not a part of them, and their babble at the merit of the work . . . It was not fair, because she craved to be included . . .

They were her Dorrie's people, damn her.

*   *   *

It was a warm spring evening.

A long valley, and the trees from the woodland threw broad bold shadows on the grassland.

It was an idyllic setting.

A father inserted a fishing hook into a writhing worm and cast the line into the hidden darkness of a slow pool, and handed the rod to his child son.

It was a place of calm, of peace.

They had worked the plan through when they had still been in the tree line of the wood, how they would shatter the evening, break the idyll, crack the calm and the peace. They had talked it through coldly, and Penn had said what he would do, and Ulrike had agreed the plan. He took off his trousers, and she unzipped her jeans and kicked them off over her boots, and there was no shyness between them, nor any humour. It was a small part of the plan that it would be better for them when they crossed the stream to keep their trousers dry. It was part of the plan, methodical and point by point, that it would be better for them when they fled with the prisoner to have dry trousers. They heard the excited squeal of the child and saw him arc his rod up, but there was no fish. It was a good moment for Penn to go.

He saw the father bent over the grass and the man, Milan Stanković, the man who was the killer of Dorrie Mowat, would be searching in a tin or a jar for a fresh worm to thread onto the hook.

Penn had such confidence in her, he did not feel the need to look back at her for reassurance.

He left the tree line, and as he ran across the weeded and untended grassland of the field towards the stream, he could see the hunched low-set shoulders of the man and the child. He took a line towards a mess of fallen willows that were up the valley from the deep pool where they fished. He was running blind, because all of his attention was on the lowered shoulders of the man and the child, and the skin of his shins and thighs was nicked by the old thistles of the field that had not been worked since the fall of Rosenovici, since the death of Dorrie Mowat . . . He saw the man straighten, and the child was pointing to where the fish had taken the worm and was trying to wrestle the rod back from his father so that he might cast again more quickly. Penn had dived to the ground, fallen among nettles that pricked at the bared skin of his legs. He was crawling towards the bushes of willow.

The worm was in the water. They were both of them watching the line.

Penn hesitated when he reached the willows' cover.

There was a high bank to the stream, cut deep by the winter's flow, where the willow branches fell into the water. Penn looked up into the closing dusk and he saw far away that the tractors were retreating towards the dulled blossom of the orchards and the climbing smoke of the village. It was so quiet . . . He slid down the bank. He dropped into the pressure power of the current. It was shallow water above the pool, going quickly. They were both of them, man and child, rapt and staring into the dark water in front of them. It was the chance that he must take. His body was bent so that the water broke against his chest as he took chopped strides on the smoothed big stones of the stream's bed. He made the crossing. He came to the far bank and grabbed at a root and dribbled the stream's water from his mouth.

Penn came up the bank.

He lay in the grass and he felt for the soaked fine rope that was a part of the plan, and for the torn cloth strip from the tail of his shirt.

He was forty yards, perhaps fifty, along the bank of the stream from the man and the child.

There was a shout.

The happiness of the child gave a moment of opportunity to Penn.

He was behind them, going cat quick, closing on them.

The rod was arched above them. They were both clinging to the rod, and the child was yelling and the father was trying to calm him.

He had the opportunity.

Penn came on them. When he was close, when he was a stride away from them, the father turned. When his hand was raised for the blow, Milan Stanković saw him. When he had the heel of his hand high, the killer of Dorrie Mowat gazed at him in bewilderment. Penn hit him. Penn hit the neck of Milan Stanković, defenceless because his hands were still clasping the rod, above the shoulder and below the ear. It was not a blow that would have felled a readied man, but Milan Stanković was in bewilderment, and his hands came off the rod and he went down. So fast . . . The man on the grass of the field, and Penn rolling him onto his stomach and driving his knee down into the man's back, and snatching clear the pistol at his waist, and dragging up his right arm as if to break the socket at the shoulder. The child held the curved and quivering rod, and for that moment did not understand. He saw Ulrike break the cover of the trees and she was running, whitened legs pumping, to the far bank of the stream. He had the noose on the wet rope around Milan Stanković's right wrist, and then he was pulling the left arm back to meet the right wrist, and binding the wrists together. It was about advantage . . . and the advantage of surprise diminished. Milan Stanković shouted in his fear, and he heaved with his hips, his buttocks, to throw off Penn. With the fear was recognition . . . It was the struggle of the animal that senses, in fear, the open doorway of the abattoir. She was coming dripping along the stream's bank, hurrying to him, and the child had thrown down the rod. They came together at Penn, Ulrike and the child.

He pulled Milan Stanković upright.

The child clung to his father's legs.

He hit Milan Stanković hard across the back of the skull with the barrel of the pistol, to hurt and to stun.

The child beat at Penn with small clenched fists.

Penn had one hand on the roped wrists of Milan Stanković, and the other hand held the pistol under the chin of the man who had killed Dorrie Mowat, and he was trying to propel Milan Stanković away and back towards the fast spate waters above the pool, and he could not move him because the child held at his father's legs and punched and kicked at his father's attacker. Ulrike was there. Penn saw the cold in her eyes. Ulrike had said that he would have to be cruel. She caught the child, she broke the child's grip. She threw the child down, viciously, onto the grass of the field.

Penn and Ulrike ran on the bank to the upper end of the pool, and they had the weight of Milan Stanković between them. They scrambled him down the bank, and into the flow of the stream. He slumped once between them, his feet slipping, and he was doused over his head and was spluttering water when they pulled him up.

Just before they reached the tree line Penn swung to look behind him.

He saw the rod sliding away into the pool.

Ulrike, amongst the trees, retrieved the backpack.

He saw the child running, demented, across the empty fields and back towards the village and the smoke and the blossom dull in the dusk.

Evica shook him, shook her Marko.

She shook him hard to kill the hysteria in her son, and then she held him against her until the panted sobbing subsided, until he could tell her.

18

She ran fast down the lane of the village, punishing herself, carrying the weight of her son.

She had pulled her coat from the hook on the door, she had left the dog in the kitchen, she had swept the food cooking in the pots off the stove. Fleetingly, she saw the Priest sitting bowed at his window table with the oil lamp lit and the chessboard laid out. She saw the wife of the Headmaster sitting hunched near to the barred window.

She ran through the stillness of the village, in the greying light, past the garage where gasoline used to be sold before the war and the sanctions, past the shop where food could be bought before the war and the sanctions. She ran through the silence of the village, her feet clattering the quiet.

She ran until she no longer had the strength to carry her son, and then she dragged him, his stumbling feet slipping in the potholes of the lane. She came to the building, used now by the Territorial Defence Force of Salika village, that had been filled with agricultural stores before the war and the sanctions. She went across the yard and past the barns where the big agricultural plant was kept, idle because it was impossible to obtain spare machinery parts and tyres and fuel. She burst into the office area. She saw the guns of the killers, and the playing cards, and the bottles heaped on the table of the office area. She was the acting headmistress of the school, and she was the woman who had been to university in Belgrade, and she saw the dislike of her in the faces of the killers.

They stared up at her from the chairs around the table that was heaped with their guns and their playing cards and their bottles.

Evica said in not more than a whisper, 'Milan . . . Milan has been taken . . . Milan is captured . . .'

She looked into each of their faces, Branko's, Stevo's, Milo's, and she had never hidden that she despised each of them equally.

Evica did not plead. 'You have to search for him . . . you have to find him . . . you have to bring him back to me . . .'

There was the stink of their bodies, and the smoke of their cigarettes, and the stench of the alcohol. She held Marko tight against her. And there had been first their amusement at the superior bitch fighting for breath, then the fuddled confusion of the drink, then they were listening.

Evica would not beg. 'Search, because he had gone fishing . . . find him, gone fishing with Marko . . . taken across the river . . .'

From the postman, 'By whom . . . ?'

'I can't know.'

From the gravedigger, 'Who took him . . . ?'

'I was not there.'

From the carpenter, 'Why . . . ?'

'I do not know . . . you have to find him . . . Marko was there . . .'

The hand of the chief of the irregulars snaked out. A rough and calloused and large hand. The hand snatched at the shoulder of her son's anorak, and the boy was pulled from her. For a moment, she tried to hold the boy. She saw fear in the face of her son, and she could not protect him. The boy was dragged to the table, her grip on him was broken. And the time was rushing, and the darkness was closing.

Rough and guttural questions, small and frightened answers . . . They had gone fishing. They were fishing the big pool up the valley. There was no one near to them while they were fishing . . .

She watched, and she realized the patience of the chief of the irregulars, that he let her son regain his confidence through the story of their fishing . . . The big fish, the good trout, had taken the worm, stripped it from the hook. They had bent to put another worm on the hook. They had cast again into the pool.

The fish had taken the worm, taken the hook. A big fish, pulling at the rod, and his father helping him to hold the rod up . . .

But the time was running and the darkness was gathering.

'Hurry, Marko, what you saw . . .'

And she was cut to silence by the slashed wave of the chief of the irregulars.

He stood amongst them, her son, and he told his story . . . The man had come from behind them as they held the rod together to fight the fish. His father had loosed the rod. He had looked round. His father was on the ground, on the grass of the field. The man was without trousers. The man knelt on his father and was binding his arms. The man had pulled his father up and hit him. He fought the man, he tried to kick the man's legs. A woman had come. He tried to stop them from taking his father. The woman had thrown him down, the woman had hurt him . . .

'What was he like, the man?'

Some of them already knew. She trembled. She remembered. She heard the voice that she had translated: 'I have the evidence for my report that Dorrie Mowat was killed by, was murdered by, Milan Stanković.' She saw the face of the man, beaten and scarred and cut. They shared the guilt.

Pandemonium breaking out of the office area of the TDF headquarters. Shouts, cries in the night, and the gathering up of weapons, and the howling of awakened dogs. And who was the leader now . . . ? The one from the irregulars, but he did not know the terrain of the valley? The postman? The grave-digger? The carpenter? And was there a working telephone line out of the village? And where was the man to link the radio to Glina military? And where should the search begin, in the wood-land across the stream, in darkness? At the deep pool where her Milan had been captured? She heard the babble of argument, and time was running.

She shouted above their voices, 'Cowards . . . you all share the guilt. It was not just him that did it . . . Idiots, if Milan is taken, your leader, it is all of you who are threatened. Murderers . . .'

In confusion, in disordered chaos, the village was armed, the link was made and interrupted and made again and interrupted

344

again with Glina military, and the search party moved out into the lane in front of the old agricultural store, and the debate of tactics began.

They had no leader.

She remembered the man, what he had said and what he had seemed to be. '. . . Tell Dorrie's mother the name of the man who killed her daughter . . .' Dignified, brave, remote from the law of the bastard village that was her home, not intimidated by the violence threatening him. If that man had her Milan . . . Evica reckoned that the man and the woman who had taken her husband had a start on them of near to an hour.

At the first halt, an hour gone since they had moved into the haven of the tree line on the west side of the valley, he had given Milan Stanković's pistol to Ulrike and he had shone the torch full into the face of Milan Stanković and he had held the small-bladed knife against the bearded throat of the man.

She knew their language, she interpreted.

Into the wide grey-blue eyes he had said that, if they were trapped, if they were intercepted, if they could go no further, he would slit that throat. And at the rest stop, two minutes on his watch, he and Ulrike had taken their turn in watching him close and they had slipped on again their dry trousers. He had whisper growled the threat to slit Milan Stanković's throat, and he did not think he was then believed.

He attempted to be cruel because it was what Ulrike had ordered of him.

And as the second hand of his watch was slipping for the end of the two minutes, he had summoned what he hoped was ferocity and he had told Milan Stanković that if he shouted, screamed, howled, he would cut his throat.

Penn dragged him forward. Ulrike led with the torch cupped in the palm of her hand so that it made a short cone of light ahead of her feet. Penn had the knife close to Milan Stanković's neck so that when they pitched or stumbled then the tip of the blade would waver against the fullness of the man's beard. It was not important to him that the man had spat contempt at him.

345

The man did not shout, but instead talked softly. He was not gagged because Penn had thought that if he were gagged with the torn strip off the tail of his shirt then his breathing would be impaired and he would not be able to go as fast as was required of him. A low and calm voice. He could hear the murmur of the voice and the staccato bursts of Ulrike's side-of-mouth interpretation.

'. . . You think you can succeed, then you are a lunatic . . . The whole village will be coming, man and boy, guns . . . You are the stranger here, don't know the ways in the forest, they know them . . . You only took me because I had the boy with me, because I was distracted with the boy, if I had not had the boy you would not have taken me . . . You are shit, shit when you came the first time, shit now . . . They will be coming after you, coming close to you . . . It is our forest, not yours, why you have no possibility . . . You say you will kill me, you would not dare . . .'

There was a change in Ulrike's voice. There was no longer an automaton translation, but something said softly in the man's language, and the man's words dried.

Penn asked, 'What did you tell him?'

Ulrike said, not looking back, 'You might not kill him, but *I* would. That's what I told him, that I would kill him. He may not believe you, he should believe me . . . and I asked him if he felt guilt.'

She was so strong . . . He wondered if she had ever felt weakness. And everything of her was denied him. He wondered where she had been five years before, when he had waited on the railway station for the delayed train and chatted to the stranger, Jane, and taken the taxi down to Raynes Park where Jane lived. He wondered if Ulrike Schmidt, who allowed no sentiment, would have looked at him then, admired him or wanted to share with him. His best friend, Dougal Gray, would have understood. Penn had heard that Dougal Gray, in Belfast, now lived with the separated wife of a policeman. In the heart of danger men and women were thrown together and thought they found love when they squirmed only for comfort. In a year, when Dougal Gray finished his extended tour, and was posted back to Gower

Street there would be no chance that the separated wife of a policeman would up sticks to travel with him . . . There was no future.

He had a hold of the wrists of Milan Stanković that were knotted with the fine rope at the pit of his back. Each time that they had gone a hundred metres, each moment that they stopped, he strained for the sounds of pursuit, and Milan Stanković was listening too, each time he bent his neck that he would hear better the first signs of the chasing pack.

They went on into the depth of the woodland, climbing from the valley.

There were some who said they should take cars and the jeep, and go up the road beyond Bović towards the Pokupsko bridge where the Kupa river was the cease-fire line. There were others who said they should drive up the Vrginmost road and then take the turning towards the artillery position and fan out into the woods from there. And there was delay while the cars were filled with gasoline from the pump in the yard of the old agricultural store, and there were some who said they should go on foot into the woodland from the Rosenovici side of the stream, and others said they should go first to where the boy had told them his father had been taken. More delay for the argument. Some said they should wait for the army to come from Glina military, some said they should do the work for themselves.

She listened. She wept.

They decided. They had filled the cars with gasoline, but they would not use them. They would go on foot. They would go across the bridge and through the village of Rosenovici, and they would make a beating line through the woodland.

She wept because she saw the wild excitement in torch-lit faces, as if they were away and off to drive a boar from thicket scrub, to rouse a deer for shooting.

She watched the column of bouncing lights, raucously tailing away towards the bridge.

Evica Stanković realized how greatly she loathed them, all of them.

And she wiped the tears off her face, and she led Marko away.

347

She went to the house of the Priest. The Priest should have been her friend, as the Headmaster should have been her friend. She gave her son into the care of the Priest and his wife. She despised the man, as she despised herself. The Priest and the Headmaster and herself were the only three souls of the village with education, but amongst them only the Headmaster had stood up for what he believed. She told the Priest that Milan had been taken as a war criminal, and she saw the shallow sneer on the Priest's face, and she knew him to be an ambivalent bastard.

He told a story in his low singing voice. It was the story of a Croat, the story of Matija Gubec, the leader of a revolt in the year of 1573 against the tyrant Franjo Tahi. He said it was the story of a little man who had risen to great power.

'. . . He wanted, Gubec, to be a big man amongst the peasants, and he made an organization of revolt. The sign of recognition with his people was a sprig of evergreen. The simple people followed him, but they were tricked by the superior intellect of the tyrant: they were told that while they went with the peasant rabble so the Turks were gathering to pillage their homes and they deserted Gubec. He was taken. He was brought to Zagreb. He was led to St Mark's Square for a coronation. But the crown was iron, and the crown was heated by fire until the iron was white hot. He was crowned, and then he was dismembered. It is a story of long ago, before we were civilized, the story of a man who reached too far.'

He would have known that she was desperate for speed, and he had held her with the mincing words of the story, and with the tail of the story he had kicked her. So many times the Priest had walked to her house and wheedled for favours from her Milan and patted the head of her Marko. The chess set was laid out on the table of rough stained oak . . . The Priest, the bastard, had not had the courage to stand beside his friend. When the Headmaster faced death then the Priest, the bastard, had stayed quiet. That the Priest dared taunt her was absolute proof of how alone she was. They blamed her, the Priest and his wife, for the humbling and the killing of a friend.

She left her son there, whimpering, with the thin-boned fingers of the ambivalent bastard resting on the boy's shoulder.

She went back to her home and she put on heavy boots and took the rusted bayonet down from the high wall hook, and she called for the dog to come with her. She knew the name of the dog, the name given it by the Ustaše Croat people, and she took the big flashlight. With the dog at her heel she went away across the fields on the east side of the river. She could see their torches going through Rosenovici village, and she could hear them. She went alone with the dog, and she called it with its Ustaše name to be close to her. She knew how it would be . . . They would search a small area, the area around the villages, their own area. They were tribal. They would not move beyond the boundary of their own area. She could recall when some of the young men of the village had been volunteered for duty, last year, outside Petrinja, in the trenches facing Sisak, and they had drifted home within twelve days because it was not their own war, beyond their own area.

Her dog would know the scent of Milan.

Her torch found the jar of worms and the landing net and one of the rods. Her dog whined at the bank beyond the pool, and her torch showed the sliding marks of boots and bodies.

She had the dog on a lead and she tugged it down into the fierce flow of the stream.

'You sort of people, you always back a loser.'

The First Secretary said it drily. He drove his big Rover along the night-empty highway from Karlovac towards Zagreb. A heavy brute to drive, but it was weighted with armour plating on the side doors and with bullet-proof glass for the windows, and the self-sealing tyres that could absorb small shrapnel and low-velocity gunfire were unresponsive.

Ham whined, 'What'll happen . . . ?'

'Good to know you care.'

'What'll happen to me . . . ?'

'God, just for one moment, for one fleeting second of time, I thought you were concerned with someone other than your own miserable self. A constant disappointment, Freefall, you have been to me. What'll happen to you . . . ? You'll be shovelled on, like any other bag of rubbish that's dumped on someone else's front step. Nagorny Karabakh, wasn't it? Not Nagorno, best you learn how to say it first . . . They're welcome to entertain you. Myself, if I were you, I'd choose the Armenian side rather than the Azeris, but knowing your track record it'll be the Azeris because they're the losers.'

He prided himself that he retained some small influence in this awful corner of Europe. He had done an insignificant deal with the Croat military, a personal arrangement with the Intelligence Officer involving an insubstantial roll of German banknotes and the promise of future contact . . . Anyone could be bought in this awful corner, surprisingly cheaply in this case. He had won the release of Sidney Ernest Hamilton, codename Freefall, into his personal custody. Just the matter of handing in the wretch's uniform, his kit, his ID, and the Dragunov, and the little list of contacts for the moving on of black market supplies of Marlboro cigarettes, and he had been given the wretch in handcuffs.

'Will you snitch him?'

'I beg your pardon, try to speak English, please.'

'Shop him, tell the Serbs where to be waiting for him, will you?'

'You should just stick to losing . . . Affairs of state aren't your business, Freefall, never were and never will be.'

'They'll make you watch. They'll put you in a chair so that you are comfortable, and they'll make you watch . . .'

It was close to dawn. They could start to see the way ahead of them and there was no longer a need for her to shine the torch in front of her feet. Penn had stopped twice to rest and he had allowed Milan Stanković to eat a small piece of bread and he had given him a broken piece of sharp cheese, and once he had unzipped the man's trousers and handled him so that he could urinate without messing his trousers. He felt exhaustion and Milan Stanković also fought tiredness, but she still had strength and she set a pace that was hard, and from the side of her mouth she gave, briskly and without feeling, the interpretation of what he said.

'When they have you sitting down and comfortable then they

will put her down onto the floor and they will strip off the trousers from her, and they will take the knickers from the bitch, and they will all come to her, all serve her. What it's like when a big boar pig comes to serve a sow, big so that it hurts. One after the other, all of them in the village, old men, young men, me last of all, and they will make you watch . . .'

He did not know how she could translate and how she could not cringe. He did not know how she could not turn on him and hit him. Each time that they made the short stops he would listen, and sometimes he would hear far distant shouts, and then they would press ahead faster. The decision that he had to make was where to lie up, whether they should go forward as the light grew and lie up until darkness at the bank of the Kupa river to wait for the inflatable to come across at the rendezvous point, or whether they should lie up through the daylight and then make the charge in the dusk to the river. He was not ready to make the decision, and he could not think clearly while the voice of the man droned on and while she gave her clipped interpretation.

'Before they shoot her, we will play with you. Which do you prefer? Electricity . . . ? Fire . . . ? Knife cuts . . . ? Electricity on your balls, is that what you would prefer? Fire on your feet, on your body, needles from the fire under your fingernails? Knife cuts at your testicles and your penis, on your fingers, at your ears, the knife going into your eyes. The last you will know of the electricity and the fire and the knife will be from me. You will be crying for me to finish it, and you will be shouting for me to go to her with the electricity and the fire and the knife cuts . . . But you can let me go free . . .'

Penn understood. He remembered the arrogant conceit, a long time ago, of an Irishman, not a big Provo but a second-rater from the feeble Irish National Liberation Army faction, who had been picked up when Five, their role as watchers completed, had deigned to call in the Anti-terrorist Branch for the formality of the arrest. The Irishman, skinny little creep, had been spread-eagled on the carpet of his pig-sty living room, and he had been silent, but the arrogance and the conceit had been large on his bloody face, as if to say they'd crack nothing out of him.

'Is that what you want? Do you want to sit comfortably

and watch all of the men, and me, screw the arse off her . . .
before she dies? Do you want to let me go free? Do you want
to feel the electricity wires on you and the fire burns and the
knife cuts, they make pain but they don't make death, not till
we are ready, do you want that? Or do you want to let me go
free . . . ?'

Ulrike spoke in his language, and his words withered.

They heard vehicles. They were straining four-wheel-drive
jeeps and they were manoeuvring in the slipping rutted mud of
the loggers' track. They were crouched down and he held the
knife so tight against the bulged adam's apple at the bearded
throat of Milan Stanković that the skin was nicked and he drew
blood. They were away from the track, in the depths of the trees,
and they could see the soldiers in the jeeps, and he could see the
guns that the soldiers held. He held the knife so close against
the throat of Milan Stanković and the images were splayed in
his mind, of Ulrike laid out on a floor of concrete and her legs
held open, and the electricity wires clipped to his skin . . . The
vehicles bucked on the track, and passed.

His decision was taken. They would go on until they reached
the Kupa river.

'What did you tell him?'

Ulrike said, 'I told him that I wanted to hear him speak of
his shame when he killed Dorrie Mowat . . .'

'What does it fecking mean, in a simpleton's terms?' He stood
in front of the wall map.

Not a military man, the Director of Civilian Affairs found the
big wall maps, so beloved of the military, to be sanitized and
cold viewing. He assumed that the neat laundered officers around
him, the Canadian colonel and the Jordanian major and the
Argentine captain, could make sense of the whorls and lines.
The wall map, nine feet in height and equally broad, covered
the entire area of former Yugoslavia and was draped with a clear
plastic sheet on which had been written in chinagraph crayon
the disposition of UNPROFOR units.

The Jordanian major held a long pointer and identified Sector
North, and then Salika village.

The Argentine captain said, 'They have a mass of radio traffic, mostly out of Glina, but hooked in to Vojnić where they have Command and Control, and linked to Petrinja and Lasinja and Skakavac and Brezova Glava which are close to the cease-fire demarcation line. We have the situation reports, from our monitoring, of their units that have been put to state red alert along the Kupa river. We have the transcripts of the radio transmissions made by the field troops that are deployed. We have visual confirmation of their movement from the DanBatt fixed observation posts, X-ray 9 and X-ray 11 . . .'

'And it means . . . ?'

The Canadian said, 'It means that he's coming, coming with his prisoner, coming to the river. It means that he's being hunted.'

'What chance . . . ?'

'They've lost him in the immediate vicinity of his snatch. They reckon to block him on the river.'

'I said, what chance . . . ?'

'If the Serbs were to know where he planned to cross the river, no chance. They do not have that information . . . He has a slight chance.'

He was looking up, and the tip of the pointer was against the bland green of the map surface, cut only by the Kupa river, no roads. He imagined it as a morass of swamp. The Director thought he was playing God Almighty with the life of a man coming to the river with his prisoner, and he thought that the man coming to the river with his prisoner was playing God Almighty with the lives of all those within reach of the artillery and the missiles. He turned his back on the map, went slowly and subdued out of the operations room. He wondered what it was like, the swamp morass to which the man was coming with his prisoner.

It was a small farm, not more than five hectares, where Zoran Pelnak and his wife lived. The farm gave, at best, a hard living and it was poorer now that his two sons were taken by the army. Before the boys had gone, one to the garrison at Osijek and one down in the south at Gospić, Zoran Pelnak had had their help in the never finished work of cleaning and deepening the drainage ditches that cut his land. The fields were too low set for good farming ground, too near to the river that flooded its banks most winters, and most winters the farmhouse of brick and wood was set upon a small island in a shallow lake. It was Zoran Pelnak's home, had been his father's home, and his grandfather's and his great-grandfather's home. His great-grandfather and his grandfather and his father had dug the drainage ditches and cleaned them and deepened them. There were three fields for the farm and in two of them he harvested a hay crop and grazed animals, and in one of them he and his wife grew their vegetables for their own eating and for sale in the market at Karlovac. He and his wife could survive the isolation of their life on the farm that fronted the north bank of the Kupa river. Their neighbours had long gone, left their homes and their farms and their livestock, abandoned them. He would not leave. He would not have cared to have gone to the graves of his great-grandfather and his grandfather and his father, sat on his haunches beside the stones, and explained why he was running from the drainage ditches they had dug. He moved slowly from the front door of the farmhouse. From the porch of the door he could see, across the field and the bogland where the cattle could go only in summer, the far bank of the Kupa river and the trees. He moved slowly from the rheumatism that came from living in a place so damp, towards the barn where his four cows were bedded, and the pigs and the goats, and the hens. On the far bank, behind the trees, maybe the bastard fuck Partizans watched him, and he was too old to care if they saw him. Zoran Pelnak knew most of what happened, each day and each night, on the far bank of the Kupa river. He pressed on into the barn, and he hoped that the soldiers would soon be down from their camp for their well water, because the soldiers would help him lift down the baled hay for the animals.

It was many hours since Evica had last heard the advance behind her of the search party, and their shouts.

She guessed they would have turned by now, cold from the night, down because of their failure. She guessed they would be

354

heading back to their village, arguing between themselves, going back to food and warmth. And going back to dispute the new command of Salika, and to fight for control of the diesel supplies and the sacks of seed potatoes. Two would fall; she thought Branko and Milo would fall. One would rise; Stevo would command the village. She thought the wife of Stevo the most stupid woman she knew, and the wife of Stevo would take her place as the village's queen. They would turn back when they reached the perimeter line of their vicious and ignorant world . . . And her village would become an armed camp, isolated, guarded close.

The dog had the scent and moved easily ahead of her, loping on the trail on which her man had been taken.

Marty was told it by an Austrian of UNCIVPOL, told that the balloon was up in Sector North. He was a good friend of the Austrian policeman because they had shared a house, when the snow had fallen in January on Bosnia, away down east in Srebrenica, and it had been goddamn cold because the house had only half a roof, a place where men became good friends. The Austrian policeman had been coming off duty, he had a new posting at the UNCIVPOL desk in the operations room, and he had told Marty that all hell was loose across in Sector North, and that the crossing points were closed at Turanj and at Sisak, that a bigshot guy from a village in Glina Municipality had been kidnapped, that it was some crazy stuff about a war crimes investigator, and more crazy that there was the German woman from the UNHCR Transit Centre at Karlovac in tow. The Austrian policeman had told him all of this and his eyes had been going past where Marty stood in the doorway of the converted freight container, hooked on the shining steel ring set in the floor of the container, and the chain that was padlocked to it, and the collapsible bed that was made up in the far corner behind Marty with the sleeping bag laid on it and the folded blanket and the handcuffs. And Marty had told him, dead serious, that because he was homesick he'd gotten a big brute of a bear, a proper grizzly, being crated in from Anchorage, and he had gotten rid of the Austrian policeman as fast as was half decent.

He drove into central Zagreb.

Marty thought of the photographs on the walls of the freight container, pictures of the weak and the outnumbered and the defenceless who had been caught behind the lines.

He parked among the new black BMWs in their sleek rows, the wheels of the fat cat bastards who were doing fine.

He went up to her room.

Marty Jones told Mary Braddock that Penn was coming with his prisoner towards the river . . . he looked for her excitement . . . that Penn had taken Milan Stanković away from the village of Salika . . . he watched for her triumph . . . that a huge man-hunt was in progress in Sector North between the village of Salika and the Kupa river . . . he expected to see her flinch . . . that the whole of the goddamn place beyond the cease-fire line was alive, roused . . . he expected to see her wilt.

'I want to look into his face. I want him to know that he murdered my daughter. I want to be there when he's brought across.'

'That's positive thinking, ma'am, and positive thinking is always good. Could just be premature thinking. Do you have any appreciation of the odds against . . . ?'

'Penn'll bring him across the river, I don't doubt it.'

He felt almost an anger. She was sitting in an armchair and her legs, narrow and fine, were crossed in elegance, and Ulrike Schmidt, the best woman he'd known, was hacking through a bucket of hell with Penn and the prisoner, and the jaws of the goddamn trap were closing tight, as they had closed on those who were photographed on the walls of his converted freight container. One thing to goddamn talk about it, one thing to make the great goddamn plan, quite another to . . .

'Ma'am, it's not a picnic.'

'He didn't have to go . . . He never met my daughter, of course not, but he talked some unpleasant rubbish about *loving* her. I find that repulsive. I don't need lectures in motherhood. But I have the right to demand the punishment of my daughter's killer . . . He took our money.'

It was like a dismissal. He said he would go ring the mercenary down in Karlovac.

★   ★   ★

It was a recklessness that pushed Penn forward.

Thought through, well considered, he would have made the decision to lie up through that long day, and then after the fall of dusk complete the last charge for the river bank.

He did not ask her for her opinion, and she did not challenge his decision. He was drawn towards the river bank, goaded towards it.

So tired, and wanting only to be there, where he could gaze out across the slow depth of the water, he was driven towards it, towards the danger of the last barrier . . . The sun was up above them and slanted down diffused by the upper branches . . . The danger would be at the last obstacle and that was where they would set their men, where they would run their tripwires, where they would make their ambushes . . . He had now used the gag cloth, wedged it between Milan Stanković's teeth and knotted the ends tight against the shaggy long-grown hair at the back of his neck. Milan Stanković accepted the gag, and at the last stop of two minutes Penn had thought he had seen the first slipping of his arrogance, the first breaking of the conceit, as if fear had begun to gnaw at the man, and Penn heard the breaking of a branch behind him.

They were away from the path.

They were far into the cover of the trees, and Ulrike had heard what he had heard and swung on her hips to look into his face.

They were frozen. The movement of the forest woodland was around them, and both were straining to hear the sound again of the breaking of a branch, and Penn held the knife hard against Milan Stanković's throat.

She broke the moment of stillness. She moved on. He went after her, pushing the man forward, and he did not know if they were followed . . . He would not tell her that it was all ahead of them, that the worst was in front of them.

The day supervisor scowled down at him.

'Oh, you're so kind, thank you so much . . . and another thing, I'd be very grateful if you could get me a few guidebooks, former Yugoslavia . . .'

God, what a miserable woman.

'. . . Yes, I'm very nearly through . . . Those books that get to the second-hand shops, full of photographs, I'd appreciate it so much.'

Henry Carter smiled his sweetest.

She walked stiffly away, and he regretted that he had insufficient courage to call after her and request a beaker of coffee . . . If she brought him coffee she would probably accompany the visit with a further dose of that obnoxious sickly air freshener . . . As a major favour, she had brought him a set of photocopied newspaper clippings. He was, indeed, nearly through. Perhaps he was nit-picking, perhaps he was far beyond his brief, but he did not care. A job worth doing, that sort of thing. He was sifting the clippings, believing they had a place in the file even though they were dated months after the events that consumed him.

The Secretary General of the United Nations, should know what he was talking about, guaranteeing his organization's support for the international war crimes tribunal:

> We will put on trial those who have contributed to civilian suffering and it will not be forgiven . . . will deal not only with the people accused of committing the crimes, but also those who inspired the human rights violations . . . We have to denounce it . . . civilians are being bombed, starved and mistreated and children are targeted by killers in the shadows.

Good solid stuff, and a pity that no one had bothered to tell the bureaucrats in their offices above Library, and not told the Foreign and Commonwealth Office, and not told UNPROFOR. Worth entering in the file because Penn, that ordinary and decent man, and maybe a bit of a clairvoyant and most certainly blessed with common sense, would not have believed a word of it. He grasped at another clipping and wrote a brief summary to go into the file with the clipping, and hoped quite fervently that, one fine day, the file would be examined by a mandarin or an apparatchik with enough honesty to feel humility . . . some chance.

FRITS KALSHOVEN: Dutch academic, had been appointed to job of Chief Prosecutor, but resigned. Cited 'refusal of Great Britain and France and Germany and Italy to co-operate'. Noted positive attitude of United States of America, Canada and Norway. Also blamed 'obstruction' of sister UN agencies.

Ah, getting better . . . Gratifying to read it. Another clipping, another digest. Henry Carter squirmed, but it was necessary for the full picture to be drawn if it were ever to be understood why Penn had made that desperate and poorly considered expedition behind the lines, into the heart of danger. Leave it to those bastards to sort out and a man may as well wait for his Bath chair . . . More brave talk.

A new PROSECUTOR named: Ramon Escovar-Salom (Venezuelan attorney-general). Total budget of $30 million. Eleven judges appointed (nice work if you can get it!), at salary of $150,000 per annum, payable regardless of whether charges are brought.

The voice was cold behind him.
'I have your guidebooks, Mr Carter. I have also to tell you that I will be complaining, most forcibly, to In-House Management about the demands you have placed upon us, and your quite disgusting lack of personal hygiene.'
Henry Carter breezed, 'Not much longer, nearly finished.'

19

The man was snivelling.

Penn reckoned Milan Stanković to be in bad shape and there were low grunting sounds in his throat that were muffled by the gag. Maybe it was exhaustion, or maybe it was the tightness of the fine rope binding his wrists. They were going slower. They were close now to the inner line of the forward zone.

He reckoned the forward zone would be five miles, a mile either way, deep, and in the forward zone would be the maximum concentration of strongpoints and minefields and tripwires and patrols, and the forward zone could not be avoided, could not be skirted. He had shown her the way they should move: weigh each footfall, stop and listen and go, and he thought she had learned well. He had the knife so hard against Milan Stanković's beard that the man no longer seemed to doubt him, and took as great a care with each stride as they did.

She would go forward, she would stop, she would listen, she would flick her fingers for him to come with the prisoner. They would both listen for a moment, and then she would move forward again.

It was when the tears were coming faster on Milan Stanković's cheeks that she began, again, to interpret what the man said through the gag.

'He is telling you about his grandparents. His grandparents were taken out of Salika village . . . There was a cordon round the village, made at first light by the Germans and by the Ustaše fascists . . . Before the German troops and the fascists moved into the village his grandparents were able to hide his father in the barn where they kept two cows and their cart. His father was eleven years old . . .'

Going forward again, stopping, listening.

'When the German troops and the fascists came into the village they took all the men and women they could find, and then the German troops stood back . . . Many of the Ustaše fascists were from Rosenovici village, and the German troops allowed them to take charge of the villagers from Salika. They were walked, his grandparents and many others, to Glina town. It was said to them when they reached Glina, without food or water, that the Serb villages provided help and support for the Partizans who were hidden in the Petrova Gora forest which is near . . . They were put into the church at Glina, his grandparents and the other people from the village and from other villages . . . He says that many of the Ustaše fascists were from Rosenovici, and many would have known his grandparents and the other people . . . The church was set on fire by the Ustaše fascists . . .'

Going forward, stopping again, listening.

'He says the German troops were from a regiment of Wurtemberg, and they were country boys and they would have no part of it . . . He says the fascists, and there were many from Rosenovici, had blocked the doors of the burning church and they fired their rifles at the windows so that there was no escape from the fire . . . He says it is the first story that his father told him . . .'

Going forward, stopping, listening again.

'He says the story of what the Ustaše fascists did to his grandparents, what the people from Rosenovici did to their neighbours, burning them with fire, is in his bones and his blood and his mind, and has been since he was a small child . . . He says that you do not understand, and that you cannot understand . . . He says that you have no quarrel with him, and that he has no quarrel with you . . . He says now that you should try to understand . . . He begs you to permit him to return to his people, to his wife and to his son . . .'

Going forward, stopping, listening.

He felt the cold in him. Even when they crossed the small clearings where old trees had rotted and fallen, where the sun caught him, he felt cold. She spoke to the man, the whisper of the local language, and again she killed the words, and the pleading.

361

'What did you say to him?'

'I asked him, could he describe the face of Dorrie Mowat when he hit her, knifed her and shot her . . .'

The man was broken.

He took the lead. He did not know how she could find the cruelty. He let Ulrike have charge of moving Milan Stanković forward. He handed her the knife and she held it against the man's throat, as he had done. She would use the knife, of that he was certain. Ahead were the strongpoints and the minefields and the tripwires and the patrols. As his defence, he had only the skills he had learned as a child, going to the badger sett or the vixen's den, stalking the fallow hind. He remembered about the INLA man, and what the detective sergeant of the Anti-terrorist Branch had told him weeks after the arrest, meeting in a pub to hand over surveillance evidence notes, that the arrogance and conceit had been stripped off the man with his clothes, that the man had sat in his cell wearing his paper overall suit and wept . . .

There was nothing definite that he could tell her. It was just his instinct.

Each time they stopped and listened, his instinct told him they were being followed, but he saw nothing behind and heard nothing.

And it was all ahead of them, the worst.

'I don't know how we'll pick up the pieces again . . .'

It was the usual way of their sessions. They were in the kitchen. The bulk of Charles Braddock's body was slumped on the table and he spoke muffled through his hands.

'I've always made the decisions for her. I've always said what'll happen. Damn it, she's always been here, waiting, available . . .'

Arnold Browne leaned against the sink. Pretty rare for him to be invited inside the Manor House and not outside to the 'snug' shed at the bottom of the garden, but it was usual that he should play the punchbag for his neighbour's monologue. He supposed that he was attracted by the power of the man, but he found the whined self-pity quite unpleasant.

'. . . Lost her to that damned child. I mean, it's hardly as if

362

she can just walk back through the door, and we carry on like nothing ever . . . Humiliated me in my own house, at my own table, with my own friends . . . I mean, it's not even for the child living, it's for the child that's bloody dead. Not what I want, not at all. I've done everything that Mary could have wished for, needed, asked for . . . Arnold, she's crapped on me, bloody ungrateful woman . . .'

He went to the kitchen door. It was not Arnold Browne's way to tell his neighbour that he thought him the most opinionated bully he had ever met. Or to inform his neighbour that he thought his wife to be the most selfish woman he had ever known. It was not his way to tell his neighbour that a young man had been exploited when vulnerable . . . And it was not his way to reveal that, in his own mind, he was tormented by guilt for his part in the matter.

He let himself out.

'Yes, Penn. He's Bill Penn . . . Might be under *William* Penn . . .'

She stiffened. Mary Braddock could endure no longer the isolation of her room. She sat in a low chair in the lobby. She waited for the telephone call from the earnest young American. She straightened, taut.

'He was here, this is where he was staying, Bill Penn . . .'

The reception clerk, bored and superior, was shaking his head, reluctantly leafing through the guest list.

'This is where he was booked in . . .'

A nasal English voice. She saw a small man, overweight and bald. He was leaning over the desk trying to read the lists as the reception clerk's pencil moved languidly over the names. He wore dirty jeans that were smeared in engine grease and an open shirt with a pullover that was ragged at the cuffs.

'Ah, yes . . . Here, but gone . . . Gone two days ago, two days ago he checked out . . . Yes, I remember, Mr Penn, I think he had had an accident . . . but gone.'

She saw his disappointment. He looked Jewish. She saw him mouth a curse, and he turned away. She was up fast out of the low chair and she intercepted him by the glass swing doors.

'Excuse me . . . you were asking for Mr Penn.'

'Right.'

'It's impertinent, but in what connection?'

'Depends who needs to know.'

'Well, if it doesn't seem ridiculous, I suppose I could say I'm his employer.'

'The girl's mother? Dorrie Mowat's mother? I'm Benny Stein, I met Bill Penn.'

'"BENJAMIN (BENNY) STEIN: Crown Agent lorry driver, Brit aid convoy, rescued me (life threatened situation) from Sector North at considerable risk to himself, his colleagues, and the future shipment of aid through Serb-occupied territory."' She had recited it, as if it were learned by heart. '. . . You were in his report.'

'We were geared up to go back today, down to Knin, but there's some flap over there, crossing points closed. We got put on hold. Seems I missed him, just wanted to put alcohol down his throat. Good guy, but you know that, lucky guy. So, he's gone home . . .'

'Not home, Mr Stein, back inside Sector North. I asked him to return there, and that's what he did. I asked him to bring out my daughter's murderer, that's what he's doing.'

She stared him straight in the eyes. She saw him shudder. She thought that for a moment his mind was working like a slow mechanism, but when they came his words had the deliberation of a quite total dislike.

'Do you know Oscar Wilde, Mrs Braddock? Maybe you don't . . . "Women have a wonderful instinct about things. They can discover everything except the obvious." What is *obvious* to me but not *obvious* to you is that over there, inside Sector North, is a bloody awful corner of hell. So, you "asked" him to go back inside . . . When I got to meet him, he was kicked half to death, they were taking him out to shoot him. You know what he said? He said that you told the worst stories about your daughter . . . "a story about her for every year of her life, the stories seemed to queue up to foul-mouth her . . ." And for your peace of mind, you "asked" him to go back into that place . . . Well done, Mrs Braddock, for missing the obvious.'

He pushed past her, hammered into the swing doors.

She thought that Benny Stein, if he had not pushed past her and run across the pavement, would have hit her.

They played it as a game, and the Director watched. The tip of the wand moved high on the wall map of the operations room, and the Canadian officer described the moves. But there was no passion to the commentary.

'Initially there was a search mounted out of Salika village, that search did not make a trace and was wound down this morning. The activity of the search is now in their prime militarized zone fronting onto the Kupa river. They've cancelled leave, beefed up the duty rosters. They believe they have sealed the militarized zone – it's out of the hands now of the rabble because their mainforce military have taken charge. We have no idea of the location of their target, whether he is pressing on, whether he has decided to go to ground while the heat's hot. From our monitoring of their radio it is clear that they do not, as of this moment, know his position, nor his approximate position. They seem, however, confident of blocking him in their militarized zone. That's about where it stands . . . You'll excuse me for asking you, sir, but do you have that information, where he's coming to?'

They waited on him. The Argentine captain held the sheaf of papers that carried the monitored radio messages. They watched him. The Jordanian major lowered the pointer from the map. They searched him for truth. The Canadian colonel smiled, dryly.

The Director said, in sadness more than anger, 'I bloody well don't. We're only the United Nations, you see, only the world body, only the one international authority that every clown politician pays lip service to. We are good enough to be derided, humiliated, insulted, kicked from one fecking end of this place to the other, good enough to shuffle aid round without being thanked. Not good enough to be trusted. It's what I've made a career at, advancement without trust . . . Thank you, gentlemen.'

He went back with heavy steps, up the flight to his office. His secretary greeted him at the outer door, messages in hand and with a gesture towards the three men sitting uncomfortably in the outer office and waiting for their delayed meeting. He waved her away. The Director closed the door hard behind him. He sat long at his desk and he smoked his cigar and loathed himself for the habit. There were many telephones on his desk. Big decision of the day . . . He reached for the white telephone, and he dialled hard, belting the buttons.

'. . . Your guarantee? He does not cross with his prisoner, I want that as a promise. I have that as an unequivocal promise? I accept your guarantee.'

He had the promise from the First Secretary of the British mission that the man who was disowned would not be permitted to cross the river that night with his prisoner. He must place his trust in the guarantee.

She did not know how much longer she could keep up the pace. The dog could hold the pace, whining for food in its hunger when she stopped to rest, sometimes veering away from the scent to lap at a pool of old rainwater, but the dog kept strength while she faded. Sometimes she had a kaleidoscope of lights in her mind, hallucinations at her eyes . . .

She knew this part of the forest, not well, but she had been there as a teenager with the Pioneers of the Party, when the young people had gone on long hiking marches with their tents and cooking gear, when they were brought to the place of the massacre. Where the dog led her was within a half-hour's walk of the place of the massacre. At the place the teenagers had been lined up by the officials, the rain dripping on them, and the Croat children and the Serb children had listened to the officials tell of the shooting in cold blood by the Ustaše men of the group of women who were taking food to the Partizans, and after the speeches the teenagers, Croat and Serb, had murmured their factional insults at each other. It was why she knew this part of the forest . . .

She had thought, all through the length of the day, that she would find soldiers, and that the soldiers would go with her as the dog led them on the scent. She had found no soldiers, and now the light amongst the trees was fading. She had only the bayonet.

Evica Stanković had seen them first an hour before.

When darkness came they would be close to the river. She had seen them for a moment, where the haphazard growth of the trees made a clean corridor for her vision. When darkness came again, when they were near the river, she would lose them. She went on and all the time her eyes, sometimes blinded in tiredness, sometimes seared by the leaping lights, searched for the shape of them.

Evica Stanković had seen, in that moment an hour before, the man leading, and the woman, and her husband who was called a murderer was dragged between them.

The two military policemen were waiting on the platform of the station. They were tall men and their heads were above the mass of passengers, friends, relations, who crowded and waited for the instruction that they should board the train.

'What I don't understand . . .'

'Wrap it up, Freefall.'

The First Secretary threaded through the crush, going towards the military policemen. Ham had spent the day, imprisoned without ceremony in the basement cellar of the First Secretary's villa on the high northern outskirts of Zagreb, among the firewood and the coal sacks with a thermos and a plate of sandwiches and a bucket.

'I don't understand . . .'

'Never was your strong point, Freefall, understanding.'

Ham was given into the custody of the military policemen and they looked at him with a savagery that stripped off his face the first trace of the cheeky smile. He was handcuffed to the younger of them. He was handed the envelope of travel documents and checked them awkwardly, one-handed.

'Why did you help me, why didn't you leave me with the bastards?'

'Now, don't dally, not in Budapest, not in Sofia, not in Istanbul. Just get yourself straight through to Yerevan. Frankly, if you survive that train journey then you'll come through any war intact, even Nagorny Karabakh's little scrap . . . Part of the code, Freefall. I don't like to leave colleagues dangling, not in mid-stream.'

The announcement was made over the loudspeakers and the passengers surged to the train's doors. The cases were being passed up, and the knotted bundles, and the cardboard boxes reinforced with string. The older military policeman elbowed a way through, and Ham was pulled forward and the First Secretary trailed him.

'You think I let him down, Penn, you think I caved too bloody easy?'

'I'm having you met off the train at Istanbul, you'll be given the ticket for Yerevan. Armenia is the side to be on, Freefall. Keep your nose clean and your bottom wiped, and you can be quite a useful asset to us there. It would be very sad if you were silly, could have dangerous consequences for you . . . Of course you let him down, of course you caved too quickly. You're a coward, Freefall, but not an idiot, that pleasant lady would have killed you if you hadn't been a coward, and she would not have lost five minutes of sleep over it.'

He was taken up the steep steps and the handcuff ring cut at the flesh of his wrist. He looked down onto the First Secretary, and the man was peering at his watch as though already bored.

'Where is he?'

'Somewhere behind that bloody line, stumbling forward . . . yes, with his prisoner . . . stumbling forward towards your promised rendezvous . . . Enjoy Nagorny Karabakh.'

The door slammed behind him. The handcuff jerked him towards the corridor of the carriage. He stood his ground, sod the buggers. There was the whistle's blast and the first shudder of the train lurching away.

Ham shouted, 'Tell him it wasn't my fault. Tell him I wasn't to blame.'

A faint reply, through the filthy window of the door. 'Goodbye, Freefall . . . If I see him, I'll tell him.'

The train ground out of Zagreb station. Three passengers, Bosnian refugees, with all that they owned around them, were cleared from their seats by the military policemen. They would be with him until the Slovenian border, then the military policemen would free him, leave him. From Ljubljana he would go on alone into Austria, and at Vienna he would start the long journey, via Budapest and Sofia and Istanbul and Yerevan, to the war in Nagorny Karabakh, wherever the fuck that was. Of course it was not his fault, of course he was not to blame.

Nothing in his life had ever been the fault of Sidney Ernest Hamilton. In the dropping light the train cleared the concrete outer suburbs of Zagreb. He was without blame. He reached with his free hand into his pocket for the carton of Marlboro cigarettes, and for his playing cards . . .

She said it softly. '. . . He says that you have seen his wife. His wife is a fine woman. He says that you have seen his boy, and that I hurt his boy. His boy is a good son . . . Everything that he knows is in the village of Salika, and everything that he loves is there. He asks you, begs you, pleads with you . . .'

He looked away from the wreckage of the man. He remembered the power of the man and the glory of him in the hall of the village's school, and his boots and fists. He could not make the link.

She said it quietly. '. . . He says that his wife should have a husband, and his son should have a father . . . He says that he will swear to you, promise to you, on his mother's life, that he will never hold a gun again, will never fight again. He says that you are a man of honour, a person of courage, and that you will understand his weakness . . . He begs you to let him go back to his wife, he pleads with you to let him return to his son . . .'

Her voice dripped in his ear. He stared again into the face of the broken man. The eyes of Milan Stanković ran wet and his mouth dribbled saliva against the folded material of the gag. The man was pitiful. He could not make the link between the man who was laden with conceit and the man who grovelled for his freedom. The birds clattered in the branches above him and there was the panting of Ulrike's breath spurts and the moaning in Milan Stanković's throat.

'I told you.'

369

Her face and her eyes and her short bob-cut hair were close to him.

'You told me to be cruel.'

'And it is hard for you to be cruel.'

'It is hard.'

'Because you do not see the evil in him.'

'I cannot make the link between what he was, what he did, and what he is now, pathetic.'

She was so strong. He could see that she did not waver, and that she had no doubt.

Ulrike said, 'It is what they are all like, it was the same long ago, and it is the same now . . . It was the same long ago in my country, when the men and women who had committed acts of evil were stripped of that power and put in the cells to await trial, and left in the cells to await execution, and when they were taken to the scaffold some had dignity and some were pitiful . . . they could not be recognized for what they had been, what they had done . . .'

Penn hissed, 'Don't worry, don't bloody worry your pretty head, because I will *try* to be cruel.'

He went on. Penn led. It came to him again, the instinct . . . He thought they might be a mile from the farm with the outbuildings where the troops were billeted. Twice he looked behind him, long and hard, and his eyes that were drifting with tiredness saw only the swaying trunks of the trees and the spreading shadows. He thought that the worst would begin after the farmhouse where the troops were billeted, and the worst would be all the way to the Kupa river and he still could not escape the instinct that they were followed in their flight.

There was no minute taken of the meeting, no stenographer present, no tape recorder in use. The room allocated for the meeting was on the third floor of the Ministry of Defence building with windows that looked down onto the central courtyard where the lights now burned bright. The room was the office of a senior civil servant, young and Harvard-trained.

'It will be done with discretion. There will be Special Forces, of the Black Hawk unit, under the direct command of the Intelligence Officer of 2nd Bn, 110 (Karlovac) Brigade. They are to be given no help, the German woman and the Englishman, in crossing the Kupa river. They are in charge of their own destiny. Under no circumstances, *none*, will they be permitted to bring Milan Stanković across the river. From what I hear, if Stanković crosses then Karlovac and Sisak will be shelled, Zagreb will be attacked by missiles. There can be no misunderstandings in this matter.'

The First Secretary leaned forward, elbows on the table. 'No misunderstandings . . . because if Stanković comes across and into your jurisdiction then international opinion would demand your own dark corners be examined, your own psychopaths be arraigned, and that would never do.'

Parked in the courtyard below was the Mercedes of UNPRO-FOR's Director of Civilian Affairs.

'The meetings that we are brokering, from what I hear from my sources on the other side, will be immediately curtailed if a Serbian is kidnapped and brought before a war crimes tribunal. Gestures are unimportant. It cannot be allowed to happen. Gestures are trivial and cost lives. A substantial window for peace would have been closed.'

The First Secretary swung back in his chair. 'And we must not block the path to the appeasement of violence, good God, no. Peace in our time, peace at any price. Why not . . . ? And you should know, what I now realize, she was a very fine young woman, Miss Dorothy Mowat, and such a shame that her murderer, by our hand, should walk free . . . If you'll excuse me . . . It's my job to be on that bloody river bank tonight.'

He had made four telephone calls and all had been deflected.

Four separate times he had dialled the number of the old police station, the number of the 2nd Bn, 110 (Karlovac) Brigade.

He had asked, in turn of the duty officer and the commanding officer and the liaison officer and the adjutant, if he could be hooked through to Hamilton, Sidney Ernest, on a matter of importance. Four times asked to wait – no problem – four times asked the business of the call – personal – four times asked his name – mumbled and unintelligible – four times told that

Hamilton was not available to come to the telephone and asked again for the nature of the business and the repetition of his name.

Marty Jones was not easily unsettled, less often now that he had been in Croatia and Bosnia for close to a year. But now apprehension crawled in him. Dusk was coming to the parade ground beyond his converted freight container . . . Hell, he was not going to take goddamn crap from them . . . After the fourth deflection, Marty telephoned Mary Braddock, told her he was coming soonest to collect her, that she should have warm clothes.

He did not know the place of the rendezvous on the bank of the Kupa river, and Ham should have rung him. He felt a bad night was taking shape.

Before he locked the door of the freight container behind him, he looked a last time, longingly and almost lovingly, at the camp bed with the sleeping bag and the blanket primly folded, at the brightness of the handcuffs, at the length of the chain and the strength of the ring set in the floor.

The last of the sun, rich gold, came from the trees on the far side of the river and made sweet lines on the moving water, and bathed the worn face of Zoran Pelnak and hurled his shadow back against the old timbers and the weathered brick of his home.

Too much of his time, he liked to joke with the soldiers who came from their tent camp for his well water, was spent gazing at the great Mother, the force, that was the Kupa river. He could spend more hours than the day gave him just watching the movement and the flow of the river. Each day, each hour, he could find something that was new in the movement and power of the river . . . And the river was something to respect, as worthy of respect as had been his own mother, because the river was strength. They did not comprehend, the soldiers who came with the scrubbed old milk churns for their water from his well, the force of the great Mother. Zoran Pelnak did . . . His respect, his awe, of the river had been with him since he was a child, since the evening that the sunken log had come without warning to beat against the bow of his small boat and trip it. He had lost his footing, fallen, scrabbled, slid into the dark cold of the water. What he could remember was the helplessness that he had felt, long ago as a child, thrashing against that force, and his father had pulled him clear. The force would never be forgotten by Zoran Pelnak, never trifled with. He had not swum in the river that bordered his fields since that day when he had struggled in panic against the cold darkness of the current. He knew the force of the great Mother . . . And there was always something new to see.

He paused at the door of his home, and he scratched the debris from the animals' fodder off the sleeves of his greatcoat.

There was a place in the first line of the trees opposite, where the herons made their nest. He could not look into the low sun at the nest, but he could see the male bird erect in the shallow water by the reeds poised and waiting, perhaps for a frog.

He considered the male heron to be the most beautiful of the river's birds.

And when he was inside, warm from the fire, his meal taken, then he would sit by the window and light his lamp and wait for the moon to climb, and the gold would have gone from the great Mother, replaced by silver.

The pistol was aimed at her.

The man was crouched down beside the tree and he held the pistol, aimed at her, with his arms extended. The woman stood beside the man and held the knife against Milan's beard, against his throat. She stopped, and she took the weight of the dog and the farm twine tied to the dog's collar cut at the palm of her hand. She stopped, and she clutched the rusted bayonet.

The pistol was aimed at her across the width of the track that divided them.

She said it in the man's language, deliberate. 'Let him go . . .'

Evica had come fast, closed the last gap, run noisily through the final metres, and she had blundered from the cover of a corner of evergreen holly. They would have heard her come the final metres, but they would only have seen her when she broke the cover of the holly. The dog strained to cross the track.

The aim of the pistol wavered.

'Let him come to me . . .'

Penn blinked at her across the track and she saw the raw tiredness of his eyes that tried to lock along the barrel length of the pistol. It was as if the birds had gone, fled the place, because the silence crawled around her. There were scars on his face. He was the man who had come into her life, the man who would destroy them. The weight of the dog cut the farm twine across the palm of her hand. If she let go of the twine, if she released the dog, then the dog, going forward, forty kilos weight, would overwhelm the man, Penn, with exhaustion in his eyes . . . if she let go of the twine.

'Let him be free . . .'

She looked away from the man, Penn, away from the muzzle of the pistol. The woman's hand did not move. The man, Penn, whispered to the woman, as if he placed and identified her. The knife was steady against the hair of Milan's beard, against his throat. She saw the chilled certainty in the woman's face, as if tiredness had not washed it clear. The knife was sharp and clean. Evica had seen before such chilled certainty, seen it on the faces of the men as they had gone away across the bridge early on the last day of the battle for Rosenovici, and she had heard later that day, and not looked from her window, the rumble of the bulldozer in the field across the stream, and heard the final shots. And she had seen the chilling certainty on the faces of the men who had gone to the headquarters to take the Headmaster from his cell . . . She knew, in her exhaustion, that the dog could take the man, Penn, even if he fired, even if he hit. She knew, in the anguish of her mind, that if she loosed the dog then the woman, determined, cold, would gouge the blade of the sharp clean knife deep into the throat of Milan, would not hesitate because it was in the certainty of the woman's face.

'Please, you should let him come to me . . .'

There was a wetness on the face of Milan, and she could see where the tears had run from his eyes and across the dirtied skin of his cheeks, and gone to the matt of his beard. And Evica saw the fear in Milan's eyes, as if he too knew the certainty of the woman.

'I beg of you, let me take him home . . .'

374

The man gazed at her, dulled. She remembered, a long time ago, many years, when she had gone with the beaters and the dogs to flush a boar, a long hard run and chase and they had found the boar against a rock outcrop that it could not climb, and it had turned to face the leashed dogs and the guns, and she had seen the dulled eyes of the boar. The man with the pistol did not have the cold certainty of the woman who held the knife so steady against Milan's beard and throat. But it was not the man who spoke.

She had a clipped voice, controlled.

'What was done at Rosenovici was a crime. What has been done through former Yugoslavia is a crime. At stake is the rule of law . . . What we do is small, because we are only small people, but it is necessary to find a point for a beginning. You are the wife of Milan Stanković, you know what he did. After the flag of surrender, he took the wounded from Rosenovici, and he had a grave dug, and he butchered those wounded . . . You are his wife, you know what he did, you know the scale of his evil . . . And with the wounded was a young woman . . .'

The young woman, the girl, coming to the school at Evica's invitation, speaking English that Evica might improve her language, coming in torn jeans and sweaters that were holed at the elbow, sitting with the fun laughter bubbling in her . . . dead and buried.

'The crime of the young woman was that she stayed when others ran. She stayed with those who were wounded. She gave them help and love. Your husband made the chain. The chain is from the young woman to her mother, to Penn, to your village, to your husband. He made the chain when he killed that young woman . . . We do what small people, Mrs Stanković, have always done through history, we make a beginning. And the law, Mrs Stanković, belongs to small people, and I am small and Penn is small, and the law belongs to us. We cannot give him back to you and to your child because the rule of law, without which we all fall, demands that your husband be brought to account . . .'

Evica thought the woman was without mercy. The fingers that clasped the knife against Milan's beard had no gold wedding ring. She could see the tight waist of the woman behind her opened coat and there was not the slackness at her stomach of childbirth. Evica thought the woman was without love.

'That night, when he came back from Rosenovici, did he tell you what he had done? Did you hold him, and tell him that it did not matter? Did you cuddle him, and tell him he was without guilt . . . ? Or did you feel shame, Mrs Stanković, did you feel that when he lay beside you he dirtied you. You should go home, you should go home to your son and tell the child that his father is a murderer, and you should tell the child that the rule of law demands his father's punishment . . .'

She looked into her husband's face. She remembered the night. She remembered how she had lain awake, how she had pushed him away from her, how he had slept and she had not, how he had cried out twice but not woken, how he had once thrashed with his arms as if to beat away a nightmare, and how in the first light of the morning she had stood at the window of their bedroom and looked across the fields, across the stream, and seen the smoke rising from the buildings and seen the grey-black scar in the corner of the field.

Penn said, 'He has nothing to fear from me. It will not be as it was for Dorrie Mowat . . .'

She let the bayonet fall from her hand.

'. . . I protect my prisoner with my life.'

She turned away.

Evica pulled the dog, reluctant, after her.

She twisted her back on her husband. The dusk was falling on the woodland. She could not answer the argument of the woman. She could not fault the promise of the man.

She heard them moving, first loud and then fainter.

Evica never looked back, never turned to see her husband taken as a prisoner towards the Kupa river.

He turned the pages.

Perhaps it had been stupid of him to ask for the books. He leafed through photographs in expensive colour that showed children in national costume, and wedding dances, and the archaeology of the national heritage, and Roman amphitheatres, and the beauty of polyptych work from churches. Henry Carter thought it an obscenity that a nation of such age-old talent should have stooped to such far-down barbarity . . . God, and since when had he been qualified to criticize? He leafed the pages, searched patiently. There was an aerial view, across two pages, of the old quarter of Karlovac, and he could make out clearly the former barracks built by Napoleon's marshal where the German woman had administered the Transit Centre.

The searching ended . . . It was a dreadful photograph, quite unsuitable for his purpose, but it was what he must make do with. The photograph showed in foreground the tables and chairs laid out on the patio of that city's principal hotel, in bright summer, with lolling and burned holiday-makers under gaudy sunshades. Beyond the patio, glared by the sun, was a pedestrian road and then there was the bank of the river. It was what he had sought to find, a view of the Kupa river. The river of the photograph was low against high banks, wide but seemingly harmless. It could give him an idea, only a frail impression, of how the Kupa river would be, at night, swollen by the winter, guarded by strongpoints and minefields and patrols, approached by the German woman and the prisoner and Penn.

His eyes misted over.

20

They stood so still.

His heart hammered and his chest heaved, and he tried to breathe through his nose because he thought that would be more quiet, and she had the bulk of Milan Stanković pressed against him, and he hoped that she had the knife so hard against the man's throat, that the man would not dare to shout.

The two shadow shapes were on the track that ran above the farm with the outhouses. The shadow shapes moved with care.

They came within five stretched paces of where Penn and Ulrike Schmidt and Milan Stanković stood, so still. The moon was high enough, full enough, to throw fierce light onto the openness of the track they used. Penn could see that the shadow shape leading wore metal rank pips on his shoulder epaulettes, and the shadow shape who followed was carrying, tensed and readied, an assault rifle. It was where it could end, and the worst had not yet begun . . . Milan Stanković might not believe him, but would believe Ulrike. Milan Stanković knew from her cold certainty that if he made a sound, the smallest sound, then the knife would be driven into the softness of his throat . . . She could try to make him cruel enough and she would not succeed . . . The shadow shapes moved away. He reached back with his hand, and his fingers found hers. He did not twist his neck so that he could see her, because he feared that the material of his camouflage tunic would rustle or grate. His fingers found her body. They held a pinch of flesh at the flatness of her waist, and he squeezed the pinch with his fingers, hard so that he would hurt her, so that he would make her concentrate, and the moment before he took the first step he pulled at the pinch as the signal that she should follow him. They went onto the path, onto the fallen leaves and the wetness of the mud. They followed the shadow shapes that were ahead of them.

There was a low whistle. The whistle was like the warning cry of a young owl, from his childhood when he had gone at night to the twenty-acre plantation. There was an answering call from the mature owl that located its position. They followed the shadow shapes that led them towards the Kupa river. He attempted all the time to keep the shadow shapes at the edge of his vision as they meandered along the track. It was a bastard . . . The whistle, the answering night call, and when he strained to hear in the close quiet of the forest there were softly spoken voices, murmurs in the trees, it was the identification of an ambush position . . . Penn understood . . . an officer and his escort moving to inspect the ambush positions that he had designated. Penn understood that it was necessary for the officer to whistle ahead so that the troops, lying up and cold and with their nerves stretched, would call back, would not blast at the shadow shapes approaching them.

It was their chance, he saw it.

He led Ulrike and Milan Stanković wide of the track each time that the officer whistled, the owl's sound, and each time the call was returned, and each time that there was the brief whisper murmur of the voices.

It was the opportunity, he must take it.

The shadow shapes of the officer and his escort took them through the network of the ambush positions. Four times they heard the whistle, the response call and the short whisper of voices, four times they were able to skirt the waiting troops. All the time the sight of the shadow shapes drew him forward, and the ache of the tension was in his legs and there was the hammer of his heart, and he wondered how it was possible for Ulrike to hold, all that time, the knife blade so steady against the beard and throat of Milan Stanković with cold certainty. There was vomit in his throat, from fear. He depended on Milan Stanković, on the desperation of the man. Would the knife go in if the man stumbled and a twig broke? Would the knife go in if the man spluttered once? It would be in Milan Stanković's mind that if

379

he stepped heavily, grunted once, then they were gone . . . He was trying to evaluate how desperate the man was . . . And if the man made a noise and Ulrike stabbed him in cold cruelty, then he and Ulrike were gone . . . They were in the hands of their prisoner, dependent on the desperation of their prisoner . . . The vomit was in Penn's throat and sliding forward and he could not spit and he did not dare to swallow. They were so close to the shadow shapes, and to the voices, and once a metal water bottle rattled against a rifle barrel, and he trembled, and did not know how the faster panting of his breath had not been heard . . . The shadow shapes turned. So still again, so frozen against a tree's trunk, so quiet, and the shadow shapes had gone away and past them, retreating until he could no longer see the blurred half-images. Weakness dribbled in him.

They went off the path.

He glanced at his watch. He estimated it had taken one hour and forty-seven minutes to cover one mile.

And he should, too bloody right, have listened better to Ham, and he could not remember the details that Ham had given him of ambush positions. He should have listened better because there would be ambush positions to a depth of a mile, and then there would be tripwires, and then there would be the patrols moving on the bank of the river, and then there would be the bloody river.

Her hand came to him. She took his shoulder and she squeezed it hard, as he had squeezed her. She squeezed the bone of his shoulder as if to tell him that she thought he had done well.

He knelt.

Penn brushed the floor of the forest with his hand until he had found a small branch.

He held the branch ahead of him, making a blind man's progress, going towards the river.

'It's Hamilton, I want, Sidney Hamilton. I expect you call him "Ham". I'm his friend . . .'

The warning was there, quick.

Marty Jones was at the sandbagged entrance to the old police station, and the sentry had come out of the protected sangar to block him, and the corporal was reaching for the field telephone in the guardhouse.

The sentry was aggressive, and the corporal was evasive.

Marty Jones hesitated. He knew it had gone foul and the aggression and evasion were the evidence. He hesitated and he did not know what his response should be, and then in front of him was the blast of the horn and the flashing of headlights. Two jeeps and a car lined up and trying to get the hell out of the inner courtyard of the old police station, and the barrier was down and blocking their leaving. The corporal abandoned discipline and the field telephone and came out to lift the barrier.

Two open jeeps came by him, and he saw the flashes on the tunic arms of the guys and he knew they were Special Forces, and there was a big Rover tailing them out under the raised barrier. The barrier came down and the corporal was reaching again for the field telephone, and Marty was running.

They could just as well have shouted a warning at him.

Marty Jones ran to where he had parked the car, flung himself inside, twisted the ignition and hit the gears.

Not until he had caught them, could see the lights of the Rover and the two jeeps, going down the big avenue, out of Karlovac, towards the river where there were the tanks' teeth of concrete beside the wide road, and the artillery-damaged apartment blocks from the war gone by, and the bazooka defence bunkers, did he kill the lights and let them lead him.

He hissed to Mary Braddock, through his teeth, 'I don't know what it is, I just know it's gone bad . . .'

He was trying to concentrate, but his mind was leaping . . .

Two more hours gone, and he reckoned a mile covered for each hour.

And no longer the surety of the moon to guide him with the flow of silver light.

He had found one tripwire. The taut wire checking the motion of the stick, and crouching until his fingers brushed the wire, and Ulrike and himself lifting the weight of Milan Stanković over the wire and the knife blade never leaving his beard and his throat.

381

The last stretch before the river, and facing the last patrols
. . . and the concentration came harder and his mind leapt faster.

The wind rising, and cloud scudding across the moon's face.

Too much damn well surging in his mind, and that was
danger. Danger was distraction from the gentle loose hold on
the stick that wavered in front of his footfall . . . Penn took them
off the path that ran down alongside the planted mines, and on
towards the river bank . . . It was a place where brambles were
thick, near to the path, and the moonlight was at that moment
gone from above the tree canopy.

A mile from the river bank . . . His mind leaping, concentration failing, *danger* . . . The flashing of the torch, shaded, and
the ripple sounds of Ham edging the inflatable into the current
of the Kupa river. The drive to Zagreb, the prisoner given over.
A taxi for the airport, first flight out. She was so strong and there
was no future for them. He would not know what to say to her.
Gazing into her eyes, staring into the depth of them, wondering
if she would cry, if she would laugh, if she would kick him on
the shin. No future for them. Her going back to the Transit
Centre. Him going back to Alpha Security Ltd, and tramping
up the stairs from the street door beside the launderette, and
seeing Basil and Jim and Henry, and Deirdre giving him the
post that had accumulated, two weeks of it. No future for them.
Heading back to Jane, and asking shyly how it had been, and a
cold kiss on his cheek that was formality, and Tom's wet mouth
on his face that was a stranger's, and nothing . . . But there was
no future for them. And the morning after . . . The morning
after he was home he would go down to the station at Raynes
Park where there was a florist and he would buy the flowers, big
bunch and bright blooms, and walk them home and fill the little
living room of 57B the Cedars with life, and he would kiss his
Jane, and tell her that he was going out of her life. And the
morning after, the day after tomorrow, he would catch the train
into London and take the Underground to Goodge Street, and
walk down Gower Street, and sit in the front reception as if it
were his right and not give a shit what the guards thought, and
wait for Arnold bloody Browne to take the lift down . . . The
day after tomorrow he would make Jane laugh, and leave her

. . . The day after tomorrow he would tell his story to Arnold bloody Browne and have the pleasure of walking out on him . . . He would go to search for space for himself, go where the dewed fields were quiet in the morning, and where the trees threw shadows in the evening . . . It was the way that Dorrie had shown him, and he would go to private places in the months ahead, years to come, and he would think of Dorrie and be with Dorrie. It was his dream . . .

The bramble stems clawed at him, held him.

He did not hate the man. He almost felt a pity for the man. And the man had a wife who had loved him, and a child who fought for him. The man was craven, bare-arsed and bare-balled because they stripped from him even the love of his wife and the pride of his child . . . For what? For *principle*, for the God Almighty 'feel good' factor of those who wanted to see 'something done', for Mary bloody Braddock's peace of mind. He wouldn't get the chance ever to talk with the man, like he would have talked to the man in a café or a bar or on the beach if they, Jane and him, had ever come for a holiday in what they called former Yugoslavia, and way back, and before the madness . . . For what? For the killing of Dorrie Mowat, what else . . . ? Was she laughing, was she bloody mocking? Dorrie Mowat . . . up high, up on the bloody mountain, looking down and laughing, mocking, had caught him.

Caught in the brambles at the side of the path. His boot kicked at the clinging bloody mess.

Caught him, caught Mary, caught Marty Jones, caught and hurt them all, like she'd hurt him, like she'd hurt Milan Stanković, would have liked to have talked with the man . . . caught in the brambles' hold . . .

The wire would have been set across the path that they avoided. His boot tripped the wire. The wire would have been fastened to a cut peg that had been buried in the brambles' mess. His boot was held for a moment by the wire as he lurched for balance. The wire might have been visible if the bloody moon had not been hidden behind the bloody cloud. His boot snagged the wire.

One movement, throwing himself back. One movement, flattening Ulrike and the man.

The thunder of the explosion numbed his hearing, cut the whistle spray of the grenade's shrapnel. He was pulling her up, then grasping for Milan Stanković, and he felt the wet run of blood because the knife blade had been against the man's beard and throat and the sharpness of the knife's blade had slashed the hair of the beard and the skin of the throat. Pulled her up, grasped and lifted him.

Going for the path and running.

Clutching back behind him for the jacket of Milan Stanković and dragging him, and Ulrike was pushing him.

It was the start of the stampede run for the river bank.

High up, above the tree canopy and below the cloud that masked the moon, away to the east, the first flare burst.

He had taken the telephone call, broken his meeting, charged from his office and gone like a mad puppy down the stairs to the operations room.

The Director stood in front of the wall map, and the tip of the pointer danced against the clear sheeting that covered Sector North.

The Canadian colonel said, 'It's what we're getting from the monitoring. He's in trouble . . . They're in close pursuit. He'll be running for his life, but there's the river ahead of him. No rendezvous, right, sir . . . ?'

In the cause of the greater good . . . The Director nodded, dumb. He stared up at the map.

The Jordanian major asked, knowing the answer, 'No rendezvous, no boat waiting for him?'

In the interest of the greater number . . . The Director shuddered, numb. For a few brief seconds the tip of the wand held the clear-cut line of the Kupa river.

The Argentine captain lit his cigarette, 'No rendezvous, no boat waiting, with or without his prisoner there is not a possibility of him coming out. It is what you wanted, sir, yes . . . ?'

Penn was running, trying to see the path, trying to take the man and Ulrike with him.

Bad pain . . .

His hand was behind him, gripped deep into the material of the man's coat.

The pain was the man's teeth buried into his hand.

Penn loosed him. He was crushed by the pain. He staggered free of the burden of the man. There was another flare falling behind them, gone from its summit arc, and the flare threw brilliant white light down through the trees' canopy, and he could hear shouting and whistles blowing. He gripped his bitten hand and he was bent and he was rocking and he squeezed at the hand as if that way he could shed the pain. The pain was his own world and private, and the pain brought smarting tears welling from his eyes.

Penn turned.

Light fell from the flare.

It gleamed on the knife's blade. She had lost the knife. Penn stood and suffered his private pain and watched. The knife was beyond her reach, as if it had fallen clear when the man had moved. She was on the floor of the wood, and she was writhing in the leaves, and she clung to one leg of the man, and the boot of Milan Stanković kicked with savagery at her body.

The flare was guttering, failing.

He saw her body bounce away from the impact of the kick, and her hands seemed to have the last clinging hold of his legs. If he had had his hands, if his hands had been free . . . If the flare had not been fired, if there had not been the light . . . Penn thought the man realized he was at the edge of freedom. One more kick, one more blow from the boot at her head, and she would loose him. It was the last moment before the flare fell. He could hear the shouts and the whistles closing. In the last moment of the light of the flare, the last moment before the final kick that would free the man, Penn tried to learn to be cruel.

With the heel of his hand he hit at the back of Milan Stanković's neck.

Penn hit with his bitten hand, and the man fell, and they writhed in the coming darkness.

He punched at Milan Stanković, as an animal at war.

Penn beat at Milan Stanković and he seemed not to hear her

385

voice in the night's blackness, and she was calling to him that he had hit enough. She had the knife.

They took the prisoner, sullen quiet, on towards the bank of the Kupa river.

The knife's blade was back at his throat.

Penn led the charge, and his bitten hand dragged the man forward. He had needed to be cruel to have hit so hard with the heel of his hand. He did not hate the man. There were flares, all the time, bursting high behind them . . . He had respect for the man . . . He knew of the deep and raw courage that was required to make a break. He felt that the man was in his care. He did not think about Mary Braddock, nor about Katica Dubelj, and he did not think about Dorrie Mowat. The man was in his care, and he owed Milan Stanković his protection. The man would not fight again . . . it was finished for Milan Stanković, he had fought and failed, but respect was won. When the flares died, when they fell back doused, then there was the full moon's light, and the fast-going clouds had moved on. They ran, stumbled, charged, pulled and pushed the weight of Milan Stanković, down the path that ran beside the single length of barbed wire that marked the minefield. He could not judge how far behind the chasing pack were, but all caution was gone . . .

Ahead, through the trees, he saw the dark mass of the Kupa river.

There were silver trellis lines on the darkness where the force of the current swirled.

They burst the last cover of the trees. They came onto the narrow path that ran along the upper bank of the great river. She was tugging at his coat, pecking at him for his attention. The cover of the trees was behind him. The reeds nestled along the bank ahead of him. The shouting and the whistle blasts were behind him. The river and the silver network of lines were ahead of him.

There was a killing flatness in her voice.

'We came too early. We are an hour ahead of the rendezvous. You said we should lie up, but we cannot . . . We came too early for Ham, for the rendezvous, for the boat. Did you not know that . . . ?'

386

She was at his back, the barrier was ahead of him.

Another flare soared high behind him, and he saw the far width of the river ahead of him. Milan Stanković rocked with muffled laughter, and he would not have understood what she said, only the tone of despair. Penn turned. Eyes going past the babbled laughter of the man who croaked under the gag, and he was trying to speak as he laughed, as if now the knife at his beard and his throat no longer terrorized him.

She destroyed him because he had not thought it through when he had led the stampede flight towards the Kupa river.

He rifled at her pockets, felt first the weight of the pistol, then the bulk of the torch. He stood on the path above the deep flow of the river and he shaded with the palm of his hand the beam of the torch.

He made the signal. He flicked the button of the torch, on and off, on and off, waited for the answering light, on and off, on and off, waited to see the boat dragged down the far-away bank, on and off, on and off.

The voice carried by the loud-hailer echoed sharply across the river width.

'Penn, you have no boat. There is not going to be a boat . . .'

'. . . You should abandon your prisoner. Penn, you and the woman, Schmidt, should take your chance in the water. Penn, Hamilton is not here, there is no boat. You should immediately release your prisoner . . .'

It was a long and straight track, and it went by a well-constructed building that was roofless and abandoned. The track went all the way to the river. Marty saw the flares that lit the skyline, and the flares silhouetted the group at the end of the track. He was leading Mary Braddock towards the group and the jeeps and the Rover car. Below the flares, beyond the group, separated by the width of darkness and silver, Marty saw the winking, on and off, of the light.

'. . . If you try to bring your prisoner across, you will be identified by flashlight. We have authority to shoot if you attempt to cross with your prisoner. Release him immediately . . .'

*　　*　　*

He had snapped off the torch.

The amplified voice bayed across the river.

'. . . You have to take your chance in the river, just you and the German woman. For fuck's sake, Penn, move yourself. Penn, are you coming? We are forbidden to give covering fire . . . Just you and the German woman, not the prisoner, get into the water . . . Penn, you don't have time . . . Do it . . .'

He could let the man go. He could walk away from the man. He could turn the man loose. To turn the man loose, to permit the man to walk away, might save her life, Penn's life . . . She could hear the voices now, behind her, carried towards the bank by the amplification of the megaphone. He had a hold of Milan Stanković, and he seemed to look into her face, and she did not challenge him, and she felt no fear. She wriggled clear of the straps of the backpack, let it fall. He pulled Milan Stanković down the bank and she slithered after them. They splashed into the cold of the water, and she clung to the man and tried to hold the knife blade steady against his beard and his throat. He never turned to her, never asked it of her, just assumed it, that she would follow him. The mud of the river's edge was over her boots, the slime was round her feet. The water was at her waist, the cold groping at her groin. There were three, four, metres of reeds at the side of the river, in mud against the bank. She had her free hand, not the hand with the knife blade against Milan Stanković's throat, tight on the mouth of the man. They made strong waded steps through the reeds, each step sinking in the mud bed. They were going away from the flares, away from the megaphone that was silenced, away from the closing crash of the pursuit.

He was, to her, a simple and decent and ordinary and obstinate man, and she felt a love of him.

They went down river, they went with the flow goading them on, and once they foundered and the chill of the water was at her shoulders and the water was in Milan Stanković's nostrils and the water was over Penn's head. She wanted so much to tell her father of Penn, tell her father how she had known always that he was a man, Penn, of *principle* . . . tell her father how they had gone down the river bank, hidden by the first summer

388

growth of the reeds. Low against the water's surface, the power of the current restrained by the reeds, she could see across the full width of the river, and it did not seem possible to her that she could ever get to tell her father of the man she loved. On and on, more mud, more slips, putting further behind them the flares and the shouting and the chasing pack. She wanted so badly to tell her father . . . if he freed the man, if he left the man, then the chance to cross was theirs, but he would not, and she did not ask it.

A long distance gone.

There was a cacophony of flapping movement in the trees above. A heron flew across the face of the moon. There was a pallet held by the reeds.

Across the river a small light burned. The light was in a window.

The pallet was one that would have had stacked on it fertilizer bags, or seed sacks. The pallet of coarse wooden strips must have been discarded in a field, upstream, and taken by the winter's flood water.

It was for the *principle*, and he did not speak to her, made no effort to strengthen her, but she saw that he took in his fingers the man's beard, the hair on his cheek, and he gave the hair a small pull as if to reassure the man, as if to give him his protection. He dragged the pallet out from the reeds and held it against the flow of the current, and he levered the torso of the man up onto the surface of the pallet.

He kicked off from the mud bed in which the reeds grew. She swam beside him. They pushed the pallet clear from the bank.

The current caught them.

Milan Stanković flailed with his legs and Penn was one side of the pallet and she was the other, and they tried to steer a course against the power.

A small light burned in the window that was downstream across the river.

They were crouched behind the wheels and bodywork of the jeeps because the Intelligence Officer had said that from the Serb side they might shoot. And he had the grim dry smile on his face, washed in the moonlight, of a man who enjoys a fucked-up failure. Beside him was the First Secretary, behind him were Marty Jones and Mary Braddock, ahead of him and lying prone were the Special Forces troops.

Marty Jones trembled.

Mary Braddock gazed ahead, without voice, without feeling.

They watched the torch beams cavort on the far bank, up into the trees, onto the path, down among the reeds, and out across the darkness and silver lines of the river.

Far down the river bank, way too far, the First Secretary saw a single light, steady like a beacon.

He fought to drive the pallet forward.

He no longer felt the cold of the water.

He seemed to hear Dorrie's mocking and Dorrie's laughter.

The man no longer kicked with his legs as if the weight of his river-logged boots was too great. Penn thought that Milan Stanković had surrendered to the power of the river. He no longer had the support of Ulrike, knew that she was beaten by the pressure of the current. They were lower in the water than they had first been, and the level of the water was above his shoulders and washed over the wood strips of the pallet, and the water lapped on the hips of Milan Stanković.

They were not halfway across.

He could see the small, constant light ahead.

Beneath them was the great dark depth of the river, pulling at them, tugging at them to take them down. If they were no longer able to drive the pallet forward, if they drifted, then the river would take them down. They went slower, and the current was greater, and the small light ahead did not seem closer. He kicked harder, kicked from the last of his strength, and when he tried to drag the night air into his lungs then he was sucking in the foulness of the river. Her body was beside him, but she could only paddle her feet, could not kick.

Penn spluttered, 'Tell them that we tried . . . Tell them someone had to try . . .'

He had a hold of her hand. It was not difficult for Penn to

break her grip on the pallet. He seemed to show her the small light that did not waver. He did it quickly. He broke her grip on the pallet, and he pushed her away from him, from the sinking pallet, from the motionless weight of Milan Stanković.

He saw that she was clear in the water.

He saw the whiteness of her face and the brightness of her eyes and the slicked hair of her head.

The man was sliding back from the pallet. She had tried to teach him to be cruel, and she had failed. He held the man as best he could, and he kicked.

The power of the current hacked at his strength.

Penn did not see her again.

The water was rising around him.

Penn did not see the light again.

'It was what I saw from my window. Because it was a full moon I saw them very easily. I saw them from the time that they made the heron fly, when they came out of the reed bed with their raft thing. They made good speed at first, and they would have felt that it was possible, but if you think that you find weakness in the great Mother that is the Kupa river, then you fool yourself. The river plays the game of tricking you, there is no weakness. The river brings you on, away from the safety of the bank, then tricks you . . .'

He sat in his chair of stained oak beside the window and the oil lamp threw a feeble light across the room. He spoke gently, but with respect, as if he had a fear of giving offence to the great Mother.

'I could see them all of the time. Good speed at first, but that is the way of the great Mother because from the south bank, from their bank, the river bed is more shallow and the current is less strong. When you come further into the flow of the river then you will find the true strength of the great Mother . . . Of course it is possible to cross if you have a good boat, if you have oars and you have been God-given good muscles, of course it is easy if you have the engine for the boat . . . but the river watches for your weakness, and if you are weak then the river will punish you . . .'

The woman sat bowed on the bare boards. She was in front of the stove, with the pistol close to her feet. She wore a faded old dressing gown tight around her, borrowed from the farmer's wife, who had bought it in the market at Karlovac thirty-one years before, and draped over the dressing gown was the farmer's greatcoat. She did not speak. Her clothes, sodden from the river, were across a chair beside her.

'The strength of the great Mother, where she finds your weakness, is when you come to the centre where the current is most powerful. At the centre, coming from the far side, is where the drag pulls at you. When they were coming, the year before the last year, the Partizan bastards, there were deer that ran ahead of their gunfire. I saw a deer come into the water, running in fear, a big stag, a good head on it, and it could swim until it reached the centre of the river . . . I can only say what I saw. It was at the centre that he pushed the woman away. I heard his voice, but I do not know what he said because it was foreign and because the river makes its own sound, the voice of the great Mother is never silenced. I think that he pushed her away so that she could swim free. She was so lucky . . . perhaps the attention of the great Mother was on him and his friend, perhaps the great Mother ignored the woman, swimming free. I could see it from my window, the man and his friend taken down the river . . .'

They listened. They were crowded into the room. The mud fell onto the board floor from the boots of the Intelligence Officer, from the shoes of the First Secretary and Marty Jones and Mary Braddock . . . She did not understand a word that was said by the old farmer, but there was a grim sadness on his face and she felt a release. They were all touched by Dorrie, her daughter. She felt her freedom.

'They were taken down the river, the great Mother held them. They could not go from the hold of the current at the centre of the river. The raft thing was lower in the water. He tried to kick a last time, but the strength was gone from him. Was his friend wounded? I think his friend was wounded because his friend had no use of his arms. They lost the raft thing. I saw him hold his friend up in the water, as if he supported him. He would not be able to save his friend, I could see that. If he had loosed his friend, given his friend to the great Mother, then perhaps, perhaps . . . I do not know . . . all the time he tried to help his friend. They went under. I saw them again and they were held in the current, and I knew it would not be long. Just their heads, for one moment I saw just their heads, and still he tried to protect him, his friend. I did not see them another time. Who was his friend that he would not leave? They were so small, they were against such power. I did not see them another time . . .'

They took the woman with them, and the old farmer was told that his wife's dressing gown and his greatcoat would be returned in the morning.

Later, the Intelligence Officer would use the field telephone to communicate a satisfactory situation to his enemy. Later, the First Secretary would send a three-line encoded message to the dishes on the roof of Vauxhall Cross. Later, Marty Jones would return to his converted freight container to dismantle a camp bed and unfasten a chain linked to a pair of handcuffs, and to arrange for ballistic tests to be made on a Makharov pistol.

Later, Mary Braddock would take her small suitcase to the airport.

Later, the shells would be taken from the artillery pieces that faced Karlovac and Sisak, and technicians would stand down the ground-to-ground missiles that could reach the southern suburbs of Zagreb.

Later, the troops of the Ustaše bastards and the Partizan bastards would search the reed beds on their side of the Kupa river, and find nothing.

They went out into the bright moonlight and walked away from Dorrie's place, turned their backs on Dorrie's war.

EPILOGUE

He had tried three times to dial the number, and each time the telephone had given him an unobtainable tone.

Henry Carter pushed himself up.

He stretched.

His hands were behind his neck and he arched his back and let out a short squeaked cry. He went to the desk nearest his own. No, she was not eating chocolate that morning. Yes, she wore a prim new blouse. She looked up at him, away from her screen, nervously.

He smiled. He apologized. He said it had been disgraceful of him to have shocked her with that quite revolting photograph the morning before, and he was reaching into his wallet. He offered her a five-pound note and said it was for the dry-cleaning of her blouse, and if there was anything left over, then she should purchase some little trifle . . . God, what sort of little trifles did young women buy with the change from the dry-cleaning of a chocolate-stained blouse? . . . And he needed her help. The senior dragon was not in sight. Please, he needed to dial an out-of-London number, and couldn't seem to manage it. Of course the telephones could only be used for in-London calls, but there had to be a way. She knew the way. She put the five-pound banknote into her purse, and blushed, and told him what digits he should dial to obtain it, and he made a little joke about a nephew in Australia. She was gazing up at him, and his fingers rubbed, embarrassed, across his cheek stubble, and he should have taken the time to find that hidden razor, and should have brushed his teeth, and should have changed his socks . . . In her face, he thought he saw simple kindness.

'Has it been awful, Mr Carter? It must have been a pretty awful file to have kept you here, all yesterday, all through the night. Is it *something really sad . . . ? Sorry, shouldn't have asked that, should I, I'm not need-to-know.'*

He said quietly, 'Do you know, my dear, there was only one thing that I ever did well when I worked here. I was good at standing in safety on the right side of some of life's most hideous barricades, waiting for some poor devil to come back from the wrong side. I wish so much that I had been there, waiting, not able to intervene, but sharing . . . So kind of you to help me with the telephone.'

He sat on his desk. He dialled again.

He heard the clip of her voice.

He kept his silence.

Who was there? What did they have to say?

He heard the annoyance of her voice.

Would they, whoever they were, not waste her time? Who was it?

He put down the telephone, cut from his ear the growing anger of Mary Braddock, mother of Miss Dorothy Mowat. So tired now . . . It had all been such a long time ago. He had cut from his ear the authority, annoyance, confidence and anger of her voice.

A little while ago, only a few minutes, it had seemed important to speak to her, to tell her that an old desk warrior had bludgeoned a file into shape, made it ready for burial on a disk. He gathered up the papers of the file, the photographs and the maps, and his own crude plan of the two villages separated by the stream.

He walked across the open-plan space of Library to the day supervisor's position.

'Finished then, Mr Carter?'

She was leafing through the material that would be transferred to the disk. She turned the typewritten pages, and the photographs of the grave site and the cadaver and of Bill Penn, and the maps, and his sketch plan, and there was that curl at her lip to indicate that in her opinion the material had not warranted the smelling socks and the stubble on his cheeks and the demands made of her staff. She came to the last page in the order he had assembled the material. He had written a heading in his own copperplate writing.

She read.

'They may be able to run but they can't hide.'
(L. Eagleburger, SofS, USA)
Geneva/Brussels airborne brief. 16.12.1992.
Eagleburger announces programme to prosecute war criminals in
former Yugoslavia.
List below of those prosecuted by UN-sponsored tribunal:

But the sheet was blank.

She flushed. She wondered if he ridiculed her.

*He intervened in her confusion, best dress smile, the one that he
kept for Christmas and family.*

*'Assuming that somebody, some day, for some reason, should actu-
ally read the file, I thought they might be interested to know what
was achieved in the two years after Mr Eagleburger's brave words
. . . If only our masters would abstain from saying things they don't
mean then life would be so much more bearable, don't you
agree . . . ? Thank you for the kindness of your staff. Whistling for
the stars, am I . . . ? Good day.'*

*He cleared his desk, packed away his empty thermos in his brief-
case, and shrugged into his coat.*

Quite chill that morning.

*It was behind him, all of it. It was as if it had never happened,
as if by conspiracy brave words became hollow and empty.*

*Quite a brisk wind off the old Thames catching him as he strode
towards the station. All of it was behind a sentimental old desk
warrior. His step was lively. Ahead of him was the short train journey, the quick change of clothes and socks, and the brushing of his
teeth, a good shave with a new blade, then the drive to mid-Wales
and the railway line at Tregaron, and the sight of the soaring freedom
of the kites. Henry Carter thought that, after where he had been, he
needed to find a place of freedom.*